Praise for Nalini Singh,
"the alpha author of paranormal romance" (*Booklist*),
and the Psy-Changeling Novels

"A must-read for all of my fans."
—Christine Feehan, #1 *New York Times* bestselling author

"Nalini is brilliant." —*USA Today*

"Singh shines with elaborate, compelling world-building
and scorching sexual and emotional tension."
—*Kirkus Reviews*

"A beautiful, amazing, heartbreaking love story."
—Fiction Vixen

"Scorching hot." —Dear Author

"I don't think there is a single paranormal series as well-
planned, well-written, and downright fantabulous as Ms.
Singh's Psy-Changeling series." —All About Romance

"Paranormal romance at its best." —*Publishers Weekly*

"A fast-moving, heart-pounding, sexy-as-hell thrill ride."
—Joyfully Reviewed

"Sheer genius." —The Romance Reviews

Shards of
Hope

❖

NALINI SINGH

JOVE BOOKS, NEW YORK

JOVE

**An imprint of Penguin Random House LLC
375 Hudson Street, New York, New York 10014**

SHARDS OF HOPE

A Jove Book / published by arrangement with the author

ISBN: 978-0-425-26404-1

PUBLISHING HISTORY
Berkley hardcover edition / June 2015
Jove mass-market edition / January 2016

PRINTED IN THE UNITED STATES OF AMERICA

10 9 8 7 6 5 4 3 2 1

Cover art by Tony Mauro.
Cover design by George Long.
Cover handlettering by Ron Zinn.

Penguin
Random
House

CAST OF CHARACTERS

In Alphabetical Order by First Name
Key: SD = SnowDancer Wolves DR = DarkRiver Leopards
BE = BlackEdge Wolves

Abbot Arrow, teleport-capable telekinetic (Tk)

Aden Kai Arrow, telepath (Tp)

Amara Aleine Psy member of DR, former Council scientist, twin of Ashaya, mentally unstable

Amin Arrow, telepath (Tp)

Andrew "Drew" Kincaid SD Tracker, mated to Indigo, brother of Riley and Brenna

Anthony Kyriakus Psy Councilor, father of Faith

Ashaya Aleine Psy member of DR, former Council scientist, mated to Dorian, twin of Amara

Axl Arrow

Blake Stratton Arrow

Bowen "Bo" Knight Security Chief, Human Alliance

Carolina Arrow child

Council (or Psy Council) Former ruling council of the Psy race; no longer extant

Cristabel "Cris" Rodriguez Arrow, sharpshooter, teacher

DarkMind Neosentient entity and dark twin of the NetMind

Devraj Santos Leader of the Forgotten (Psy who defected from the PsyNet at the dawn of Silence and intermingled with the human and changeling populations), married to Katya Haas

Edward Arrow

Faith NightStar Psy member of DR, gift of foresight (F), mated to Vaughn, daughter of Anthony, cousin to Sahara

Ghost Psy rebel

Gregori BE Lieutenant

Griffin BlackSea Changeling, Lieutenant

Hawke Snow SD Alpha, mated to Sienna

Ida Mill Psy, leader of group that believes the Silence Protocol is the only right path and that the empaths should be removed from the gene pool

Irena Arrow

Ivy Jane Zen President of the Empathic Collective, married to Vasic Zen

Jaya Empath

Jen Liu Psy, matriarch of the Liu Group

Jojo Leopard cub

Judd Lauren Psy member of SD, Lieutenant, former Arrow, mated to Brenna

Kaleb Krychek Leader of the Ruling Coalition, psychically bonded to Sahara Kyriakus

Lara SD Healer, mated to Walker

Lucas Hunter DR Alpha, mated to Sascha, father of Naya

Malachai BlackSea Changeling, Lieutenant

Max Shannon Human, Security Chief for Nikita Duncan, married to Sophia Russo

Mercy DR Sentinel, mated to Riley

Miane Levèque Alpha of the BlackSea Changelings

Mica Arrow, Lieutenant of Zaira Neve, based in Venice

Ming LeBon Former Psy Councilor, military mastermind, cardinal telepath

Nathan Ryder DR Senior Sentinel, mated to Tamsyn, father of Roman and Julian

Naya Hunter DR cub, daughter of Sascha and Lucas

Nerida Arrow, telekinetic (Tk)

NetMind Neosentient psychic entity said to be the guardian and librarian of the PsyNet, twin of the DarkMind

Nikita Duncan Former Psy Councilor, part of the Ruling Coalition, mother of Sascha

Pax Marshall Head of the Marshall Group, grandson of Marshall Hyde

Pip Arrow child

Riaz Delgado SD Lieutenant, mated to Adria

Riley Kincaid SD Lieutenant, mated to Mercy, brother of Drew and Brenna

Ruling Coalition Formed after the fall of Silence and of the Psy Council; composed of Kaleb Krychek, Nikita Duncan, Anthony Kyriakus, Ivy Jane Zen for the Empathic Collective, and the Arrow Squad

Sahara Kyriakus Psy (uncategorized designation), psychically bonded to Kaleb Krychek, niece of Anthony Kyriakus, cousin to Faith

Samuel Rain Psy, genius, robotics engineer who developed experimental biofusion

Sascha Duncan Psy member of DR, cardinal empath, mated to Lucas, mother of Naya, daughter of Nikita

Selenka Durev BE Alpha

Shoshanna Scott Former Psy Councilor, head of Scott Enterprises

Sienna Lauren Psy member of SD, cardinal X, mated to Hawke, niece of Judd and Walker

Silver Mercant Senior aide of Kaleb Krychek, in charge of worldwide rapid response emergency network that spans all three races

Sophia Russo Former J-Psy, married to Max Shannon, aide to Nikita Duncan

Tamar Civilian member of the Arrow Squad, financial and data analyst

Tamsyn "Tammy" Ryder DR Healer, mated to Nathan, mother of Roman and Julian

Tavish Arrow child

Vasic Zen Arrow, teleporter (Tk-V), married to Ivy Jane Zen

Walker Lauren Psy member of SD, mated to Lara

Yuri Arrow, telepath (Tp)

Zaira Neve Arrow, telepath (combat)

Smoke and Mirrors

SPRING IS IN full flower in the year 2082.

It has been four months since the fall of Silence, the protocol that bound the Psy race to a cold, emotionless existence. Telepaths or telekinetics, strong or weak, the Psy are now free to feel, free to love and hate, free to laugh and cry. Emotion is an intoxication to many, but to others, it is a deadly threat.

For the Silence Protocol was put in place for a reason.

The ten-year debate preceding the implementation of Silence was fractious and raw for a reason.

Millions of Psy decided to condition all emotion out of their young for a reason.

The Psy gave up joy as well as sadness for a reason.

That reason was the violence and madness endemic within their race. To be Psy was to have a far greater chance of criminal insanity, a far greater chance of striking out in a moment of uncontrollable anger and ending the life of a loved one. To be Psy was to be cursed.

In 1979, Silence was a beacon of hope. To a desperate people on the verge of a violence-fueled extinction, it was the *only* hope. They ignored the smudges on the beacon, the flickers of darkness within, the whispers that perhaps Silence was all smoke and mirrors. Driven by love for the very children they were condemning to a loveless existence, the Psy accepted

the harsh tenets of the Protocol, accepted the hope held out by
their leaders.

Today, the smoke has dissipated, the mirrors have
shattered.

And the darkness at the heart of the Psy race is once more
a vicious truth no one can ignore. For what happens to the
murderers and the insane in this new world? What happens
to the broken?

They still exist.

They still kill.

Chapter 1

ADEN WOKE ON a cold, hard floor, his head throbbing. Another man might have hissed out a breath, might have groaned, but Aden's training was so ingrained that his sole response was to lift his lashes a bare sliver, only fully opening his eyes once he realized he was surrounded by darkness. He wasn't, however, alone. He could hear breathing—quiet but jagged. As if the other person was trying to maintain silence, was unable to do so for reasons Aden couldn't yet identify.

Remaining exactly where he was, he scanned outward with his telepathic senses . . . and had to capture a scream before it traveled to his vocal cords. The pain was blinding, the agony leaving his vision white. Controlling his breathing and his body through sheer strength of will, he fisted his hand, gritted his teeth, and made a second attempt, this time to reach the PsyNet, the sprawling psychic network that connected all Psy in the world but for the renegades. A Net connection would give him a viable way to alert the squad about his capture.

The backlash of pain almost led to a blackout.

Quietly lifting his arm when he could function again, white spots burning in his vision, he reached to the back of his head and the center of the starburst of pain. He expected to find blood-matted hair that denoted a cracked skull. What he discovered instead was a raised bump close to the lowest part of his skull, near the area that housed the cerebellum and beyond it, the brain stem. No, it wasn't a bump but a *scar*—it shouldn't have been there and it still felt tender.

That wasn't the only anomaly. From the dryness in his throat and the stiffness of his limbs, Aden calculated that he must've been unconscious for hours. Long enough for the squad to realize he was missing and to locate him. Vasic alone should've been able to accomplish that. Except it appeared even the best teleporter in the Net hadn't been able to lock on to his face, using it as an anchor to get to him.

The only other times Vasic had failed to lock on to people was when those individuals had created complex shields designed specifically to thwart teleporters capable of locking on to people rather than simply places, *or* if the individual concerned didn't know his or her own identity—such as those whose minds were broken.

Aden's mind was whole, but whatever it was that had been done to his brain via the barely healed incision he'd discovered, it had screwed up his psychic wiring. Vasic's absence told Aden his psychic signature must've also been affected on a deep level. He knew of no surgical technique—or technology—that could achieve that aim without a full psychic brainwipe, but he didn't make the mistake of thinking he knew everything.

He ran a mental checklist of his body and the items on it. All his weapons were gone, as were his belt and his boots. Whoever was behind this had been thorough.

Having maintained an ear on the other person breathing in the room, he crawled silently toward the rasp of sound. His cellmate hadn't moved the entire time, and there was something in the unsteady rhythm of the breathing that had him certain the individual was hurt. With his eyes having adapted to darkness ameliorated only by a thin edge of light that came in under what must be a door, he could see that his cellmate's body lay in a corner of the windowless room—as if it had been thrown there. That body was small and with the wrong proportions to be a man. Either a child or a woman.

Close enough now to see the curve of her hip, the fine line of her jaw, he realized it was a woman. A woman who smelled of blood. He moved his hand to her face, brushed away the dark curls that were impossibly soft . . . and found his wrist gripped in a punishing hold. "Move and I'll rip out your throat."

"Zaira," he said in the same low whisper she'd used. "It's—"

"Aden." She released his wrist. "I'm injured."

"How bad?"

"I was shot." Taking his hand, she placed it on the viscous stickiness above her stomach, her thin but should-have-been-bulletproof top soaked with blood and her lightweight body armor missing. "It passed through the left side of my abdomen."

Aden might not have any equipment or supplies, but he was still a trained field medic. "Do you have any source of light on you?" It was possible their captors had overlooked something.

"Negative. No tools or weapons. They even took my boots."

He shifted so close to Zaira that, under any normal circumstances, he would've been invading her personal space. When he pushed up the long-sleeved black top that hugged her body, she didn't protest. Her skin was clammy under his touch, and though he felt the edges of a bandage, it had clearly been an inexpert job—blood had soaked through, was continuing to do so. "I need to touch your skull."

"No need. I've been cut, something done to my brain. I'm psychically blind. Any attempt to use those abilities results in extreme pain." She took a shallow breath. "Since rescue hasn't arrived, I'm assuming you're in the same position."

"Yes." He checked her head wound to make certain it wasn't bleeding, too, discovered a roughly sealed incision identical to his own. Their unknown captors had the technology to do brain surgery advanced enough to block psychic abilities, yet they'd left Zaira badly hurt and in pain? "They want you weak."

"Yes." Her next words were so quiet he heard them only because he was close enough to feel the soft warmth of her exhale. "I didn't know it was you, but now that I do, I think our captors plan to use me to break you. One entered the room earlier, said, 'He'll talk or we hurt her,' to another individual."

"Arrows aren't so easy to break."

"And you aren't fully Silent, Aden. You never have been." Another strained breath. "Everyone in the squad knows that—now someone outside the squad has figured it out."

Aden decided he would correct her about his Silence later. "Conserve your strength. I need to be able to count on you when we escape." There was no "if." They *would* escape.

"If you can get me a weapon," Zaira said, "I'll cover you as you go. I'm weak, will slow you down. You'll do better on your own." She said that as if it was a simple fact, as if she wasn't talking about the end of her own life.

Leaning in until their noses almost touched, until she could see his eyes as he could see the jet-black darkness of hers, he said, "I don't leave my people behind." He knew what it was to be left behind, and though it had been done for the best of reasons it had marked him on a primal level. "We'll go together."

"You're being irrational."

It was a complaint he'd heard multiple times from her. And not because her own Silence was flawless.

The truth was that Zaira had never needed Silence. What had been done to her in childhood had caused her to retreat deep into her psyche, shoving her emotions into a dark hole in a bid to survive. In their place had grown an iron will and a harshly practical mind. Silence had only ever been a tool she used to create a civilized shell.

Without it, she was close to feral but no less ruthless, her brain having learned long ago to put survival above all else.

It made her the perfect soldier.

Some would say it also made her a psychopath, but they didn't understand—unlike a psychopath, Zaira had the capacity to feel the full range of emotions. That capacity was in permanent cold storage, but it gave her a conscience regardless. It also gave her the capacity for unflinching loyalty: because Zaira's violent survival instincts didn't always equal her *own* survival. She'd already walked into the path of a hail of bullets aimed at him during an operation three years before, had barely survived her injuries. He wasn't about to allow her to sacrifice herself for him again.

"You should've toppled me from the leadership years

ago," he said as he moved to lift up the bandage, see what he could make out of the wound. "My irrationality where my people are concerned is apt to continue."

"I thought about it, but I don't have the patience for politics."

He knew that despite her icy words, Zaira would take down anyone who challenged his right to lead the squad. For him to lose her loyalty, he'd have to do something so horrific, he couldn't even imagine what it might be. "How were you shot?" he asked, wiping away the memories of how close to death she'd come the last time. "How many hits?"

"One," Zaira replied. "They came for me while I was some distance from the Venice compound. Five men. I blasted a telepathic request for assistance but no one made it to me in time."

"How many did you kill?"

"Three. Fourth injured. Fifth would be dead, too, if he hadn't made the shot."

Five men against a very small woman and she'd nearly defeated them. Deadly and smart, she was one of Aden's top people for a reason. Now her breathing grew harsher as he checked the edges of her wound by touch. "Must be a new bullet designed to penetrate our armor," she said through what sounded like gritted teeth.

"Is this top made of the new material developed by Krychek's company?" The thin and fabriclike innovation was meant to be as effective as much heavier body armor.

"No. I put myself low on the priority list—others on the frontline needed it more."

Pressing the pads of his fingers on different parts of her abdomen, he asked her to tell him what hurt and what didn't, and stumbled upon an unbandaged wound on her side. "I'm fairly certain the abdomen wound is the exit site," he said after investigating it as carefully as he could, "but there are signs the bullet ricocheted inside you before it left your body." Causing internal damage he couldn't determine without a scanner. "Are you coughing up blood?"

"No."

"That's good." Her abdomen was also not swollen or tense. "If there is internal bleeding, it's not severe yet."

Pressing the bandage back into place, he pulled down her top, then shrugged off the leather jacket he was still wearing and got her into it. It was too big on her, and he rolled up the sleeves before she could ask him—Zaira would not want her hands hindered in case of a fight.

That done, he stripped off his T-shirt and, tearing it using brute force, managed to make wadding for the entry wound on her side. If he'd been wearing his uniform top, this would've been impossible; that material was designed not to tear. It was as well he'd been in civilian dress except for his combat pants. Knotting together strips of fabric, he got it around her waist and tied the wadding into place. It'd provide some pressure at least, help stem the bleeding. "Too tight?"

A shake of her head.

"I'm going to try to stop the bleeding." He had minor M abilities that meant he could seal some wounds, though he had no capacity to see inside a body to gauge injury.

"No," Zaira said when he would've touched his hands to her skin. "That sucks energy. Save it. We'll need it to get out of here."

He didn't like leaving her hurting and in pain, but she was right: he was a trained field surgeon and medic *because* his ability was so limited. It was useful when he had healthy backup, but it became a liability in a combat situation. Far better for him to rely on his skills. "Warn me if you're about to lose consciousness," he said before he realized a grim truth. "I need to test if my M abilities even work." No matter if it was about healing the body, not the mind, it still required a psychic energy burn.

Pain was a hot poker down his spine, his vision blurred for over a half minute.

"No?" Zaira said softly.

"No," he confirmed. All their psychic abilities were out of reach.

Tugging her top back down again over the makeshift bandage he'd created, he put his lips right against her ear, one of her curls brushing his nose. "How long will you last?" He was well aware that though her injury was bad, she wasn't as frail as she'd made herself appear.

"Seven minutes at full capacity, but that capacity has been halved by the wound and the shock from the blood loss."

That still made her a hundred times deadlier than most people on the planet. "We wait for a chance. My signal."

"Agreed," she said, just as there was a rattling sound.

Leaving Zaira on the floor in her guise of a small, weak, wounded creature, he rose to his feet. The light that poured into the room was dim, but it told him multiple things.

This room had no other exits and was created of hard plascrete.

There was a corridor outside, but no sounds of machinery—even the hum of background technology or traffic—invaded the room.

Either they were far from civilization or the plascrete was well insulated.

The heavily muscled man in the doorway was dressed in camouflage pants, a jacket of the same mottled shade, and black combat boots. He stood like a special ops soldier . . . stood like an Arrow.

Aden ignored the male's masked face and took in his height, his body weight, his musculature, ran it against his mental database of Arrows. No match. He and Zaira hadn't been betrayed from the inside, but this man was a high-level soldier. Black ops most likely.

He carried a weapon.

That was his weakness. He thought the weapon made him invulnerable.

Pointing that weapon at Aden, the male said, "Sit."

Aden had noted the dented metal chair in the center of the cell at the same time that he noted the plascrete; he'd also weighed up its value as a weapon. Still calculating his options, he walked to the chair, took the seat. "If you're intending to interrogate me," he said, confirming the presence of another guard outside when that guard's shadow hit the opposite wall, "you should know Arrows are trained to die rather than break."

"Oh, you'll talk. I have plenty of time and everyone has a breaking point." Cold words. "From what I hear, Arrows are nothing if not loyal. This one—she means something to you." Having walked into the room, he kicked Zaira's body.

Chapter 2

SHE MOANED, BUT Aden knew it was for effect. That didn't mean the kick hadn't hurt. It only meant that Zaira would never permit anyone to hear her in pain unless it was to her advantage.

Aden memorized the location of the kick, made a mental note to check Zaira for further injuries after they were free and the man who'd kicked her was dead. The latter was a certainty. "All my Arrows mean something to me."

Their captor continued to stand by Zaira. "But this one you go to see every week."

Zaira needed the oversight, not because she wasn't a good Arrow, but because of her psychological makeup. She was independent and strong and she had a conscience, but she was also damaged in a way that might cause her to make certain decisions that could not be unmade. So Aden ensured he was available for her to use as a sounding board.

That was what he told himself, what he'd always told himself.

"Do you intend to torture her to break me?" Aden asked, his eye on the guard outside—who had stepped partially into the doorway now. Well trained, like this one, and careful never to take his attention off Aden. Not well trained enough, then, because Aden wasn't the only threat in the room.

"Yes," the guard answered. "Tell me—are Arrows trained not to break under sexual torture?"

Aden felt his muscles lock. Relaxing them with conscious effort of will, he watched the guard by the door while pretending he hadn't even seen him. "Pain is pain," he said. "We've had more body parts broken, burned, crushed, and otherwise injured during our childhoods than you can imagine. During anti-interrogation training, I once had my fingernails pulled out one at a time before a hot poker took out my eye."

The medics had fixed the eye, the other injuries, but they'd left him in brutal pain and half-blind for days, the next round of training based on exposing psychological weaknesses. Aden hadn't splintered. He'd been ten years old at the time.

The guard kicked Zaira again. "You might think it's all the same, but we'll see. First I'll make you watch as she's sexually tortured by my human compatriots, then I'll ask them to do the same to you. In the end, you'll give us everything."

Aden needed to know the why behind this captivity, but he'd already made the determination that both these men had to die. It was the most efficient way to secure an escape. "Only two guards for two Arrows? A mistake."

"There's nowhere for you to go—and we have the guns, while your minds are chained by those implants the docs put in." A vicious telepathic blow that made Aden's head ring.

It also gave him an accurate gauge of the male's psychic ability.

"Low and hard," he said in Arabic, the language Zaira had spoken with the parents she'd ended up beating to death with a rusty metal pipe. *"He isn't strong enough to kill with his mind."*

Though her breathing had gone shallow, she moved like lightning, her legs scissoring to take out those of the stupid, stupid man who'd stood so close to her. As he slammed to the ground with bone-cracking force, Aden was already moving, picking up the chair and throwing it at the second guard, who'd come in, bullets firing. The chair hit the other man in the chest hard enough to make him stumble back and nearly drop his gun.

"Aden."

He grabbed the gun Zaira shoved across the floor, having taken it from the guard she was choking to death using her thighs. Lifting and firing it in a single smooth motion, he hit the second guard dead center in the forehead.

"Cris would be proud," Zaira said, then sucked in a pained breath.

Aden shot the guard on the floor, guessing the male had attacked Zaira on the psychic plane. What he didn't realize until he hauled Zaira to her feet and felt the wetness on her side, the scent of iron suddenly bright, was that the man had also jabbed his hand into her wound, doing further damage. "I'm fine," she said, though her shivers indicated otherwise.

Conscious they didn't have much time, Aden left her for a second—she swayed but stayed upright—and ripped the ski masks off the two men. No one he recognized, but he had faces now.

"He's human," Zaira rasped, eyes on the second guard. "Has to be, given the lack of a psychic component to his attack and the other guard's boast about his human compatriots."

"Agreed." Aden stripped the blood-flecked camouflage jacket off the second guard, pulled it on, then took the male's knives and guns to strap them on himself and Zaira. Their one advantage was that any other guards wouldn't have heard the altercation—all the weapons were silenced and Aden and Zaira had kept their voices low throughout.

Zaira pushed him away when he went to wrap his arm around her waist to steady her as she walked. "No. We'll only succeed if you have both arms free. I'll be behind you."

He knew that wasn't what she planned, but he allowed her to believe he did. "Let's go." Reaching the door, he scanned for surveillance feeds, found nothing. Low-tech—but low-tech could be a defense against discovery: if nothing was hooked into a network, then no one could hack in.

He didn't like exiting into the corridor not knowing what awaited around the corner, but there was no other option. He and Zaira were all but silent, each movement careful, but a guard saw him as he looked around the corner. Aden fired to silence the guard's shout of alarm. The guard fell without making a sound, but he had his hand on the trigger as he died; the gun spit fire, the bullets hitting a small steel grille that covered an air vent.

The hard, pinging noise echoed against the plascrete.

Aden heard a door bang open the next second, more footsteps heading toward them. Checking to make sure Zaira remained with him, he covered the distance to the dead guard and, hauling up the body, used it as a shield against the bullets and laser shots that peppered the area. Ice-cold wind swept down the corridor as more guards came in from what had to be the outside of this building.

The door was slammed shut seconds later.

Zaira didn't try to come around him; she knew as well as he did that he needed her alive. Not wasting his ammunition, Aden took one shot at a time, eliminating two of the guards before they got smart and started trying to target him in turn—except Zaira was laying down fire that meant the men couldn't poke their heads out from the side corridor where they'd taken shelter.

The psychic attack that accompanied the weapons fire was haphazard and not as powerful as it should've been for the number of men he'd seen. Despite the inexplicability of such an alliance, it again indicated that some of these guards had to be human. "The door," he said to Zaira, pointing out their escape route.

It lay in almost a straight line from their current position.

Continuing to move toward that door under a covering hail of gunfire, the dead guard's body absorbing the hits, Aden waited until he was almost at the corridor junction, then shoved the corpse onto the dead man's former comrades. They weren't expecting that, had underestimated Aden's strength, as people often did, and were momentarily stunned.

That was all he needed.

He ran.

As he'd expected, Zaira stayed behind, continuing to lay down fire so he could get out. When he slammed through the door, it was into a sullen darkness, the sky above starless and heavy with clouds that threatened to crash open at any moment. Lightning flashed in the distance but that was the only—fleeting—source of light.

No sound of vehicles.

No high-rises.

No sign of a road.

Nothing but trees in every direction . . . and gunfire behind him.

ZAIRA saw Aden make the door, felt a sense of satisfaction that wasn't strictly Silent. He was important, Aden; he was the future of every Arrow in the squad and those to come. She was a senior commander, experienced and useful, but she was also disposable in this circumstance. Compared to Aden's, her life had little value—its value lay only in protecting his.

She'd done that. She'd served her purpose.

Side burning and head thumping, she continued to fire even as she slid to the floor, but her bullets eventually ran out. She dropped the weapons to show her captors she had nothing, was no threat. If they came close enough, she could get at least one with a knife.

Regrettably, the guards appeared to have learned their lesson. Though they emerged from their corner, they kept their guns trained on her and maintained their distance. "Go after the male," a bearded man commanded two others. "He won't get far in this terrain. We need him alive."

Two of the camo-gear-clad men ran out, leaving two in the room.

"If you need me alive," Zaira pointed out, "you should get a medic." Death didn't worry her, had never worried her. But she would've liked to have seen the future into which Aden would lead the squad. She was a murderer who'd never felt an ounce of remorse for her crime. She could never shrug off the coat of Silence without becoming that pitiless killer again, but she'd thought maybe she could take part on the shadowed periphery.

Vasic and Ivy Jane's wedding had made her see that there was hope for many of her squadmates, hope for a life beyond the regimented existence of an Arrow. Those like Zaira could stand sentinel against the darkness so others could be free to grab at life. It was no sacrifice, not when the end result was that some of that life spilled over onto Zaira and her brethren.

She'd been invited to Vasic and Ivy's home more than once since the wedding, had thrown a stick for their inquisitive dog, had even helped Ivy repair a trellis the other woman used for climbing berries of some kind. Normal things that had, for a short window of time, made Zaira feel normal, too.

And Aden . . . she would've liked to see him make it.

"Get the medkit," the bearded guard said without taking his eyes off her. "And call in an update, tell the team in the chopper that we have the situ—"

A bloody flower bloomed on his forehead, his body thumping to the ground a split second before the other guard's.

Zaira looked up to see Aden in the doorway. "You came back." No one had ever come back for her for no logical reason. No one but Aden. Because this wasn't the first time he'd done it. "Foolish."

"Not from where I'm standing," he answered, striding into the room to check her wound. "You need medical attention."

"They said there's a kit here." Taking the gun he put in her hand, she tried to stay conscious as he disappeared, to return with a small metal box four minutes later.

"This installation is compact—I've cleared the entire area," he told her before opening the kit and quickly cataloguing the items within. "Communications system is voice-code protected."

Which meant it was out of their reach; voice code locks could be broken, but it took time and a very specific set of tech skills. "I think there's a backup team on the way in a chopper."

Aden gave a short nod to acknowledge her intel, but didn't stop what he was doing. "The kit's not advanced enough to fully take care of the gunshot injury, but I should be able to stop the major bleeding at least." He took out a handheld scanner, tried to switch it on. "Dead. Water damage." Throwing it aside, he picked up a disposable laser.

Biting down on a leather belt Aden pulled from one of the dead guards, she tried to contain her pain as all Psy were taught to do, but her mind wouldn't cooperate. Aden looked up at her flinch. "Whatever is in our heads is interfering?"

She nodded, but told him to continue with her eyes.

He did, his jaw a brutal line. Why did he persist in

believing himself Silent? He *cared*. Aden had always cared. It was the biggest open secret in the squad. It was why they all fought so furiously for him and with him. Because Aden came back for his people. He'd come back for her.

No one else might mourn or care for an Arrow, but Aden would. Aden *did*.

She knew that Marjorie Kai, the woman from whom Aden had inherited the Korean part of his heritage, would consider his capacity to care a black mark against him. Marjorie was an Arrow of old, one who'd helped set the rebellion in place—and who had given up her son to it when he was just a boy.

His Navajo-Japanese father, too, would say the same: *Strength is control. Control is power.*

Zaira had heard Naoshi Ayze say that at least a hundred times during the past five, going on six, years. Marjorie and Naoshi had settled in Venice after their "deaths" in an explosion at sea two decades past, and the compound there wouldn't have existed without them. But while the squad owed them a great debt, Zaira had come to realize the two Arrows no longer understood the son they had created and shaped to be an avatar of rebellion.

Aden was stronger, *better* than both of them, and he followed his own path.

Throwing aside the laser when it burned out, he picked up another one from the kit, worked on her. There was pain, but it was the burn of the laser, the deep ache of being gutshot fading slightly.

"I think I've cauterized the major bleeds," Aden told her, rebandaging both the entry and exit wounds using sterile gauze packs before making her drink two small bottles of a high-nutrient compound in the kit. Soon as she'd done that, he thrust a solid energy bar at her. "It'll increase your energy levels, stave off unconsciousness."

While she forced down the tasteless bar, he went looking for their boots. "Got them," he said a couple of minutes later. "Socks were on the floor but they're dry."

He'd also unearthed a green camo canvas daypack and, once he'd pulled on his socks and boots, started filling the pack with any food he could find, the remaining medical supplies, and technical equipment they might be able to jerry-rig. "We're in mountainous and heavily forested terrain, low visibility because of thick cloud cover and the fact it's full night," he told her. "A storm seems imminent. Strip the guards, put on as many extra warm layers as you can; ditch my jacket and find a rainproof one."

Already moving, though she was sluggish compared to her normal speed, Zaira went to the guard who'd taken a bullet in the skull and fallen forward on his face, leaving his clothing mostly unbloodied.

"Here." Aden threw her an olive green sweater from a small metal trunk he'd dragged over from around the corner. "Looks like their spare supplies." Shrugging off the lightweight jacket he was wearing, he pulled on an identical sweater over bare skin, though what was baggy and loose on her sat easily across his broad shoulders. "It's empty aside from a few more energy bars."

Having unzipped and shrugged off the leather jacket, she put it back on over the woolen sweater. She could easily fit a heavier waterproof jacket over it. "Do they have sleeping bags?"

"No. I found pallets in a small room down that corridor." He paused. "I think I saw a jacket that might not swamp you."

Zaira made her way to that room while Aden stuffed the daypack with the last supplies and extra ammunition. The heavy hooded jacket she found hanging on a hook on the wall must've belonged to the short, slight guard who'd run outside after Aden. It was still large on her, but not so large as to be unmanageable. Seeing another thick, weatherproof jacket crumpled in the corner, she picked it up and shook it out, then scanned the room until she located a pair of gloves.

Aden had just finished packing the supplies when she got back. Nodding thanks for the jacket and gloves, he snapped closed the clasps on the daypack and began to get into the jacket. Her senses prickled fifteen seconds later, while he was zipping it up. "Let's go. I hear a chopper."

Aden didn't argue, both of them aware her hearing was more acute than his—a simple genetic quirk that often gave her a slight advantage in stealth operations. Her father had once credited a long-ago changeling ancestor for that familial genetic trait. Zaira didn't know if that was a true assertion or not, but she appreciated the usefulness of it.

Slinging on the daypack, Aden led the way out. The bodies of the guards sent to find him lay on the ground outside, their eyes staring at the sullen night sky and their skin leached of color. Ignoring them, Zaira and Aden made straight for the cover of the dark green firs that spread out in every direction around them, birch trees with lighter green leaves scattered in among them. Right now, intel wasn't as important as survival.

Chapter 3

THE GROUND WAS uneven, rocky, as they ran, the air cold in her lungs but not knife sharp. Of course, that was now, right after she'd had an infusion of energy thanks to the drinks and the bar she'd eaten. The real test would come in an hour or two, when her injury began to make itself felt again. "Chopper's about to land." She could hear the jets that made it a high-speed vehicle. "Has to be a clearing nearby."

"Probably a natural one. Nothing to raise suspicion to anyone doing a flyover."

Shouts carried on the air soon afterward, but while this terrain might make for a good holding pen, it was so thickly forested that it also made for a very bad area to search. Especially when hunting two Arrows. Except one Arrow was badly wounded to the point that she was a liability.

"I'm slowing you down," she said, her breath coming too hard and too fast for someone with her training and endurance.

Aden's answer was to point down, to what she was just able to make out as flowing water. *A river.* Seeing his point, she headed in that direction, slip-sliding down the hill covered with small flowering shrubs and leaving a visible trail on purpose. Aden did the same. With luck, their pursuers would think they'd both slid right into the river.

Going in a straight line to the river once they'd reached

the bottom, she and Aden scuffed up the dirt near the water's edge to further the illusion that they'd fallen in.

"If we get wet," she said, "we're dead." The water was a hard rush, as if swollen by rain upstream. Not even the strongest swimmer could fight that current, keep from being smashed up against rocks or into broken tree trunks caught in the torrent. That is, if the cold didn't stop the heart first.

"Rocks," Aden said, pointing out the jagged stepping-stones she'd missed in the darkness. If her hearing was acute, Aden's night vision was just as sharp. It had made them an excellent team on the rare missions they'd worked together.

"We get to the other side and we have a much higher chance of survival. They won't expect it."

"Because I can't make it." She knew her balance was off, her body weak; she currently didn't have the physical agility to cross the "bridge" of stones, especially when each stone was covered with a thin and no doubt slippery layer of wet green moss. "You go that way and I'll lead them left."

Aden took off the daypack, gave it to her. "Put it on." When she went to open her mouth, he said, "For once, Zaira, don't argue."

"I only argue when you're wrong." She put on the pack against her better judgment because time was their enemy. "You need the supplies and I can't go far."

He turned his back to her. "Get on."

"Aden, that's a bad decision. We'll both go into the water." The sounds of pursuit were getting louder. "Go. I'll lead them off."

Looking over his shoulder, he held her gaze, the deep, liquid brown of his irises so intense it felt like a physical weight anchoring her where she stood. "Either we both go or neither one of us goes. Choose."

"I'll challenge your leadership the instant we're out of here," she threatened, then jumped onto his back, locking her legs around his waist and sliding her arms up under his own to clamp over his shoulders.

She knew she was comparatively light, probably weighed around half of Aden's body weight, but she also carried the pack, and he was walking across a river in the dark on stones that weren't exactly meant to be used as steps. Focusing only on staying as relaxed as possible, so as not to throw him off, she breathed in the chilly air and thought about all the ways she would torture those who had taken her and Aden.

The guards had just been the brawn. Someone else was behind this.

Aden stepped onto the first stone, his muscles flexing against her as he maintained his precarious balance. A second step. A third.

Water frothed around the rocks, the river's passage rushing thunder around them.

Aden's body dipped and she held on though her training told her to let go so he'd have a better chance of survival. She knew Aden. He'd come for her again. He'd dive into that dangerous water in a stupid, irrational, un-Silent decision and he'd *come for her.* So she'd stay with him as long as possible, until there was no other option and even he would agree with her.

Only she wasn't sure he ever would.

He really was a very bad leader in that respect—and it was why his Arrows gave him their unswerving dedication. All of them rejects from the world, from their families. No one else had ever come for them, ever would. Silence or not, it mattered that Aden would. Perhaps that exposed a flaw in the heart of the Protocol and perhaps it was simply a sign that even Arrows had a soul.

Halfway across the river and she could hear shouts that indicated their pursuers were heading to the ridge she and Aden had slid down. "I estimate they'll see us in another two minutes."

Aden didn't answer, but she knew he'd heard.

Four more stones, the other side starting to appear closer, but then Aden's foot slipped. Zaira would've released him and chanced the water except that he locked one hand around her ankle. A silent statement that if they went, they'd go together. Irrational, she thought again as they both almost fell in before he righted himself.

Two more stones.

The sounds so close now, flickers of light flashing on the ridge when she glanced over her shoulder.

Aden slipped and slammed down to his knees . . . but it

was on the bank. He made sure his body tumbled sideways so she fell on the bank beside him rather than backward into the water. Pushing up on her hands, she looked up toward the ridge. "We need to get into the trees."

They made it barely in time; the chopper was in the air now and sweeping the area with a spotlight. Pressing themselves to the ground and covering their bodies in enough forest floor debris that they no longer looked people-shaped, Aden and Zaira waited.

Zaira breathed into her hands, the gloves she'd found in the coat's pockets too large but warm. She couldn't hear Aden breathing and for a second, her heart stopped. *Alone,* whispered the stunted, murderous child hidden in the darkest corner of her psyche, *alone.* A second later, she shook it off. He was being silent, that was all. Aden could be more silent than any other Arrow she knew, even the most capable assassin. She'd asked him once how he'd learned to do that. His answer was one she'd never forget.

When I was a child, my parents told me to be invisible, so invisible that no one would ever consider me a threat, so invisible that I would be forgotten.

Zaira didn't understand how anyone could have failed to see the relentless strength and raw power that lived in Aden, but they had. Ming LeBon had barely paid Aden any attention, until one day, their former leader suddenly realized someone else was holding the reins and that he'd been deposed. No more would Ming treat the Arrows as his personal death squad, using them up then putting them down as if they were lame dogs.

They belonged to Aden now. And they would follow him into hell itself.

She felt the spotlight sweep over her at that moment, the light seeping through her damp tomb with its smell of the earth and the musty wet of decomposing forest debris. The light didn't linger. The sound of the chopper grew more distant heartbeat by heartbeat as the search went downriver, the voices of the searchers on foot also heading in that direction.

"I think they're gone," she said at last.

"Slowly." Coming up from his prone position with painstaking care as she did the same, Aden picked up the pack she'd thrust under a tangle of undergrowth, then looked up at the smattering of stars exposed by a small gap in the cloud cover. "We're in the northern hemisphere."

Since it was spring in that hemisphere, they had to be either at a high elevation or in one of the generally colder areas such as Alaska. "Can you narrow it down further?"

"No, but this might." He retrieved a small device from the pack, stilled before turning it on. "It could have a tracker that could lead the search straight to us."

"Don't use it," Zaira said. "The risk outweighs the gain. In fact, leave all the tech behind. They may not have thought of it yet, but if there are trackers, they could activate them remotely."

Aden took out every piece of technology they'd carried this far, venturing to the river's edge to throw them in the water before returning. "How good is your knowledge of astronomy?"

"Bad. I've always had access to the PsyNet for reference." The psychic network overflowed with data. "And after my defection, I could telepathically contact others if I needed location data." Zaira had played dead for five years and eight months in order to provide a safe haven for "broken" or used-up Arrows for whom Ming had signed execution orders, but now the Net needed her alive and part of it. A large number of the Venice contingent had returned to the PsyNet with her, none of them any longer at risk from Ming's assassins and pet medics.

It had been a strange homecoming, the formerly stark night sky landscape of the Net now webbed with delicate golden threads created by the empaths whose presence protected the Psy race from a deadly psychic contagion, but it had been a homecoming all the same. In a heartbeat, her world had gone from a small, contained network she'd had to constantly remind herself wasn't a cage, to a vastness without boundaries.

It felt as if she'd taken her first real breath in years.

As a result of the work she'd done protecting empaths, thus interacting with them, one of those fragile golden threads had reached out to her and, despite her instinctive defensive reaction, she'd allowed it to connect. She had no desire to end up insane and foaming at the mouth as a result of the infection that had almost destroyed the Net before the empaths created the Honeycomb.

Thinking of the Honeycomb as armor helped her accept it. Knowing that on the other end was an empath with absolutely no survival skills whatsoever helped even further— Zaira had more chance of being eaten alive by scarab beetles than she had of coming under attack by an E whose gift helped create that protective web.

"Tell me when you start to flag," Aden said, pack back on. "We can't go far in the dark anyway, especially with no landmarks."

Zaira knew that had she been uninjured, they would've kept going. "I say we put more distance between us and our pursuers regardless."

They walked in silence, surrounded by trees on every side, with thick shrubs forming the undergrowth—which meant they unavoidably left a trail—and jagged rocks hidden beneath that they tried to avoid. Aden was the one who stopped. "Look."

Following his arm, she narrowed her eyes to see better. "A cave?" It was more a serrated slash in the rock face, but when they squeezed through, it proved large enough to fit them both. However, the instant they were inside, they shook their heads and moved back out. To be in that cave was to be protected—and to be trapped.

Instead, and keeping an eye on the increasingly ominous cloud cover, they eventually made a shelter at the tangled roots of a forest giant, breaking off branches from a nearby fir tree to create a carpet and then a kind of tent. Zaira ate the energy bars Aden gave her, made sure he ate his share, and forced him to drink half of one of the high-density nutrient drinks from the medkit.

"You're no use to me dead or hypothermic," she said when he told her to finish it. "Drink it."

Filling the empty bottle with water from a nearby stream, Aden put it back in the pack and lay down beside her. Snug against one another in the small space they'd deliberately structured that way to maximize heat retention, she said, "How did they take you?" Aden was as experienced as she was, and while she was the more deadly in one-on-one combat, he was smarter when it came to tactics. No one should've been able to outmaneuver him.

"Blitz attack," he said. "Four men hit me on a city street in the split second while I was out of public view—they came in shooting. I took a stun to the face."

That explained the spreading bruise on the right-hand side of his face. "They respected your skill more than mine."

"That's why you've always been so dangerous. People see you and think woman first and soldier second."

"I used to think my shape a hindrance before I realized the effect it had on males." At a height of five feet and two inches, she was relatively short, and while she was in lethal shape, her body tended toward curves rather than straight lines. "Now I see it as camouflage." The soft, unthreatening exterior hiding a razored blade that could cut your throat and not blink.

"Good." Aden put his hand on her forehead. "Your temperature is slightly elevated. Rest."

Tired from the continued pain in her gut and aware she had to become stronger if she was to function as his backup, she didn't argue. "Will you take first watch?"

When he said, "Yes," she closed her eyes and went to sleep. Because Aden was the one being on the planet she trusted never to harm her. He was too irrational to be sensible.

Chapter 4

"IT'S CONFIRMED? THE Arrows have escaped?" That was the last thing the organization needed.

"They won't get far," said the blunt-faced man who was the leader of the cleanup squad. "At least one is badly injured, from the report we received before it went to shit. Bandage we found inside was soaked with fresh blood. She'll die soon and save us the trouble of hunting her down."

"Arrows don't worry about camaraderie so she's probably already been dumped to survive on her own." The group of elite assassins was composed of piercingly intelligent and highly trained rabid dogs who'd do anything to complete a mission—or to survive capture. Leaving an injured squadmate behind wouldn't even be a question. "The retrieval of her body isn't a priority." Zaira Neve was no longer useful. "Concentrate on Aden Kai."

The human male on the other side of the screen chewed the tobacco he insisted on using, and spit out the yellow-brown residue in a disgusting display. "Yeah, well, he won't survive long, either. Massive storm front's about to hit the mountains and he's got nowhere to go."

That, at least, was true. The group had chosen the location in part because of the privacy afforded by its inaccessibility. "Continue tracking." The only way to be certain an Arrow was dead was to see the corpse.

"I will, but I need to know if I have authorization to take terminal action if necessary."

"Yes, but only if you can't contain him." Once broken, Aden Kai could be a critical intelligence asset. "Do *not* use the fail-safe solution. Not yet."

"No offense," said the tobacco-chewing subhuman creature, "but I was told real strict to only take orders from the whole group when it came to this kind of a decision, never just one of you."

There wasn't time for a group meeting, but he was right. This groundbreaking and brilliant organization worked only because each member believed himself or herself equal to the others. That equality was a carefully constructed sham, but the belief was important for the end goal. "The others will contact you within the next five minutes."

There would be no dissension, not on this point. Because if it was a case of a live Arrow with vengeance on his mind or a dead one, the equation was simple. Should Aden Kai prove problematic, the organization would have to live with the loss of data, change plans accordingly, adapt.

Adaptation was the key.

Chapter 5

ADEN SENSED ZAIRA fall into a deep sleep, her breathing even. Her skin, when he checked it after about what must've been an hour, was no longer as clammy. Though they were in a cold climate, which the rising wind was turning even more bitter, they were well clothed and had enough food to last another day. After that, they'd be in trouble, and Zaira was already dangerously weak as a result of blood loss.

Making sure the hood of her jacket covered her head, he curled his body around hers in an effort to keep her warm, his mind alert. However, that mind was bound in chains he had to force himself not to test. It went against his instincts, but he couldn't afford to do any damage that might debilitate him—his knowledge as a medic told him that whatever implant they had in their heads, it was unstable.

Technology this advanced *could* be created underground, but the Arrows worked in the shadows, worked in that underground. They would've picked up hints if this had been a long-term project. No, what he suspected was that the implant was some nightmare combination of the Human Alliance implant that shielded against psychic intrusion and the "hive-mind" implant developed by Ashaya Aleine while she'd been under the control of the Council.

Her research had been destroyed, a large part of it by Aleine herself, but it was possible that someone had smuggled out a prototype or had siphoned off enough of her research before she pushed the destruct button, to reverse engineer her creation and fiddle with it in concert with the Alliance implant to achieve this psychic-blinding effect.

If his hypothesis was true, the implant in his skull and in Zaira's couldn't be as well constructed as either of the originals—Aden had cause to know that Ashaya Aleine had helped the Alliance develop their implant, too. She was a genius on a level rarely found, and she worked in tandem with her sometimes psychotic but always brilliant twin. It'd be difficult for any lab in the world to procure a team that could match their combined abilities.

There remained a slim chance that he was wrong, that this was an independent creation, but if he was right, these implants could well have a remote self-destruct built in, as with the *original* Alliance implants. Their abductors could kill them from a distance. If so, the only reason he was alive was likely because they wanted to interrogate him about classified data.

Zaira, however . . .

He sat up, staring down at her. She'd been taken because whoever had been watching him believed she was a weakness in his armor. That fact had kept her alive up until now, but it wouldn't last. Their captors might think Zaira was already dead, but if they didn't find her body they'd push the detonation key in order to make certain. She'd die in a matter of seconds unless she was out of range. The same applied to him. They wanted him alive, but only to a certain point.

No one was stupid enough to hurt an Arrow, then set him free to come back with retribution on his mind.

"Zaira."

She woke silently and with Arrow swiftness. "Yes?"

"We need to move." He explained why as she sat up, a slight catch in her breath the only indication of pain.

It was an hour later, when she stumbled while they were crossing an exposed, treeless area that had only a thin covering of some kind of foot-high shrub or grass with tiny white flowers, that he realized something was seriously wrong. "Your wound?"

She halted in among the grasses. "Significant pain, some

light-headedness." Chest heaving in shallow breaths, the softness of her lips bracketed by white lines, she held his gaze. "I'm not going to last much longer."

He knew what she was telling him—to do what Arrows were trained to do and make the rational, logical decision: leave her behind. Gripping her chin, he said, "We are not that anymore. We are not only assassins trained to die and to kill. We do not abandon the weak or the hurt. And we never, *ever* leave our own behind." That, he decided at that instant, would be the new motto of the squad, be what all trainee Arrows were taught. *No Arrow is disposable. No Arrow is to be left behind.*

Zaira's eyes held his for a long moment, the thickness of her lashes throwing shadows over the rich black of her eyes. "You've changed," she said. "You were never Silent, but now you're . . . different."

Aden didn't disagree because she was right. Touching Vasic's bond with Ivy had altered him on a fundamental level. His fellow Arrow and closest friend guarded that bond with intense protectiveness, but Vasic had permitted Aden within his shields, permitted Aden to see the shimmering power of the translucent yet unbreakable strands that bound Vasic to his empath. Not only that, but he'd permitted Aden to touch one of the strands, *feel* the power of the emotions that locked him and Ivy to one another in an intricate, intimate tapestry.

Aden didn't know if it was because he'd been permitted so close, or if it was because Vasic was his blood brother and Ivy an empath, but when he'd touched their bond, he'd felt a sharp stab of emotion that was as painful as it was beautiful. A knife blade that slid in through muscle and bone and heart to make him bleed. "Vasic allowed me through his shields," he told Zaira. "After his bonding."

She went motionless. "What was it like?" A whispered question.

"I don't have the words." A slumbering part of him had awakened at the contact and that part craved the feeling of belonging that he'd sensed from Vasic. As if the world could fall, but Vasic knew Ivy would always be there, no matter what. Aden wanted the same. Not yet, not when so many of his Arrows needed him to remain their leader, alone and strong, but one day in the future, he wanted that intimate, absolute connection with another being. "Even before that experience, I wouldn't have left you behind. You know that."

"You *have* to go ahead," Zaira said, pressing her hand over his mouth when he would've spoken again. "Listen to me. If you go ahead, there's a chance you can find help, bring it back. We won't get half as far with me slowing you down."

Waiting until she removed her hand, he wrapped his arm around her waist and began walking. She came rather than hold him back. "Aden."

"Do you think," he said, "that I could continue on as I've been doing knowing I'd left you to die alone in the cold dark?"

Zaira's arm came around his waist; the sign of capitulation had his muscles tensing. Because it meant she was far worse off than she'd let on. Zaira never held on to anyone, never accepted help except in extreme circumstances.

Seeing movement a bare half minute afterward, he froze, his eyes tracking the lumbering shape until it resolved itself into the form of a black bear. The creature wasn't interested in them, disappearing off to the left while Aden and Zaira went forward.

"We need to get the implants out," he said, realizing she was right in one sense—they *were* too slow to outrun a chopper and if their captors had any intelligence they'd eventually do a low sweep over the entire possible search area while transmitting the command that would cause their brains to implode. "It's possible I'm wrong and there might not be a fail-safe switch, but we can't take that risk."

"Agreed." Zaira's response was immediate, her voice rough. "If we remove them, we might regain our abilities, be able to contact the squad."

Scanning the unforgiving landscape around them, he found a thick grove of trees that would provide cover and a shield against the wind. When Zaira stumbled, he picked her up and carried her there. Pain shot down his left leg from where he'd been injured in the fight outside the bunker, but it was nothing he couldn't handle.

Placing Zaira on the ground, her back against what

looked like it might be a young chestnut tree, he found the medical kit and started to go through the supplies. "Two disposable lasers left." One for each of them. "Power grade means it should be strong enough to cut through the skull since the area is already weakened, but it might not be enough to fully seal the wound."

Zaira took one laser. "I should do you first. Talk me through it before I lose consciousness."

It was a smart request but impossible. "I need to figure out how to get it out without paralyzing or killing us." If the implants had integrated into their brains and/or had filaments woven into their spinal columns, both were very real possibilities.

"What are the chances they've put it in a part of the brain you can't reach?"

"I won't know until I remove the bone. Our only advantage is that the surgery was clearly done recently and in a hurry—there's a high probability the implants won't have fully integrated." Fewer connections meant less chance of a fatal mistake.

Zaira handed back the laser. "My head's swimming. If you operate first, I might not remain conscious long enough to remove your implant."

"I have a longer window of life—they want to break me. Execution is a last resort." He looked up at the sky as he felt a spit of rain on the back of his hand. "Now, before the clouds open up. Angle your entire body to the left."

When she did, he dug out a penlight he'd taken from a guard. The beam was too thin to be useful anywhere but in close quarters, but it was bright enough at that range. Holding it between his teeth, he gathered up Zaira's barely shoulder-length hair and used a rubber band from the medkit to tie it up off her neck, exposing her nape and the area immediately above. Then he tucked a bandage between her collar and her spine to soak up the blood.

That done, he snapped on a pair of disposable surgical gloves. "This will hurt."

She reached out to grip one of the tree roots that had curled out over the earth before flowing back in. "Go."

Thin beam of light shining on the reddened and jaggedly

sealed flesh low on her scalp where a rough square of her hair had been shaved off, he frowned. "Damn it, it's infected." Whatever their captors had shoved in there, Zaira's body was rejecting it. Grabbing the disinfectant, he wiped the area and knew he'd have to hurt her again later by washing out the wound.

His muscles threatened to tense, but he couldn't allow that to happen. Not now, not when he needed to have rock-steady hands and iron focus. Thinking back to the lessons on the brain he'd had as part of his training, and of everything he'd learned as a result of his attempt to find a fix for Vasic's gauntlet, he put one hand on the back of Zaira's head to hold her in position, and very carefully made four incisions along the lines of the scar to cut through the skin and muscle and into bone.

She bled and it was a clean red, no sign of deep infection. Good.

Wiping away the blood with a swab he'd dampened with disinfectant, he put down the laser and disinfected a disposable scalpel, then used the tip to gently check if he could lift out the tiny piece of bone. No. He had to go deeper. Squeezing Zaira's shoulder to warn her, he used the laser again. It took three careful series of cuts to get the bone out. Zaira's breathing was beyond shallow by that point, but she was holding on to consciousness.

"There's a rough suture in the membrane that protects the brain," he told her. "I'm using the lowest setting on the laser to cut through it."

Relief punched through him as soon as he opened the suture. "I can see it. It's as if they literally just shoved it in."

"Wrong part of brain," Zaira managed to say as he replaced the blood-soaked bandage he'd thrust below her skull.

"Yes. So it must somehow be able to send signals to the right sections." There hadn't been enough time for filaments to weave their way through the neural matter.

Using the penlight to examine the implant, he said, "It has six very thin arms that are clasped around a part of the cerebellum." Like a spider gripping its prey. "I think the arms are meant to hold it in place until the final biological connections are made."

A crackle of blue-white light in the implant, powered either by Zaira's body or by a tiny battery within the implant itself. "It looks like it might work via electrical impulses."

Zaira took a deep breath, exhaled slowly. "Is that good?"

"Yes. It lowers the risk of dangerous neural connections." He tried to look very carefully under the implant to confirm, but he didn't have the right tools.

"If I'm wrong, I'll kill you." One more death on his conscience. And this time, it would be this woman he'd known almost as long as he'd known Vasic. Tortured and bruised black-and-blue, skinny and suspicious, she'd glared at him during that first meeting, then lied to his face, and he'd known he had to make sure she survived.

The squad needed her fire, her relentless spirit.

He wasn't sure he'd succeeded—Zaira lived, but that fire of the soul had gone into deep hibernation. The disobedient, wild, dangerous girl he'd met had become the perfect Arrow . . . who continued to argue with his decisions fifty percent of the time and who'd once shot him in order to make a point about a threat assessment.

What were you saying about the angle being impossible?

It had been a measured, glancing hit to his upper right arm that had barely taken off a layer of skin, but the memory gave him hope that the fire wasn't hidden so deep that there was no hope of its return.

Because it wasn't just the squad that needed it. Aden needed it most of all.

He'd been trying to provoke her since the fall of Silence in an effort to reawaken that part of her nature. Now he might be the one to end it all, to forever stifle the flame. "The risk of death is significant."

"I'm dying anyway," she said as rain hit his back, the canopy above not enough to totally shield them, though he angled his body to give Zaira as much protection as possible. "I'd rather go honestly, trying to fight this thing, than have my brain explode because I did nothing." A shuddering breath. "You'd make the same choice."

It was still the hardest thing he'd ever had to do.

Holding the penlight clamped between his teeth again, he used the laser at the lowest possible setting to burn the "legs" off the implant. When the tiny metallic square didn't fall away after all the legs were gone, he used the tip of the scalpel to lift it off. It stuck for a stubborn second and he held his breath at what could be a sign of further connections beneath, but then it was falling into his hand.

And Zaira was bleeding again.

Dropping the implant in the medkit, he said, "Disinfectant." It was the only warning he could give her before he washed the blood out with the burning liquid—the brain might not technically feel pain, but the skin and muscle at the incision site would. He would've never done this had he been in an infirmary, but out here, the risk of a fatal infection through the open wound was too high.

He had to take the chance the disinfectant wouldn't do further damage.

Her spine went stiff before her body slumped. Catching her, he leaned her against the chestnut tree on her side and, repairing the membrane, lasered the piece of bone back into her skull, hoping to hell he hadn't done permanent harm. The wound finally closed, if raggedly so, he put a small bandage over it, then got rid of the blood-soaked bandage below her neck by placing it, his gloves, and any other detritus in a small disposal bag and putting that in an unused pocket of the daypack.

If their pursuers brought in tracking dogs, he wouldn't leave such a rich blood supply for them to scent. At least he and Zaira had the rain on their side—it would wipe away any tracks, wash away scents. The rising wind might also ground the chopper, which would take any heat-sensing technology out of the running; even if the chopper stayed up, the presence of bears in the area would bring up false hits their pursuers would have to investigate.

He didn't immediately have to move Zaira.

Decision made, he slid the implant into a small plas bag that had held pain relief pills before he emptied the pills into the medkit. He placed the bag in the bottom of the medkit to protect it from the elements, weighing the bag down with the burned-out laser and putting all the remaining supplies on top before he shut the kit. That done, he used fallen leaves to line the floor of another small hide under the thickest part of the canopy and carried Zaira's unconscious body to lie on it, building a tent around her using low-hanging branches he snapped off from the trees around them. It would make them invisible from the air and provide protection from the elements.

By the time he finished, the rain was hard pellets whipped into a harsh slant by the wind, but the canopy was holding off most of it. He checked the hide, gathered three more heavily leafed branches to cover the spots where water might get in, then slid inside himself. He'd stay awake, maintain a watch, but he needed to be close to Zaira.

Her breathing was too faint, her pulse sluggish.

No.

Turning her over carefully onto her back, he unzipped her jackets, pushed up her sweater, and found her Arrow uniform once more sticky with blood. When he peeled it up and examined the bullet wound, he saw it was bleeding steadily. Grabbing the last disposable laser, he gripped the penlight again and sealed multiple torn veins. By the time the laser flickered, she wasn't leaking fresh blood.

He had to fight himself not to try to use his M ability to reach the internal wounds he couldn't see. Given the viciousness of the pain feedback to any attempt at using psychic abilities, she could wake to find him burned out, unconscious. And much as Zaira liked to tell him to leave her behind, he knew damn well she'd never leave him behind. She saw him as critical to the survival of the squad—he'd never been able to make her understand that she was as important. So if he went down, she'd stay, guard his back. Die.

That fact and all the others weighed against testing the padlock on his ability.

That didn't mean it was an easy decision.

Bandaging the wound, he found another one of the small, nutrient-rich drinks in the medkit and, lifting up her head, coaxed it down her throat, drop by tiny drop. Afterward, he placed her head on his thigh and kept his finger on the pulse in her neck, under the hood he'd tugged up over her head so she wouldn't lose heat through her skull. The fact that the top of her head was tucked up against his abdomen should also help her maintain her body temperature.

"Stay with me," he said as her pulse refused to grow stronger.

Zaira had survived a childhood so hellish, she should be insane or broken or a monster. Instead, she was one of the strongest Arrows he knew; she'd protected their most wounded, most broken for over five years. That many long years she'd stayed dead to the world, stayed in a tiny network that he knew must've felt like a prison to a woman who'd grown up in a barren locked room.

And still she'd gone because he'd asked her.

He would not allow her to die now, when, for the first time, she had a chance at a real life. This desolate landscape would not claim her fire. It had no right. "You *will* stay," he ordered, his lips against her ear. "You promised me." That promise had been made nearly twenty-one years ago, but he'd never forgotten, never would forget.

Even after months of sufficient food and daily outdoor exercise, she'd still been so skinny and small and with such anger inside her. Barely four feet tall back then, at least a foot shorter than him, and yet she'd said, "I won't run anymore. I won't try to leave. I've decided to stay and protect you."

"Why?"

Midnight black eyes afire in a sun-browned face that was all sharp bones. "Because you don't have a monster inside you."

"Keep your promise," he said now. "Don't leave. Stay with me. *Stay*."

His only answer was a pulse so faint, he could barely feel it.

Chapter 6

STANDING BELOW A star-filled North Dakota sky, Vasic tried and failed for the hundredth time to get to Aden or Zaira. "I can't sense either of them," he told Ivy where his wife stood next to him on the wide verandah both his lost squadmates had helped build.

The light above bathed the area in a gentle glow that didn't penetrate the night darkness beyond. "I've never not been able to sense Aden." The idea that his failure meant his closest friend was dead was a possibility he refused to consider.

Dark circles under the translucent copper of her eyes and lines of tension around her mouth, Ivy took the phone from her ear and thrust it into a pocket. "Sahara says Kaleb's continuing to try, too, but he's getting nowhere."

That was bad. Vasic was a born teleporter and Kaleb Krychek a cardinal telekinetic who could also lock on to people rather than simply places. If the two of them couldn't locate Aden or Zaira, no one could. "I can't even tell if they're together or not." The timing of the abductions suggested the same foe at work, but they couldn't rule out two separate actions or two separate prisons. "The Es connected to Aden and Zaira—they're still sensing nothing?"

Ivy rubbed her face. "Yes. They're saying it doesn't feel like death . . . just as if they're lost."

Vasic had never known Aden to be lost. Even as a child,

his best friend had known where he was headed, known what he wanted.

Wrapping her arms around him, warm and soft and loving, Ivy said, "Aden's strong, resourceful, incredibly smart, and Zaira's lethal, with a mind that thinks in ways no one can predict." The bond between them rippled with her passionate belief. "Whatever the situation, I know those two will come out on top."

Vasic held her tight with the single arm he possessed; Samuel Rain's attempts at designing and building him a working prosthetic had continued to fail. Vasic could've halted the entire thing, but after what the brilliant robotics engineer had done to save his life, it was a small enough thing to indulge Samuel's eccentricity and determination to succeed.

"He needs constant challenges," Aden had said a bare week earlier, while he and Vasic were going through a martial arts training routine in the open area to the left of the verandah. "Right now, you're it." A small pause. "Sooner or later, he *will* succeed or go mad trying, so you'd better decide if you do, in fact, want a prosthetic."

"Since I was eight years old," Vasic said to Ivy, the side of his face pressed to the soft black of her hair, "Aden's always been there." A quiet rock that didn't shift or give way no matter how vicious the deluge. "The idea of not being able to speak to him . . . I can't process it." Vasic had once had a death wish; it wasn't until this instant that he understood what it must've done to Aden to believe he'd have to watch Vasic die.

Ivy leaned back to reach up and stroke his hair off his face, her gaze potent with emotion. "He's your brother." She swallowed past the thickness in her voice. "And he's our family."

She understood; she'd always understood. Never had she begrudged him his friendship with Aden. Never had she failed to include Aden in their new family.

Love isn't finite, she'd told him, it is infinite and it has infinite facets.

"I love him, too," she whispered. "Even though he's a year younger than you, he's like a big brother."

"Yes." Vasic cupped the back of her head. "Aden's always

been older than he should be." Always carried too much weight on his shoulders.

"And Zaira." Ivy's hand fisted against his chest. "She plays with Rabbit, you know."

"What?" He'd never seen the commander throw so much as a stick for his and Ivy's pet, had always thought she was too deep in Silence to pay attention to the needs of a small white dog.

Ivy nodded against him, fine strands of her hair catching against his jacket. "I've seen her when she thinks no one is watching. She'll play-fight for his stick with him, and once, I saw her give him a treat she must've bought herself."

Raw hope grew in his heart, dulled only by the dark fact that both Aden and Zaira were missing. "Is she capable of breaking Silence?" He'd never forget the defiant, bruised, and bloodied girl he and Aden had first met, the girl Aden had stayed in touch with even when he and Vasic had been transferred to a training facility on a different continent.

Vasic and Aden had shared so much growing up, but Aden's relationship with Zaira was and had always been, separate. Vasic had never questioned it, seeing it simply as Aden being Aden and keeping an eye on a member of the squad who needed it. That was before Ivy. Being bonded to an empath had given him new eyes; he'd begun to glimpse odd inconsistencies in Aden's interactions with Zaira, things that didn't line up with his behavior when it came to the rest of the squad.

Vasic hadn't said anything but he hoped that his friend would find with Zaira what Vasic had found with Ivy. He wanted that for Aden, wanted him to know what it was to find home in his lover's eyes. Even more, he wanted the laughter for Aden, the joy of figuring out how to navigate this new territory of love and affection and tactile contact that wasn't about pain or training or anything but pleasure. The only problem Vasic had foreseen was Zaira herself—the Venetian commander had never shown any signs of desiring a life beyond Silence.

"Zaira's shields are so strong I never pick up anything," Ivy told him, running a hand up and down his back in a petting gesture she didn't seem to be aware of making but that was deeply familiar to him by now. "I don't know if she feels or even *wants* to feel, but anyone with the capacity to be kind to a small animal who can offer her no advantage, has a heart." Ivy looked up, a sheen of emotion in her eyes that punched him in the heart. "She has this blunt and deeply honest way of looking at the world. No filters."

"You're friends," he said, the realization a surprise.

Ivy wiped at her eyes. "Not yet, but we're getting there. I really like her even if she keeps telling me I have the survival skills of a newborn puppy," she added with a wet laugh. "She's planning to teach me self-defense moves tailored to my size and weight."

"Did you tell her I'm already giving you lessons?"

A shaky smile. "She said the things you're teaching me are fine if I plan to grow a foot and put on ninety pounds of muscle. Otherwise, I need to move smarter and be more sneaky."

He felt his lips curve slightly. "Yes, that sounds like Zaira." Pressing his forehead to Ivy's when she drew in a trembling breath, Vasic cupped her face in his hand. "You said it—they're tough. They'll survive and we'll find them."

"I know." Ivy closed her fingers over his wrist. "I just hope they're not being hurt." Anger and worry and frustration. "It's enough, Vasic. *Enough.* Why can't the world just leave the Arrows in peace?"

Vasic had no answer for her, but he knew his next move. "I'm going to head to Venice," he said, continuing to hold her face in his hand, her skin so soft under his touch and her love so sweetly fierce that he was astonished all over again that he had the right to hold her, to call her his own. "We still aren't certain where Aden was taken, but Zaira's team has pinpointed the exact location of her abduction."

"I'll come with you." Ivy pressed her palms to his chest, his empath who was so generous with touch, with affection. "I might be able to help some of Zaira's people. Especially Alejandro—he's not functional without her."

IVY had been right to worry about Alejandro.

The Arrow, who was only in his twenties, had imprinted on Zaira after his brain reset following an overdose of a drug Ming LeBon had used to turn Arrows into mindless weapons.

As a result of Zaira's absence, he was in a violent rage. Corralled in a secure room in the Venetian compound, he was crashing his body repeatedly against the door in an effort to get out.

"Be careful," Vasic told Ivy, well aware she had a full measure of the empathic tendency to give too much, even at the cost of her own safety. "His brain is compromised. He may not react to empathic help in a predictable way."

"He's afraid." Ivy's voice held an echo of pain that wasn't her own. "I can sense it from here—Zaira is his only anchor to sanity and he's terrified he's falling back into the abyss. More than that, he's terrified for her." Her head turned toward the door behind which Alejandro screamed in fury. "Keeping him trapped and unable to assist in the search for her isn't a good idea."

Vasic wanted to free the other male, but he also knew that to be an impossibility. "He's a deadly threat. He'd think nothing of killing tens if not hundreds of people in his hunt to find Zaira." The commander was Alejandro's sole priority but not in a healthy way. "The best we can do is sedate him so he doesn't harm himself." And hope Zaira wasn't lost forever, because if she was, so was Alejandro.

The clarity of Ivy's eyes reflected her awareness of that terrible unspoken truth. "I'll see if I can calm him enough that the process of giving him a sedative doesn't turn into a bloodbath—and doesn't cause him even more psychic pain."

Waiting in the predawn darkness that cloaked this part of the world, he watched until he saw her reach the closed door guarded by two sentries who came toward her, no doubt with a report about Alejandro. Only then did he follow Zaira's lieutenant, Mica, out of the compound that had functioned as a secret bolt-hole under Silence. It was here that many of their "dead" had come, the ones deemed useless by Ming and targeted for execution.

Aden, Vasic, Zaira, and the others at the heart of the rebellion hadn't been able to save all their brethren and each loss lingered, an open wound on their souls, but they'd saved enough that the squad was now the strongest it had ever been. Many of Ming's useless Arrows had decades' worth of experience to pass on to those coming through the ranks.

Even Alejandro had something to contribute—quite aside from being a fully trained Arrow who could provide backup as long as Zaira gave him the order, he was a genius with delicate explosives.

Ming hadn't seen any of that. All he'd seen were men and women who were "imperfect," and thus not worth the time or the effort to ensure they could remain a part of the squad. That made him a fool.

"What was Zaira doing outside the compound?" he asked Mica.

"I think she just needed downtime." The dark-haired and stocky male, whose jaw was currently heavily shadowed by stubble, glanced around to ensure they couldn't be overheard. "Some of the older Arrows occasionally do their best to make her brain explode."

"I've always told Aden I'm surprised they're all still alive." Zaira was not known for her patience.

Mica's expressionless facade didn't crack. But when he spoke, Vasic understood why he was Zaira's lieutenant. "I've offered to disappear them where no one would ever find the bodies, but Zaira says they'll come back from the dead, they're so stubborn about doing things a certain way."

It would, Vasic thought, take time for the old guard to adapt to this new world. "Did she often take the same route on her walks?"

Mica shook his head. "She was scrupulous about never following a pattern . . . but she did go for a walk away from the compound at some point every two or three days."

So someone had to have been watching her, waiting for her to get far enough away that the chances of backup reaching her in time were low.

"We're here, sir."

Though the canal water sat dark and placid beside them, the evidence of violence was easy to spot not far from where two older Arrows stood watch and kept away the robe-and-slipper-clad spectators who'd spilled out of the nearby homes. Splatters of blood marked the cobblestones, distinctive even under the dull yellow of the light seeping through the old glass of the ornate streetlamp.

Krychek appeared beside Vasic right then. Dressed in

black combat pants and a black T-shirt, the cardinal telekinetic appeared more akin to the Arrows than to the political
sharks with whom he swam daily. "This is the location?" His
eyes, cold white stars on black, scanned the scene.

Vasic gave a short nod before looking toward Mica. "The
bodies?" There was too much blood for one person; he'd
have known Zaira had taken down at least one of her attackers even without the telepathic briefing he'd received when
Mica's team first arrived at the scene.

"We have three in a cold storage room at the compound."
The lieutenant stood at parade rest, his eyes watchful of the
civilians who lingered beyond the perimeter. "Someone used a
high-powered laser to burn off the dead men's faces and their
fingerprints show signs of having been burned off months ago."

"Crude but effective." Kaleb looked at Vasic from the other
side of the splatters of blood, having walked slowly around, his
eyes cataloguing the evidence as he moved. "Obliterating the
faces wouldn't have taken longer than a minute at most. DNA?"

Mica answered only after glancing at Vasic and receiving
a nod. Vasic wasn't officially Aden's second in command,
had never believed he was stable enough for the position, but
his squadmates had always treated him as if he was—and
now, the mantle was beginning to fit.

"No DNA hits."

It was possible to wipe someone that deeply from the official record, but it took considerable power and access.
"Psy?" he asked the lieutenant as Kaleb crouched down beside the bloodstains as if attempting to analyze the pattern.

The answer was a surprise. "One Psy, two humans."

Krychek's head came up at Mica's response, the flawless
physical lines of his face betraying nothing, despite the fact
that he was the man who'd taken down Silence. Many people
believed it was a twisted double bluff, that Krychek was
holding on to his own emotionless conditioning while nudging others out of it. Those who believed the latter thought he
planned to take advantage of the confusion engendered by
the breakdown of a way of life that had lasted more than a
hundred years.

Those people seemed to have conveniently forgotten the

psychic bond that tied Krychek to Sahara Kyriakus. The man wasn't Silent—he was just very, very, *very* good at showing only what he wished.

"Psy and human?" he said to Mica, his dark hair gleaming blue-black under the streetlight.

"Yes. We double-checked the genetic screen."

That was highly unusual. Psy and humans *could* work together, and the Human Alliance had recently assisted in helping those of Vasic's race control the infection that had turned so many Psy blindly murderous, but it was a fragile relationship at best. Humans had no trust in the Psy, given how often unethical Psy had used their abilities to manipulate and rape human minds. For members of the two races to work together to abduct an Arrow was so beyond the realm of what was known as to be nearly incomprehensible.

"Did the humans show signs of mind control?" Long-term control could leave physical lesions on the brain.

Mica shook his head. "It was the first thing the pathologist looked for."

Vasic wasn't surprised—it made no sense to use enslaved humans against a high-value target. The puppet master couldn't know when his slaves might collapse from the strain of fighting against psychic coercion. "Any other useful data?"

Mica's eyes met Vasic's. *Sir, should I answer aloud?*

Vasic knew Mica wasn't worried about the bystanders— they were too far away to catch anything. *Did you find any signs Krychek may be involved?*

No, though investigations are ongoing.

Answer aloud for now and run any sensitive data past me. The fact was, Kaleb had tentacles in every corner of the Net—he was an asset they couldn't afford not to utilize. And so far in their alliance, the cardinal had kept his word.

"Zaira managed to telepath certain details before she was incapacitated," the lieutenant said. "Five trained operatives working as a unit, in silence."

That eliminated any possibility of mind control. Zaira was very experienced. If she'd described the five as a unit, they had to have been consciously cooperating. Mind control was never that smooth, especially in high-pressure situations.

Krychek rose to his feet. His telepathic voice was as cold and obsidian as his eyes when he said, *There's been nothing, not even a faint rumor, of any such Psy-human cooperation.*

It appears we have an intelligent and careful enemy. One smart enough to plug all leaks and skilled enough to abduct the leader of the Arrow Squad and one of his most experienced commanders. Before today, Vasic would've said that was impossible.

Chapter 7

ZAIRA WOKE WITH a throbbing head and a mouth filled with cotton wool, the pillow under her head hard yet tensile. Scanning out with her mind, she gasped, the shattering pain sparking fireworks in front of her eyes.

"Zaira." A familiar masculine voice in the pitch-dark inside what had to be a hide, Aden's hand brushing away her hood to expose her face, his blunt-tipped fingers on her pulse. "How is your head?"

"Water first," she said, her voice coming out a croak as she managed to sit up after bracing her hand on her pillow—which turned out to be Aden's thigh. He was warm under her touch and she didn't immediately break the contact. Being alone inside her head . . . it threatened to wake the feral, inhuman creature she'd once been, the one who had planned two murders and executed the plan so flawlessly that Justice had wanted to execute her.

The fact she'd been seven years old at the time had been seen not as a mitigating factor but as an aggravating one.

If the subject is capable of this level of violence at her current age, she will undoubtedly be a threat to society if allowed to grow to adulthood.

That had been the conclusion of the joint PsyMed-Justice report done on her at the time, a report she'd accessed after she was an adult. They had been right in a sense; left alone, she would've no doubt become even more violent and out of control. It was Arrow training that had taught her discipline . . . and Aden who had taught her that she had value beyond her ability to mete out violence.

"Here."

Taking the water bottle from Aden in her spare hand, the fingers of her other one curling into the taut muscle of his thigh, she drank the whole bottle. "We'll have to get more."

"The weather's going to make collecting water a nonissue."

Eyes acclimated enough to the darkness that she could make him out, she saw Aden reaching inside the pack for more water. "No, not just now." Putting down the empty bottle, she lifted her hand to touch the incision site, but he tugged it away before she could make contact.

"It's out," he told her after releasing her wrist. "Don't mess with it. Your head?"

"As if there's a live jackhammer in there." The final sparks of the fireworks finally faded away to leave her conscious of the sound of thunderous rain outside. No wonder Aden wasn't worried about their water supply. "How long was I out?"

"I don't have a timepiece but I estimate three hours."

"The chopper?"

"I heard it circling maybe an hour after you went down, and just before the rain got this bad and the wind turned into a gale."

So they were safe enough for now. Their pursuers would be idiotic to try to track them in this terrain in the dark in such inclement weather. On the flip side—"They have to know we'll have holed up."

Aden nodded. "We'll have to be ready to move as soon as the weather clears up enough that the chopper can take off again." Lifting an index finger, he made her follow it from left to right, then took her through a battery of other tests to check for any lingering impairment. "You're physically fine."

"No PsyNet link," she said, answering his unasked question. "I instinctively did a telepathic scan when I woke and the pain was severe enough that I think a second attempt could cause me to black out again."

The aloneness was a huge thing inside her, stretching and

growing and swallowing her up until soon all that remained would be the rage that had burned in her as a child. "We should do your surgery now." Not only was her mental state unstable, her abdomen didn't feel right. "I think I might still be bleeding internally."

Expression grim, Aden got her to pull up her blood-matted top and palpated her abdomen. "Yes," he said afterward. "I clearly didn't find all the damage."

"It's not your fault." She put the top—plus the sweater—back down and zipped up his leather jacket, then the waterproof one she wore over it. "The fact you've kept me alive this long is a credit to your skill." He was only meant to be a field surgeon and medic, but Aden had never been "only" anything. "Let me pay back the favor. This weather makes it likely they'll press the kill switch the next time they can get up in the air. No point leaving you alive if they have doubts about being able to get to you."

"There's just enough charge left in the last laser that you should be able to unseal the bone following the lines of the original surgery. You'll have to do the rest using a scalpel."

She stared at him. "Aden I'm a combat telepath trained in hand-to-hand fighting and various weapons. I know how to slit a throat using any knife at hand, but I don't know how to do complex surgery." It would've been difficult enough with the laser. "I'll butcher you." End up with hands drenched in blood again.

Her mind flickered with frozen snapshots of her palms stained a rust red that had an orange tinge, her arms splattered with flecks of brain matter. Each mental photograph was from the point of view of the child she'd been, the ground below far closer and her bare feet wet with the blood in which she'd walked as she brought down the pipe over and over again.

Small, smeared footprints surrounded the bodies.

Gritting her teeth, she slammed shut a mental door that hadn't opened since the day she perfected her shields. That screaming, bloodied girl was gone. Dead. "I can't do it."

"You have to." Aden dragged the daypack closer and pulled out the medkit.

"Aden," she began, fingers still curled tightly into his thigh.

His eyes locked with hers in the darkness inside the co-coon he'd created for them. "I'm dead otherwise." An in-escapable truth. "As you said, I'd make the same choice."

To die attempting to fight their captors rather than allow them to blow up his brain from a distance.

Breathing in and out, she tried not to hear the scrabbling nails of the murderous ghost she'd put back in her cell, and said, "Tell me how."

HUNDREDS of miles away, another meeting was taking place, the attendees hooked in via comm screens set to audio only, except for the one that showed the man in charge of the operation to retrieve Aden Kai.

"A much bigger storm is scheduled to hit within the next hour." His jaw moved as he chewed. "We'll have a roughly five-minute window in about ten minutes—the current front is moving away from us and the real storm's not yet arrived."

"Chances of retrieval?"

"Low. I've got people on the ground but they're trapped on either side of swollen rivers and streams, or hampered by low visibility." A foul dark brown stream coming out of his mouth, his spit aimed at the ground. "We can take the chop-per up in the window between the smaller storm and the big-ger one. What do you want me to do? Search or eliminate?"

"Please wait." Muting their side of the feed so he wouldn't be able to hear the discussion, the attendees spoke among themselves, their voices distorted by technology. The deci-sion was unanimous: Aden Kai could have been a serious asset, one that would've significantly accelerated their long-term plans, but they couldn't risk him getting out alive.

"Eliminate," they told the search leader. "Take the chop-per up as soon as it clears and sweep the area while emitting the destruct signal."

That signal had a range of two miles. The leader of the Arrows would be dead long before the second storm hit.

BLOCKING out the noise of the howling wind and the pounding rain, her heavy rainproof jacket off so she could move more easily, Zaira knelt behind Aden. He was taller than her but he'd taken a cross-legged position and bent forward so she could work on him.

She gripped the penlight in her teeth, shining the beam onto the crudely sealed incision on the back of his head, and after cleaning it as he'd told her, picked up the laser and cut along the lines of the previous surgery. Aden had instructed her to do it three times, going a fraction deeper each time. The laser died midway through her third set of cuts.

"You should be able to use the tip of the scalpel to lever up the bone," Aden said with no pain in his tone, though she knew from experience that this had to hurt. "The previous seal is weak enough now that it should break."

Taking the disinfected blade, Zaira followed his instructions. Any hesitation could mean the difference between getting the implant out in time or not, the difference between Aden's life or his death, so she put her mind into the icy-calm state where nothing could reach her and used a knife on the one person she'd sworn to protect, to never harm.

"Bone's out," she said around the penlight.

Blood welled and she had to wash it out using the disinfectant. "I can see the suture in the membrane."

"Cut it open—use a delicate touch."

She made the cut before she could overthink things. "Done."

Aden's shoulders locked, his breathing rough, but he said, "You should see the implant."

"It's not there." She made sure the beam was shining right at the wound, and that the blood had been cleaned out. A glint caught her eye. "Wait. I can see the very edge of what might be one of the 'legs' you described."

"They did the surgery in a rush. The implant may have moved." Aden released a harsh exhale. "You'll have to widen the hole in the bone using the blade."

The ice threatened to crack, her stomach churning. A single tiny error and she could stop his breathing. But if she didn't, she reminded herself, then the cowards who'd done this would kill him from a distance.

"Get ready," she said from around the penlight and began to saw at the bone.

The disposable scalpel bent a minute later and she had to switch to a barbaric-looking hunting knife. Disinfecting it, she continued on, having to clear away blood multiple times, the knife doing far more damage than a laser would have.

She couldn't hold on to the ice. This wasn't some random target. This was Aden. And she was hurting him, blood slick on her thin surgical gloves.

"Zaira."

Realizing she'd frozen, she slammed the memory door shut again and continued to slowly, painfully widen the hole in his skull.

Sweat trickled down her temple but she kept her hand steady. This was Aden's life. She *would not* fail. Putting down the knife after removing an inch-by-inch square of bone, she washed out the blood using the disinfectant because they had no other sterile liquid. Aden went rigid but stayed conscious. "Do you see it?" he gritted out.

A glimmering square of metal in among the flesh and blood. "Yes," she said just as there was a tiny flicker of blue at the site, an electrical impulse passing through the device.

"This'll be the hardest part," he said, his breathing rough. "You can't laser through the legs so you'll have to use the tip of the scalpel to lift them up." He asked to see the bent scalpel. "Yes," he said after she showed him. "The tip is still sharp and flat enough for it to work."

It was like asking a giant to pick up a single fine sewing needle off a floor slippery with blood.

But Zaira would do it. There was no other choice.

"The rain's stopped."

Zaira hadn't noticed, but now she felt the stunning quiet. No rain, no wind. The chopper would be in the air soon, their pursuers moving on the ground. It meant they, too, had to move, but she wasn't about to rush this and paralyze or kill Aden.

She carefully disinfected the scalpel again using the near-empty bottle of disinfectant. She was just about to slip the angular and sharp tip under a metallic spider leg when she heard the faint, faraway echo of the chopper. Ignoring it, she went back to work . . . and suddenly the implant lit up, the electrical impulses turning it into an electric blue storm.

Every muscle in Aden's body locked as the impulses started to snake up at rapid speed, going for his cerebral cortex. She didn't even think about it. Sliding the tip of the blade directly under the main part of the implant, she tore it off without finesse and threw it aside. "Aden? Aden!" He was bleeding badly, his head hanging forward.

She washed out the wound with the last of the disinfectant and, with no way to repair the membrane, slotted in the pieces of bone she'd removed and slapped on a thick piece of gauze to soak up the blood while she tried to find a pulse in his neck. "Don't be dead," she said. "Don't be dead." It was a low, staccato mantra as she searched desperately for a pulse, her blood-slick fingers sliding over his skin. "Don't be dead, Aden." *Don't leave me all alone. You promised I would never be alone again.*

Tearing off the gloves, she replaced the blood-soaked gauze and searched for a pulse again. Aden couldn't be dead. Aden was the squad's future. Without him, they'd crumble, fade away, break into a million pieces. "Don't be dead," she said again, and this time it was an order. "Wake up!"

Thud.

She halted, listened with her fingertips, and felt it again, the thud of his heart pumping blood. Removing her fingers from his throat, she quickly lifted the gauze and checked the state of the bleeding. Bad. There was nothing in the medkit to seal it up, so all she could do was tape a fresh gauze pad over the site and try to put pressure on the wound.

It wasn't enough. He needed proper medical attention.

Her abdomen cramped at the same time, pain shooting through her torso. Breathing past it, she found the second-to-last bottle of nutrient drink and, tilting Aden's body back toward her own so that his head was supported by her shoulder, dripped the enriched liquid into his mouth. When he didn't swallow, she stroked his throat. "Swallow, Aden, or I'll cut your throat and pour it straight in."

There was little chance he could hear her, but he swallowed with the next stroke of her fingers, so she continued the action. "A little more. I need you conscious and able to walk." If necessary, she'd put his body against the tree behind her and kill anyone who came close, but he'd have a much higher chance of survival if she could get him farther from their pursuers.

It took time to finish the bottle and the chopper got close to them more than once. If it came too close, the heat-seeking equipment would capture their images and betray their location, but the rain pounded down again just in time, the wind even stronger. So strong that it howled through the copse of trees, tearing apart their hideout in a matter of seconds and scattering their supplies.

Chapter 8

ZAIRA TURNED HER back into the wind, protecting Aden's face as the rain and the wind hit the leather jacket she wore. Realizing she couldn't afford to lose body heat through exposure, not if she was to get Aden to safety before her own body gave out, she tried to search for the larger rainproof jacket and could see nothing in the darkness and the rain. It was only when she shifted to better protect Aden that she realized she'd accidentally knelt on the jacket.

Placing Aden's head very carefully on her thigh and making sure his hood was on, his jacket zipped up, she pulled on her own. She had to fight the wind to do it, water running from her drenched hair down her spine. That wasn't good, but hopefully the jacket would keep out the worst of it now. Pulling on her hood, she tied the drawstring under her chin tight before slipping on the gloves she'd stuffed into the pockets.

Three hours she'd been out. If Aden was going to be unconscious that long, she had to come up with plan B, find some way to protect him from this vicious weather. She'd have to dig, she decided. Use her hands to make a shallow indentation where—no, the water would fill that up. If she lost consciousness and didn't keep his head up or keep the rain off his face, he could drown.

Unable to sense his pulse through her thick gloves, she bent her face to Aden's, tried to feel his breath as she continued to

consider and discard possible options. If only she could carry
him, but he was too heavy. She might be able to create a litter,
drag—

"Zaira."

Jerking up, she looked down at his closed eyelids, wondering if she was having an auditory hallucination as a result
of the fragmentation caused by the aloneness, but then he
lifted the thick, curling lashes so unexpected in the otherwise clean lines of his face. "Out?"

She spoke against his ear so he'd hear her. "Yes, I got it
out." When he tried to sit up, she helped him, leaning his
back against a tree. "Keep your head down!" she said into his
face, the rain and the wind loud around them. "I'm going to
see if I can find any of our supplies!"

"Line. Of. Sight." It was ground out between his teeth,
and she saw more than heard the words.

She understood regardless. "I won't go far!" It'd be easy
to become turned around in this terrain and weather, lose
one another.

Crawling on her hands and knees in an effort to get below
the wind, she banged her knee into the sharp corner of a
metal object. *The medkit.* Immediately taking it back to
Aden, she put it by his thigh. It held the implant he'd taken
out of her head; Zaira knew it was critical they protect that.
Even if she and Aden didn't make it, if the squad found the
implant, it would offer some answers.

She protected the medkit with her body as she opened it
to retrieve the last tiny bottle of concentrated nutrient drink.
"You need strength," she said when Aden would've pushed it
toward her. "I'm not leaving you and we need to move." This
group of trees had appeared strong earlier, but the wind was
all but pushing them over now, revealing their dangerously
shallow roots. "I can't carry you. You're too damn big."

As if in a period to her words, a tree not far from them
crashed to the earth with a sound so loud it cut through the
weather, the impact reverberating along the ground. Another
tree fell soon afterward, snapped in half like a matchstick.

"Quick," Aden ordered, and took the drink.

Crawling forward again, in the direction of the wind, she
found the now empty daypack plastered against a tree. The

only other things she found were three solid energy bars trapped in the roots of a tree and, oddly enough, the penlight, which had become stuck against a large rock.

She put the items in the pack, crawled back to Aden's side, and added the medkit to it. "Can you walk?"

In answer, he levered himself up and seemed to find his balance after a shaky start. Getting up, she rose on her toes as he bent forward so they could speak. "The energy hit helped," he said. "My head's pounding, but I can function." Taking the daypack, he pulled it on, then slipped his arm around her waist. "Stay together!"

She gripped the back of his jacket. "Go!"

Another tree slammed to the earth only inches from them. It was no longer safe to stay here but heading out onto open ground left them brutally exposed to the elements. And those elements were in a punishing mood. Lightning lit up the sky in a jagged white-hot burst in the distance, thunder boomed, and each drop of rain hit like a tiny shard of ice, cutting at their faces and soaking everything not covered by the rainproof barrier of their jackets.

Her combat pants had some built-in weather protection but nothing designed to deal with this kind of a storm. She could feel water trickling into her socks, knew her feet would be ice-cold before long. Aden had to be in the same situation. Cold, however, was a problem they'd handle when it became an issue. Right now, it was about making it to safe harbor, any safe harbor. They could not stay expos—

Her stomach suddenly cramped again and this time, she couldn't control the nausea.

Bending forward to throw up, she tasted blood.

ADEN helped Zaira up after her convulsive retching, shivers wracking her body so uncontrollably that it felt as if she'd shatter. Holding on to her more tightly, he used all his energy to help her move.

"I'm going to lose consciousness soon," she said against his ear when he bent toward her. "I'll be dead weight."

He'd carry her until he couldn't walk anymore. Because he would never again watch one of his people die without doing everything in his power to stop it. "Do you know how many Arrows I had to let go?" he asked her. "How many I couldn't assist, couldn't get out when they began to fracture?"

"They understood, Aden. We all did." Her fingers clenched in his jacket, her left leg beginning to drag. "You were fighting for our survival and they died in battle." Harsh breaths. "Don't take that honor from them by using their deaths as a whip with which to punish yourself."

His shin hit a rock hidden in the dark, the impact hard enough to bruise bone, but he kept going. "Stop talking. Conserve your strength."

"And stop winning the argument?"

If Aden had known how to smile, he thought he may have at that instant. Zaira's razor-sharp words told him she was still fighting. But he didn't know how to smile, his emotions crushed beneath the heavy weight of Arrow training until he wasn't sure they existed—but he wanted to find out.

"Thank you," Zaira said unexpectedly the next time he bent toward her. "For not leaving me alone in the dark." A breath that didn't sound right. "For keeping your promise."

You'll never be alone again. I will always be there for you.

He'd made that promise to the suspicious, ferocious girl she'd been. Tonight, on this desolate landscape under an unfriendly sky, he made it again to the strong, determined, just as ferocious woman she'd become. "I will never leave you. No matter what."

No answer.

"Stay awake!" He shook her slightly, only breathed again when she made a protest. "Tell me about your first assignment."

"I cocked it up." Her voice was sluggish and almost inaudible in the howling wind, but she was still breathing, still conscious. "I was sent in to retrieve evidence of a serial killer and I got caught in the room with him."

"Since he ended up dead, I don't think you erred."

"Everyone ends up dead around me. You should be careful."

"You've kept those in the Venice compound alive and functional and they're some of our most fractured." He squeezed her when she didn't reply. "Zaira."

" 'm awake," she mumbled as the rain suddenly slowed to a light drizzle then cut off altogether, almost as if they'd passed the line of demarcation of a heavy cloud bank. Aden knew the lull wasn't going to last, so he took the chance to scan the area, saw a large stand of trees not far in the distance. They appeared much more solid than the ones under which they'd previously taken shelter—and as far as he could see, none was in any danger of collapsing.

If he and Zaira made it there, they could hunker down and he could try to figure out how to fix her injuries. Part of his brain tried to tell him it was too late, that he didn't have the equipment to fix the damage, but Aden wasn't about to give up. He would fight for her till the last beat of his heart and hers.

"Aden, my mind wants to reach out."

"Fight it." Another burst of pain could incapacitate her. "Think about the next dinner at Ivy and Vasic's house."

"Do you think," she said between gasped breaths, "Ivy expected so many Arrows to take her up on her offer of an open door?"

"Ivy is an empath. She likes people—she even likes Arrows."

Zaira's body got heavier, but she continued to drag her feet forward. "I think I'm hallucinating."

She sounded too lucid to be hallucinating. "What do you see?" He couldn't see anything of interest.

"Giant paw prints in the mud."

Stilling, he glanced toward the ground. He hadn't focused on it except to make sure they didn't run into anything, but Zaira's head had been hanging down. He lowered her into a seated position against a large rock and, wiping his hand over his face to rid it of the water dripping from the hood, took out the penlight.

"You're not hallucinating. I can't be certain, but I think they're feline." And very fresh. The prints had to have been made since the rain stopped, and that couldn't have happened more than two minutes earlier.

"What kind of cat has paws that big?"

Using the penlight to trace the edge of the print, he saw the shape of claws, measured the size of the pad using his gloved hand as a comparison. "A changeling cat. One of the large predators. Tiger, leopard, jaguar."

Zaira's body rocked with another wave of shivers, her teeth clattering together as she tried to form words. "A-a-r-re we—" Clenched teeth, clenched fists as she brought the shaking under control with icy strength of will. "Are we in the Sierra Nevada?"

While the Sierra was SnowDancer wolf territory, the SnowDancers had some kind of a treaty with the DarkRiver leopards, so Zaira's question was a valid one. "We might be, but probability is low—the chopper would've never escaped SnowDancer notice."

Everyone knew the wolves were very unwelcoming when it came to outsiders—"shoot first and ask questions of the corpses" was their rumored motto. "A small cabin, a small group—that could've flown under the radar in such a vast territory, but the chopper would've lit up their surveillance satellites and, bad weather or not, we'd be drowning in wolves by now."

"Terrain wrong for DarkRiver."

"Yes. I don't think we're in Yosemite." It was possible they were near the territory of another feline pack. On the other hand, given the cats' reputation for roaming far distances in their youth, it was equally possible they were near a single solitary changeling. If Aden could locate the owner of these paw prints, that changeling could go for assistance— if he or she didn't attack them on sight. Many changelings remained leery of Psy.

It was, however, their only chance.

They walked as fast as they could, hoping to beat the rain that was starting to spit again. If it poured down, the trail would be erased in a heartbeat, and with it, their first real chance of survival. Zaira finally lost consciousness what must've been about eight minutes later, and from the blood she'd coughed up, he knew she'd die if she didn't get medical attention soon.

No, he thought, *you do not get to die.*

Lifting her into his arms, he carried her tucked against his chest. She was so small in comparison to the others in the squad, but she was deadly and strong and part of their future . . . part of his future. When he went to his knees in the mud, he got up again, muscles straining and arms locked around her. His body protested, the leg injury he'd sustained in the fight outside the bunker starting to make itself felt, but he was still functional, still able to walk.

Following the tracks of the changeling deep into the trees just as the rain pounded down again, he wasn't prepared for the tracks to simply disappear. Not with the canopy offering enough protection that he should've had another minute or two at least. He put Zaira down very carefully before taking out the penlight again and checking the ground. Nothing . . . but big cats could often climb.

He turned just in time to see the glowing eyes of a large jungle cat coming at him.

The impact crushed the air from his lungs, slamming his body into the rain-soaked forest detritus. His training told him to fight, but he lay quiescent. "My partner is badly injured and in need of medical attention. Will you offer assistance?" If the answer was no, Aden would use the knife he'd palmed, get away from the changeling.

It might not be an easy fight, but he wasn't going to fail with Zaira's life at stake.

Growling, its teeth flashing in the dark, the changeling walked over to Zaira's body. Aden could see spots now, realized this was a leopard, but, judging from the "welcome," not any leopard he knew. Sending Aden a glowing yellow-green glance after sniffing at Zaira, the leopard bared its teeth and took off, moving so fast that Aden had no hope of following him.

The darkness swallowed him up a heartbeat later.

Either the cat was going for help or his answer was no to the request for assistance. Regardless, Aden had to keep going, try to locate a vehicle so he could get Zaira to a medic, or find a comm beacon he could hot-wire to send a message to the squad. Simply hunkering down was not an option. She'd die.

He refused to think too hard about the fact that so far, they'd glimpsed no signs of civilization, no evidence that there might be a comm beacon or station in the vicinity, much less roads or traffic. That was self-defeating behavior and he was an Arrow trained to survive.

Rising, one of his ribs feeling as if it had cracked under the impact of the leopard's pounce, he picked Zaira up again and continued on. As long as his body functioned, he would walk.

A hard droplet of water penetrated the canopy to hit his cheek, then came another and another and another, until all around him was a torrential rain that sought to shove him to the earth. And then the wind slammed into him, the gale so strong that each step felt like fighting his way through a brick wall.

So be it.

"Stay alive," he said to Zaira, then gritted his teeth and took the next step.

That was when the bullet wound in his leg finally tore wide open.

Chapter 9

REMI RACED THROUGH the rain, the pads of his paws soundless on the wet mass of leaves and branches under the trees, surefooted over the grassy open area that threatened to turn to mud at any instant. When the rain thundered down again, he growled low in his throat. On the list of his leopard's least favorite things in the world, icy cold rain rated very high, but that was an easily shrugged-off concern, his mind on the two people who'd been tracking him until he turned the tables on them.

He'd kept his claws sheathed as he slammed into the man, intending only to pin the stranger down so he could figure out if he'd attracted unwelcome attention that could pose a risk to his pack. It was only as he hit the man that he'd caught the acrid scent of wet iron, a scent the wind had hidden from him until that instant.

The woman, he'd realized almost at once, was bleeding badly. Her companion might be conscious, but he wasn't in much better condition.

Remi had recognized the man's face a heartbeat after Remi's paws made contact with his chest. No way to mistake those sharp cheekbones, the intense eyes, the ruler-straight black hair that had become visible when his hood slid off: Aden Kai. The reputed leader of the Arrow Squad, according to the reports Remi had seen on various news platforms.

No one seemed to know too much about the Arrows. Rumors ranged from calling them a death squad to a highly trained black ops team, but everyone had witnessed their actions in the past months. The black-clad men and women had saved Psy, human, and changeling lives across the globe—and they hadn't stuck around to lap up praise or play to the media.

Arrows apparently did what needed to be done and didn't bother with the niceties.

Remi could deal with people like that—if he didn't end up having to kill them. Right now, though, the question of what the fuck two Arrows were doing out in the middle of the Smokies could wait. A woman was dying and Remi would do everything in his power to attempt to save her. That didn't mean he wouldn't execute her if she proved a threat to his pack. It just meant he'd do it after she was healthy.

Reaching the spot where he'd parked his rugged all-wheel-drive vehicle after deciding to use the cover provided by the storm to come up here to spy on RainFire's reclusive neighbors, he shifted into human form and hauled on his jeans. Once in the driver's seat, he didn't switch on the head-lights. The jet-chopper he'd heard earlier in the night had disappeared, but it was possible it was simply circling above the heavy cloud layer, ready to drop down through any clear patches—and given the fact that the Arrows had headed away from the sound of the chopper, it was a good bet the two had company they wanted to avoid.

Normally he'd have let the two parties fight it out among themselves, keeping his fledgling pack out of it, but every part of him rebelled against such an unfair fight. The Arrows were wounded and on foot, with a tiny knapsack of what he assumed were supplies, while the other side had a jet-chopper and likely ground forces. There was also the fact that his leopard had never liked the scents left behind by the neighbors who owned this tract of land.

Sour sweat and cold metal had been the most prominent elements.

Another growl rumbling in his throat, he drove on. Even with the torrential rain, his night vision and knowledge of the terrain meant he was at no risk of a fatal crash. RainFire might not own this land—yet—but no alpha worth his salt wouldn't be fully aware of every aspect of the landscape around his pack.

The odd rock scraped the undercarriage, a few branches hit his windows, and he definitely lost a side mirror as he maneuvered through the forested landscape, but the vehicle was whole when he reached the farthest point he could go. Getting out, he ran on bare feet to where he could scent the Arrows. That scent was dull, buried under the rain that pounded his bare upper body and plastered his jeans to his legs, but the wind was on his side this time and those two didn't belong in this environment.

The leader of the Arrows was down on his knees, but he still held on to his gravely wounded partner, shielding her face from the elements by curving his body over hers. Even as Remi ran to him, Aden attempted to get up. Stubborn fucker. But will alone couldn't overcome a body that had apparently been through the wars, and Aden was unconscious by the time Remi reached him, his body curled protectively over his partner's.

Leopard and man both growled in approval.

Psy, especially combat-trained Psy, were meant to be heartless bastards who balanced every action on a cost-reward ratio. Remi had picked up that fact from a couple of Psy he'd worked with on an oil rig back when he was nineteen. The two had been cold enough, but according to them, they were sunshine and roses compared to their more dangerous brethren. In this situation, leaving his partner behind would've given Aden a better chance of survival, yet he hadn't, was still protecting a fallen member of his squad.

Assassin or not, Remi decided Aden Kai had at least one redeeming feature.

Taking the woman first, after tugging her from Aden's tight grip, Remi put her in the backseat, then went back for Aden. The bastard was heavier than he looked, and he woke as Remi was hauling him to his feet, a knife suddenly in his hand. "Stand down," Remi growled, his claws slicing out of his fingers to prick at Aden's side. "I have your squadmate in the truck."

A nod, Aden managing to stay conscious as Remi helped him into the backseat with the other Arrow. As he started to drive down to the pack's base, he saw Aden check the woman's vitals. "How far?" the Arrow leader asked.

"Thirty minutes." He was driving hell for leather.

"She won't make it. Go faster." An order from a man used to giving them.

Remi was a predatory changeling alpha—he didn't take orders from anyone—but his cat didn't snarl. He could forgive a man trying to protect someone who belonged to him. "Strap in," he said, waiting only until Aden had put the safety belts around both himself and the other Arrow before he accelerated to a breakneck pace that would've equaled certain death for most people.

Remington Denier wasn't most people. He wasn't even most alphas; he'd spent five years of his life working on race cars before he decided he didn't want to roam alone anymore, his hunger to set up a pack of his own a bone-deep pulse in his body. He'd set it up all right, but now he had to hold it together. Today, however, his days testing how cars handled on the track, combined with his night vision and heightened hand-eye coordination, kept them from going over cliffs or slamming into trees.

"Cat." A faint sound from the back.

"What?"

"Zaira—internal bleeding. Gunshot wound. Abdomen."

"Got it," Remi said, knowing the pack's healer would need every detail he could give him. "What else?"

"Small implants. Embedded in our brains," Aden ground out between short, rough breaths. "We got them out, but there could be damage."

Fuck, that did not sound good.

"Zaira's laser seal needs to be broken, the internal repairs checked."

"I'll tell Finn," Remi said, but when he asked Aden to explain further and received only silence in return, he realized the Arrow leader had lost his battle with consciousness. Just as well—at least Remi didn't have to worry about revealing the location of RainFire's central base. He'd taken his cue from the DarkRiver leopards and set up a public HQ, while ensuring the pack's heart remained protected and off the grid.

However, unlike with DarkRiver, RainFire cats weren't spread out across their territory. Such closeness could've been a source of primal tension since leopards weren't natural pack animals. It was the human side of changeling felines that made them want to create large extended families; in ordinary circumstances, the cat's need for space was accommodated by having plenty of land area between packmates.

That wouldn't work for RainFire. They just didn't have enough people and resources to function as a united pack while scattered over the territory. One day, that would happen, but for now, their struggle for survival as a pack had trumped the need for space. Not that packmates didn't go off on their own now and then—he'd convinced a number of loners to join him in setting up RainFire, after all. But they always returned because RainFire was now home, their loyalty sworn and unbreakable.

Screeching to a stop beneath the sprawling network of aeries built in the massive trees in the heart of their territory, permanent bridges connecting aeries and retractable rope ladders going down trunks, he hit the horn in the emergency pulse. Senior packmates boiled out into the rain-lashed dark a heartbeat later, including their healer, Finn.

RainFire had lucked out snagging Finn—at a couple of years past forty in age, he was highly skilled and had full medical qualifications as well as a powerful gift. His birth pack had been sorry to see him go when he joined RainFire as one of the founding members, but had understood his choice; the healer who'd trained Finn had decades more life left in him, as well as another apprentice, and Finn was too strong to be anything but the senior healer in a pack.

As it was, he'd spent his adult life volunteering to assist packs who'd lost their healers and who didn't have a trainee old enough to step into the position. It had given him an incredible breadth of experience—he'd been to even more places in the world than Remi, mentored countless young healers who needed time to come into their own—but he'd been desperately lonely. Healers needed their own packs to nurture, needed family around them. Remi had never met a healer who was also a loner. It appeared to be an impossible combination.

Having hauled open the back door, Finn went to check Aden.

"No," Remi said. "He was clear she was the more critical. Internal bleeding, abdomen."

Finn went clawed and just tore a hole through the woman's clothing to check her stomach. Swearing hard and low seconds later, he grabbed her in his arms. "Get the male inside!" he said as he began to turn to run to the infirmary. "He's losing blood from somewhere!"

"Shit." Remi had thought the scent was all from the woman, that Aden had simply surrendered to exhaustion and cold.

Throwing the Arrow leader over his shoulder in a fireman's carry, as the other man didn't appear to have gut wounds, he followed Finn to the infirmary—a large open room in a ground-level cabin—and placed Aden on a bed next to the one where Finn was already working on Zaira. Finn's shirt was plastered to his body and his light brown hair dark from the rain, but Zaira had his unflinching attention.

Finn's nurse, Hugo, and another member of the pack who had some medical training took over the instant Remi had Aden on the bed, stripping the Arrow leader of his camouflage green jacket and cutting through his sweater in their search for his injuries.

"He said they had some kind of an implant in their heads," Remi told Finn. "They got it out—fuck knows how—but there could be damage."

"Jesus." Having turned Aden onto his side, Hugo hissed out a breath, the long braid in which he wore his black hair falling over his shoulder. "No wonder the back of his sweater is soaked in blood." A pause as Hugo peeled away a bloody bandage. "Oh, hell, he's got what looks like an unsealed wound at the back of his head."

"Are you fucking kidding me?" Finn muttered, his eyes focused on the woman; her abdomen didn't look right even to Remi's untrained eyes, the jagged tear of the bullet that had violently exited her body a further insult.

Finn ran a scanner over her stomach. "This is bad. She should be dead, would be if someone hadn't sealed the major bleeds."

"Fix her first," Remi said, knowing in his gut the Arrow

leader would've made the same call. He hadn't missed the fact that Aden had focused totally on her injuries when he'd been losing blood from what, to Remi's eyes, looked like a seriously bad head wound.

"Finn," Hugo said, having slit Aden's pant leg along one side, "he's got a bullet wound to his upper thigh. Bullet's still in there, I think."

As Finn barked out orders, Remi stared at the Arrow who'd walked who knew how long a distance through storm-lashed terrain with a bullet in his thigh and a bleeding head wound, all while supporting his wounded squadmate. The man was a serious threat, but Remi would have a difficult time killing him now. He was starting to like the stubborn Arrow.

Leaving Finn and his people to their work, he walked out into the wide corridor outside the infirmary to find his sentinels gathered around. Lark, Angel, and Theo all had damp hair, had no doubt made sure the all-wheel drive was safely parked and RainFire's perimeter clear of threats. "Are we on generators?" He'd caught the telltale flicker of the lights a minute before.

"Just switched," Lark said, her ebony skin flushed from within, as if she'd been running. "Comm lines went down fifteen minutes before the electricity. Best guess is that a lightning strike fried the conduit."

"Damn." RainFire was now effectively isolated from the rest of the world. The pack's territory was in a dead zone as far as current satellites were concerned, which meant that if RainFire wanted satellite comms, they'd have to pay for a satellite of their own. The pack was too young to have that kind of money.

"How long can we run the generators?" Changelings were more resistant to cold than humans or Psy, but RainFire had cubs who wouldn't last long if the heating went out. Should that be a risk, Remi would find a way to get them to civilization.

"Days," Theo said, his tanned skin belying the current weather. "That's why Lark and I blew the budget. We got the green version that we can run with fucking vegetable scraps if that's all we have."

"Sometimes," Remi said, "I remember why I asked you degenerates to join the pack."

The cousins bumped fists. They'd been roaming alone when Remi first met them, having been on their own since they were teenagers after their tiny pack imploded as a result of a frankly selfish power struggle that had savaged pack bonds, but he'd never met any two who were *less* suited to being loners.

Big, quiet Theo had a marshmallow heart when it came to the cubs, while competent and outwardly hard-assed Lark was never as happy as when she was poking her nose into packmates' lives and doing everything she could to smooth over any flare-ups or personality clashes.

Beside them, Angel, much more self-contained and solitary by nature, folded his arms. His "straight-from-a-marble-statue" bone structure, as described by Lark, combined with eyes of deep ultramarine and flawless brown skin, made him a magnet for both men and women—only Angel seemed to prefer to walk alone in every way.

Of all the people who had agreed to help Remi set up Rain-Fire, it was Angel's agreement that had most surprised him.

"We've got plenty of supplies," the other man said. "We can wait this out, though it might take a few days. Last comm transmission I caught before lines went down said the meteorologists were calling this a once-in-two-hundred-years storm."

"Yeah." Lark's elfin face twisted into a scowl. "Damn mountains seem to have forgotten it's spring."

Weather was always changeable in the Smokies during this part of the year, but the sentinels were right: it was never usually this bad. While RainFire had only been in the area approximately two and a half years, Remi had kept a sharp eye on the region over the past five years, ever since he'd targeted the land for the pack he wanted to build, and not once had the mountains turned this dark and wet and cold in spring.

"Our position on a rise should protect us from any mudslides," he said. "Theo, I want you to take a team and make sure there's nothing to worry about around us regardless— be careful, but check to see if the ground shows signs of becoming unstable."

"Will do." Theo rubbed at his jaw, as if his stubble itched. "I think we should be good. These trees have roots so deep nothing but the earth cracking open's going to shake them."

That was why Remi had chosen this place for the pack's heart. These "aerie trees" had been planted over three hundred years before by a small pack named RainStone. Then had come the Territorial Wars; RainStone had been decimated in the ensuing fighting, their land passing into the trust created after the wars to hold pack lands that no longer had a living pulse.

Remi and the other founding members of RainFire had flat out bought a great big chunk of land around this section for their new pack and they had certain changeling rights to areas in public ownership, but the heart piece, they'd had to request from the trust. The trust's founding document decreed that the entrusted pack lands could never be sold, only be given—to new or old changeling packs that needed it.

As a result, the testing process for those who applied for a land grant was stringent. For an inexperienced alpha who wanted to set up a brand-new pack, it was brutal. That process was overseen by the ten most powerful alphas in the country at any given time. Remi had had to show those tough men and women not only that he had enough committed people and resources to set up a pack and hold the land against outside threats, but also that he had the strength to keep his new pack safe.

Not every changeling with the dominance to be alpha has the heart for it.

It was Lucas Hunter, alpha of DarkRiver, who'd said that to Remi at the start of the three-month period in which he'd acted as Remi's mentor—a condition of the land grant. His task had been to give Remi a crash course in what it meant to be alpha of a vibrant, growing pack, *and* assess if Remi had the goods to be entrusted with the task.

Lucas had gone on to add, "You have to create bonds so strong that your packmates know you'll always have their backs."

"That's not even a question." Remi would fight to the death for his people. "It might've taken time for my alpha nature to assert itself, but it's fucking wide awake now. All I want is my own pack, my own sprawling family to protect."

Lucas's green eyes had glinted in approval. "Never forget that—your pack is the heart. The alphas who fuck up are the ones who start to think they're the most important element of a pack." A shake of his head, his hair gleaming blue-black in the sunlight, the savage clawlike lines that marked one side of his face clearly delineated. "We're just the lucky bastards who have the honor of protecting the heart."

Remi would allow nothing to harm that heart. He intended for RainFire to put down roots as deep and as strong and as unshakable as those of the trees in which they'd made their homes. "Cubs?" he asked, his mind on the most vulnerable of their packmates.

Theo was the one who answered. "All accounted for and where they should be." His smile reached the warm brown of his eyes. "I did have to chase a couple who thought we were playing hide-and-seek."

Lark pointed her chin toward the infirmary, her pixie cap of hair standing up in all directions after she ran her fingers through it. "What's the story with those two?"

Remi gave the three sentinels a rundown of everything he knew to date. With the comm lines down, he couldn't touch base with Lucas, find out if the more experienced alpha—who also had direct contacts among the Psy—knew what the hell was going on. It looked like he'd simply have to wait for the Arrows to wake up.

If they woke up.

Because right now, from the grim look on Finn's face, he knew that wasn't a guaranteed outcome. "How bad?" he asked the healer when Finn paused to gulp down some water.

Wiping off his mouth, Finn just shook his head.

Chapter 10

SELENKA DUREV, ALPHA of the Moscow-based BlackEdge wolves, glanced at the report one of her senior lieutenants had just brought in. Her wolf's claws immediately pricked at the tips of her fingers, a growl building in her throat. "This is confirmed?"

"As far as it can be." Gregori's expression was harsh. "The bones of a hostile competing company are all there—Krychek's gone so far as to buy the Cavzi plant out from under us."

Selenka wrestled her wolf into patience, flipped through the report again. As one of the strongest and most established packs in Russia, BlackEdge had a diversified business base, but a large part of the pack's income came from producing environmentally friendly components for various vehicles. They'd been building up their reserves to go into the full-on production of vehicles within the next three months. Except it appeared Kaleb Krychek had stealthily put his own plan in play to serve the same market.

It was exactly what Selenka might expect from the most ruthless man she had ever met, but for a single fact. "Something smells off." Krychek and BlackEdge successfully coexisted in the same region because they took care not to step on one another's toes. "The payoff isn't big enough for him to sacrifice his relationship with us."

That relationship had taken time to build, and while Selenka would probably never actually trust Krychek—and vice versa—they respected one another as adversaries who should not be messed with. "Why this venture? Why not just attempt to mount a hostile takeover of our already established businesses?"

Gregori folded his arms, the tattoos that covered them going taut as his eyes took on a flinty cast. "Maybe he's decided he doesn't have to play nice anymore now that he has that black ops squad on his side. The Arrows."

Selenka could see Krychek unleashing the squad against the pack. If he thought it would be a quick, quiet execution, he had no idea of the strength and ferocity with which Selenka's wolves would fight. Only . . . Krychek *was* aware of that truth—he'd also always struck woman and wolf both as a man who'd make it a point to know the other powers in the area—so he had to realize that not only would the wolves howl for blood at an unprovoked attack, so would the other predatory packs.

Krychek was too smart and too politically cutthroat to incite bloodshed in his territory, bloodshed that would suck up his resources at such a critical time. He needed Moscow and the surrounding areas to remain stable, especially now when he was dealing with the aftermath of the deadly psychic infection that had claimed so many lives. BlackEdge had stepped in to help contain the insane violence, as had the StoneWater bears.

All three parties had ended that exhausting, painful, and sad period feeling as if the fragile balance in the region had become far more deeply stable. Krychek kept an eye on the Psy and the humans, while between them, BlackEdge and Stone-Water handled the changelings, predatory and nonpredatory.

And yet, what was this business maneuver if not the opening salvo of a silent war? The alpha wolf in Selenka curled its upper lip over its teeth, blood hot. Containing the urge to go for Krychek's throat took every ounce of her human control. "Can we dig any deeper?" She held up the report, her fingernails painted a vivid pink courtesy of one of the pups who'd waylaid her that morning.

Gregori shook his head, his blond hair tumbled from the wind outside. "We've gone as far as we can."

Which meant the ball was in Selenka's court. Even a year ago, she'd have taken immediate countermeasures, likely by subverting one of Krychek's own business interests. However, a year was a long time. As Krychek no doubt kept tabs on the pack, Selenka did the same when it came to him. So she understood that Krychek had changed in a way Selenka didn't think most people realized.

He had a mate now, and the one time Selenka had seen them together, she'd realized it was a true mating, not a false front. Of course, mated pairs could fuck things up together as easily as those who were single, but no matter what people said about Psy in general and Krychek in particular, a man who had the ability to mate was capable of an intense level of loyalty and commitment.

His relationship with BlackEdge was a cold thing in comparison to the raw fury of a mating, but he'd given Selenka his word that he wouldn't attempt to encroach on her territory. It was why the pack had never made any aggressive moves against him.

"I'll talk to him," she said. "Find out what the fuck is going on."

And if Krychek wanted a war, she'd give it to him.

KALEB was still in Venice with the Arrows when he received an urgent message from Silver. "Sir," his senior aide said, "Selenka Durev is demanding an immediate meeting. She wouldn't give me details, but her tone makes me believe this is serious."

"Is BlackEdge showing any signs of aggression?"

"Negative at this point."

"Monitor the situation. I'll connect with Selenka." Walking to the edge of a canal, he made the call. "Selenka," he said in Russian when she answered. "I received your message." Even without Silver's determination, he would've known there was a problem: Selenka had the inbuilt arrogance of any predatory alpha, but she never demanded a meeting unless it was necessary. Like him, she was too busy to waste time on petty politicking.

"I need to talk to you," she replied. "Face-to-face. Can you make the usual spot in a half hour?"

Having already come to the conclusion that there was little further he could do in Venice, Kaleb agreed to the meet, then located Vasic. The other man had been checking up on a sedated Alejandro, who Ivy Jane had apparently managed to put into a natural sleep before the sedatives were administered.

"I'm heading out to handle another situation," he told the teleporter, "but I'll keep trying to get to either Aden or Zaira every ten minutes."

Vasic fell into step with him as they walked out into the courtyard in the center of the compound. "I'm still sensing nothing."

That was not a good sign. Of the two of them, Kaleb was the more psychically powerful, but Vasic was a Tk-V, a born teleporter. He'd also worked with Aden for decades. If Vasic couldn't find him, then Aden was either dead or had suffered a traumatic brain injury. The fact that the NetMind, the guardian and librarian of the PsyNet, was confused about both Aden and Zaira, and unable to inform Kaleb if they were alive or dead, further pointed to massive neural damage.

"Did Santos confirm he had a meet with Aden?" he asked instead of stating a fact of which Vasic had to be well aware. The squad had finally narrowed down the time period in which Aden had to have been taken, and it aligned closely to his meeting with the leader of the Forgotten—descendants of those Psy who'd dropped out of the PsyNet at the dawn of Silence.

"Yes." Vasic's eyes met those of another Arrow a short distance away and Kaleb knew telepathic orders were being given or data shared. The teleporter had always been the less vocal member of the partnership with Aden, but this incident made it clear that Vasic was fully capable of stepping into the leadership breach if necessary.

A Psy such as Ming would've taken the opportunity to stage a coup, permanently pushing out Aden. Vasic, on the other hand, was holding things together for his partner's return and using all his resources to find him. Kaleb wouldn't have understood Vasic's choice once, but that was before he'd built friendships of his own and gained the loyalty of men and women who would never sell him out.

Kaleb would never betray any of them, either.

"There's nothing to indicate Santos had a hand in the disappearance," Vasic added. "Visual records confirm Aden left the building after the meeting."

That didn't completely clear Devraj Santos, but the other man had no reason to make an enemy of the Arrows. According to Kaleb's intel, the squad was assisting the Forgotten in figuring out a way to handle the violent new psychic abilities that had started to appear in their population. "I'll go to New York after my meeting," he said. "I have contacts there, may be able to run down more information."

"I've already dispatched an Arrow unit to trace Aden's trail," Vasic said, his next words unexpectedly blunt. "You have direct access to the NetMind. Can you work on that level?"

Kaleb did have direct access to the guardian and librarian of the PsyNet. He also had access to the NetMind's dark twin. "I've already initiated a search." He told Vasic about the neosentient entity's confusion as to Aden's and Zaira's status, saw grim realization on the other man's face. "There's nothing else," he added. "No data, no rumors. The only way this could've been done so cleanly was if everything was kept off the PsyNet."

Vasic stopped in the shadow of a wall covered by a trailing vine, his eyes chips of winter in the early morning sunlight. "More evidence of intelligence and planning."

"Yes." None of this pointed to an impulse act, or one driven by mindless fanaticism. "I also have a team of hackers wading through the Internet and setting up alerts." Unless the abductions had been organized by a crack ops team, someone somewhere would eventually make a mistake.

"You'll share any other information you uncover?"

"As soon as I get it." Kaleb had no friendship with Aden, but he considered the Arrow leader a critical asset.

Leaving Aden's second in command on the heels of that agreement, Kaleb teleported to his Moscow office and spoke with Silver about a number of other outstanding matters before teleporting out to the windswept and isolated outcrop where he was to meet Selenka.

The wolf alpha was waiting for him, a tall woman with dark eyes and dark hair streaked with purple against coolly white skin. Clad in black jeans, boots, and a hip-length electric blue leather jacket over a white tee, she could've been mistaken for a stylish human female if not for the aura of untamed power she carried with her.

Selenka was very much an alpha wolf.

"You've suddenly decided to go into the automotive industry?" was her opening salvo.

This was why he liked dealing with Selenka: her directness cut through all the fat. "No," he said, just as directly. "Except for my shares in Centurion, of which I'm sure you've always been aware."

Waving that away, Selenka passed him a sheaf of papers right as the dull gray sky began to spit with rain. He created a telekinetic shield around them without thought, keeping off the rain so he could read the printed material.

"Handy."

Kaleb ignored the pithy comment, his attention on the documents that purported to show him mounting a ruthless assault against the pack's largest business enterprise. "A complex bit of illusion." He shot telepathic orders to Silver to get to the bottom of these corporate filings.

Hands on her hips, Selenka raised an eyebrow. "You're saying this isn't you?"

Kaleb responded with a bluntness he knew she'd appreciate. "I have more important things on my plate right now than starting a fight with a wolf pack known for its aggression."

A slight smile curved her full lips, her eyes suddenly wolf-gold. "If it's not you, then things become far more interesting," she said, the predator inside her adding a gritty roughness to the words.

"It appears someone is attempting to disrupt the peace between us." He was well aware that should he have truly attempted to go head-to-head with BlackEdge, Selenka's pack was more than capable of causing hell in his region.

"Say I believe you." The wolf inside Selenka continued to

watch him, its gaze unblinking. "What does anyone get out of pitting us against one another?"

"If the strongest Psy in the region and the strongest pack in the same region suddenly become enemies, the ripple effect would be significant." Impacting every aspect of life. "Psy afraid to go near changeling territory, changelings worried about fatal psychic rapes, humans feeling pressured into choosing sides. A steady build until things explode into violence."

Selenka gave a slow nod. "You'd also lose the goodwill of other non-Psy groups."

"Yes."

"Someone was counting on us not talking to each other."

Kaleb didn't reply in the affirmative because there was no need. "My aide is currently canceling any offers I've purportedly made. You have a clear run." As for the person stupid enough to try to use his name to foster dissent in his region, Kaleb would make certain that individual regretted the mistake.

No one played games with Kaleb.

Chapter 11

ADEN WOKE TO darkness for the second time. Keeping his eyes closed, he listened. Movement around him, the sound of male voices in conversation.

". . . stable, but I won't know for sure until she wakes up." A blown-out breath. "She's tough as a leopard—just refused to die. As for him, I have no fucking idea how he was still walking."

His memories cleared enough that he remembered the yellow-green eyes of the leopard who'd slammed him to the ground. Those same eyes had glowed in the face of the man who'd hauled them to his vehicle. *A leopard changeling.* Having put the pieces together, Aden lifted his lashes.

A tall man with a heavily muscular build, his shaggy hair multiple shades of brown and roughly tumbled, his jaw shadowed with stubble that was dark against golden skin, was talking to another male. That one had a leaner build, but it was paired with a layer of muscle that made it clear he wasn't used to sitting behind a desk.

The bigger man was dressed in black cargo pants and a dark gray T-shirt, the other in a checked blue shirt with the sleeves rolled up to his elbows, worn untucked over jeans. Neither appeared to be armed.

"The bullet exited all right," said the one in the checked shirt, "but it ricocheted off her ribs and nicked several of her organs on the way out." The man, who had to be a medic, touched points on his own chest, as if indicating the impact sites. "Someone patched her up just enough to save her life—left alone, she'd have been dead long before you found her." He rubbed his face, the honed line of his features placing his age in the late thirties or early forties.

The bigger man, by contrast, had to be around twenty-eight or twenty-nine.

"You get the bullet from his leg?" he asked.

A nod. "It's so distorted it's pretty much useless."

Aden didn't have to listen any further to know the muscular man was in charge—predatory changeling alphas had a certain unmistakable bearing. Young or old, they carried responsibility as well as power.

The alpha turned to him right then, his eyes a striking, clear topaz striated with light. Eyes that looked feline, though the alpha was in his human form. Despite the change in eyes from leopard to human, Aden immediately recognized him as the man he'd met on the mountain.

"You're awake," the alpha said, walking over. "I'm Remi. This is Finn."

Not about to have this meeting lying on his back, Aden sat up, quickly getting a visual of Zaira on the infirmary bed next to his as he did so. His skull throbbed violently but he wasn't as weak as he might've expected. It appeared he'd been given something to maintain his strength, his fluids replenished. "How long have I been out?" he asked, noting that he was wearing only loose black drawstring pants.

Remi threw him a white T-shirt from a shelf to one side of the room. "Eighteen hours."

An eternity for an Arrow in hands that were not those he trusted, but these hands had saved his life. Pulling on the tee, he reached back and gingerly touched the spot where Zaira had dug out the chip right as Aden had sensed it build up to explosion point, lightning bolts of electricity crawling through his neurons on a direct path to his cerebral cortex.

His fingertips met a thin-skin bandage. "Any permanent damage?"

"I can't tell." White lines bracketed the medic's mouth, his leaf green eyes grim. "Whatever it was you two had in you, it was jammed in—hack job. You probably did less damage taking the things out than was done putting them in."

Aden couldn't risk testing his telepathic muscles. If he suffered a backlash of pain, it might leave him helpless again even if it didn't do any further damage. As it was, he didn't think the news would be good—he'd consciously dropped his psychic shields when he woke. Instead of sensing a loud background hum that denoted the minds of the people around him, he'd heard only echoing silence.

The fact that he was around changelings didn't explain that silence. Changelings might have strong natural shields, but they *existed*. And from things Judd had said now and then, he knew most packs had human members as well. He should've at least felt a faint murmur that was created of the surface thoughts of a group of sentient living beings.

Controlling his psychic need to reach out took harsh effort. Akin to a changeling leashing his animal, or a human not using her dominant hand while attempting to complete a delicate task. "The current date and time?" he asked, trying not to think consciously of the absolute silence inside his head . . . and of what that silence would do to Zaira if she was in the same condition.

When Remi answered his question, Aden did a rough calculation and realized his and Zaira's captors had only had him for twenty-three hours prior to their escape. Zaira had to have been taken after him, else he'd have heard of her abduction. Rushing the surgery had been their unknown enemy's biggest mistake. A longer time frame and the implants would've likely become too deeply embedded to easily remove.

"I'd like to take your vitals." Not waiting for an answer, Finn picked up what Aden recognized as a top-of-the-line medical scanner and closed the distance between them.

Cooperating with Finn's requests because the medic clearly knew what he was doing, Aden said, "You didn't contact the squad?" It was very possible this unknown pack had no contacts in the PsyNet, and thus no way to get a message back to Vasic and the others.

Remi shook his head. "Communications are out because of the storm. We figured you'd get in touch with your people once you woke." He tapped his temple in a silent reference to Aden's psychic abilities.

"I'd feel better if you had a specialist look at you," Finn said, putting down the scanner to physically check Aden's wounded leg. A lock of his light brown hair fell across his forehead but he ignored it to continue his task.

Flexing the limb for the medic and feeling no pain, Aden said, "You appear to have done an excellent job." It was simple enough to seal a minor wound with the correct laser, but repairing all the tiny blood vessels, torn ligaments, and other shredded internal mechanics would've taken hours of concentrated and careful work.

And Aden's wound had been far less complicated than Zaira's.

Finn didn't speak until after he'd tested Aden's reflexes on that side of his body. "I'm a qualified and certified doctor as well as a healer," he said, switching to the other side, "but I'm no neurosurgeon. I can't guarantee I didn't miss something."

Remi stirred, eyes locking with Aden's. "I don't want to end up with two dead fucking Arrows in my territory," he said with brutal frankness. "Call in one of your teleporters, go see an M-Psy."

Aden had to make a decision—tell the truth and reveal his vulnerability, or make up a lie. For now, he decided on the lie. Remi could've killed him while he was down, but the leopard alpha's assistance could also be a cunning double cross. Remi had been in the same isolated area as their captors, after all. Aden couldn't afford to trust the alpha or his packmates until he'd categorically confirmed their lack of involvement in his and Zaira's abductions.

"I'll need to realign my mind before I can make contact," he said, banking on these changelings not being close enough to a Psy to know his words meant absolutely nothing. "The insertion of the implant disoriented my pathway to the PsyNet."

Remi frowned but nodded. "It'll be at least a day, maybe two before you can get out if your people can't get in. Rain's caused landslides lower down the mountain, blocked most of the roads, and last forecast we caught before the systems went down say this weather isn't going to let up anytime soon."

There was a massive boom just then, the thunder loud enough that both changelings visibly reacted, Finn with a grimace and Remi by going preternaturally still. Acute hearing, Aden realized, had to be a disadvantage in these circumstances.

"I have technical training," he said. "I might be able to jerry-rig a transmitter."

"You're welcome to try." Remi folded his arms. "But the conduit lower down the mountain has most likely been fried by lightning and my techs tell me the interference caused by the combination of the weather and our location makes it unlikely any lower-strength signal will get out."

Aden wasn't certain that was a drawback—because if this pack was friendly, then he and Zaira had a safe haven in which to recover from their physical and psychic wounds. Their psychic blindness could well be seen as an invitation for further violence in the outside world.

Aden, in particular, couldn't afford to have his lack exposed. It would pin a target on the entire squad's back if their leader was shown to be "human" in his vulnerability. Arrows survived not just because they were dangerous but because people saw them as dangerous. Else they were simply threats who needed to be put down.

As PsyMed had once wanted to put down Zaira.

Allowing himself to look toward her for the first time, he made certain to keep his tone neutral as he said, "I heard you note Zaira was stable."

"She is, but she'll only be out of the woods once she wakes up." Finn shifted to give Aden an unobstructed view of the other bed.

Zaira's body lay motionless in a way it never was in life. The rebellious, brilliant fire in her whispered its continued existence in the way she fought, so quick and smart, in the way she spoke with such rapid-fire intelligence, in the way she protected those who were her own with icy fierceness.

Aden made himself look away before he betrayed the depth of his concern for her.

"You aren't fully Silent, Aden. You never have been."

He'd thought it was his contact with Vasic and Ivy's bond that had changed him, but maybe Zaira was right about his Silence. He cared, had always done so for the people he saw as his own. And Zaira . . . she'd never been just another Arrow in his squad. Always, he'd been drawn to the fire in her, that untamed wildness that was so unlike his own controlled nature.

Aden had been taught discipline from the cradle, been taught to never draw attention or be anything but unremarkable in the eyes of the world. Zaira was like the storm outside in comparison. She'd become the perfect Arrow, but even that, she'd done on her own terms. Since the day they met she'd been disagreeing with him about everything under the sun, never watching her words, never offering him anything but the searing truth and her absolute and unflinching loyalty.

The room suddenly flashed with a shocking brilliance of purple-white light.

"Given your unworried demeanor," Aden said when neither Remi nor Finn made a comment on the closeness of the strike, "I assume this building is protected from lightning strikes?"

A teeth-baring grin that was very feline. "Careful, Arrow, or I might think you were insulting my ability to look after my pack."

"No insult intended." Aden fought his compulsion to hold the alpha's gaze in a primal power struggle, the instinct one he'd learned to rein in over the years. Instead, he returned his attention to Finn. "Zaira's condition?"

"She has less severe bruising at the implant site, but her internal injuries were significant." At Aden's request, the healer listed those injuries one by one. "I made damn sure I fixed each and every tiny shredded piece—that I can promise you."

Aden believed him. There was a strong sense of competency about the other man, added to which, he'd picked up on injuries even Aden might have missed. Finn wasn't just a doctor and a healer, he was a very good one.

Taking Aden's pulse again after asking him to stand beside the bed, Finn said, "If she doesn't regain consciousness, though, there's nothing else I can do at this point except try the drugs I have. None are calibrated to Psy physiology."

It wasn't what Aden wanted to hear and he could tell it wasn't the news Finn wanted to give.

"The best-case scenario is that she wakes on her own in the next few hours," Finn continued. "At that point, the major issue will be with the site of her gunshot injury; it'll be tender for a period, and her body will tire more easily for roughly a week, but she'll be fine as long as she doesn't do anything to tear open the new skin."

Making a note on an electronic chart, the healer walked backward several feet. "I had to stimulate growth of her own skin because none of the patches I had would bond to her, so it's more fragile than she might expect."

When Finn urged Aden to walk toward him, Aden knew the other man was judging his balance. "Anything feel off?" the healer asked, his eyes intent as another burst of lightning lit up the lightly tanned skin of his face.

"No." Except for the painful silence in his head.

"Headache?"

"Yes."

Finn asked him several more questions to gauge the amount and exact type of pain and Aden had to think not like an Arrow but like a civilian to answer him. An Arrow's pain threshold was far higher than most people's, but that could be dangerous in this circumstance.

"Okay," the healer finally said. "Nothing unexpected here, and the pain should ease up after twelve hours. If it suddenly increases in strength, or changes in some way, I want to know immediately." The words were an order. "Any delay could be fatal if there's an unexpected bleed."

"Understood." Thanking the healer for his work, Aden turned to Remi. "I can't recall if I ever identified myself to you." Neither could he place the leopard changeling in any known pack.

"I recognized you," the alpha said, keeping his hands on his hips rather than extending one. It was either a courtesy because Psy were known to be uncomfortable with the kind of touch the other races took for granted or a sign of reticence because he didn't yet trust Aden enough to shake his hand. "You're with RainFire, in the Smokies."

The pack name didn't raise a red flag, but neither did it

come with knowledge. He did, however, now have a general location. Since the Great Smoky Mountains sprawled across a large area of land, he'd have to gather additional data to figure out the specific location. "This weather is unusual for the region."

Finn rolled his eyes. "You win the prize for understatement of the century. There was a tornado warning not long before the comm blackout, so yeah, this isn't usual. Not unheard-of, though—just rare."

The extreme weather had given Aden and Zaira a critical advantage, one their captors couldn't have anticipated. Injured as they'd been, with the implants in their heads and their captors in a jet-chopper, they wouldn't have made it far without the rain hampering the chase by washing away their trail.

"Think you can keep some solid food down?" Finn asked and, at Aden's nod, left the infirmary to organize it.

Unable to fight the urge any longer, Aden walked around his bed to get to Zaira's. Her breathing was even, her skin tone back to its normal warm shade between cream and golden brown rather than clammy and bleached of color. When Aden picked up a·scanner Finn had left nearby, Remi didn't protest. Aden checked her vitals, focusing on the areas of injury, and was satisfied the healer had done a stellar job stitching her up. All that remained was for Zaira to punch through the veil of darkness behind which she was currently trapped.

Keep your promise, he said silently. *Stay.*

Aloud, he spoke to Remi. "Thank you for the assist."

Remi raised an eyebrow. "Why exactly did you need an assist? Arrows are usually a law unto themselves, from all I've heard."

"Even Arrows can't heal bullet wounds on their own." Not strictly true. There was one Arrow who could, but Judd Lauren's ability was so rare it was nothing most people would ever know.

"It wasn't a criticism." Remi shook his head. "I don't know how you walked on that leg if you came from where I heard that chopper circling."

Aden had walked on it because he'd needed to walk on it

to save Zaira. He'd been hit on his way back inside to her, had quickly bandaged up the wound while searching for supplies. The black of his combat pants had hidden the blood from Zaira, his decision not to tell her a conscious one. He hadn't trusted her to agree to come with him once she knew he was wounded, too. She'd have fought to stay and hold off the enemy, give him a head start. Since Aden would've dug his heels in, it had been quicker to prevent the argument in the first place.

"Do you know who occupies that land?" If the RainFire alpha was willing to share data, Aden had nothing to lose by gathering it. He would, of course, double-check all information after he left the pack.

"No. They fly in and out." Remi's T-shirt stretched across his wide shoulders as he leaned back against the wall and folded his arms again.

A relaxed pose if you didn't notice that watchful, dangerous gaze.

"We've kept an eye on them since they moved in about four months back," the alpha said, "but they don't impinge on our territorial boundaries so we generally mind our own business." He glanced toward the doorway. "I can scent food on the way. Eat, wait for your squadmate to wake up, then we'll talk."

Returning his attention to Zaira, Aden willed her to wake up, but the brain monitor remained static.

Two hours passed.

Three.

Three and a half.

Chapter 12

ZAIRA DREAMED, WAS aware she was doing so. It was the first time in a decade that her discipline had faltered to this extent, but she was wounded, weak, and the dream pushed its way inside before she could slam the door shut. Only it wasn't truly a dream but a memory so surreal it could've been a figment of her imagination.

"Zaira."

She looked up from the table where she'd been strapped down. Bruises and cuts marred her legs and her arms, her collarbone still fractured but her ribs feeling as if they'd been fixed. She didn't wonder why someone had fixed one of the injuries she'd sustained in the fight for her survival yet left others untouched—people liked to hurt her, that was simple fact.

The pain didn't matter; pain was something she'd learned to handle long ago. It was the confinement, the aloneness that threatened to drive her to madness. The ones who'd come for her after she'd beaten her parents to death had trapped her in matte-black shields she couldn't breach, the psychic loneliness crushing. "What?" she snapped in response to the sound of her name, willing to talk simply to hear another voice.

"Are you there?" she asked when there was no immediate answer, not sure she hadn't imagined a companion. She'd

done that before, had full-color "delusions," as her parents
termed them. Delusions that had been her friends. Delusions
that had made her feel less alone as she existed in the place
that was her cage.

"Shh." A slender boy with dark eyes slanted above sharp
cheekbones, his straight hair gleaming black and his skin
light brown, walked into her line of sight. He was silent,
quieter than anyone else she'd ever met. She didn't know how
he did that. Every time she tried to walk quietly, she stumbled or thumped or gave herself away.

That was why she had a fractured collarbone—she'd
made a noise in her ambush and her mother had turned and
hit Zaira with the datapad in her hand hard enough to slam
Zaira off the chair on which she'd been standing. It hadn't
saved her mother or her father, though. Zaira's bone might've
cracked, but she still had a mind that had stealthily grown
beyond her parents' ability to leash.

And she'd still been able to swing the rusty metal pipe
afterward.

When the boy who walked so quietly touched her restraints,
she began to struggle, the bracelets cutting into her wrists and
the manacles into her ankles. "Don't touch me," she said in a
hiss of sound. "Don't touch me." The feeling of helplessness
made her want to scream, but beneath was a cold rage.

"Quiet," the boy said, the command in his voice so strong
that she stopped speaking.

"I'm going to undo your restraints," he told her. "If you
start struggling or screaming or fighting with me, it'll alert
the trainers and they'll come strap you down again."

Zaira just stared at him. The instant he released her, she'd
do everything in her power to take him down. He was bigger
than her, but she'd killed her parents. She could kill him.
Once she'd done that, she'd escape this place where they tortured her by making her alone just as her parents had done.

The boy with the dark eyes and the silent feet held her
gaze. "Don't," he said, and it was another order, though one
given in a soft, solemn tone. "Do you know where this facility is? Have you looked outside?"

"Mountains," she said, remembering what she'd seen
from the vehicle that had brought her here. "Some green

things. No trees." She'd been born in Jordan and though she'd rarely been permitted out of her cage and never beyond the walls of the family compound, she'd glimpsed enough of the landscape through the bars of the gates to know she was no longer anywhere near the region where she'd been born.

But the air outside had felt as dry, the sun as warm, so maybe she was just in another part of Jordan?

"That's all there is for miles and miles and miles," the boy said. "Even if you somehow manage to outwit all the security protocols and escape, you'll die of thirst and heat exhaustion within hours."

"So?" Dying was preferable to being trapped.

"So we can't win if we all die."

She didn't understand him, didn't want to understand him. He was a stranger and even if he was a boy, that didn't mean he wasn't allied with the adults. None of her siblings or cousins had ever helped her. Instead, they'd reported on her when she went out of bounds and tried to squeeze through the bars of the main gate. "Okay," she said, just so the boy would do what she wanted.

He moved to the ankle manacles and used something she couldn't see to unlock them. When he paused at the second one and glanced at the door, she froze. Was there someone there, someone who would stop him before he set her free? But he returned to his task a second later.

Fighting the rage inside her that made her want to scream and kick, she forced herself to pretend to be following his order to behave, even once her ankles were no longer bound. Except the boy didn't free her wrists. He just stood beside her and watched her.

"What?" she asked, so *angry* that she just wanted to beat him until he had no face.

"I know you'll run," he said. "If you do, the trainers will realize Vasic and I can get into these rooms, and they'll punish us. That means we won't be able to help anyone else until the punishment is over."

What did Zaira care about anyone else? No one cared about her. All she wanted to do was get out of here. "I won't run."

"Yes, you will," the boy said, and then he put his tool to her wrist manacles.

Zaira wanted to stay silent, but he was confusing her. "Why are you letting me go, then?"

"Because," he said in that quiet voice that made her listen, "I won't be like them. I won't use threats or pain to keep you from doing what you want."

Zaira didn't understand him again. So she just waited. And as soon as he freed her, she jumped off the table, ignored the throbbing pain all over her body, and bolted.

The boy and the taller one who'd been waiting outside for him went in the opposite direction from her, and then she was through a heavy door on the other end and the alarms shrieked. Her heart in her throat, she kept running, her bare feet slapping the cold surface of the floor.

She didn't know what made her glance back. When she did, she saw the boy had come back and was now by the doors that had set off the alarms. Their eyes met, and at that instant she knew he was going to pretend it had been him who'd set off the alarm.

He was giving her time to hide.

ALL of them had been caught, of course. Zaira didn't have Aden's stealth and she didn't know the facility. Aden and Vasic had been punished far more brutally than Zaira, a fact she didn't learn until over ten years later, when she'd become skilled enough to hack into secure records databases.

All she knew then was that the boy with the dark eyes and the quiet feet had come back for her. When he unlocked her shackles a second time, she didn't beat him with her fists . . . and she didn't run despite the need inside her. Because another need was stronger.

"Why do you do this?" Zaira asked him as she lay curled up on the examination table, under a heat blanket he'd smuggled in for her. He'd told her he couldn't treat her wounds except in subtle ways no one would notice, but he could make her more comfortable. "Why do you help me?"

"So you'll be strong enough that they won't break you when I'm transferred," he said, continuing to work on a crushed bone so it wouldn't hurt as much when they came back and forcefully switched off her psychic pain controls.

Her parents had taught her those controls so she wouldn't pass out before they were done with her.

"Where are you going?" she demanded, infuriated. "When?"

"I'm being sent to another facility in ten months," he told her. "Does the bone hurt less now?"

"Pain doesn't matter," she said, trying not to think about the fact that the only person who had ever treated her as something better than garbage would soon be gone, leaving her once more alone in the darkness. "I can think past pain."

"I know. But the spirit can also be broken."

"What's that?"

"It's . . ." He paused, thought about it. "Have you seen the birds in the sky?"

"Sometimes." She'd spent most of her life in a cell without light, but there had been times when she'd been let outside, when she'd had to interact with other children. Her parents had called it "socialization" training so she wouldn't be "an uncivilized monster" as she grew. Zaira didn't think it had worked, but she was talking to Aden like a real person, so maybe she was wrong and it had.

"I think of the spirit as being a bird with wings that can fly free."

Zaira tried to imagine that, failed. "My spirit's already gone. It flew away a long time ago."

"If it had, you wouldn't want to run, wouldn't want to escape." He lifted away the laser he'd been using on her bones. "Your spirit is strong—it's a wild, angry fire inside you. I need you to hold on to that fire."

"Why?" she asked again. "Why do you care?"

"Because you're mine now."

ZAIRA woke to find the boy by her bedside, dream merging with reality. Only he wasn't a boy any longer. He was a tall, strong, powerful man, but he still moved with silent grace, and he still had the same dark eyes. Eyes that told her she had to be strong, that he needed her to be strong.

Yet if she stumbled, he wouldn't call her a failure; no, he'd simply break her fall and help her back up. Even after he'd been transferred out of the Turkish facility where she'd spent the rest of her childhood and teenage years, he'd found ways to tell her he hadn't forgotten her, that she existed to him as a unique individual and not just another trainee.

Once, it had been an e-mail he'd managed to route past the firewalls and the security. Another time, Vasic had broken the leash on his mind and teleported Aden to her. The visit had lasted five minutes before they had to leave or risk being caught, but in those five minutes, Aden had made Zaira remember that she was a sentient being and not the robotic killer her trainers wanted her to believe she was.

He'd made her remember that she was her own person first, and his, second.

No one else had a claim on her.

"Zaira." His voice was calm now, his expression betraying nothing. "We were rescued by the RainFire leopard pack. We're safe."

There were cues in his words her fuzzy, aching brain struggled to comprehend, but then he did something highly unusual. He took his hand and closed it over her own, squeezed. The physical link jerked her to full consciousness, anchoring her in the present even as her brain scrabbled for a psychic connection that would dissipate the silence inside her skull.

A vast aloneness.

No PsyNet.

No telepathic link with Aden.

Not even the vicious backlash of pain she'd felt earlier.

Nothing but crushing isolation.

As in that dark room of her childhood where no one could hear her scream.

Her breathing threatened to turn uneven. Squeezing her fingers around Aden's, their connection concealed by her body and his, she regulated her respiration by falling back on basic Arrow training. As her brain cleared, she realized he didn't want her to betray their psychic weakness.

So she didn't.

Allowing him to help her into a seated position, she took the opportunity to scan the room. They were alone except for a lithely muscled male with light brown hair and eyes so brightly green that she wasn't certain his irises were real. Identifying himself as Finn, the medic ran her through a barrage of scans and tests after checking to make sure her brain was registering the correct patterns.

Zaira cooperated in the checkup, the loose drawstring pants she wore bagging around her ankles until she bent and folded up the hems. Her white top was also too large and made of a cotton so fine Zaira didn't know what use it was as clothing—it wouldn't effectively stop a scratch from a child, much less a bullet.

At least the medic seemed to know what he was doing.

"You had some pretty bad internal injuries, never mind the brain stuff," he said after he'd completed the tests. "I've fixed you up, but you'll be tender for a few days, possibly up to a week. Take it easy. Not that you'll have much choice, given the weather." A grimace. "And ignore any snarly cats you see—we're not used to being penned in."

Aden didn't speak until Finn walked out of the room to retrieve something. Then, placing his lips close to her ear, he said, "Changeling hearing is acute." When she nodded to show she understood the warning, he spoke again in that near-inaudible whisper. "Do you have access to the PsyNet?"

Fingers clenching on the edge of the bed, she admitted the terrible truth. "It's silent inside my head."

In Zaira's eyes, Aden saw a hollow darkness. "You're not alone," he said, aware Zaira's reaction to extended psychic aloneness could spin in either direction. As a seven-year-old new trainee locked inside a trainer's shields, she'd gone into a berserker rage in an effort to break out; the trainer had been forced to knock her out lest she claw out his eyes. A week later, in the same situation, she'd gone catatonic for five days.

A permanent note had been made in her file: *Zaira Neve is not to be confined on the psychic plane. This flaw does not negate her usefulness as an Arrow—once out of training, she will never be in such a situation.*

No one could've foreseen their current circumstances. "You're not alone," he repeated, though he knew words wouldn't be enough. The damage done to her as a child had been some of the worst seen by the squad's mental evaluation panel—according to the records, the debate on whether or not she was even worth the effort had been long and intense.

In the end, it was her intelligence and proven strength that had saved her: Zaira hadn't broken under the childhood abuse. She'd fought back and she'd done so with a cold intelligence the squad appreciated. "I need you to stay strong," he said, speaking to the part of her that was the fire. "Zaira."

She gritted her teeth and gave him a nod, betraying nothing of her psychological state when Finn returned to the room with Remi. The alpha held his silence until Zaira drank some water and waved off an offer of food.

"So," he said, "now that you're both awake, who shot you?"

Chapter 13

ADEN GAVE HIM the facts—there was no reason to hide the truth. Either RainFire was already in on it, and knew, or the pack might be of assistance in unearthing further information. "The men who were holding us were a combined Psy-human team."

"Human?" A skeptical look. "You sure?"

"Yes." The surprising development lined up with one other factor in this situation. "The implant Zaira and I had in our heads," he said, reaching into a pocket to retrieve the small, flat container in which he'd earlier put the surviving implant, "shows signs of being a patch-up job involving human and Psy technology."

Aden had borrowed Finn's microscope to have a closer look at it. He was no expert, but he'd previously seen both the Aleine implant and the Human Alliance one, and the one he held clearly showed evidence of both. "A roughly done fusion."

"Goes with the sketchy nature of the surgery," Finn said, his tone unforgiving. "They might as well have used a hacksaw, it was so badly done."

"Yeah, but these ham-handed butchers managed to abduct you two," Remi pointed out with a directness Aden was coming to expect from the RainFire alpha. "Everything I've heard about Arrows tells me you aren't exactly easy prey, so the abductions were well planned."

Aden looked at the rough-edged male with new respect. Aden had never disregarded changelings, never underestimated their intelligence as so many Psy did, but he'd come perilously close to downgrading Remi's threat level because the other man appeared so ruggedly physical. He wouldn't make that mistake again.

"Either the implants weren't ready when the opportunity arose to abduct us," he said, "or they were never meant to be long-term."

"I wouldn't keep a threat alive, either, not after I had what I wanted." The alpha's gaze shifted to Zaira. "You don't talk?"

"Not when I have nothing to say," Zaira responded with glacial calm, though Aden knew she was at the edge of her endurance.

He had to get her away from the changelings. "Is there any reason for Zaira to be confined to the infirmary any longer?" he asked Finn.

"No, but I want to do a couple of final scans before I spring her. I also want to check your bullet wound now that you've been on that leg for several hours."

Aden stepped aside so Finn could complete Zaira's scans, but remained within her direct line of sight. Aloneness was Zaira's secret horror, the one foe she couldn't beat.

Being isolated and alone and hurt day after day changes a person, Aden. It turns a child into . . . into a thing that isn't quite human and not quite animal. Like any trapped creature, that child will gnaw off its own limb to escape—but if that child is a Gradient 9.8 combat-grade telepath named Zaira Neve, it'll first ask if it can gnaw off its attackers' limbs instead.

She'd said that to him at fifteen, the self-portrait both icily honest and disturbing.

You aren't an "it," Zaira.

You're right. I'm not an it. I'm a nightmare.

AS Finn worked on the female Arrow, Remi could feel Aden weighing him up. Fair enough. Remi was weighing up the Arrow—and his silent partner—in turn. Though Remi was predisposed to like him, he wasn't about to give two lethal strangers free rein of the compound.

"There's a small aerie just above the infirmary that you're welcome to use until the weather clears," he told them. "Or until your transport arrives."

Finn had suggested the reason a teleporter hadn't turned up already was because the two Psy had residual bruising from the implants that might be interfering with their psychic abilities. That made sense to Remi and it also made him a fraction more sympathetic to their guarded caution. If someone shoved an implant in his head that stopped him from shifting, he'd be a whole lot pissed and suspicious, too.

"Thank you," Aden said in that calm, cool voice that nonetheless held the power of a fellow alpha. "Do we reach it via an outer door?"

"No, it's connected through an internal trapdoor at the end of the corridor outside." He jerked a thumb over his shoulder. "The ladder's shielded from the wind and rain so you won't need outdoor gear."

Finn had asked for the modification as that particular aerie was used mostly by patients who'd recovered enough to leave the infirmary but that Finn wanted close by for two or three more days. In this case, it'd keep the Arrows within easy watching distance—there was no way to leave the aerie except through the trapdoor that led down into the infirmary corridor.

Aden and Zaira could attempt to climb down the tree itself, but then they'd be stuck outside in the storm; the weather was an excellent security measure right now. Hell, Remi had pulled back all of his sentries and ordered everyone to stay within a tight circle around the heart of the pack—anyone who went out any farther at the moment had a death wish. If the rain didn't wash you away, the lightning would fry you where you stood.

"If you have surveillance footage of your neighbors," Aden said, "we can study it while in the aerie."

Remi shook his head. "No footage." It wasn't a lie—the pack didn't have the time or the resources for in-depth surveillance of their neighbors, especially since those neighbors had minded their own business and left RainFire to mind theirs. "We can sneak up to investigate once the storm's died down. I'm betting they'll have cleared out on the off chance you two made it out."

The female Arrow, the one who was attempting to appear harmless—Remi's leopard huffed in laughter—stared impassively at the food Finn had brought in. "You need to eat," Finn said, his expression stating he'd brook no refusal this time. "Aden told me Psy prefer plain food, so I tried to find the plainest but highest-protein items I could—mixed nuts, a lentil-based spread on high-energy bread, and an energy bar."

When Zaira still didn't take the food, Aden spoke. "Eat. If you don't, you'll be weak."

Zaira took the plate from Finn on the word "weak." "Thank you."

After she was done, Remi showed them up to the aerie. "Lock the trapdoor," he said, demonstrating the mechanism, "and you'll have privacy." Not bothering with the ladder, he jumped through the trapdoor and straight down to the infirmary level. His cat ensured he landed lightly on his bare feet, his body in a slight crouch.

Walking into the infirmary, he met Finn's perceptive gaze. "Well?"

"Muscle tone on both is as good as your own," the other man replied with a grin. "Aden and Zaira are as dangerous as each other, I'd say."

That's what Remi had figured. Anyone who discounted the woman because of her size or gender was an idiot who deserved to get his head ripped off. "Anything about their injuries say they're lying to us?" Finn was a healer to the bone and he'd done his best by the two Arrows but his first loyalty was to RainFire.

"No." Finn brought up two scans side by side on the screen beside the beds. "Aden and Zaira were shot like they said, and had those barbaric things implanted. I also found signs of multiple stuns to the body."

Frowning, he tapped a laser pen against his datapad. "I guess it's the only way to contain an Arrow if you don't want to use drugs."

"Wouldn't drugs be faster, quieter?"

"Tammy told me Psy don't react well to most drugs," Finn said, referring to the DarkRiver healer. "You never know when even a specially calibrated drug will have the unintended effect of sending their psychic abilities out of control." Frown turning into a scowl, he shook his head. "I counted four stuns on her, more on him. Their abductors were playing with fire—their bodies could've overloaded at any point past three."

"That bruise on Aden's face from a stun, too?"

"Yes. I cleared it up some, but it'll take at least forty-eight more hours to fully disappear."

Remi stared at the scans that provided unmistakable evidence of violence that could've easily led to death. His focus was on building his pack, but he wasn't about to ignore a threat on his border, especially when that threat might ignite an all-out war with the Arrow Squad. Soon as the storm cleared, he'd do everything in his power to find out what the fuck was going on up there.

THE howling aloneness inside her skull threatening to awaken the bloody rage that had helped her survive and almost led to her execution, Zaira stood in the center of the aerie and watched Aden secure the trapdoor. Task complete, he walked over and did something that made every muscle in her body lock tight.

He put his arms around her.

"What are you doing?" Arrows didn't make physical contact except in exigent circumstances.

"You're in distress at being cut off from the PsyNet." Aden didn't release her stiff form, his body heat passing easily through the thin material of his T-shirt and her top. "You need contact."

Zaira didn't know how to answer that. She wasn't used to being in distress about anything—if she'd ever had any softness in her, it had calcified long ago. Even as a child, she'd refused to permit herself to be weak. She'd much preferred to be angry. In anger was strength, brutal and deadly.

In rage was power.

Arrow training had taught her to corral that rage, but she knew it lived inside her, as vicious as always and ready to do damage. Even now it twisted in its bonds, eyes red and only two things in mind: escape and retribution. Escape from the nothingness and retribution against those who'd put her in this position.

She had never been this alone.

Even when her parents beat her without mercy while holding her trapped within their telepathic shields, she'd had their minds within touching distance. When her Arrow trainers had locked her in *their* shields—all of which were constructed to ensure she didn't break out as she'd done from her parents' weaker efforts—she'd felt their presence in the shields themselves.

It wasn't the same, having Aden's arms around her while her mind was numb with aloneness, but the incipient rage took a wary look and withdrew from the surface of her thoughts. Aden wasn't its target, and the contact, the feel of his muscled body pressing against hers, his strong arms around her, was a living barrier to the nothingness that threatened to suffocate her.

And it was Aden, the first person who had ever treated her as a sentient being worth knowing. He'd asked her opinion on things at a time when others had seen her as a vicious monster to be broken to the bit. He'd told Zaira her ideas had value. Later, he'd also ordered her not to lose herself in the hard black box that was Arrow training.

You, Zaira, are priceless as an individual. Don't ever permit them to erase you.

In Venice, she had an Arrow who'd imprinted on her as a result of a catastrophic drug error—Alejandro followed her orders without question, would die for her in a heartbeat. While Zaira would always question Aden if she didn't agree with him, she sometimes thought she'd imprinted on him in a similar way: for her to ever turn against him, Aden would have to betray her in ways of which he was simply incapable.

Where she had a twisted conscience at best, he was that shining knight human and changeling children read stories about. The good man who would fight on the side of right and who would never abandon those to whom he'd pledged his loyalty. She knew he could be ruthless, had witnessed it, but Aden's ruthlessness fed into his overwhelming protective instincts, never into the selfish pursuit of power or glory.

Stepping in the path of danger to protect him had never been up for discussion for Zaira. It was an absolute fact: as long as she lived, she would do everything in her power to keep Aden safe. Coldly planned murder, torture, she'd do whatever was necessary in an eyeblink. He might not agree with her actions, but she was quite willing to disobey him should his life be on the line.

Every white knight needed a deadly black sword at his back.

Relaxing against him on that thought, she allowed the heat of his body to seep into hers. It wasn't protocol, but Silence had fallen, so they broke no laws. There was also no risk to the unforgiving and constant discipline that kept her sane and nonviolent; this was an aberrant circumstance that would cease to exist as soon as their brains recovered from the trauma of the implants.

Zaira couldn't afford to believe anything else, the idea of endless aloneness a horror that made the rage inside her threaten to boil over into unthinking insanity. "Are you in distress, too?" she asked Aden while maintaining a white-knuckled grip on the sleeping death that lived within her.

"How do the other races deal with this silence in their minds?" he said in response.

"Maybe that's why they make so much physical contact." She'd never before come close to understanding the tactile nature of the humans and changelings. Being physically close to Aden wasn't like being in a psychic network. It was more immediate and oddly more intense despite the fact that there were only two of them in this physical network.

Aden moved his hand to the back of her head, but the strength and warmth of his palm in such a vulnerable location didn't rouse her instinct to fight. Always, she'd thought that if she was trapped again in any way, she'd fight. However, she'd never considered the depth of her trust in Aden, never understood that being held wasn't always a prison. "I heard the healer. Your leg was injured."

"I've survived worse."

"You're supposed to keep your partner apprised of your situation."

"Not if the partner will then argue against the best course of action."

Zaira opened her mouth, closed it a heartbeat later. His decision had saved both their lives—she would've never made it out without his help, and he'd be dead from the implant had he gone out on his own. Sliding her arms around him to strengthen their two-person network, she listened to his heartbeat strong and steady under her ear . . . and thought that perhaps the other races understood a truth she'd only just realized: that even a tiny physical network connected by trust held a potent, raw power.

Chapter 14

"I NEED TO shower," she said a long time later, the howl down to a low whisper she could almost ignore and the rage curled up in a drowsy sleep deep inside her psyche.

Releasing her, Aden watched her walk toward the only internal door in the aerie.

Behind it, the facilities were neatly laid out, small packages of soap and shampoo on the counter that held the sink. One package was labeled as being for females, the other for males. Zaira didn't know why men and women would need different cleansing supplies, but she used the female set because she liked the pale blue shade of it.

Liking anything had been prohibited under Silence, but Zaira had never been able to break her pre-Arrow habit of coveting pretty things. As a child, she'd once collected shiny components from organizers discarded in the family's recycler; she'd made herself a toy that sparkled in the thin beam of sunlight that seeped through the narrow window high up in her cage.

Her parents had taken it mere days later, taken the only pretty, shiny thing she had.

A month after she met Aden, he'd noticed her staring at a faceted black button he'd taken from his pocket. Exending his hand, he'd given it to her. "You don't have to hide it," he said when she curled her fingers over it. "I'll tell the trainers I gave it to you to anchor you to the squad."

Holding it so tight the edges cut into her palm, she'd said, "Why are you giving it to me?"

"Because everyone should have something of their own."

It was much later that she'd discovered the "button" was actually a subtle indication of rank and that it had belonged to Aden's mother before she was promoted. Aden secretly kept it with him when his parents were out in the field. Despite that knowledge, she'd never returned it. At the moment it was safely hidden in the false bottom of a trunk in her room in Venice. It was hers; he'd given it to her.

Nobody else but Alejandro had ever given her anything. And Alejandro didn't count—he didn't have a choice. His imprinting drove him to offer her everything he owned. He would do the same even should she kick him bloody morning, noon, and night. Aden, however, had always had a choice, and he'd given her not just the pin but also other small things over the years. All of which she would never return.

Opening the shampoo, she lathered up her hair. A scent reached her nose soon afterward but it was light enough that she could ignore it. It was only as she was stepping out of the shower ten minutes later that she realized she hadn't thought about fresh clothes. A knock came on the door right then. "Zaira—a RainFire pack member dropped off a change of clothes a few minutes ago."

Cracking the door open, she took the bundle he held out.

"Most of it is borrowed from pack members," he said, "but they were able to find some new things in their stores."

"Thank you."

In the pile was an unopened package that held three pairs of panties. She broke the seal, took out a dark blue pair, and found it fit well enough. No bra, but the bandeau provided had enough hooks that she could cinch it tight around her frame. The fact that she had relatively generous breasts on a small frame had always been a source of annoyance, but she'd never considered having them reduced, for the simple reason that she didn't trust anyone to play around with her body while she was unconscious. Being injured and forced into it was bad enough—why do it on purpose?.

The dark green cargo pants were big in the waist, but whoever had chosen the clothing had included a belt and punched in extra holes for her. She had to roll up the bottoms a couple of times, but otherwise, the pants were strong and warm. If necessary, she could wear them for several days before they'd need to be washed.

On top, she pulled on a black T-shirt. Since she didn't like loose fabric that an opponent could use to pull her toward him or her, she undid the belt and tucked in the tee. The short sleeves were still too big, but she'd just have to manage that risk. Her used clothing she put into the small basket in the corner, guessing that RainFire had central laundry facilities she and Aden would be able to access.

Aden went in as soon as she stepped out.

She'd shared quarters with squadmates before, usually on missions, but this felt different. Maybe because these quarters were unlike any she'd ever before had, and maybe because the blackness and continuous rain outside turned it into a cocoon. Yet despite its compact size, the aerie didn't have any sense of being a prison.

There was a large window on the opposite wall and, when she checked, she saw the clasp was unlocked so she could open it at will. Also bringing the outside in was the equally large skylight above the bed. Currently covered by fallen leaves, it nonetheless also had a latch that could be opened.

Zaira decided she liked changeling architecture.

On the left wall was a small set of cubbies in which Aden had placed the rest of the clothes the changelings had dropped off. Zaira went through them, then looked around until she found her boots. They'd been placed beside the bed, no doubt by Aden. Bare feet could be a serious disadvantage in a fight, so their boots were designed to ensure they could literally roll out of bed and slam their feet into them and be ready.

The bed itself was large enough to accommodate them both, the mattress firm but the bedding soft. Quite unlike the plain cotton sheets and scratchy blanket she used in daily life. The large, flat cushions on the floor in front of the small comm screen confused her until she realized she was in a changeling living space—the cushions were meant to accommodate both human and feline bodies.

Trained to adapt to any environment she was in at the

time, Zaira went down and touched the cushions, then took a seat on one.

"Comfortable?" Aden asked as he left the bathroom.

"I don't know," she said, bracing herself with her palms on either side. "The body sinks into these."

"I think that's the point." He came to stand beside her, his damp hair pushed off his forehead and his body clad in jeans and a white T-shirt that had a sports emblem of some kind in black on the front.

He looked young. Like a man who had nothing more important on his mind than a sports game. The illusion only lasted if you didn't look into his eyes. Because in those eyes lived the unwavering determination of a man who'd toppled a former Councilor from power and who had long ago won the fidelity of the most dangerous men and women in the Net.

Moving to the small area to the right that appeared to be for food preparation, he opened the cupboard and pulled out a sealed container. "It's a high-energy drink mix." He made two mugs of it, brought her one. "Likely too sweet for us, but we need the energy if our injuries are to heal."

"You made it with hot water." Ivy Jane did that because she wanted her guests to be warm; for some reason, no one in the squad had pointed out to her that their uniforms insulated them from the weather.

Aden took a seat on the floor opposite her, his back against the wall and one leg stretched out on the polished wood of the floor, the other bent at the knee. Bracing his left arm on that knee, he said, "Perhaps Ivy has inadvertently conditioned me that such drinks must be warm if given to another."

"She is very insistent." Zaira sipped from the mug—the taste was far richer than her senses were trained to handle, but she continued the intake. "Ivy is . . . different. As you said before, she likes us." Nobody actually liked Arrows. Sometimes Arrows were useful, other times dangerous, but they were never considered friends. "I don't think anyone has ever liked me before."

Aden stilled, those intense, quiet eyes locking with her own. "I like you, Zaira."

The words made the rage inside her stir, but not in violence. In a biting possessiveness she'd spent a lifetime trying

to leash. Aden didn't belong to her. Aden was too important
to the squad to belong to any one person, and never could he
belong to someone as fundamentally broken as Zaira. "Don't
say things like that," she warned him.

He didn't break the eye contact that fed the rage's possessiveness until the leash threatened to snap. "Why?"

"Because I might take you seriously." Aden saw her, *knew*
her, but Zaira wasn't sure he appreciated exactly how dangerous she could be. "I might decide to keep you." Locked
tight in a box with her other treasures and available to her
alone because the rage, it didn't know how to share things that
meant the most. It had no concept of "civilized" or "acceptable" behavior. That part of her had grown in a place nearly
devoid of light and was permanently twisted as a result.

"Would you harm me?"

Not if she was rational—but when the rage woke, she was
different. "Soon after I was transferred to the Arrow training
camp, I saw a butterfly." A glorious creature with pink and
black and white in its wings. "I'd never seen anything so
pretty and I wanted it. So every time I had an outdoor period,
I would stalk it, until one day, I caught it in an empty jar I'd
stolen from the mess hall."

She could still remember her happy excitement. "I could
see the butterfly struggling to get out, but I kept telling it I
would keep it safe." It had been an earnest, serious promise.
"I, who grew up in a cage, put another living being in one
and didn't understand it was wrong. That's who I am."

Aden didn't look away, didn't tell her she'd been showing
psychopathic tendencies in hurting the helpless butterfly.
"Did you capture a second butterfly after the first died?"

"No." Heartbroken at having destroyed its beauty when
she'd wanted only to keep it, protect it, she'd tried over and
over to talk her butterfly back to life. "I didn't lose the compulsion, however. I still want to put treasures in a box."

"Yet you understand why you can't."

Zaira wasn't sure she did, the foundation on which she'd
rebuilt her psyche riddled with cracks, because below that
foundation burned the rage that had never died. "Perhaps I'm
just good at pretending." Even now, she wanted to cross the
distance between them and snarl at him for forcing her into

a corner where she had to acknowledge the scarred and frankly insane girl inside her.

Zaira normally only ever let that girl out under controlled circumstances, such as when she was alone in her room with the door locked and barred. Then, for a short time as she went through her treasures, she allowed that rage-fueled girl to emerge, soothing her with the shiny, pretty things she'd so coveted when locked in the dark.

"You know what I want for the squad," Aden said, seemingly dropping the subject of her sanity or lack of it.

Zaira wasn't so easily fooled. Aden might move silently and speak in a tempered tone, but once he decided on a path, he *did not budge*. "You want Arrows to have lives like real people," she said, placing her half-full drink on the floor.

"Yes." Aden rested his own mug on the taut muscle of his thigh. "We don't have to be defined by our identities as Arrows. We can choose to be more."

Aloneness sank its fangs into her again. Her hands fisting at her sides, she tried not to listen to its mocking laughter. "Most of us aren't like you," she said to this man who was the best of them. "We can't handle the stresses of life beyond a regimented existence." Rules, boundaries, that was what kept their violent and deadly abilities in check. "We become monsters if released from the cage."

"No." A single flat word that hummed with power. "I refuse to accept that my Arrows are frozen in amber. They've given their blood, their hearts, their entire lives to the Net." He sliced out his hand. "Enough."

His passionate conviction reached the insane thing inside her, made it try to look through her eyes. Tremors shaking her form as she fought the dual assault of aloneness and an old, twisted insanity, she tried to speak, couldn't.

"Zaira." Aden set aside his mug and hauled her against his chest, his arms muscled steel around her. "You aren't alone, will never be alone. You are an Arrow."

It was the only group into which she'd ever fit. "Have you seen my intake report?"

"Yes."

"My parents used to lock me in a cabin on the grounds of the estate. It had only a single window high on one wall." Her

family had wanted to retain her powerful telepathic ability—
and its later financial value—rather than giving it up to the
Council or the squad, but they hadn't had any idea how to train
someone with such violent power. As a result, they'd attempted to crush her spirit, beat that control into her.

"Except for my socialization training, I was alone for the
majority of my early life." Dark, dark anger burned in her
soul. "Trapped inside their shields so I couldn't even access
the PsyNet." A rough breath. "If anyone ever wanted to torture me until my sanity snapped, this is what they'd have to
do. Cut me off from the Net, leave me alone again."

Aden's hold tightened. "I told you, you won't ever be alone
again. I'm here. I'll always be here." The old, aged anger in
his tone gave lie once more to his professed Silence.

The quiet, dark-eyed boy she'd met had been angry for
her from the start.

Spreading her hand over his heart, the rhythm lulling the
rage into peace again so she could think, she said, "You have
to lead from the front." It was the only way his plan could
work. "The squad will follow you into hell and back if that's
what you ask—all you have to do is show them the way."

Air moved above her, as if he was shaking his head. "The
squad needs me to remain as I am, needs the stability."

Rising to face him, though she kept her hand on his heart,
she said, "That's your parents talking." Zaira had lived with
Marjorie and Naoshi since she'd taken over the Venice compound, knew every one of their views on how Aden should
lead the squad. He had always gone his own way regardless,
but every so often, he hit a blind spot. Like now.

"You're the *only* one who can convince the others that
change is possible for more than the youngest of us." Even she
would go as far as she was able, holding the rear and watching
over those who'd successfully made new lives for themselves.

Aden's jaw was a clean, hard line. He'd shaved, she realized suddenly. His skin would be smooth should she touch it.
Then he spoke and the possessive compulsion quieted. "My
job is to make sure no one is left behind." Aden would never
abandon any of his men or women in the dark.

"It *was*," said the woman who was perhaps the most perfect Arrow he had. "Now your job is to forge a new path."

Her words clashed against his parents' advice to hold things steady, to make himself a cold power in the eyes of the populace so that no one would ever consider the Arrows a viable target. But his parents also thought Vasic "lost" to the squad because of his bonding with Ivy. They didn't understand that Vasic had been lost for years, had come back to them because of Ivy.

For the first time in more than a decade, Aden's best friend was *alive*.

"You know I'm right," Zaira said into the quiet. "If I wasn't, Vasic's bonding as well as Abbot's would've already initiated the change you want." Her fingers dug a touch into his skin through his T-shirt. "Wide-scale change can only happen if it spirals out from the center. And you, you're the center."

It was her reference to Vasic that made Aden see her words for truth. The other man was part of the core of the squad, Aden's second in command, his mate an empath who had opened her home and her heart. And yet the squad hesitated on the precipice. Waiting, Aden saw now, for a signal from the top that such "rebellion" from the rules was acceptable on a squadwide basis.

"If I do this," he said slowly, "I can't do it alone." If his men and women needed him to go into the unknown first, that was what he'd do. He'd been born—*created*—to be what the squad needed and it was a mantle he'd accepted long ago. "Any change in my personal psyche is useless unless I bond on some level with another individual." It wasn't simply about moving out of the shadows, but about making deep, emotional connections beyond the ties of loyalty that bound one Arrow to another.

"I can offer you a number of suggestions for a suitable partner," said the only woman he could ever see by his side. Strong, fierce, and with a fire in her heart that could spark the same in every Arrow heart if she'd only set it free.

Aden looked into the midnight black of her eyes and shook his head. "I want you. No substitutes."

Chapter 15

"I THANK YOU for choosing me, Aden," Zaira said after a long, long quiet, and it was a solemn statement that glittered with a brittle beauty. "I will never forget that you did and the insanity in me wants to accept, to take you and cage you up as I did that butterfly, but you know I'm one of the lifers. I won't ever be anything but an Arrow—or a monster." She touched her fingers to his jaw. "I'm broken too badly to fix."

He thought again of the bruised and battered girl who'd run out of the treatment room even though she'd been hurt and in pain, of the woman who'd argued with him during their escape. "If your parents had broken you," he said quietly, "you would've never killed them, never survived." She'd made the only real choice in horrific circumstances. "You might have fractures inside you, but so do I."

Her eyes turned obsidian, no whites, nothing but ink black. "You're the best of us." A potent statement. "The *best*. The strongest, the smartest, and the one with a heart stubborn enough that it resisted Silence and cared for the most damaged among us." She clamped her hand over his mouth when he would've spoken. "I'm tough and I'm violent and I will slit the throat of anyone who tries to cause you harm, but I will never choose to go beyond the rigid black walls of an Arrow's life. I can't. You know exactly why."

He tugged away her hand. "I know what you believe."

That the visceral rage that lived in her made her a lethal risk outside the confines of regulation Arrow life.

Zaira had once broken the jaws of two male trainers who'd tried to hold her down. She'd been twelve at the time and had spent the next year being taught ice-cold discipline after being given an ultimatum: learn control or be kicked out of the squad, out of the only family she had. The threat and the training had worked—she'd had no more nonsanctioned violent episodes—but Aden knew the rage lived within her.

"The anger is part of your fire," he told her, not for the first time. "Why do you persist on seeing it as a threat to your sanity?"

"And why do you refuse to understand that it isn't anger?" she retorted. "It's a kind of insanity and I inherited it."

Pushing off him, she rose to her feet. "What my parents did wasn't 'normal' in any sense of the word. They said they intended to teach me psychic control, but what mother or father could possibly think that beating a child with a leather belt until that child had no skin on her back, her blood flecking the walls of her cage, would lead to anything but a kind of feral madness in the child?" She folded her arms. "No sane parent. Mine weren't sane, and I carry their genetic legacy."

It was an argument the two of them had been having since childhood. He could remember the first time with crystal clarity.

"I'M crazy." Small and with dirt on her face from an outdoor exercise, Zaira ate the nutrition bar he'd saved for her from his own lunch—she was given exactly enough for her caloric needs, but Zaira was always hungry. As if part of her couldn't forget being starved as extra punishment.

"You're not crazy."

"I am." She chewed a bite of the bar. "Not crazy like the human who used to scream outside the compound some days about the end of days, but crazy like I have a mean, bad thing inside me."

"Does the mean, bad thing tell you to kill everyone? Kill me?"

"No. It only tells me to kill people who hurt me and who

*hurt you." Her eyes zeroed in on a trainer Aden knew to be
particularly brutal. "I lie in bed and I think about how I
would cut his throat. I know how to get into his room. I could
do it while he was asleep." Another bite of the nutrition bar.
"I like to imagine watching his blood turn his pillow all red."*

"Don't. They'll execute you for it."

*A sideways glance. "I won't. I want to be there when you
grow up and take over."*

ZAIRA had always believed he'd take over the squad, even before he'd shared his plans with her. "All of the reasons you've
stated," he said instead of getting into the same argument
again, "are the same reasons it has to be you." An Arrow no
one expected to make it out *and* one who was deeply respected.
If she was the only woman he could see by his side, Aden had
long ago accepted that his relationship with Zaira wasn't like
the relationship he had with others in the squad.

Vasic was his closest friend, but Zaira . . . Her spirit
burned hot enough even under so many layers of control that
it had warmed him through the coldest winters of the soul.
When Vasic was determined to die, to the point that he'd
allowed himself to be fitted with an experimental and unstable biofusion gauntlet, it was Zaira Aden had gone to,
Zaira with whom he'd shared his frustration and his concern.
She'd suggested knocking Vasic over the head and forcibly
removing the gauntlet before it became too integrated.

Of course Aden hadn't been able to take her advice, but
in speaking with her, he'd found the strength to keep going,
keep fighting for Vasic's survival. Zaira had used to send him
regular mission specs for how the two of them could incapacitate Vasic so the gauntlet could be removed. Since they'd
both known he wouldn't take Vasic's choice from him, it had
been nothing but an intellectual exercise that had given him
a break from the crushing knowledge that he would soon
lose the only man he called friend.

It was why she'd done it, though if he asked her, she'd no
doubt say she'd been deadly serious.

"You," he repeated when she didn't answer. "It must be you."

Zaira didn't respond to Aden's words, to the relentless

determination in his voice. *Stubborn, irrational, obdurate Arrow.* Taking both mugs to the food preparation area on that thought, she finished her drink while staring out through the window lashed by rain, then washed the mugs clean. And fought to keep from giving in to the violently possessive creature inside her, the one who wanted to grab at Aden's offer and never let go.

"Don't try to tell me my madness is a result of nurture," she said when she could think rationally again, referring to one of his strongest counterarguments. "Every single generation of my family has been plagued by it. My grandfather was rehabilitated because of his violent episodes, and in the generation directly before Silence, we had two murderers." A father and a son responsible for the murders of forty-seven women between them. "My parents abused me until I beat them to death. I was *seven*. What does that tell you?"

"Each one of those facts could be used to support the idea of nurture." Aden's voice never rose, and he remained in his relaxed position on the floor, but the thread of steel in his tone was unhidden. "The father forced the son to help him stalk and torture his victims. Your grandfather saw his own father be executed for murder. Your parents drove you to violence."

Zaira strode to the other side of the room as the maddened rage creature shoved at her skin, *wanting* him all to itself. "Choose. Another. Partner." She could put steel in her voice, too.

"Someone better suited? Younger? Without as much blood on her hands?"

"Yes." Even as she spoke, Zaira saw the flaw in her argument. For this to work, for Aden to demonstrate to the squad that even their most broken could have a second chance at life, his partner had to be strong and deadly and kissed by darkness.

Getting to his feet in a smooth motion that betrayed his strength, he unexpectedly didn't push the point. "Rest," he said. "We're both weaker than we should be."

Zaira knew the discussion wasn't over, but she could use the respite to regroup. "You need to rest, too." Aden had a tendency to put the squad first, forgetting about himself in the process. "There's no need to stand watch—if the changelings meant us harm, they had plenty of time to take action while we were out, and no one from the outside can get in through the storm."

Aden walked to the right side of the bed as she headed to

the left and slipped beneath the fluffy comforter. She'd seen the large T-shirt the changelings had provided as sleep clothing for her, but she preferred to sleep fully dressed while in unfamiliar territory. It would be much easier to defend herself against attack if she wasn't tangled up in fabric.

Aden, too, didn't bother to change as he slipped into the bed that was as unlike an Arrow bed as possible. He touched the comforter, lifted it up, put it down.

"I like it," Zaira said, patting the softness of it.

Aden turned his head toward her. "You would."

Shifting onto her side, she looked at his face. She liked that, too, always had. He was formed of clean lines and smooth olive-toned skin, his damp hair starting to turn silky as it dried. "I'm going to buy one like this for my bed." Small things were no threat, wouldn't make her snap . . . and the insane girl inside her deserved pretty things. It was little enough compensation for the fact that Zaira never let her out in public, never allowed her to taste true freedom.

Aden shifted onto his side, too, their breaths mingling as they spoke, the intimacy a warmth around her that muted the aloneness.

"For the perfect Arrow, you have a rebellious streak."

"I buy Alejandro ice cream." She put her hand on the pillow in front of her face. "It makes him happy." The brain-damaged male was childlike in many ways, could spend hours staring in fascination at the way the sun glittered on the canal water or how the clouds moved in the sky. Ice cream with its colors and flavors engendered the same fascination. "I always ask him what flavor he wants and give him an hour or two to decide because he likes to think about it."

Zaira hadn't spent even a second weighing up her decision to indulge Alejandro's fascination once she became aware of it. His life was destroyed. If ice cream gave him pleasure, then he could have ice cream. "Your father thinks I'm making the situation worse. He says Alejandro should be locked up alone so I don't have to 'babysit' him."

Aden closed his hand over hers, pushing the aloneness even further away. "Why is my father still alive?"

She shifted her hand so that it lay on top of his, not because she was asserting dominance, but because she wanted to touch

Aden, not just be touched by him. "He's your father; that's the only reason why." Zaira didn't feel any special loyalty toward either Naoshi Ayze or Marjorie Kai. She accepted that they'd sown the seeds of rebellion, and that they'd run countless dangerous missions to protect their brethren, but she also knew that had they been in charge of the squad, she'd either have been executed or turned into a pitiless, unthinking assassin.

Their vision for the Arrows was both great and blinkered.

Aden's parents had fought to claw back control of the squad from the Council after it became clear the leaders of the Psy had forgotten the mandate of the Arrows. Zaid Adelaja may have formed the squad to support his parents' vision of Silence, but the squad's driving force had never been to advance the personal interests of the Councilors; it was to protect the Psy race.

"The Council turned an elite squad into a mockery," Marjorie had said to Zaira more than once. "They used us as a whip on the backs of those who would oppose their rule, while allowing the true threats to roam free."

Zaira had no argument with Marjorie's thoughts on that point. The other Councilors had been bad enough, but Ming was the worst—less a leader than a parasite using up the lives of good men and women in his lust for power. Zaira could also respect Marjorie and Naoshi for laying the foundations of the rebellion, but she would never forget that they had sacrificed their son to their vision. According to Marjorie, Aden's parents had made the decision to "die" after discovering that Ming intended to get rid of them because they held too much sway over their fellow Arrows.

"For a long time," Aden's mother had said, "we believed Ming was one of us, that his political ambition was a weapon he used to protect the squad. Naoshi almost told him of our plans to break away from the Council. A day later, we discovered his intentions for us, learned that he was capable of murdering his fellow Arrows in order to hold on to the leadership. It was the first sign of what he would one day become."

Zaira couldn't imagine ever trusting Ming, but she had to remember that to Marjorie and Naoshi, he'd been a compatriot, a fellow Arrow with whom they'd no doubt run missions. "Yet you abandoned Aden to his control," she'd responded. "Even if Ming didn't kill him, he could've easily ejected him from the squad."

In one way, Zaira could understand Marjorie's and Naoshi's choice to trust their son to be a sleeper agent, to carry on the stealthy battle from within while they acted from the outside. Even as a child, Aden had been too old; he was a worthy keeper of his parents' dreams. But he'd still only been a *boy* left to survive under a leader who saw no value in him.

Marjorie's response had been impassive. "Aden was Ming's ace in the hole, or so he believed." Nothing in her expression or tone said she regretted her decision. "Ming wasn't stupidly arrogant back then. He knew part of the reason we'd threatened his power base was because the other senior Arrows trusted and respected us. Our status was why Aden was allowed into the training program in the first place, despite his low rating on the Gradient."

The older Arrow's eyes had met Zaira's, the ice in them impenetrable. "What better way to 'honor' our memory than to allow our weak child to remain in the squad? Aden bolstered Ming's image as an Arrow who abided by the wishes of his squadmates—in our case, even after death."

Marjorie had meant it when she'd called Aden "weak." Even after all the extraordinary things he'd done, his success in achieving what Marjorie and Naoshi couldn't and freeing the squad from the Council's clutches, Marjorie saw him only in terms of his known abilities. She had *no idea* of the man her son had become, no comprehension of just why the squad followed him with such steadfast loyalty, and no understanding of his leadership methods and dreams for the squad.

Quite frankly, neither Marjorie nor Naoshi had the imagination or the heart to see any other path but the cold, ascetic one Zaid Adelaja had laid down over a hundred years before, when he became the founding member of the squad.

"I thank you for your forbearance in letting my father live," Aden said at that moment, not protesting when she began to explore the back of his hand with her fingertips, the craving inside her too huge a thing to totally stifle.

Zaira ran her thumb over his knuckles. "I did warn Naoshi that if he ever mentioned locking Alejandro away again, I'd snap his neck." Aden's father was bigger than her, but they all knew she was one of the deadliest Arrows in the squad. Never had she failed to acquire or dispose of a target unless she'd made a conscious decision to disobey orders. And when she disobeyed, she made sure her proposed targets went under so deep that no other assassin would ever locate them.

Ironically enough, Naoshi appreciated Zaira's insubordinate streak, appreciated that even under Ming LeBon, Zaira had remained her own person. What Naoshi failed to understand was that Zaira was only that person because Aden had taught her she was an individual in her own right, one who had the right to make her own decisions, have her own opinions.

In contrast, Naoshi's and Marjorie's vision of the squad would've produced interchangeable carbon copies. And while they might not have done as Ming had and executed "malfunctioning" or "worn-out" Arrows, she didn't think they would've given those Arrows any real quality of life, either.

"Alejandro won't make it if we're trapped here more than another day." His compulsions would tear him apart from the inside out. "I have to find a way to let him know I'm alive."

"Ivy knows about him," Aden reminded her. "She'll help keep him calm, and if that's not possible, Vasic knows to sedate him." He spread his fingers so she could weave her own into them, strengthening their private two-person network. "That's why else you're perfect," he said, returning to the argument he had no doubt decided he would win. "You have the capacity to stand against the old Arrows who many obey without question."

A valid point, but it didn't alter her decision. "You've seen me snap, seen the carnage I can cause." Broken bones, broken faces, broken bodies, she'd created it all with little more than her hands and the power of her mind. "Your partner can't display such irrational rage, and if I break discipline to embrace a 'normal' existence, I can't guarantee I won't have an episode."

And she couldn't guarantee the violence wouldn't one day turn on him. It could be his face she smashed in, his bones she crushed, his incredible mind she turned to mush. "The risk," she murmured as his eyes turned jet-black in repudiation, "is too high."

"No."

"Yes."

Stalemate.

PSYNET BEACON: BREAKING NEWS

Aden Kai, rumored leader of the Arrow Squad, has disappeared. Sources say he was abducted over forty-eight hours ago and is presumed dead. The squad could not be reached for contact at time of press. Further updates to come.

PSYNET BEACON: LIVE NETSTREAM

Who is your source? Until you name him or her, this is nothing but scaremongering.

K. Benedict
(Tunis)

Who would dare abduct an Arrow? The individual or individuals involved must have a death wish.

Z. Ek
(Vancouver)

If even the Arrows aren't safe now that Silence has fallen, how can we expect to survive?

Concerned Citizen
(Bogotá)

. . .

Deep in a quiet room in a reinforced building deep underground, senior Arrow Blake Stratton considered the *PsyNet Beacon* report. News of Aden's disappearance had spread through the squad, but Blake hadn't seriously considered that anyone could kill Aden. If this report was true, however, his path was now clear of obstructions. Aden was the only one who might have stopped him, the only one who might have put all the pieces together.

Without Aden, no one aside from his mysterious "friend" would ever know.

Aden alone had seen Blake as a child. Aden alone understood the jagged crag on which he stood. On one side lay the screaming abyss of insanity and violence that made his mouth water and his blood thunder. On the other side a civilized existence where his instincts and desires were kept under strict control . . . and fed just enough blood to keep him from giving in to the furtive hunger that beat beneath his skin.

Ming had fed him that blood. Ming had known that his soul was parched without it, needed the sustenance. Not that Blake had ever felt any loyalty toward the ex-leader of the squad. The other man had simply been useful. Ming had sent him on assassinations his fellow Arrows wouldn't carry out, assassinations against people who had simply gotten in Ming's way.

Blake could still feel the slender neck of the twenty-three-year-old technician who'd been his last kill. He'd taken his time with her. Ming didn't know; he thought Blake had completed the task that first night. But why should he rush things? No, he'd kept her alive for a month. Watching her bleed and beg and die had given him something he thought might be labeled as pleasure though it didn't register as emotion on the dissonance triggers in his mind.

There had been no punishing starburst of pain, no warning stab inside his head.

Aden had removed dissonance triggers from the minds of many in the squad, but not all. Either he suspected their mental state and/or their impulse control, or the task was too complex in certain situations. It didn't matter, not to Blake. He'd worked out that he was a psychopath. He had no empathy for others.

The term "narcissist" was also used to describe those like him.

It struck him as a great irony that the most Silent among his kind had apparently always been the narcissistic psychopaths. Maybe it was amusement he felt at the thought, but that, too, didn't register on the dissonance triggers. If he did possess emotions, they were buried so far beneath his psychopathy that they were like stones trapped beneath the surface of a frozen lake.

He wasn't sorry about that, didn't care.

He didn't care about anything except his own needs.

Sliding out a knife from his boot, he looked at the gleaming blade. It had been months and months since Aden had deposed Ming. No one had fed him since, and he'd known better than to ask Aden. He'd also known better than to exercise his need. It was a secret thing. Not a thing that could be exposed to the light.

He thought again of the message that had come directly to him, the message that invited him to feed and told him he was safe from discovery. The source had even given him the details of a target who fit his tastes.

Was it Ming? He was almost certain it must be—the former leader of the squad was clearly attempting to undermine Aden by nudging one of his senior Arrows to unsanctioned murder. If so, he'd chosen the wrong target: Blake might be a psychopath but he was a smart one.

Politics didn't interest him. All he wanted was to feed.

"You should've used me, Aden," he said aloud. "You should've believed in the monster you glimpsed as a child." Instead, the squad's leader saw Blake as a soldier he could trust, a soldier who had risen above his past.

Aden didn't understand—or didn't accept—that some wounds could never be repaired. Blake knew he'd been born this way, but the fact that he'd been abandoned by his family unit only to be tortured by the squad's trainers had polished his psychopathic tendencies to a gleaming shine. Without that history, he might've simply become a narcissistic CEO or a coldly venomous politician, but that ship had sailed long ago.

He was who he was.

The light glinted on the surface of the blade.

Chapter 16

ZAIRA WOKE TO find her back pressed up against Aden's chest, her head pillowed on his arm. She froze, the position one that should've never happened. The fact that she'd been asleep shouldn't have mattered; her training should've held, had always before held when she'd had to rest in close quarters with another member of the squad.

But when she went to pull away, she felt a stubborn hesitation within herself. If she stopped touching him, she'd be alone again. As she'd been in that cold, barren room so long ago. Aden was warm, was alive, was a living being she could trust. And her head, it remained a dark, empty place filled only with her own thoughts and her own madness.

Her stomach tensed, a dull throb of pain reminding her of her recently mended injury.

In a psychic network bursting with data feeds and broken fragments of other people's conversations, she could forget the twisted thing inside her, forget the stunted creature that had been deprived of light and kept in isolation for the first seven years of its life, until it was permanently deformed, its thoughts disturbing.

That rage creature had taken over her body the day she'd beaten her parents to death, taken over her mind, too. She'd come to covered in blood and screaming like a being created of horror as others in the extended family unit attempted to pull her out of the room she'd turned into an abattoir. Seven years old and the creature had given her such strength that it had taken two adults to rip the bloodied pipe from her hands, force enough to rip off the skin on her palms.

And the screams . . . that had been the creature's laughter.

It was quiet now, but it was very much awake and aware and with her. It always was. She could simply ignore it better in the tumult of noise created by other minds. The instant she left this bed, she wouldn't have Aden's presence to assuage the rage, turn it quiescent. In the quiet, in the aloneness, it would whisper to her.

But she couldn't stay in this bed forever. And she couldn't depend on Aden's proximity to control it—because with each instant that passed, the possessiveness inside her grew and grew. If she wasn't careful, she might one day wake to find that she'd murdered him as she'd murdered that butterfly, permanently stopping his heart with its capacity to care that astonished her.

Lurching from the bed on that thought, she used all her strength to shove away the insane part of her psyche and slammed the door shut on it. The psychic lock wouldn't last. The stunted, enraged creature would emerge again, sly and slippery and vicious. It always did, always would—because it was an indelible part of Zaira, its black tendrils entwined around the core of her soul, a malignant tumor no operation could remove.

Her eye fell on the clock by the bed. Six thirty a.m.

Morning, and the rain continued to lash the window, the tree leaves in her line of sight twisted back in the wind that pummeled the aerie.

More time alone with Aden.

It was a secretive thought born in the possessiveness that might one day end him.

Her heart pulsing with the same wild beat as the storm, she stripped and showered under an ice-cold spray to remind her body and her mind of the discipline necessary to ensure she stayed sane. Any fracture could turn her once again into that girl who'd smashed her parents' brains to pulp with her telepathic abilities, then beat their weakened bodies to death with a piece of pipe she'd found on one of her excursions outside; the creature had hidden it inside her hole in a rare moment when no one was watching.

It was the latter that had led PsyMed to label her a deadly risk.

A child striking out in a moment of physical danger is understandable. However, a child who shows this level of premeditation at such a young age is a candidate for re-habilitation.

Zaira didn't often think about the time she'd spent strapped down in the PsyMed center as they dug around in her brain. When she did, she wanted to ask the psychiatrists and medics what exactly they thought a seven-year-old girl should've done against much larger and older opponents.

She'd known her parents were going to beat her. That was a given. She'd known they were going to try to break her so they could enslave her abilities. That, too, was a given. She'd also known that if she struck out in an attempt to protect herself, they'd just hurt her more. They'd trapped her in their shields so her screams didn't hit the outside world, and her small hands and body couldn't do any real damage.

She knew because she'd tried. So many times.

The only rational, reasonable thing to do had been to plan it. She had to make her parents incapable of keeping her in their shields, incapable of ever again hurting her. That was why she'd discarded all possible weapons she'd come across—planks of wood, a brick, even a small sheet of metal—until she'd found a piece of pipe she could swing, but that had enough heft to it to stun at least. That was why she'd put her chair by the door; so she'd have the height to swing from behind as soon as a parent entered.

It was also why she'd cunningly built shields beneath her public mind. Her parents thought they saw everything she thought and felt, but they had no idea about the angry and twisted part of her that had lots of secrets. Including the capacity to plan and carry out a murder.

The only problem, of course, had been the fact that she had two targets, both with powerful shields even a Gradient 9.8 telepathic child couldn't simultaneously destroy. So she'd had to wait for a day when she was certain they'd arrive one after the other, giving her just enough time to debilitate one and get the other before the second person realized what was happening.

In the interim, she'd taken beating after beating, her body bruised black-and-blue. And each morning, she'd pressed her ear to the door and listened, until the day she heard her mother become delayed by a conversation with an older child, while her father continued on to Zaira's cage.

That murderous patience had saved her life and turned her into a menace in the eyes of PsyMed. If not for the squad stepping in to claim her for their own, she'd be a drooling vegetable by now, suitable only for menial tasks.

The child shows tendencies toward criminal psychopathy.

Switching off the shower as the words from the PsyMed report continued to scroll in her mind, that report having become available to her once she was no longer a minor, she shook her head. "I am not a psychopath." Insane in a way that meant she could never lower her guard, but not an individual devoid of conscience or empathy. "I am *not* a psychopath."

She didn't realize how loudly she'd spoken until Aden's voice came through the door. "No, you're not."

Another breach in her discipline, those words spilling from her lips. "I need fresh clothes." That, too, was a mistake. She'd been so off center that she'd forgotten to prepare. "I can wear the pants again." A few wrinkles were nothing when the fabric was strong and warm.

"I'm leaving a change by the door. Finn came by a few minutes ago with a T-shirt that should be a closer fit—he borrowed it from a pack member who's willing to share more if the size suits."

Picking them up, she got into clean panties and the same bandeau as the night before, then pulled on the cargo pants. Over that, she tugged on the white T-shirt Aden had left. It fit much, much better than the T-shirt in which she'd slept, but only once it was on did she realize it had a sparkly pink pony on the front. She stepped out of the bathroom. "Are they trying to subtly insult me?"

Aden followed her pointing fingers to the pony that pranced over her breasts, a flicker in his eyes she couldn't quite read. "It appears the only person in RainFire with a build close to yours likes color and sparkle," he said. "The secondary option is for you to wear the larger clothes, but I thought you'd prefer a pony over having your movements hampered."

"I'm not so sure. It's very pink." Going to the cubby that held the other clothes, she found that the uniform top and pants she'd worn the night of her abduction had been meticulously repaired, laundered, and returned. Finn, she realized, must've dropped these off with the T-shirt. The scars of the repaired tears in Aden's leather jacket made it appear as if someone—the healer?—had literally torn through the tough material with his claws. A note sticking out of the pocket said whoever had done the repair had wiped off all traces of blood, but hadn't otherwise cleaned it, worried about causing damage.

"That solves it." Grabbing the uniform items, she headed toward the bathroom . . . and hesitated. "Are we attempting to blend in?"

"We can't blend in, but we should do our best not to appear so other that they close their minds against us."

Zaira looked down at the pink pony again. "For the good of the squad." At least she could throw the leather jacket on over it. Because she wasn't going to give that back to Aden. It was hers now. He'd given it to her. If he wanted it back . . . well, he couldn't have it.

Some things of his, she might give back to him if he really wanted them, but not the jacket. It smelled of him and when she wore it, she didn't feel alone. "I'm keeping this," she said to him in case he believed any different.

His lashes, thick and long and curling, came down over his eyes, rose back up again. "You'll have to shorten the arms."

"I'll just fold them." She began to do exactly that. "If I cut them, you won't be able to wear it."

"I thought you were keeping it."

"I'm going to lend it to you sometimes." Then it would smell like him again. "But it's mine."

A slight incline of his head before he walked into the bathroom to refresh himself after their long and deep sleep.

The changelings clearly had no problem finding clothing that fit him. When he came out after a quick shower, he was wearing the same pair of faded blue jeans as the previous night, but his T-shirt was plain gray, his feet bare, and his hair slightly damp in front and tumbled.

It was the most casual she had ever seen him.

"You look normal," she said as she finished putting on her boots. "Not like an Arrow."

His eyes met hers, and there it was: the thing that made him an Arrow, the same thing that made her want to own him, keep him.

"Good." Sitting down to pull on his own boots, he said, "We should go to breakfast—but first, why did you feel the need to remind yourself you aren't a psychopath?"

Zaira should've answered him. It was a perfectly reasonable question from the leader of the squad. What she did was open the trapdoor that led to the corridor outside the infirmary and go down. Aden followed seconds later. Heading toward the breakfast area Finn had given Aden instructions on how to find, Zaira considered her own irrational behavior and found no answer.

"This is it," Aden said, nodding to a door on her left.

Opening it, she found herself going up narrow steps that opened out onto a path laid along a sturdy branch. The outside world was blocked out by thin sheets of transparent plas, but there was no heat, the chill extreme. "Strong construction," she said, tapping on the plas to find it was near-glass quality, the rain beyond rolling down the outer surface in crystalline beads. "Glass would be more dangerous if they have children around."

"It's also more durable," Aden pointed out. "And easier to disassemble."

"Of course. They must remove the panels during clear weather." They were leopards, after all, likely prowled freely along the branches of this tree and those of the other forest giants around them.

The dining aerie was located in a smaller tree to their left, though "smaller" was a relative term, given the size of the trees.

Just after they'd made their way inside and hung their

jackets on the hooks by the door, a small changeling child ran over to Zaira. It was female, she thought, its curly black hair tousled and standing up every which way, and its body clad in what looked like pajamas with feet. The pajamas were pale yellow fleece with white sheep on them.

Around two years of age, she judged. Possibly two and a half.

The child also appeared to have clawlike scars on the right-hand side of her face, but a second look made Zaira question their origins. It didn't appear as if she'd been mauled; the marks were integrated too flawlessly into her skin and facial features. As if she'd been born with them . . . and then Zaira recalled an image she'd seen of Lucas Hunter.

The DarkRiver alpha bore identical markings. Either the child was somehow related to the alpha or this was a changeling genetic quirk.

"Hi!" the child said, staring up with yellow-brown leopard eyes against skin of a glowing deep brown.

Zaira didn't know how to interact with children but she replied to this one so as not to offend their hosts, many of whom were in the room. "Hello."

The child pointed. "Pony!"

"Yes."

That was when the child raised its arms with a bright smile.

Zaira had no dealings with children. Not even Arrow children. "What am I supposed to do?" she said to Aden.

"Pick her up."

"Like a sack of supplies?"

"A bit more carefully." But he was moving even as he spoke, going down on his haunches to say, "How about me instead?" He opened his arms and the child went right into them.

Absolutely no sense of self-preservation, Zaira judged. "She's taking a risk."

"She doesn't have to worry about risk management—do you know how many eyes are watching us right now?"

Zaira scanned the room without appearing to do so, acutely aware of her lack of telepathic senses. Aden was right—the changelings seemed to be going about their business, talking and eating, but they were keeping a close eye on the situation at the entrance. Zaira knew how fast change-lings could move, realized that should either she or Aden appear the least threatening, they'd be under attack from multiple sources in a split second.

Having made that determination, she made sure to keep her distance from the child Aden carried easily in one arm while she babbled in his ear. Since Aden had that arm and hand busy, she put food on his plate while he held it out, then filled her own, the food items available from a community table against the left wall.

"Pony!"

She turned to find the child stretching its arms toward her. "I will never again wear this T-shirt."

Her words made the child giggle and stretch even farther out of Aden's arms, as if she'd launch herself at Zaira.

"Aden."

"For the good of the squad."

"It won't do any good if I drop her on her head." Zaira liked small, delicate things, was very careful with the trea-sures she collected, but none of them was a living being. She didn't trust herself with living beings. She killed living beings even when she wanted to save them, admire them.

"As I've seen you handle a laser pistol with rock-steady hands, I think you can handle a child."

Zaira wasn't so certain, but, placing her plate on the near-est table, she gathered the child into her arms, copying Aden's hold in order to support the small body. However, she quickly realized she couldn't hold the child in one arm as he'd been doing— her muscle strength wasn't the same as his, and the child was heavier than it looked.

"Hi!" It grinned at her before throwing both arms around her neck and ducking its head against her own, the softness of its hair brushing her neck.

Frozen in place, she stared at Aden. "Now what?"

Chapter 17

A CHANGELING FEMALE appeared in Zaira's line of sight just then, her hair and the shape of her face making it clear she was the child's mother or other close relative. "I'm so sorry," she said with a smile that didn't seem apologetic at all. "She loves ponies. Come on, cublet. Let Zaira eat."

The child—the cub—clung on tighter. "No." A puff of hot air against Zaira's neck. "My friend!"

Lips twitching, the other woman raised an eyebrow. "She can be like a barnacle. You mind?"

"No." Alarming or distressing the child would hardly create goodwill, and right now she and Aden needed RainFire's assistance.

"Be good, Jojo." Leaning in to kiss the child's cheek, the woman stepped back and returned to another table.

"Jojo good," the child said into Zaira's neck. "Zai good?"

Surprised the cub had so quickly picked up on her name from the context of the conversation, Zaira sat down at a table and looked at her new companion with more interest. "Not always," she said with utmost honesty. "I can't always control myself."

Sitting up in her lap, the child stared at her, frown lines marring her forehead above eyes that had shifted to a soft brown. A second later, she clapped. "Cookies!"

As the word seemed apropos of nothing, Zaira downgraded

her estimation of Jojo's intelligence until Aden said, "Do you find yourself unable to control yourself around cookies, Jojo?"

A firm nod from the black-haired girl. "Cookies. Nom nom." She made chomping movements with her jaw and mimed putting cookies into her mouth with hands that suddenly had tiny claws at the tips of her fingers.

Zaira looked at Aden. "Are all children this small this intelligent?"

He wasn't the one who answered.

"Kids are full of surprises," Remi said, taking a seat across from them. "Good morning, Jojo."

Beaming, Jojo pushed herself up by bracing one hand on the table and blew kisses at Remi.

The alpha grinned. "This one, though, she's a smartypants."

Plopping back down in Zaira's lap, claws retracted, Jojo reached out and took a triangle of toast off Zaira's plate. She made a face after taking a bite. "Pea butter?"

"Gimme." Taking the slice, Remi put some kind of spread on it from a small jar on the table. "There you go, complete with peanut butter."

Happy, Jojo relaxed against Zaira and busied herself eating. The small, warm weight was . . . odd. Picking up an undoctored slice of toast, Zaira was very careful with all her movements so as not to inadvertently harm the child.

"She won't break, you know." Remi's stance was unaggressive, his arm placed easily over the back of the chair next to his. "Jojo's a leopard cub, probably has bones stronger than yours."

"Her spine remains fragile. I could snap it in a second," Zaira said before she remembered she was supposed to be blending in.

The growl that rumbled from Remi's throat had Jojo going still. Zaira did, too, aware of Aden ready for a fight beside her.

"Apologies," she said before the situation could escalate. "I didn't mean I would harm the child. I was just pointing out that you're all being very trusting in allowing me to hold her. You should be more careful." Jojo was tiny, easy to harm, easy to break.

Remi's eyes remained leopard as he stared at her, but the growl was gone from his voice when he said, "You couldn't lay a finger on her before you'd be dead." Absolute conviction. "The fact that you'd warn me about yourself tells me that even if we had trusted you, we'd have been right to do so. Do you kill children, Zaira?"

"No, only adults." Ming LeBon had twice ordered her to retrieve a child he'd wanted to experiment on. Both times, Zaira had seen to the child's safety, well aware Ming needed her covert skills too much to punish her for her actions.

Remi's lips curved, his gaze flicking to Aden. "Is she always this honest?"

"Yes," Aden said from beside her, his shoulder brushing hers.

"Lying wastes energy." Zaira ate another bite of toast. "Also, it's pointless. No one would believe it if I smiled and wore frothy clothes and pretended to be helpless." She was dead certain the alpha hadn't fallen for her weak act in the infirmary so there was no point in carrying on the subterfuge.

Remi chuckled, the sound making Jojo laugh, her face smeared with the spread on her toast. The sound was high, soft, and it was a sound Zaira had never heard from an Arrow child. She didn't know if children with vicious psychic abilities could ever be this carefree, but as she watched Jojo laugh, she began to truly understand Aden's vision for the squad.

ADEN didn't monitor Zaira while he conversed with Remi. He knew she wouldn't harm the child. Because Zaira, as she'd said herself, wasn't a psychopath. She was simply wired differently. Put her in charge of a group of children and she probably wouldn't touch them or comfort them without prompting. But she'd make sure they were protected from all harm, even if it meant giving up her own life. Not because they were children, but because they were weaker than her.

Zaira's weakness was weakness.

If she was sent against a target who was vulnerable to the extent that she considered the person unfair prey, she wouldn't move. She might assassinate a pedophilic CEO without an eyeblink, but she'd refuse to touch a teacher who had angered someone in power. Then there was the hacker she'd saved even though the younger woman had been attempting to break into Arrow Central Command, and the outwardly respectable doctor she'd executed.

It had turned out the doctor was killing vulnerable patients after getting them to sign over their estates to him. Unlike in that case, Aden didn't always understand the judgments Zaira made, but he knew that children were simply never on her hit list. Perhaps because she remembered the helpless child she'd once been, the one no one had helped and everyone had hurt.

"How's the head?" Remi asked in a deceptively laid-back tone.

"Problematic," Aden said, since it was clear the alpha had an idea something was seriously wrong.

An incisive look. "Yep, that's the truth." Seeing the question Aden didn't ask, he shrugged those big shoulders. "For all I knew, you'd recovered and were staying here for reasons of your own. Spying maybe. What the hell for, I don't know—we're a dot in the ocean when it comes to changeling pack hierarchy."

Aden had a feeling it wouldn't remain that way. While he'd waited for Zaira to wake yesterday, he'd heard the alpha mention Lucas Hunter to Finn. The DarkRiver alpha was a power and he clearly respected Remi if RainFire had direct contact with him.

"I am spying in a sense," Aden said, deciding to lay these cards on the table. "This is the first time any active Arrow has been inside a changeling pack." Judd lived in one, but his loyalty to SnowDancer stopped him from sharing information about the pack with the squad.

"Nothing much to see." Remi smiled thanks at an older packmate who gave him a mug of coffee on her way across the room. "We're a big family."

"A family with rules."

"Of course." Putting down the coffee after taking a long swig, he said, "You Psy, you think you're the only ones with control issues, but we have these." His claws sliced out to dig into the tabletop as if the hard wood was made of butter.

Jojo clapped. "Meow! Meow!"

Shoulders shaking, Remi shook his head. "We don't go 'meow, meow,' Jojo. We go 'grr.'"

"Grr."

Remi retracted his claws to the little girl's laughter. "Those claws are only the start of it. If two Psy fight, you might go mind to mind, but we go claw to tooth, can rip out each other's throats if we're not careful. That's why we need rules."

"No biting," Jojo input into the conversation. "Bad Jojo." A sad face.

Reaching over, Remi tapped her on the nose. "You took your punishment. You going to bite again?"

The little girl shook her head and lifted her arms.

Remi plucked her from Zaira's lap and into his own, using a washed-soft white napkin to clean her face before holding her against his body . . . where she turned into sparkles of light. Aden watched, having never seen the transformation close-up. Beside him, he was aware of Zaira sitting stock-still. And then where the child had been was a very small leopard cub trying to climb up Remi's body.

Laughing, the alpha lifted her up onto his shoulder, where she curled happily, her tail hanging down Remi's chest. "There goes another set of pajamas," he said, but his tone made it clear he wasn't worried about the clothing loss.

"You spoke of punishment," Aden said, seeing in the child's response to the alpha an answer to a problem for which he so far had no solution. "How do you punish a child so she isn't broken or hurt? Especially a child that could do serious damage?"

"Tell me that's not how you train your children." Snarling anger in Remi's words.

"It's how we were trained," Zaira answered. "Now we want to change things, but we must have a framework."

REMI couldn't imagine harming any cub, any child. Whether that child belonged to his pack or not. Deeply disturbed at the idea that the Psy had done—might still be doing—that to their young, he picked Jojo up from his shoulder and held her against his chest. Curling against him, she began to purr, the contented sound easing his leopard's agitation.

"Punishment depends on age," he said when he realized the Arrows were serious and waiting for his response. "For the littlest, making them sit alone in a corner without toys for a few minutes is enough." He stroked Jojo's soft fur, her body fragile under his touch. "They don't really remember what they did wrong if the punishment goes on any longer, but if we're consistent in punishing them for bad behavior in that way, they eventually make the connection."

"A kind of conditioning," Aden said.

Remi shrugged. "It's about instilling discipline, teaching in a way that suits their age and ability to learn. You want to call it conditioning, go for it."

Aden and Zaira looked at each other, and while their expressions didn't change, it was clear they were silently considering the matter as a pair. Remi wondered if the two knew how often they did that. If they hadn't been Psy, he'd have thought they had something going on. Then again, things had apparently changed for the Psy race recently—for all he knew, these two were having dirty, sweaty sex every night.

His leopard grinned at the idea.

"What about older children?" Aden asked after about thirty seconds.

"Longer periods of time-out usually work for those of elementary school age," Remi said. "We also start limiting privileges." He rubbed the spot between Jojo's ears and her purr increased. His own leopard purred in his chest in reply.

God, he'd missed cubs when he'd been roaming alone, missed the sense of family that was at the core of a healthy pack. He'd needed those solitary years to realize how little such an existence suited him, but every now and then, he wanted to give himself a swift kick in the ass for taking so long to understand his own intrinsic nature.

"Older cubs also start being hauled up in front of the maternal females, or the alpha, for bigger transgressions." His grin grew wider at the memory of his teenage years. "I was once assigned to dig outdoor latrines for a camping trip, then fill them back in. By myself. In winter." The ground had been like rock. "At least it didn't smell."

"What did you do to earn the punishment?"

Aware of the sharp little ears listening to him, he shook

his head instead of answering Aden's question. "Doesn't matter. And the details of specific punishments don't matter—what matters is that the cubs understand they did something wrong, and that people care enough to correct them." Kissing Jojo on top of her head when she rose up on her feet, he put her on the ground.

She padded over to her older brother and began to pretend-attack his leg.

The teenager pretended to growl back.

Seeing the Arrows watching the interplay, he waited until they returned their attention to him. "The most important thing," he said, "is that the child knows he or she is loved, is wanted, belongs. It makes the toughest punishment bearable."

He held Aden's gaze, the other man's expression unreadable. "It's the alpha's responsibility and his privilege to create that environment—we are the guardians of every heart in our care." Aden Kai might not be changeling, but he was an alpha and he held within his hands the power to change his people from the inside out.

THE most important thing is that the child knows he or she is loved, is wanted, belongs.

Zaira didn't know what it was to be loved, didn't understand the emotion, though the insane girl in her had often pressed its hands to the windows of her eyes in wordless yearning as it watched those of the other races. Living in Venice, Zaira had seen fathers and mothers with their children, siblings laughing arm in arm, lovers walking wrapped in one another, and she'd sometimes imagined a future in which she, too, had someone who liked to be with her just because she was Zaira.

Her brain had trouble with that concept, but oddly the rage creature coveted it. Even when it appeared to Zaira that love was as huge a thing as rage, that it would fill her up should she ever understand it.

Not far from them, the boy Jojo had "attacked" was laughing as he picked her up by the scruff of her neck and nipped at the tip of her nose.

Rage was a selfish, covetous emotion that wanted to swallow

her whole. Love, it appeared, spread outward. And still the twisted, deformed girl inside her, the one filled with rage, looked at that scene and cried. The tears were old and silent and hidden deep in the vault of her mind. Zaira hadn't cried true tears since she was maybe three, but deep in that vault, the girl shaped by rage sometimes did so surreptitiously.

Zaira tried to ignore her, but it was hard, her cries echoing in the silence in her head. Stomach tensing, causing her new skin to ache, she waited till Remi left the table before saying, "How can we teach Arrow children about love if we don't understand it?"

Aden's eyes went to where Jojo was now sitting up in the lap of the boy who had the same eyes and skin as the little girl, her paws on the tabletop and her ears pricked as she listened to the conversation around her. The teenager had one hand on her back, steadying her, while with his other, he was spooning up cereal, his eyes turned in the direction of another boy with whom he was holding a conversation.

"Look at her," Aden said in that quiet tone that always brought people to attention. "She's happy to be there though no one is currently paying her any particular attention."

Zaira saw what he meant. "She's being touched by someone she trusts not to hurt her and she knows that should she need care, it will be given." As Remi had so easily prepared that slice of toast for her.

"Yes." Aden touched his hand to her own back, as if he'd sensed the vicious wolves of aloneness biting at her. "We can give our children a safe haven where they never have to fear being hurt simply for being who they are."

Zaira thought again of that long-ago infirmary room and of the solemn boy who'd patched up her wounds. He'd been her safe place. And in giving her that, he'd given her a reason not to take unnecessary risks, not to get herself killed, and never, ever to give up the fight against the insanity that wanted to envelop her mind. "I can do that." Her voice came out raw, the insane, angry girl nodding in silent agreement. "I can help make a safe place for Arrow children."

Aden's lips brushed her ear as he leaned down to speak, the scent of his body in her every breath. "If you can do that, then you can be my partner."

Zaira wanted to say yes, but her wants could be deadly. It was because of want that she collected things that were Aden's and kept them close, why she took those things out late at night and carefully looked through them one by one. "If you'd made me this offer when I was sixteen, I would've taken it."

Would've taken him.

Always, she'd been jealous of the attention he gave others, had wanted him only and always for herself.

"What's changed?" Aden asked.

"Now I understand that my obsessive desire to own you comes from the same dark place as my rage." That truth was one it had taken her years to grapple with, to comprehend. "It'll crush the life out of you." Because if she broke discipline and took Aden's hand, then all bets were off. She'd regress to the feral creature she'd once been, murderous and violent and so full of need that she would take and take and take and take.

Because Zaira couldn't walk the middle road: either she could be a disciplined, cold Arrow or she could be a savage, possessive, obsessive creature capable of any madness to get her own way. "I'd snap the neck of anyone who tried to get between us, anyone who dared take your attention from me," she said, allowing him to see the sinuous darkness that lived in her. "I'd destroy you with my want and my need."

Chapter 18

HIGH IN THE Sierra Nevada, where the snowpack hadn't yet melted, SnowDancer alpha, Hawke, was stretching out into a run in his wolf form when Riaz ran up alongside him. The lieutenant was also in his animal form, his fur a rich black in contrast to Hawke's silver-gold. Glancing over to meet the dark gold of Riaz's eyes, Hawke asked a silent question, received a silent answer.

Riaz needed to talk to him, but it wasn't so urgent that Hawke couldn't run.

Satisfied his pack was well, Hawke flowed into the run across the still night-draped snow, dawn yet to come to these mountains. His wolf needed to stretch its muscles, needed to be free. He hadn't sought out company, but now that Riaz was here, it was good. Pack was always welcome. The lieutenant was also fast enough that Hawke didn't have to temper his pace, and they ran hard and smooth for miles before circling back toward the den.

The wind rippled cold fingers through his fur, small creatures darted into hiding, the air scented with pine and the landscape endless. The morning sun was making the snow glitter by the time he and Riaz returned to the stone tunnels of their home, separating out to shift, shower, and dress before they met again just outside the den.

Wolf happily tired, Hawke leaned up against the den wall

and watched the cubs play in the area in front of the den. SnowDancer's home base was at an elevation that meant there was still a good coating of snow on the ground, though given current conditions, it would be gone soon.

It was because of the latter that the cubs had been allowed out of school as a special treat. All had clearly been too excited at the chance for one more snow play day to sleep in. Watched over by a number of adults, they were having great fun building snowmen. The ones in human form were bundled up and tasked with doing the delicate work paws couldn't accomplish, while those in pup form gathered up snow and patted it into place.

Hawke gave the postcard-peaceful, heartwarming scene approximately ten more minutes at best. His wolf's jaw opened in a lupine laugh inside him—it knew as well as the human part of him that someone would give in to the temptation to throw a snowball at any minute and then the melee would begin.

Scenting Riaz, he waited for the lieutenant to join him. "What did you want to discuss?"

He frowned before Riaz could reply. "Is that a lipstick mark on your neck? How the fuck did you have time to find Adria, get a kiss, then get back here?" Hawke hadn't seen Sienna since she'd gone out on patrol, and his wolf wasn't happy.

Giving him a smug smile, Riaz leaned on the den wall beside him. "I have priorities." He ran a hand through his shower-dampened hair. "So, business—this morning, I received a message from a group of minor wolf packs we're friendly with. They say the Human Alliance has been buying up land marked for expansion of their territories."

"Adjoining lands?" Packs did occasionally buy land parcels not immediately connected to their main territory. If that was the case, the Alliance might simply be making valid business decisions that happened to run up against the needs of the packs involved.

Riaz's nod took that possibility off the table. "The packs involved all had informal agreements in place with the landowners, but the Alliance came in with much higher bids."

"How long's this been going on?"

"Past month. The first pack thought it was an isolated—if asshole—move, but then they heard about it happening to another pack. Long story short, the alphas started talking and, so far, five have reported the same land grab."

Hawke scowled at what appeared to be a deliberate and calculated attempt to fence changeling packs in, stifling their natural growth. "Alliance trying to pick a fight?" Business was business, no matter how ruthless, but this felt more like passive aggression.

"Sure looks like it." Riaz chuckled as the first snowball was thrown and the peaceful scene erupted into laughing chaos. "The weird thing is that none of the land is of any use to the Alliance. Most of it is nowhere near a city or any of their business interests. Even if they intend to subdivide and sell it off, they won't make back the ridiculous amounts they've paid."

Hawke's instincts were starting to bristle. "You talk to Bo?" Riaz had a good line of communication with the Human Alliance security chief, who they all knew was the effective leader of the Alliance.

"Not yet. Wanted to run this by you first."

"Tell me your take on it." Hawke's lieutenants held that position for a reason; each was capable of independently making major decisions.

"I think Bo's smart enough to pick on smaller, weaker packs if he did want to initiate a fight, but I also think he's too smart to waste his resources on a stupid game. Especially when the Alliance is finally starting to find its footing again after the mess created by their previous leadership."

Hawke agreed—but he also remembered Bo making a certain other stupid decision in changeling territory. His wolf didn't yet trust the younger male not to make the same error a second time.

"Make contact," he told Riaz. "If the Alliance is trying to play 'my dick is bigger,' remind them those small packs have big friends." SnowDancer might not be allied with these particular packs, but as the biggest pack in the country, it accepted a certain responsibility when it came to matters like this. "I'll speak to Lucas, find out if this is isolated to wolf territories."

He had an answer within two hours—the DarkRiver alpha had just received a disturbingly similar report from a bewildered deer herd that had all but signed on the dotted line for some grazing land when the Alliance swooped in. A little further investigation and Luc discovered the Alliance was playing its money-wasting game across the country.

"I've got confirmed reports from at least three nonpredatory packs," the leopard alpha said over the comm, his face as grim as Hawke's own mood and his green eyes more feline than human. "A small wildcat pack is currently attempting to get in touch with a landowner who was supposed to accept an offer today." The other male's voice held a low-level growl as he added, "He hasn't called them back so I'm guessing that takes the tally up to four on my end."

Hawke's claws pricked at his fingertips. "If Bo doesn't have a fucking good explanation for this, I will personally rip his head from his body."

"Get in line, wolf."

FAR from SnowDancer territory, an Arrow stood in the shadows of a building that fronted a shimmering white sand beach. Blake made sure to be out of sight of the cameras pointed at the crowd as investigators worked the scene of a gruesome stabbing that had taken place in the dark hours of early morning. His Arrow training stood him in good stead here—only the stupid got caught. He was a phantom.

A phantom who'd bathed in blood.

Part of him was concerned by his descent into bloodlust. His plan had been to follow the slender and aesthetically pleasing human male, incapacitate him silently and quickly, then transport his target to an abandoned factory where he could play with him as long as the male lasted.

It was the target's fault he'd lost control. The human had seen him and started to run—it was in the struggle to bring the male down that Blake had nicked him with the blade.

The smell of blood had overwhelmed; he'd had to have more.

Afterward, his shoulder and arm had hurt—still twinged now. He was also covered in blood, but the black of his uniform hid that, as his gloves had protected him from the man's clawing hands as he fought for his survival. The target had never managed to reach Blake's uncovered face.

That face was now clean, wiped off. As for his bloodied uniform, he'd stashed a spare change of clothes at the factory. No one would ever know of the breakdown in his discipline. It had been an aberration in any case. He'd simply gone too long without exercising his natural urges.

He wouldn't make that mistake again.

Chapter 19

ZAIRA PACED THE corridor outside the infirmary in an effort to reorder her increasingly disjointed discipline. An hour after breakfast and, with nothing but time on their hands, Aden had offered to teach a hand-to-hand combat class to a small group of RainFire soldiers, while Zaira had done the same for a group of older trainees.

She'd been impressed by the teenagers. Though they laughed and spoke to one another far more than Arrow trainees, they also paid close attention and had a distinct advantage when it came to sheer physical coordination. Not that she couldn't put each and every one on the ground, but she hadn't had to—it turned out these predatory changelings didn't make the mistake of judging her weak simply because she was small and female.

The session had kept her from thinking about the aloneness, the silence inside her skull, but now her class was over and she couldn't outrun the rage creature any longer. It slammed against the bars, fighting to get out, to take her over, to grab at what Aden was offering and hoard it greedily close.

"Pony!"

Stilling, she glanced over her shoulder to see Jojo running toward her. The little girl had to have come through the connecting stairs. She was now dressed in purple corduroy overalls over a white sweater. Someone had gathered up her hair into tiny pigtails all over her head and tied them off with different-colored ties. The care evidenced by the act, especially when Jojo could shift at any time and undo the work, fascinated the insane girl inside Zaira.

No one had ever spent such time on her. No one ever spent such time on Arrow children. Zaira didn't know if she had the patience for it, but if it would create children as happy and as stable as Jojo, children without psychic wounds that led them to become twisted within, she'd learn that patience.

"Pony!" Jojo cried again when Zaira didn't reply.

"Zaira," she reminded the cub as things deep inside her stretched and tried to wake. "My name is Zaira."

Stopping her headlong rush at Zaira's feet, Jojo looked up with an intent expression on her face, her soft brown eyes unblinking. "Zai," she said at last and gave a firm nod.

"Zai-ra," Zaira sounded out, because the child was intelligent enough to understand.

Frowning, Jojo very slowly said, "Zai-ra," then beamed. "Zai-ra."

"That's correct." Remembering how Remi had interacted with her, she added, "Well done."

A proud smile that created cracks in the walls that held back the murderous girl she'd been. That part of her wanted to come out, play with this small, trusting child. In front of her, that child pointed at herself. "Jojo."

"I know." Distrustful of her crumbling shields, Zaira nodded at Jojo and began to pace again.

The little girl followed, running on small legs beside her. "Zai, walk?"

"Yes." She slowed her speed slightly; even she knew that hurting a child's self-confidence was not care. Her parents had told her she was stupid a lot. It hadn't helped her become a better person—it had just made her rage bigger.

"Why?" Jojo asked, thumbs hooked in the pockets of her overalls. "Why Zai walk?"

"I'm not used to being inside this way." Walls stifled her; even the windows weren't helping anymore. The silence inside her head only multiplied the sense of suffocation, threatening to return her to the small room in which she'd gone insane as a child.

"Grr." Jojo hooked her hands in the air, releasing tiny claws.

"Why are you growling?"

Jojo retracted her claws, reached up to take Zaira's hand. "Come." She tugged. "Jojo show."

Not quite sure what the child was talking about, Zaira decided to follow her for the same reason that she'd lowered her speed. There was no reason to make Jojo feel as if her thoughts and views were without value. It wasn't as if Zaira had any other pressing engagements.

"Come, Zai." Jojo walked excitedly, pulling at Zaira until they stepped onto the outside passageway that led to the dining aerie.

"Wait," Zaira said. "You don't have a coat."

"Jojo, cat," the little girl said. "Zai cold?"

Realizing changelings must have an advantage in regulating their body temperature, Zaira said, "No, I'll be fine." She'd left Aden's jacket in their aerie, but a short trek wouldn't cause any physical issues—she'd been thrown into freezing rooms as part of her Arrow training, had learned to bear it.

Allowing Jojo to lead her along the walkway, Zaira was aware of other adult and juvenile changelings always nearby—not overtly watchful, but close enough to intervene if necessary. A number nodded hello as they passed, tugging at one of Jojo's pigtails or brushing the backs of their hands against the little girl's cheek.

Touch, contact, she noted. Constant and normalized.

Jojo would never feel alone, never feel like a forgotten piece of trash.

The child took her into a connecting walkway, then another, until they scrambled down a rope ladder into a large open area that was nonetheless protected from the elements by clear plas shielding against which the unrelenting rain hit soundlessly. In comparison to the walkways, however, the temperature in the space was comfortable. That wasn't the only surprise: the area was filled with climbing frames, complex rope ladders, a rock wall, and more.

"See!" Jojo jumped up and down. "Zai play here!"

Zaira looked down at the child who'd managed to make the connection between her need for freedom and a cat's need for the same. "Thank you, Jojo." Consciously copying what she'd seen the adult changelings do, she ran her knuckles gently over the delicate softness of Jojo's cheek.

The little girl leaned into her, unafraid. "Play?"

"I would like to climb the wall over there." If she was careful, it shouldn't break open her healing skin.

Jojo nodded and walked with her to the foot of the climbing wall that sloped in a faintly concave shape, making it more difficult to traverse.

"Jojo, too small," the little girl said. "Jojo play there," She pointed to a colorful climbing frame that was clearly sized for children, complete with rope bridges and slides to the ground.

Waiting until she was sure Jojo was capable on the frame, Zaira stepped up to the wall and took the first grip. Ten seconds after she began, she realized it was a much more difficult course than appeared at first glance. For someone with a shorter reach like Zaira, it was close to impossible.

Perfect.

When she slipped, she was aware of Jojo crying out.

It was . . . odd that the child should care so much about a near stranger, but it cost Zaira nothing to make the effort to respond. "I'm fine," she said, feeling the strain in her abdomen. She ignored it. It'd be worth a dressing-down from Finn to unleash some of her pent-up energy. "This is a difficult climb."

"Yup," Jojo said. "Cat climb."

Zaira's mind clicked, the almost unclimbable difficulty of the course suddenly making sense: the cats must use their claws to compensate. Since she had no claws, she used the comparative lightness of her body to swing off one hold to the other. Again and again and again. It was a climb that required extreme concentration, logical thinking, and a careful use of strength.

She was cognizant of sounds behind her, and she kept a peripheral eye on where Jojo played on the frame, but the climb held the majority of her attention.

Never was she unaware of individuals who might become a threat, but she evaluated the overall threat level automatically and assigned it a negligible rating. It was becoming increasingly clear that these changelings didn't want to kill or harm or torture her or Aden. RainFire had offered help simply because it was the right thing to do.

So she climbed until her biceps were quivering, her hamstring muscles and quadriceps tight, and her new skin painful. By the time she hauled herself up to sit on the top edge, she had the feeling she *would* be getting a serious dressing-down from Finn. Gathering noise from below had her looking down to see a large group clapping—for her.

Jojo was jumping up and down and waving.

Zaira lifted her hand and moved it in a wave motion for no reason except that no one had ever indulged her as a child and she thought of what it would've meant. A single instant of kindness could've changed everything, could've kept her from becoming a murderer.

ADEN watched Zaira wave at Jojo. Others might've been startled at seeing his normally ice-cold commander do that, but Aden had always noted how Zaira treated the young. She wasn't warm and cuddly, but if she was in the vicinity and a child needed something, she'd provide it.

In one case, she'd broken the arm of a trainer who'd been about to do the same to an eight-year-old boy. After that, Ming ensured Zaira was never around any of the training centers. Aden wanted her to help him choose the teams to run what was now a centralized training area for the same reason. Zaira's thinking might be problematic in a number of senses, but never when it came to the welfare of children.

"If I hadn't seen that," a male changeling said from beside him, "I wouldn't have believed it."

Aden glanced at the man, who'd introduced himself as Theo. "What?"

"That fucking climb." The brown-eyed, black-haired changeling whistled. "It's built to be completed using claws. Never seen anyone do it without."

"She's an Arrow."

"Don't tell me you can all do that. I won't believe you."

No, they couldn't all do what Zaira had just done. Zaira was unique and not simply in the physical sense. As she began to climb down, Aden found himself moving closer, but he made sure not to go so close that the changelings would notice.

Remi came up beside him, his eyes trained on Zaira. "You want us to put a net under her?"

Zaira slipped right then, caught herself, hanging precariously from one hand.

"No." One thing Aden knew about Zaira—she wouldn't want herself to be seen as weak by strangers—not in any way. If he permitted that, it'd be a breach of trust she would never forgive. "She has it under control."

He had to consciously regulate his breathing as Zaira continued down. Ever since he'd touched Vasic and Ivy's bond, he'd felt his Silence slipping away and he hadn't fought hard to hold on to it. He knew he could still be the leader the squad needed without that straitjacket.

Except, according to Zaira, the fact that he cared for each and every life under his command was no secret in the squad. It was also something his parents would term a serious deviation from their aims and plans. More than that, they'd see it as a failure. Marjorie and Naoshi had created and molded Aden for a specific purpose; he had achieved that purpose, but he'd done so on his own terms—and the depth of that success continued to perplex his parents.

To them, he had always been the child who was a pale shadow of the one they wanted. Their aim had been to create a merciless cardinal telepath who could take on even a Councilor. What they'd got instead was a solemn, quiet boy who registered as a 4.3 telepath on the Gradient, along with an even more minor M ability. A child who had been permitted into the squad only because of his parents' stellar records and because he was useful in a secondary capacity.

Someone needed to be trained as a field medic for his year group—why not the disappointingly low-Gradient child of two Arrows? After all, that child was already loyal to the squad and understood how it functioned. His appointment to the medic position would also free up another more powerful child to devote his or her full attention to combat training.

Aden could still remember his mother's hands on his shoulders as she hunkered down in front of him when he was nine years old, on the eve of her and his father's planned "deaths."

You aren't what we wanted, but we'll have to make the best of it. As you aren't fit to lead, your task is to find a suitable stronger child and do everything in your power to support him to the leadership. An Arrow must be at the helm, one who remembers who and where he came from. We thought Ming was that Arrow, but he isn't one of us—never forget that, no matter what face he wears.

The irony was that Aden had already found an outwardly stronger child; through no effort of his own. Vasic's teleportation and telekinetic abilities made him a far more suitable candidate—but Vasic didn't want the position, and he'd seen in Aden what Aden's parents never had.

So had Zaira.

You'll lead, Aden. You already do.

Both the most important people in his life had said that to him at different times, in different words. Their belief had been enough to temper his parents' disappointment and lack of faith. Marjorie and Naoshi had started then nurtured the rebellion with a number of critical actions, and Aden would never downplay their contribution, but they had never treated their son as anything but a regrettable mistake. Yet they wondered why that son didn't treat them as elders, didn't heed their words. They didn't comprehend that they'd given up that right long, long ago, even before their defection.

The *only* two people who had the right to question Aden on that level, or to challenge his decisions, were Zaira and Vasic.

At that instant, Zaira slipped a second time and little Jojo ran over to grip tightly at Remi's hand. Aden, meanwhile, held his position with sheer strength of will, keeping his face expressionless and his eyes resolutely on her.

He was also calculating odds—if she fell from her current height, she'd still break a bone, but she'd survive. He would've raked her over the coals for taking the risk but he understood why she'd done it: Zaira did not do well under any kind of confinement, even that forced by the weather in the middle of a sprawling natural landscape.

Why do I have to sleep in a room? Why can't I sleep outside?

She'd asked him that mutinous question when they'd both

been children. He couldn't remember how he'd convinced her to grit her teeth and go to sleep in the small dorm, but as soon as he had the power, he'd made sure she never had to do the same again.

When the decision was made to turn the slumbering Venice base into an active asset, he'd had to select a commander to lead the op. He hadn't chosen Zaira because of her need for space, for freedom; he'd done so because she was one of his best commanders, one who could think independently *and* who had a nature rebellious enough to stand firm against the older defectors who'd assumed they would be the ones actually calling the shots. But the fact that she had a large room with a balcony in Venice was his doing—that balcony was over a canal, meaning Zaira always had a secondary escape route and the option to sleep with the balcony door open if she wished.

Never again would anyone lock her in.

Zaira missed a grip, was left hanging by her fingertips.

Chapter 20

MORE THAN ONE changeling ran closer, as if to catch her, but Aden stood exactly where he was, willing her to recover. She did. With a deliberate focus and an intelligent strength that had Theo shaking his head, eyes gone leopard in admiration. "Man, she's got *serious* fucking balls."

Aden made a note to repeat the comment to Zaira; she'd appreciate it.

"Just so you know," Remi drawled from his other side, "a whole lot of the dominants in the pack are going to be trying their luck with her now."

Aden was starting to become used to feline slyness, so he understood that Remi was needling him to find out if he and Zaira had a relationship. He answered regardless. "They're too late." She was his, had given herself to him long ago. He wasn't planning on returning the gift, no matter if she believed herself too broken to walk with him.

"Yeah." A grin in the alpha's voice. "That's what I figured."

When Zaira's feet finally hit the ground after several more risky moves, Jojo laughed and ran over to hug her legs. "Wow! Zai, cat climb!"

Aden's heart thundered, his breath finally coming easier.

Sweating, and with her features giving nothing away, though he knew she had to be in pain, Zaira placed her hand gently on Jojo's head. "A cat with no claws."

Zaira's eyes met his as the little girl laughed; her gaze was opaque, inscrutable. "I should head off to shower."

"Not until you tell us how you did that." Theo looked up at the wall, shook his head again. "It should've been impossible—that's an elite-level climb *with* claws."

Zaira tugged very carefully on one of Jojo's pigtails to get the tiny girl's attention. "May I lift you for a second?"

An unconcerned shrug. "Okay."

Shifting her hands to under the child's armpits, Zaira lifted her a few inches off the floor, then set her down again. "Thank you."

Jojo leaned against her leg in answer.

Remi, meanwhile, had raised an eyebrow. "Theo should weight lift Jojo?"

"No. I was testing my hypothesis." Zaira put her hand back on Jojo's hair, the touch seeming to come more naturally this time. "To me, Jojo weighs more than she should for a child her size."

Theo nodded. "Changelings have heavier bones. Yours are more fragile."

"Yes. So even if a changeling woman who looked exactly my size stood next to me, the two of us indistinguishable to the naked eye, she would still be heavier than me in weight."

Aden glanced up at the climbing wall while Remi nodded, his hands braced on his hips. "Your lightness gave you an advantage," the alpha said.

"But," Aden responded, "she also thought strategically." That was what made Zaira such a good commander; her capacity to look at the bigger picture and plan accordingly. "If you trace her path, you'll see she achieved maximum distance with each move."

The four of them discussed the climb further for several minutes, during which a number of other packmates joined them, before Zaira left to have a shower. Aden wanted to order her to see Finn to make sure she hadn't torn any of her newly healed injuries, but he held his silence since they had an audience. If, once they were alone, he discovered she hadn't been to the healer, he'd rectify that immediately.

"I went out earlier to gauge the weather," Remi said to him once everyone else had dispersed, but his eyes were on the climbing frame where Jojo played with several other cubs. "Storm's looking like it'll hold through tonight at least." He didn't interfere when a child tumbled off into a fall, but did stride over and wipe away the child's tears as he lifted the boy to his feet again.

The child ran off to play again a bare minute after.

When Remi returned to Aden, Aden took a risk. "I need to learn how to do what you do." If he was going to create a real family from the dangerous and the rejected and the scarred, he had to be more than a leader who understood politics and how to keep his people safe.

He had to be an alpha.

That there was a difference between the two, he'd only started to understand since being in RainFire. "I need to learn how to be alpha of a pack."

Remi's eyes turned yellow-green, a leopard watching him out of a human face. "Two things make an alpha—one is an inborn dominance and a primal drive to protect. You already have that." His lips quirked slightly. "That's why the leopard keeps trying to outstare you and why you have to force yourself to look away."

Aden hadn't realized Remi had picked up on the latter. "What's the second thing?"

"Guidance that instills you with a bone-deep knowledge," Remi told him. "When cubs have the scent of an alpha about them, we keep an eye on them and teach them how to be a good alpha by example and through gentle nudges, until by the time those cubs become aware of their alpha tendencies, they have the right skill set. Though," he added dryly, "a refresher course is needed for those of us who figure things out a little later."

"I know how to hold a group together. I also have the strength to do it." He'd been created to be a tool of revolution, his DNA changed in ways that had had an unpredictable effect, the end result so unique that Marjorie and Naoshi still believed him to be only a low-level telepath.

Aden had never been told them the truth; he'd told only five people, and those five people he'd trust at his back without question: Vasic, Zaira, coolheaded sniper and trainer Cristabel, rock-steady telepath Amin, and deadly Axl, who many in the squad had considered Ming's right-hand man, but whose loyalty had always been Aden's. Only one other person knew. Walker Lauren had figured it out while Aden had been a child in his classroom. The telepath, who must now be in his early-to-mid forties, was the only other person Aden had ever met whose base telepathic abilities worked anything similarly to his own.

"What I don't understand," he said to Remi, "is how to make the group into a family." Given the violent abilities of those who became Arrows, the squad would always be a military unit that specialized in teaching its members how to harness their strength so that strength didn't spin out of control, but it didn't have to be only that.

Remi blew out a breath as the two of them walked to watch a juvenile attempt a less aggressive climbing wall. "Family is what connects us. I don't know that I can break it down." He rubbed at his jaw, his stubble scraping his fingers. "What ties you to your men and women?"

"Loyalty."

"Good foundation." The RainFire alpha folded his arms. "I guess family is about people knowing you'll be there even when they can't pull their weight because they're sick or hurt or just plain tired. Family's there even when you stuff up and do everything wrong."

Remi glanced at a pair of cubs who were playing with a ball nearby. "Doesn't mean everyone doesn't have a place in the pack, or responsibility—that's important, too, that everyone has a role to play. No one's disposable."

He put two fingers in his mouth and whistled sharply when one of the cubs swiped at the other, and the cubs immediately separated. "It just means that when you screw up," Remi added, "you don't lose your place in the family. You might get a reaming, might be punished, but you'll always have a home where you're loved and where you feel safe."

That made sense to Aden. The problem, of course, was that he was dealing with people badly damaged on every level —the adults who had to become the families of the current generation of Arrow children had never had any kind of warmth or family in their own lives.

As for the children themselves, each knew he or she

wasn't wanted by his or her biological family. Many had been declared dead on their family trees, but Aden decided then and there that there was no rule that said Arrows couldn't be placed on a new family tree. A created tree, within a family of Arrows who understood what it was to inadvertently hurt someone with their abilities.

"I may need further advice as I continue," he said to Remi. "Will you offer it?"

"Yeah, what the hell. We can be remedial alphas together." Grinning, the leopard changeling slapped him on the back. "Come on. You want to learn how to be a family, you can hang with me while I go read the riot act to some of the older juveniles. They fucking fried a generator doing an experiment with lightning."

PSYNET BEACON: BREAKING NEWS

Confidential sources have confirmed that Arrow leader Aden Kai is not missing. He is taking part in a covert mission to unmask certain problematic insurgent elements within the PsyNet. The Ruling Coalition would not confirm or deny this fact when contacted, and the Arrow Squad remains unreachable as per its long-standing operating protocol.

PSYNET BEACON: LIVE NETSTREAM

What did I tell you? The Arrow leader is doing what Arrows do—being a shadow in the Net.

I. Erskine
(Iowa)

I'm disturbed by the implications of this report. It appears we are back to the ways of the old Council.

Anonymous
(Luzon)

The old Council kept a firm hand on things and that's what we need now.

Anonymous
(Shiraz)

. . .

Kaleb dropped out of the Net after scanning the feeds. Things had gone as he'd predicted, as he'd wanted. With the news of Aden's disappearance threatening to rock the fragile equilibrium of the Net, he'd immediately initiated damage control. Instead of making a direct statement, however, he'd used his more clandestine skills to initiate a useful rumor that was then confirmed off-the-record by one of his outwardly junior people who had deliberately cultivated herself as a source for news media.

The information took longer to hit the public news streams this way, but when it did, it held more veracity for having been "uncovered." The populace would now spend their time worrying about the direction of the Ruling Coalition rather than speculating about what had happened to Aden. At present, that was the better option.

The subterfuge wouldn't last if Aden remained missing for longer than a day or two, however. Especially if whoever had leaked the news of his abduction continued to leak further disturbing details. A single image of Aden unconscious or dead could throw the Net into chaos. Arrows might be the bogeymen of their race, but they were also a silent symbol of Psy power. And Aden represented the squad.

While Aden was the politically higher-value target since Zaira wasn't known as an Arrow by the general population, seeing her caged or in a degrading position would also have a devastating impact. Because if someone could hurt the bogeyman, then no one was safe.

The PsyNet was so vast that even Kaleb couldn't suppress all such data—there was no knowing when or how it might filter in. He could, however, prime the NetMind and DarkMind to alert him the instant anything related to Aden or Zaira hit the dataways so he could take quick and effective countermeasures.

He gave the order and the twin neosentience of the NetMind and DarkMind curled around him in agreement before disappearing into the Net. The situation was contained. At least until the shadowy enemy that had taken Aden and Zaira made their next move.

HIDDEN in a thick grouping of trees in the underground green space attached to Central Command, Blake read the new *Beacon* report about Aden and realized he may have made a mistake . . . or maybe not. Even if Aden was alive and around, the squad's leader would have no reason to connect an "out-of-control blitz killer," as Blake was being described by the media, to an Arrow who'd taken a little too much pleasure in his work but who had always disposed of his victims where no one would find them.

As long as Blake was careful not to choose a victim who was in Aden's orbit, the leader of the squad would never know and Blake could continue being part of a group where he had the greatest chance of finding a like mind. Power often came paired with deviant urges. He'd have to be careful as he searched, but the chances of success were high.

Because while killing alone was a rush, killing with a partner would double that. All he had to do was find the right person, a person who was broken inside like him but who owned that brokenness, who accepted that there was nothing wrong with their psychopathic tendencies. They existed, and therefore, they must be right to exist.

Chapter 21

ADEN TRACKED ZAIRA down to their aerie late that afternoon, having already run into Finn and discovered that she had in fact dropped by the infirmary to ensure she hadn't done any damage to her healing injuries.

The healer had scowled. "Boneheaded move, climbing that wall, but what can you expect? Dominant females are a law unto themselves."

"Did she need treatment?"

Finn had shaken his head. "She came within an inch of tearing the new skin, though—I've told her if she does it again, she could set back her recovery by a week or more." A glint in his leaf green eyes. "You sure she's not a cat? Not only does she apparently climb like one, she gave me the same look I get from the RainFire women when I lay down the law."

No, Zaira wasn't a cat. She was an Arrow. And right now, she was wearing his jacket over her clothing and lying curled up on top of the bedspread, her body rigid. Taking off his own jacket, he got in behind her, wrapping his body around hers.

At that moment, he felt her fragility, her bones so easy to break—and yet he knew she was one of the strongest people he had ever met. Zaira was afraid of no threat, no predator, not even death.

It was only isolation that hurt her.

"The aloneness is like tiny animals biting and clawing at me," she said, the tendons in her neck standing out taut against her skin, her breathing harsh. "I need to rejoin the Net or I won't be able to maintain discipline. I'll regress."

Her curls brushed his chin as he held her more tightly. "No matter what, you won't become a psychopath, Zaira." It was her greatest fear, though she didn't call it that; she called it an inevitability she had to fight.

"You can let go with me. I won't report you."

"No. If I let the monster out of its cage, I might not be able to put her back in."

"There is no monster in you, only a survivor."

"She liked it, Aden. Beating her parents to death . . . the monster liked it."

They'd had that conversation via a cell phone he'd managed to smuggle to her; it had been three years after she was brought into the squad's training program. Aden had never disregarded her fears, well aware that some wounds were permanent. Zaira *had* been changed by her childhood and ignoring that fact would be to ignore a fundamental part of her.

However, he also knew that she had never, not once, harmed anyone who wasn't a legitimate target. She had a conscience, understood right from wrong. And somehow, she'd retained the ability to feel empathy. It was why she'd broken that trainer's arm when he would've broken a child's, why she brought Alejandro ice cream, and why she'd sent Aden those plans on how to incapacitate Vasic so they could remove his gauntlet.

In her resilience, he saw a ferocious strength where she saw only a monster.

"If you want to see for certain what you become without strict Arrow discipline," he said, "this is the perfect opportunity. No PsyNet, no other Psy, no one but me." And she knew he'd take her secrets to the grave. "I won't allow you to hurt anyone." He didn't think she would, but he had to speak to her fears. "We might never again have this chance." He wanted to see her without shields, to strip his own self bare so she'd know once and for all who and what she was to him.

Not just a commander. Never just a soldier.

"All my life," he said, taking the first step, "I've done what was best for the squad. I've never resented it, never wished I'd been born in another time or place." *This* was his time and he was right where he was meant to be. "But now, I have a moment when I can simply be Aden and there is no one I'd rather be with in this moment than you."

Keeping her eyes on the window and the rain that hit it in heavy slaps, Zaira said, "My need for you keeps growing, a violent fury of want that seeks to possess." She turned toward him on the final words.

He cupped the side of her face, his handspan wide enough to cradle the entire side. "Will you do me harm?"

"I told you. If I set this thing inside me free, I'll cage you." Her breath mingled with his. "And I would murder anyone who tried to take you from me."

He knew her desire was pathological, and yet he didn't back off. Because if Zaira had a ravenous want for him, he had just as ravenous a need to be wanted. At that instant, he asked the question he'd avoided till now because the wrong answer would savage him. "Who is it you want? Aden, or the leader of the squad?"

Shifting so close that their bodies pressed along her entire length, she slid her hand into his hair, gripped it in a fist. "The squad means I have to share you. I don't want to share you. You're Aden and you're mine." Her eyes turned midnight in front of him, the whites disappearing. "Do you see it?" she whispered. "The want? It'll devour you."

"Let it try." Their lips brushed when he spoke, brushed again as she closed her eyes and moved her head slightly.

For a single heartbeat, the fit was perfect.

Then, fingers tight in his hair, she lifted the lush fan of her eyelashes, her breasts rising and falling against him and her midnight eyes vibrant with the fire that had always burned in her. A fire that had warmed him through the years. Every time the weight on his shoulders became too heavy, his heart threatening to ice over from the constant and grueling darkness, he'd gone to her and in her endless fire, he'd found his strength again.

"You heard what I told you?" Zaira pulled at his hair. "We do this and I might not be able to put myself back in the box."

"I never wanted you in a box." He ran his thumb over her cheekbone. "I told you the squad needed your fire and it does, but I need it most of all."

"If I take you," she said, and it was a warning, "I'll keep you. Always."

No one had ever been so possessive of him. Just him. Just Aden. "Take me."

She shuddered, her lips parting for an instant before she nipped at his lower lip hard enough to draw blood. Making a harsh, rough sound in her throat afterward, she pulled away and sat up with her legs over the edge of the bed, her breathing erratic. He lifted his hand, wiped the back of it over his mouth. It came away streaked with red.

The bite throbbed but when he sat up, it was to wrap his arm around Zaira's waist and pull her toward him. Her nails dug into his bare forearm and when she whipped her head around to look at him, he saw the girl he'd seen long ago: the one who was beaten but never broken, the one who had lied to his face, the same girl who, three years ago, had walked into the path of bullets meant for him, then told him to deal with it when he tried to dress her down for putting herself at risk.

"I'm not afraid," he said to her, holding her as tight as he could without hurting her still tender injury. "Not of any part of you." Including the rage that was woven inextricably with her fire.

"You should be." Twisting away and out of his hold, she jumped back on the bed to crouch a foot from him. The sound that came from her throat was a wordless warning. "I'm devolving." A grimacing look, her jaw clenched tight. "I. Can't. Devolve." Her face was flushed, her breathing rocky. "I don't want to beat your head in. I don't want to destroy your face."

He didn't flinch at the stark words. "You beat your parents' heads in for a very good reason."

"What if I decide to beat in the heads of everyone I see as competition for you?" Midnight receded from her eyes with the arctic question, as she gritted her teeth and hauled herself forcefully into that unyielding, Arrow-black box. "Think about that, Aden."

• • •

TEN minutes later and Aden was in the infirmary. He'd finally left the aerie after Zaira flat-out told him to go, her tension so vicious that he was worried she'd rupture a blood vessel if he didn't give her space.

What if I decide to beat in the heads of everyone I see as competition for you?

He didn't believe she'd do that, but he had no way to prove it to her.

"Can I borrow a microscope again?" he asked Finn, needing to distract himself.

"Sure." The healer nodded to the right. "That one's high powered. You going to examine the implant?"

"Yes. I may see something I missed the first time."

"You might want to fix up that lip before you get to work." The medic threw him a small medical laser, a very feline expression on his face. "Of course, you could leave it and strut around like the cat who got the cream."

"How do you know she didn't punch me in the face?"

Finn laughed without reserve, his eyes going leopard. "Hell, dominants have been known to take that as foreplay."

Aden sealed the wound after a moment's thought. What to him was an indication of want that filled the emptiness inside him, Zaira would see as a reminder of a dangerous break in discipline.

That done, he set up the scope and put his eye to the lens.

He wasn't a neural tech by training, but as a medic, he had some familiarity with the Human Alliance implant. The squad had made sure to get their hands on one, in order to ensure it posed no threat to the Psy race. Aden had no argument with humans shielding their minds against unscrupulous Psy. Should, however, the implant have shown any signs of having been engineered to be embedded into Psy minds as well, in an effort to manipulate them, the squad would've stepped in. No such features had been found.

Under the microscope, he saw the same thing he had the first time: segments of construction that reminded him of the Alliance implant—but those segments weren't identical to the original. As if the design had been cannibalized to another purpose.

That didn't rule out the Alliance.

Of all those who had cause to hate the Psy, and the Arrow Squad in particular, humans undoubtedly had the biggest grievance. Prior generations of Arrows had targeted high-level human scientists and businesspeople on the orders of the Council. It'd be no surprise to find the Human Alliance had decided to take steps to eliminate any further such ugliness. Bowen Knight, the Human Alliance security chief, was more than ruthless enough to initiate that type of an operation in an effort to protect his people.

However, the Alliance wasn't the only possible perpetrator, especially given the existence of segments that pointed to the closely guarded and Council-funded "hive mind" implant. A number of Psy groups and individuals found the Arrows a threatening inconvenience, including those who saw the Es as a weakness rather than a strength. On the flip side, both the Liu family group and the Chastain family group had attempted to manipulate more-naive Es into indentured slavery. Aden had personally taken care of the extraction.

Both families had more than enough money to contract out a hit.

There was also Ming LeBon—the ex-Councilor had lost control of the squad and might believe that eliminating or besting Aden was the way to get it back. He couldn't forget Nikita Duncan, either. She might be on the Ruling Coalition and more interested in finance than military tactics, but she'd survived this long for a reason: she was smart and cutthroat. She could well have decided the Arrows had too much power and put out a hit or made a mutually self-serving alliance with Ming.

It was a surprise when someone around Nikita *didn't* end up with a metaphorical knife in his or her back.

He couldn't totally discard Kaleb Krychek as the mastermind, either. The other man had agreed to an alliance with the squad and didn't appear to want personal control of it, but Aden never made the mistake of thinking he could predict Kaleb. He also hadn't forgotten that during the Alaska incident—when part of the PsyNet suffered a catastrophic collapse as a result of a psychic infection—the cardinal tele-kinetic had caught a glimpse of Aden's true psychic strength.

Kaleb could've decided Aden was too big a threat to leave alive.

Another former Councilor on the list was Shoshanna Scott. She'd lost her standing in the PsyNet with the recent changes, might want it back, but Shoshanna had little access to military muscle. As with Nikita, she could've hired mercenaries and Aden would look into that, but from all appearances, it seemed as if Shoshanna was focusing on further growing her financial power base at present, likely so she could mount a political offensive in the future.

There were also two new players who had begun to flex their muscles. One was Pax Marshall, grandson of assassinated Councilor Marshall Hyde and a Gradient 9 telepath. Some of the most ruthless people in the Net were noncardinals but high Gradient. The second was Payal Rao, eldest daughter of the Rao family group out of India. The Rao Group had a stranglehold on a large sector of the energy industry in Southeast Asia, but ever since Payal had taken the reins, it had become more active as a regional power.

Last but possibly the most dangerous group of suspects on Aden's mental list were the Mercants. Silver Mercant was Kaleb's aide, but Mercants looked after Mercants first and the family had long been a shadow power in the Net. This kind of a power play would fit their modus operandi—the Mercants dealt in information and Aden had been kept alive so he could be broken and mined for data. That had Mercant written all over it.

"Any luck?" Finn asked from where he was patching up a young woman's broken arm using healing abilities that were changeling, not Psy, and yet that indisputably had a psychic component.

Aden had checked to see if they wanted him to leave when the patient came in, but both had motioned him to stay. "Nothing new," he said in response to Finn's question.

"Done." Finn patted the shoulder of his packmate, and she headed out, her embarrassment at having slipped in the rain and fallen off her aerie balcony still evident in the faint red flush of her skin. Apparently, she hadn't thought to use her claws in time.

Coming over, the healer looked through the microscope. "Yeah, this is way beyond my pay grade."

Aden took the implant, put it back in its case, and slipped it into his pocket. He had a feeling the answer to his question about its origin wouldn't be an easy one. He was considering which scientists could be trusted to examine it, should the Aleines not agree to help, when a sharp sound cut through the room.

Finn's head jerked up, his eyes flashing to brilliant yellow with faint traces of green near the pupils. "That's the emergency siren."

Chapter 22

REMI'S VOICE CAME on over the speaker system seconds later. "We have a lost cub. Jasper may have snuck outside and become turned around. All trained personnel head out now." What followed were numbers and compass points.

Aden realized the alpha was sectioning off people to make sure the entire area around the network of aeries was searched. "I can assist," he said to Finn when the healer grabbed a coat. "I'm fully trained for search and rescue and so is Zaira." It was a little-known facet of the Arrow mandate, but they'd quietly assisted in a number of difficult rescues over the years.

"You think you can keep from getting lost out there?"

"Do you have a compass?"

Finn took off his watch and threw it to him. "It's got one built in. You two should go to the northeast quadrant. It's the biggest. I have to stay close to the aeries in case they locate him and he needs medical attention." Then he was gone.

Aden hit the corridor to see Zaira coming down from their aerie. She was already wearing the big outdoor camouflage jacket the changelings had repaired after Finn ripped it getting to her wounds, and she was holding his. "I assumed we would help," she said, no sign on her face of the woman who'd bitten his lip.

The sense of loss in his gut was raw, but he was used to

putting his own needs aside for the good of the squad. Today, he did it for the needs of a scared, lost child. Having already strapped on Finn's watch, he shrugged into the jacket and told her to stay within visual sight of him. "We don't have the advantage of following scents and the location is unfamiliar. You may become disoriented without a compass."

"Understood."

Hoods up, they headed out into the pounding rain, the area already at near night-darkness because of the heavy cloud cover. Other searchers shouted out the boy's name multiple times, their eyes flashing night-glow in the darkness every so often when the different groups came close before separating again. Realizing it was possible the child could hear them, given the acute nature of changeling senses, Aden and Zaira also called out at regular intervals.

With every minute that passed, the risk to the child rose exponentially. Aden understood changelings had greater immunity to the cold, but he had a feeling cubs were nowhere near as strong as their parents.

When Zaira held up her hand, head tilted, he stayed silent.

"This way," she said, running left over ground that had become slippery and muddy, her face dripping water. "It may be nothing, but I thought I heard a faint growling sound."

Reaching a heavy copse of waterlogged trees that looked like they might be maples, they began to scan the area. Aden saw nothing . . . then his foot slipped out from under him in the mud. He would've gone sliding down into a steeply sloped gully if he hadn't grabbed on to a tree limb. His mind immediately putting the pieces together, he followed the line of sight to where he would've fallen if he hadn't stopped himself, and saw a glint of golden fur through the wind-driven sheets of rain.

"Zaira, I see him!" He slid down the embankment in a controlled descent as Zaira shouted to the other searchers.

Bringing himself to a stop a couple of feet from the tiny leopard cub curled nose to tail on himself, his fur pasted to his body, Aden opened his jacket and lifted the child against him before checking for a pulse. He couldn't feel a beat and the small body was so cold. Zipping the jacket closed, he ran back to the embankment and began to climb it. He'd taken only a single step when Remi bounded down.

Aden unzipped his jacket to hand over the icy body of the cub. "Get him to Finn." Remi was faster and more sure-footed in this terrain and the child was critical. "I can't feel a pulse."

Racing up the incline using claws that had sliced out of his boots, Remi disappeared back toward the aeries. It took Aden longer to climb up the muddy incline and Angel was there to help haul him over the final edge when he reached it.

"Thank you." He could've done it himself, but the help had been offered in good faith and should be acknowledged.

The man slapped the side of his neck in a nonthreatening manner, holding his hand there for a second before letting go. "Good spotting, Arrow."

The three of them made their way directly to the infirmary once they reached the aerie trees. There were a number of changelings in the corridor outside, each with a strained face. Someone threw Aden, Zaira, and Angel towels and, taking off their jackets, they wiped their faces. Changing out of their waterlogged pants and socks would have to wait.

"How did he get out?" Jojo's mother asked, her arms hugging her body. "We're so careful."

"He's seven." A packmate linked hands with the woman. "That's what cubs do at that age. Sneak out, explore. The poor baby just got lost."

Beside Aden, Zaira spoke in a muted tone. "He's so small."

"Yes." Aden could still feel the boy's fragile bones, the chill of his body. "I'm going to see if I can offer any assistance." When he reached the infirmary door, it was to see Finn and Remi bent over the small feline body, faces grimly intent. Two more people, a man and a woman who had their arms tight around one another, stood not far from the bed.

Seeing no other patients who needed medical aid, Aden was about to step away when he saw Lark enter the corridor, a bloodied towel wrapped around her hand. "I'm fine," she snapped at a packmate who made a sound of concern. "Just a stupid cut while I was fixing one of the generators. How's Jasper?" Her wet hair and clothes said she must've headed directly to the generator after Jasper was located.

Aden had ducked inside the infirmary by then and returned with the tools he needed. "I'm a trained medic," he said to her. "I can seal up your wound."

Her lips curled up into a snarl. Before she could snap at him, a packmate nudged at her and spoke in a subvocal whisper—Aden could see the man's mouth moving but could not make out the words.

Snarl turning into a deep smile almost at once, Lark held out her injured hand. "You found Jasper?"

"Stay still."

"Definitely a medic," Lark said dryly. "Clearly has the bedside manner down pat."

A faint ripple of laughter that quickly faded.

Ignoring it all, Aden ran the sealer over the cut once he'd calibrated it to the right strength and after he'd used a scanner to make sure there was no nerve damage. "It's done," he said. "The skin will remain tender for a day or so, so be careful not to injure it again."

"Got it, doc."

When high-pitched and scared crying suddenly sounded from the other room, the relief was palpable. A minute later, Remi officially confirmed that Jasper would be all right and the crowd dispersed. Aden and Zaira, however, remained. Walking quietly to the infirmary door, the two of them looked in.

What they saw was the cub, now in his human form, curled up in his mother's lap while his father stroked his hair, his face. One of the boy's hands was in Remi's, the other in Finn's. He was sobbing, but Aden saw no despair on his face, none of the hopelessness that was so often on an Arrow child's face.

Zaira was the one to articulate it. "He feels safe. He can cry because he feels safe."

"Yes." It was something neither he nor Zaira had ever known.

Unlike Zaira's sadistic mother and father, Aden's parents hadn't beaten him, but they had left him alone in a squad of assassins after making sure he knew he was a sleeper for their rebellion. He'd never been able to lower his guard, never been able to forget that should he be discovered, he'd end up dead and buried.

Chapter 23

BO WAS HAVING a rare night off from his duties as the security chief of the Human Alliance, kicking back with close friends at a trattoria on a Venice sidewalk, when his phone buzzed with an incoming call from Riaz. Even though it was after midnight in Venice, Bo didn't hesitate to answer—the SnowDancer lieutenant never called simply to chew the fat.

He said, "Be a few minutes, guys," to his friends and, grabbing his beer, answered the call while walking to a bridge that overlooked the sleepy canal next to the outdoor table where he'd been seated. "Riaz."

"Bo, I got a question for you."

"Shoot." Up on the ornate bridge—which led to a half-submerged building that still had people living on the upper floors—he leaned his back against the railing and took a sip from the ice-cold bottle in his hand.

"What the fuck is the Alliance doing buying up isolated patches of land marked for expansion of changeling pack territories?"

Bo paused with the beer bottle halfway down. "Say again?" Frown getting deeper and deeper as Riaz explained, he said, "Look, I'm away from the office. Give me a couple of hours to figure out what the hell is going on and I'll call you back."

Once at the office, he brought in his senior people and

they dug through the documents Riaz had e-mailed. The general reaction was, "What the fuck?"

"We own these parcels of land," the lawyer in the group told him. "The titles are all in the Alliance's official name, complete with our correct real estate identification codes. Those codes aren't secret, so anyone could use them to make a purchase." He scratched his head. "That's never been an issue because the code equals ownership, so people make damn sure they enter their own."

"Did we pay for these parcels?" Heads would roll if that was the case—Bo knew damn well the Alliance needed that money for other initiatives. "Are we looking at someone acting without authorization?"

The CFO held up a hand and swiped through several of the flat-screen computers laid out in front of her. "There's definitely no money missing from our accounts."

"But why?" Bo's lieutenant asked, confusion in her eyes. "Someone just randomly buys all this land for way beyond market rates and *gives* it to us?"

"We'll figure that out later." Bo turned to the lawyer. "No question it's ours."

"Certified and legal."

"I want you to start proceedings to transfer it across to the changeling packs who were intending to buy it." He had to repair the Alliance's relationship with the changelings—it wasn't yet solid enough to bear this kind of blow, especially since Bo hadn't exactly been a prince the last time he'd been in SnowDancer and DarkRiver territory.

"They'll insist on paying fair market value for it, so take the money and put it in a reserve fund in case we do get hit with unexpected bills." Frowning, he added, "Place the fund under the conservatorship of me, Hawke Snow, and Lucas Hunter." If no one turned up to claim the money, he and the alphas could hash out what to do with it.

"We'll get on it."

Bo knew that would take care of the short-term problem, but it didn't answer the underlying questions: who the fuck had bought that land and why?

Chapter 24

ZAIRA LAY IN the dark staring up at the skylight. She couldn't actually distinguish it from the rest of the ceiling, the aerie under the cloak of night and the world outside lashed by rain. Beside her, she could hear Aden's steady breathing, knew he'd put himself into a resting state that nonetheless meant he was alert to any threats. She should've done the same, but her mind was too full of thoughts that kept circling.

And her self, it was too full of aloneness again.

Curling her fingers into her palm to keep from reaching out to Aden as the feral and violently possessive want inside her pushed her to do, she focused on her breathing, regulating it to the point that she could control her heartbeat; and sometime in the hour after she first began, she fell not into a resting state, but into true sleep.

A sleep so deep that, once again, she dreamed.

Of the heaviness of the cold pipe in her hands, of how the rust had stained her palms, of the wet sound of metal hitting the pulpy mass that had once been a skull. Her arms kept rising and falling, rising and falling, until strong, pain-causing hands hauled her away, her heels dragging on the floor.

In front of her, she saw the crushed ruins of her father's head, her mother's, and felt nothing but a vicious satisfaction. They wouldn't hurt her again. When others tried to take the pipe from her, she refused to let it go, though her hands were slippery with blood from the blisters that had formed on her palms; her skin tore off as the pipe was forcefully wrenched from her grasp. The blood that covered her hands was orangey, mixed with the iron of the rust. More blood flecked her face, her clothing.

Later, when the ones who had pulled her off her parents called her a monster, she didn't protest. Because they had made her a monster and she owned what she was.

Jerking awake on that thought, heart thumping, Zaira could almost smell the blood, almost hear the sound of the pipe doing catastrophic damage. No, that wasn't right. The pipe had just finished the job and given the rage inside her an outlet. It was Zaira's mind that had turned her parents' brains to soup.

It hadn't been enough. She'd had to destroy their physical bodies before she could allow herself to believe that it really was over, that they were dead, that they wouldn't hurt her anymore.

A rustle beside her. "Zaira." Aden closed his hand over the back of hers, warm and strong.

Blood a roar and her mouth dry, she didn't speak, just stared up at the ceiling again . . . and then she turned her hand so that her fingers locked with Aden's. "I was as small as Jasper when I did it." She sucked in air that hurt going in. "As small as him when they hurt me."

"You were smaller," was Aden's grim response. "They hurt you for years."

"How could anyone do that?" In her mind, she'd always been the monster; she'd forgotten she'd also been a tiny, scared child fighting for her life.

"Because some people are evil—and some are not. You're not."

Bones feeling as if they were shaking within her, she tried to hold her focus, couldn't. "Aden." She didn't know what she was asking him, but when he broke their handhold, it was a brutal shock.

"Lift your head." His breath against her ear, his body closer.

Able to feel herself devolving into panic, she obeyed his order because it gave her a way to hold off the collapse. He slid his arm under her head and, curling it around her stiff shoulders, tugged her toward him. "Turn in to me, Zaira," he ordered when she remained rigid.

Touch had never been Zaira's friend. It had meant pain and abuse when her parents had her, cold-blooded training and more pain when she was with the Arrow Squad. But this was Aden, who had held her so many times already. She was the one who'd done the hurting. Forcing herself to turn, she didn't protest when he rolled onto his back and tugged her down over his chest, her head on his shoulder and her breasts pressed against his chest and side.

They were both dressed only in T-shirts and sweatpants, and the thin cotton fabric of the tees didn't stop the heat transfer between them. Zaira wasn't sure how long she lay there unmoving before her bones began to stop trembling and her heart calmed, the scent of Aden in her every inhale. It was warm and quintessentially masculine and deeply familiar.

Lifting her hand, she placed it on his chest, right over his heart. His pulse, steady and strong, gave her a rhythm to lock on to and use to normalize her breathing. When he ran his hand up and down her back, she didn't protest, the contact further easing the excruciating tension inside her. His hand was big, strong, and so was he. Most people didn't consciously realize it, but Aden wasn't a small man. He was lithe with muscle, his strength intense.

"I'm sorry I bit you." She didn't know why she'd done that; maybe she'd wanted to scare him, but part of her thought she'd done it because she wanted to keep him. Like an abused animal clawing at someone trying to do it a kindness because it didn't know any better.

"I saw one of the RainFire females bite her mate earlier."

"Was she angry with him?"

"No. It appeared to be an affectionate act."

Her mind thought that over, considered it from every angle. "They're changeling, have more primal drives."

"Some drives are universal."

She jerked at the feel of his teeth biting down on her ear. "Why did you do that?"

"Now we're even and you have no cause to feel as if you crossed a line."

Reaching up, she rubbed at the bite, the abused, broken, uncivilized thing inside her not quite certain what to do. "You bit me," she said again.

He brushed away her hand and ran his thumb over the spot. "Does it hurt?"

"No." It had just been the unexpected nature of it that had bewildered her. "Biting is acceptable in changeling society, not in Psy."

"I haven't heard that rule."

Thrown off center by his behavior, she turned and tucked her back against his side, holding his arm possessively where it curled around her upper body. "Are you going to bite me again?" The insane rage that was part of her needed parameters to handle this.

"Maybe."

She frowned at that answer, too confused to be worried about the breakdown in her discipline in allowing the facial expression. "I'll bite you back."

"Okay."

Her frown deepened as she realized he was determined to win the argument, determined to show her that there was nothing wrong with the fact she'd gone vicious on him. Since she couldn't think of a good counterargument, she decided to see how far he'd take this—twisting around, she bit him again, this time on the jaw.

The only difference was that she made sure not to draw blood.

He flipped her, and suddenly they were locked in hand-to-hand combat. Neither one of them, however, was trying to punch or hit. Instead, they were trying to get in under each other's defenses. He was heavier and stronger than her, but she'd always been better at this; she'd taken him down more than once, and now, managed to flip him onto his back.

But when she would've leaned in and bitten him again in this contest that was a game, he pulled off a difficult maneuver that put her on her back and then he was over her, the two of them breathing heavily.

Chapter 25

"DON'T DO IT," she warned, feeling the rage inside her claw to the surface.

He did it.

The bite was on her lower lip this time, almost exactly on the spot where she'd bitten him earlier. He didn't hurt her, but the rage crashed outward, only it didn't want to harm him. It just wanted to keep him, possess him. Twisting her legs in a move she knew he'd never expect from her, given her lighter weight and body mass, she unbalanced him and suddenly had him on his front, while she knelt with one knee on his back, her hand on his nape.

"I win," she said.

She half expected him to rise up and throw her off. Since she wasn't actually going to break his neck or hurt his spine, the countermaneuver would've worked. But he spread his hand and patted the bed twice in a silent signal that acknowledged her win.

Smiling—and conscious deep inside that this was bad, very bad, the two sides of her nature now existing in one moment—she came down over him, her entire body lying along his. He brought in his arms so that his head was resting on his hands, but didn't ask her to move. "You smell good," she said, wishing she was bigger so she could touch all of him at once.

"It must be the soap and other toiletries."

Playing her fingers through the heavy silk of his hair as she lay on him, the uncivilized rage creature a living pulse in her every cell, she took a deep breath. "Yes, but it's also you." Beneath the faint scents of the toiletries was the scent of the boy she'd first met, but it had matured, become deeper, more richly masculine.

He lay still as she ran her hand along his arm and over the taut curve of his biceps, the sleeve of the T-shirt bunching under her touch. It made her feel drunk to touch him like this, made her feel as if she was spinning out into a darkness that had no end. But, like an addict, she couldn't stop. When she rose up enough to push up his T-shirt, he tugged it off over his head.

She rubbed her cheek against the warm, smooth skin of his shoulder, sliding her hand over the muscles of his back at the same time. Under her, his breathing altered, became more erratic. Lying against him, she stroked her hand over his biceps again. "You like this," she murmured. "You like being touched by me."

"Yes." Lifting up a little to warn her of his intent, he began to turn.

She shifted enough to allow it but straddled him as soon as he was on his back, her hands on the smooth skin of his chest. His pectorals were defined, as were the ridges of his abdomen right down to where his muscles created a vee low on his body. She'd never really spent any time thinking about the differences between males and females, except in the context of how male physical strength gave her opponents an advantage she'd have to learn to counter, but now she found herself fascinated by the ridges and valleys of his body, her hands eager to explore every inch.

When he raised his own hands to her thighs, she decided it was acceptable: he could touch her. Leaning down, her forearms braced on either side of his head, she ran her lips along his jawline and down his throat, to the hollow there that made her want to lick. The raw depth of that desire nudged awake the part of her that had kept her alive and sane all these years.

"I . . . can't be like this," she said, the words coming out in a halting pattern as she fought the twisted, dangerous half of herself. "It could be deadly." Inside her was a violence so horrific it had caused the first responders to flinch—all of whom had been fully conditioned adults. "I did so much damage to my parents' faces they weren't even recognizable as male or female from the neck up."

The deep memories were locked up behind a psychic wall she'd built as part of her Silence training. She could still remember what she'd done, but she didn't relive it, didn't experience what it had felt like to bring that pipe down over and over. Or she hadn't. "My shields are breaking down. I'm remembering, Aden. I can't remember and function."

Tugging up her head with a gentle grip in her hair, Aden said, "Isn't this worth fighting for?"

She thought of how she'd felt touching him before she remembered the risk, how she'd given him pleasure. Never had she given anyone pleasure. "The risk," she began, but Aden interrupted.

"We're in a unique situation," he said. "No one will ever know what happens here unless we tell them. I promise you I *will not* let you cross any violent lines."

Zaira flexed her fingers against his shoulder, the temptation extreme. With their minds numb, if she made a mistake, it wouldn't ripple out into the PsyNet, wouldn't betray her instability to those who might take advantage of the weakness.

And Aden would never tell.

Dipping her head, she licked that spot that had tempted her and his hand clenched on her thigh, his heart thunder under her palm. The rage that wasn't rage around Aden taking her over again, she began to kiss her way down and across his chest. His nipples were flat disks but he tensed when she touched them, bit at them lightly, then licked.

She filed away the response in her private folder of all things Aden and continued on her journey down his body. When his hand closed around her nape, it didn't break the moment. This was Aden, who had never hurt her and would never hurt her. He could touch her there.

He tugged.

Frowning, she looked up. "I'm busy." Underneath her, his

body was hard, hot, a strange and wonderful new landscape for her to explore.

His eyes darker than she'd ever seen them, he said, "Take off your top."

Deciding the request was fair enough since he was half-naked, she rose and stripped it off, her breasts still covered by the bandeau. Aden's hands on her waist felt bigger, hotter without that thin barrier. A shiver rippled over her and when he tilted her toward him, she went.

Sprawled out over his body, she met his lips with her own, instinctively seeking the intimacy. One hand returning to the back of her neck, he gave it to her, the two of them exploring the contact slowly and deeply. When they broke the kiss to suck in a breath, Aden nudged her onto her back.

Zaira didn't fight it.

Neither did she fight when he came over her and traced the path she'd taken on his body on her own, his hand sliding over her ribs to spread on her back as the cool strands of his hair ran over her skin. His lips were warm, his kisses wet, and at some point, Zaira stopped trying to think and gave in to the raw insanity of the sensations.

This night was secret. Was theirs.

No one would ever know.

Chapter 26

STILL GLUTTED ON the experience of stabbing the man on the beach to death, Blake stood at the window of the main training building and watched the teenagers in the compound. They were being led through an early morning martial arts routine by a twenty-five-year-old he'd previously approached about a partnership. She'd thought it would be an ordinary partnership, of course, and he hadn't disabused her of that notion.

As it was, she'd turned him down because their fighting styles didn't mesh.

He'd made a counterargument that their differences could complement one another but when she'd stood firm, he'd realized she was too dominant a personality to allow him to be the alpha in their partnership. He'd have to find someone else. Scanning the trainees almost desultorily, he considered other Arrows in their early twenties.

That was when his mind whispered—why not someone younger?

He had never before considered a younger accomplice, but as he watched the trainer move, the teens following in seamless formation, he realized it was the best possible option. He'd have both a partner with whom to share the kill, and a weaker, less confident individual he could control.

When he examined the teenagers more carefully, he found

his eye caught by a brown-haired girl in the back row he didn't recognize. That should've been impossible—like the majority of senior Arrows, he knew the juniors coming up, had taken the age group for training at various points in time.

Yet this girl flicked no mental switches.

Sliding out his portable organizer, he found the list of attendees at the session and eliminated them one by one until he was left with a seventeen-year-old girl who was a strong telepath, but who also had a notable ability in the rare illusion range.

The latter would be useful when it came to the abduction of victims. On the negative side, she also registered as stable and loyal to the squad.

Of course, he did, too, but he knew how to manipulate the tests. Did she?

He scanned several other files, all of teenagers who were old enough to be fully trained but young enough to mold to his specifications. But he kept coming back to the girl; she even looked like the female victims he preferred when he had a choice. Every other kind of victim was a mere snack—this specific type fed his hunger.

Brown haired, pale skinned, not slender, not overweight, with small breasts.

She was the one.

He just had to find a vulnerability, a crack.

Chapter 27

ZAIRA WOKE CURLED up on her side with Aden behind her. Even as her eyes opened, she remembered the previous night, remembered the warm flex of Aden's chest under her exploring fingers, the taste of him under her lips, his hand in her hair. They'd come to a halt not long after he began to kiss her body, her mind overloaded by the unfamiliar influx of potent sensual sensation, but the intimacy of it had been searing.

As it was now.

She didn't feel alone, didn't feel lost. Not with Aden's pulse beating strong and steady against her. Beyond that sound was the pounding barrage of the endless rain, though it sounded less powerful than before. "Aden?"

He stretched against her before curling himself around her again, one of his arms crossing her chest to close over her shoulder. When he spoke, his voice was unusually lazy. "Is it time to get up?"

Zaira wanted to say no, to stay in this warm, safe cocoon where there were no rules and she could touch him, claim him without fear—and where he could put down the responsibility on his shoulders and rest—but this was bigger than her needs or even Aden's. It had to do with the survival of the squad. "The rain."

Sudden alertness in the tension of his body. "I hear it."

They got up and completed their morning routine in

silence, both of them aware their secret time was close to over. By unspoken agreement, they dressed in the clothes in which they'd come to RainFire. The repairs were more than good enough to stand the test, and if the two of them were to face the outside world, they had to do it as Arrows.

"Zaira." Aden curved one hand around the side of her face. "This doesn't have to end here." Quiet words containing a strength that had won the loyalty of the deadliest men and women on the planet; only today all that intensity was focused on her alone. "I don't want it to end." He drew her closer, his voice dropping, becoming even more quiet, impossibly more luminous with power. "I want you by my side."

Zaira didn't trust herself in a world without boundaries. And yet she'd never wanted anything as much as she wanted what he was offering. Perhaps she was shortchanging them both. Maybe Aden was right and she had the control to become more . . . to become his, without ending up a murderous monster drowning in rage. "We can try," she said, taking a risk that could change everything or destroy them both. "I'll try."

Aden's fingers tightened against her face, a tremor shaking his body. "Thank you." Rough words.

"For what?" She was the one who might get to keep him.

"For giving me you." He drew back while the staggering impact of his words was still slamming through her. "Let's go to breakfast, find out when the changelings think the terrain will become navigable."

Remi met them in the breakfast room. "My gut says the last of the rain will clear within the next couple of hours."

"Land stable enough for vehicles?" Aden asked while Zaira knelt down to listen to something a pajama-clad Jojo was excitedly telling her.

Remi nodded. "The sentries have been sweeping out to survey the landscape over the past hour. So far, they've found nothing overtly problematic."

Aden had a feeling it wasn't only the sentries who'd been out; Remi had a fresh cut under his eye where a branch might've whipped his face and his hair was damp and roughly tumbled. More, the RainFire alpha struck Aden as a man who wouldn't send his people out into a situation he wouldn't enter himself.

"We can drive you out to where you can contact your people," the other man said once Zaira rose to her full height, Jojo having scampered back to her mother. "Or we can return to where I found you, see if we can retrace your route to where you were held."

Aden didn't glance at Zaira before he answered. They both knew there was only one possible decision. "We go up to the bunker."

"Be ready to move in ninety minutes. The rain should be trailing off by then."

Finishing breakfast, the two of them returned to their aerie to make sure they were leaving everything in order. Aden then headed to fulfill a commitment he'd made to offer another training class to RainFire's younger soldiers, while Zaira chose to remain behind. The fact was, she'd experienced several stabs of pain in her head since soon after waking.

With each stab came a hint of porousness in the thick black fog around her mind. She could almost catch glimpses of PsyNet traffic. Nothing concrete, more ghost shadows of what might be, but if she was in the process of going psychically active, she had to put herself back into the right frame of mind.

Her first instinct was to shove all her emotions into a box, but she didn't want to pretend last night had never happened, didn't want to lose the untamed power of the memory. And she'd promised Aden she'd try to be the partner he needed. So, instead of the box, she spent her time creating a solid layer of intensive shielding. Silence might have fallen, but Zaira didn't intend for her emotions to leak out into the PsyNet.

No one had a right to those emotions except the people she chose.

Feeling in control afterward, she went through the trapdoor and heard Jojo's voice chattering to Finn in the infirmary. The child sounded happy and healthy. Zaira should've continued on to find Aden. Instead, she made a detour.

Seeing her, Jojo broke out into a huge smile, as if they hadn't already spoken less than ninety minutes earlier. "Zai!"

Zaira caught the girl in her arms, such soft skin and fragile bones.

"Play?"

"Not today, Jojo." It no longer felt so awkward to do this, talk to a child, hold a child. "I'm going to be leaving soon."

"Go bye-bye?"

"Yes."

Jojo's lower lip quivered and she threw her arms around Zaira's neck. "No!" It was an order.

Walking over, Finn stroked the little girl's back. "Zaira has to go back to her own pack, sweetheart. They must miss her."

Jojo eased her embrace so she could look into Zaira's face. "Go home?"

"Yes."

Hugging her again, Jojo said, "Come back, okay, Zai? Play with Jojo. Cat climb."

"I will." She'd make the time for this child who didn't know what it was to be ignored and hurt; Zaira wouldn't be the one to teach her.

Leaving Jojo not long afterward, she made her way to the large ground-floor cabin that functioned as an indoor training space. Aden's session was over by the time she arrived but he wasn't alone. A tall RainFire female with rich brown hair woven into a loose braid and bright blue eyes was standing only inches from him. She had one hand on a hip she seemed to have cocked out, her body clad not in the clothes of a fighter, but in lighter gear, her top too airy and gauzy for the weather.

As Zaira watched, she reached out and put her hand on Aden's forearm.

And the rage, it roared to the surface.

ADEN was in the midst of breaking the unexpected physical contact made by the RainFire female who'd come by with fruit juice for the trainees, then stayed behind to talk to him about self-defense—though he'd belatedly realized she had little interest in defensive maneuvers—when his instincts screamed an alert.

"Run," he said to the changeling woman, who was no fighter and who'd die in seconds if Zaira got to her. *"Run."*

To the woman's credit, she took one look at the threat

about to bear down on her and ran straight for the door on the other end, going at full changeling speed. Aden, meanwhile, got in Zaira's path, her body slamming into his with bruising force. He didn't try to fight her, just clamped his arms tight around her and tangled her legs so they went to the floor.

She could get free, of that he was fully aware. However, to do that, she'd have to severely hurt him. He didn't think Zaira would do that. Even as a child, she'd never struck out at him. "Zaira, look at me."

Her eyes remained locked on the doorway through which the RainFire female had disappeared. "You're mine." It came out a low, tight rage of sound. "She touched you."

Aden pressed his weight fully on her, her smaller body twisting in an effort to break his hold. "A mistake she won't make again."

Dark eyes burning with fire met his. "Did you touch her?"

"Would you snap my neck if I did?"

Lines formed between her eyebrows before she gave a decisive nod. "Yes."

"Liar," he said, hearing reason in her tone again. But when he went to brush his lips over hers, she turned her face away, and the tension in her muscles, it was different.

Rolling off her, he sat up as she did the same, her arms on her raised knees.

"I would've killed her," she said into the silence, her respiration yet uneven. "Not only would I have killed her, I wouldn't have stopped beating her until someone dragged me off." When she turned to look at him there was so much pain in her that he reached for her instinctively.

Except she wasn't there anymore, having stood in a fluid motion and moved out of reach. "That's who I become when I step outside the box." A pitiless whisper.

Aden's fingers curled into his palms. "You can fight it."

"No." A rasped inhale. "My possessiveness toward you is obsessive. If I give myself permission to feel it, I can't control it." She placed a fisted hand against her abdomen, exhaled. "I will be the best soldier you ever have." It was a vow. "I will protect you to my dying breath."

An indelible line in the sand.

"Zaira." He lifted his hand toward her, but he had no

words with which to convince her to fight for this, for them. Because she was right—she had demons and those demons were unforgiving. She would've hurt the RainFire woman had he not stopped her . . . and he couldn't always be there if something set her off.

It was a truth he didn't want to face.

It was a truth he *had* to face.

Because he wasn't just Aden, the man who had always wanted to be permitted next to the fire of her, allowed to see the wild, tempestuous heart of her. He was Aden Kai, leader of the Arrow Squad, and she was a senior commander the squad couldn't afford to have compromised. "What do you need?"

"Distance." She backed away with that, the single word more destructive than any weapon, and with each step she took, he saw the lines fade from her face, the bleak pain from her eyes, the passion from her breath, until by the time she reached the door, she was Zaira Neve, an Arrow commander who would die to protect the leader of her squad.

The curious, sensual woman who had kissed Aden, touched him, was gone.

Chapter 28

FIFTEEN MINUTES AFTER Zaira shut the door permanently on a beautiful, secret moment that she would never forget, she and Aden rode out from the pack's center in a rugged all-wheel drive. Remi was at the wheel of this one, while a second, identical vehicle followed them. It held three other men and one female, all of whom Zaira had identified as soldiers or sentinels in the changeling pack structure.

She'd expected to be asked to wear a blindfold, but Remi had shrugged at the question. "You have visuals of the aeries now that you could share with teleporters, so I'll just have to trust you." Despite his apparently casual stance, his eyes had been leopard, his tone dead serious.

"You can," Aden had replied, once more the contained, private leader of the squad, no trace remaining of the man who'd shivered with pleasure under her fingertips, under her lips.

The part of her that had been with him in that secret time was . . . disturbed. She couldn't go forward without causing carnage, but he was better than this, had the capacity to have a life like Vasic had with Ivy. Zaira wouldn't hurt the woman he chose, not once she'd rebuilt herself to who she'd been before waking up in that bunker. If another woman became Aden's heart as Ivy was Vasic's, Zaira would protect her, too.

No. A vicious snarl inside her mind, the insane and dangerous part of her wrenching at its chains. *He's mine.*

It took all her concentration to make sure the chains held. Now that the monster in her had tasted freedom, known what it would be like to have Aden for its own, it hungered for more. That fragile discipline was why she'd taken the backseat while Aden sat in the front passenger seat, the heavy rain having turned to a light shower around them.

"I saw you not far from here." Remi brought the vehicle to a stop in a clearing below an outcrop that would conceal the all-wheel drive from even someone who was right on top of it. "I'm guessing you came from over that ridge in the distance. Any specifics?"

As they stepped out into the now rainless air, the sky clear of clouds but heavy with the misty fog that gave the mountains their name, Aden said, "We crossed either a swollen stream or a small river immediately below the ridge."

"I recall some of the particular types of trees." Zaira noted the species she'd seen.

"There would be a large clearing nearby for the chopper," Aden added, standing as far from her as possible without it being suspicious. He was giving her the distance she'd requested so why did she feel this hollowness in her gut, this screaming, howling sense of loss?

"Got it." Remi nodded at his people and they disappeared behind the vehicles. When they came back out, it was in leopard form, except for the final male.

"A tiger." Zaira took in the large predator who stood quietly on the waterlogged grass. "I thought they were the most solitary of all changeling cats."

Remi's answer was a feline smile that gave nothing away. "We can't take the vehicles any farther in this terrain. It's some ways to the river—you two okay to keep up?" Eyes on Zaira. "Especially you. You were the worst injured."

"I'll be fine."

Scanning her up and down, Remi nodded. "I'll let you make that call, but if you're going to go down, warn me." With that, he began to move, his packmates in animal form racing alongside them.

Zaira was fast, but she knew there was no way she would ever be able to keep up with the changelings should they unleash their full capacity. The Psy race's greatest advantage was the mind; the changelings', the body. Right now, the RainFire group was maintaining a hard pace, but one she and Aden could carry for a long period as well.

Only when they were almost to the river did Remi call everyone to a halt. "The river's long and that ridge is wide." He looked to Zaira and Aden, and it was clear he was barely winded. "The trees narrow it down, but if you can recall anything else specific, things will go faster—I've been up in this area, but never right to their base."

Aden's profile was clean against the green and foggy backdrop as he said, "We crossed the river by using a set of rocks as stepping-stones. They were almost in a straight line to the other side."

The tiger growled.

Remi met the unusual blue-green of his gaze. "You know the spot?"

A nod.

"Go, see if you catch any fresh scents." He faced Aden and Zaira as the tiger melted away into the trees. "Your captors are probably gone, since the op went sideways, but getting cocky gets people killed."

Aden nodded. "Reconnaissance is always a good idea."

"We'll follow Angel's scent trail at a slower pace."

The sentinel rejoined the group three minutes after they reached the concealing trees near the river. Looking at Remi, he just gave a simple nod.

"That's the all clear." Remi turned to his people. "Spread out, sound an alert if you sense anyone nearby."

As the others scattered, Remi looked at the rocks Aden and Zaira had used as a bridge. He whistled. "You did that injured and in the dark?" A shake of his head. "I'd have you in my pack."

The three of them went to the stones without further discussion. As Zaira followed Aden across, she wasn't sure *how* exactly he'd done it—it was treacherous even in the light. Heading up the hill once they were all on the bank on the other side, they took care regardless of Angel's information, but Remi's packmate had been right. There were no signs of life.

"I don't scent anything, fresh or otherwise," Remi confirmed, his eyes gone leopard. "They must've cleared out in the chopper before the storm became too bad." A glance as they walked forward. "Definite scent of blood inside, but nothing fresh."

"That's a very useful ability," Zaira said.

A raised eyebrow. "I think so. Of course, talking mind to mind is also one hell of an advantage."

"True." Her eyes went to Aden to see that he was pressing two fingers against his temple while he scanned the area with his eyes.

They hadn't spoken since the incident in the training room, but she was near certain he was experiencing the same stabbing pains as her. Like a numb foot waking up, except this pain denoted the resurrection of their psychic abilities. Zaira couldn't predict if she or Aden would be back to full strength once the process was complete or if the damage was permanent. If it was—

She cut off that line of thought almost as soon as it took form. Thinking about the aloneness was a sure path to madness.

The building took shape out of the mist in front of them. A flat, square bunker covered by camouflage netting and dead foliage that had been carefully arranged to obscure it so it'd be invisible from the air. Not a rush job, or one done by amateurs.

They listened intently for any indication of someone within before entering low and quiet.

The bunker was as cold inside as it was outside, rust-colored stains on the walls when they switched on the lights. Those lights flickered weakly but stayed on. "They must be on a localized power source," Aden murmured. "Precharged battery likely. Our captors probably took the generator."

He was proven right; the entire place had been stripped. It had to have been done in a rush, but it had been efficient. And they'd taken their dead. All signs of a trained unit.

"You were held here?" Remi asked when they walked into the room with the overturned chair near the doorway. "Caught your scents."

Aden nodded. Even if Aden's instincts hadn't said he could trust the RainFire alpha, there was no reason to hide the facts—and Remi could easily return to the scene alone and do as much investigating as he wanted. "Do you have a problem with us bringing in a forensic team?"

"Not my land, but don't fly over RainFire territory and don't come into it without permission." A hard look. "I'll give you direct contact lines. Comms should be back up in the next few hours, so next time you want to visit, you call."

"Understood." Aden continued to go through the bunker, but there was nothing that pointed to the identity of their captors. He was crouched beside a shelf, checking to see if something might've fallen underneath, when the psychic fog that had been thinning in painful stops and starts over the past hour suddenly burned away in a final excruciating blaze of pain.

It was as if he'd been breathing through smog this entire time, and suddenly, he got a clean draft of air, the PsyNet opening up around him in a rolling sweep of data and minds and psychic noise.

A flicker beside him an instant later. "I'm fine," he said, rising to his feet to meet the ice gray eyes of his best friend. "Zaira—"

"—is also fine," came another voice, one he didn't expect.

You brought Krychek into it.

You'd disappeared and I couldn't 'port to you, Vasic replied. *He's the strongest Tk in the Net. I made a judgment call as your second in command.*

At least you've finally accepted the role. Aden turned to look at Krychek. "I'll give you both a briefing shortly. First, I need an Arrow forensics team in here."

"I'll get them." Vasic 'ported out a split second before Remi returned from outside in a rush of cold air.

Folding his arms, the alpha stood with his feet braced apart just inside the doorway. "I guess your pickup's here," he said, eyes leopard-bright and dangerous as he took in Krychek.

"Yes." Aden reached out with his mind at the same time. *Zaira? Can you hear me?*

Her response was simple and coated in the frost expected of an Arrow. *Affirmative.*

Walking to Remi, Aden held out his hand in a gesture he knew the changeling male would appreciate. "Thank you for your help. We wouldn't have survived without it."

The alpha took it, shook. "You found our cub. We're even."

"Regardless, if you ever need Arrow assistance, the line is open. Finn has my contact details."

An unreadable expression on Remi's face. "That's some offer." Breaking the handclasp, he said, "If you ever find out who owns this land, you tell me. RainFire intends to buy it." A pause before he headed out, his gaze locking with Aden's, alpha to alpha. "Stay in touch, Arrow. You haven't learned everything yet."

ZAIRA made certain she was alone when she walked into the chamber where she and Aden had been held. Her eyes went immediately to the corner where she'd been thrown. The dried patch of blood was larger than she'd expected. That didn't concern her. What did concern her was the reaction she'd had to their captor's threat.

Tell me—are Arrows trained not to break under sexual torture?

His words had made her blood run cold. Clearly, there was a serious flaw in Arrow training; they weren't desensitized against that kind of abuse. The reason why it was so different from other kinds of physical pain was something she hadn't understood until she'd touched Aden last night, until she'd understood what it meant to choose to share her body with a man she trusted inside out.

A violation would be akin to having her innermost shields torn open.

Zaira.

Shifting on her heel at the sound of Aden's voice in her mind, his telepathic voice as controlled and quietly powerful as his speaking one, she found him walking toward her. For one small secret instant, she allowed herself to remember what it had felt like to touch him, what it had felt like to be with him without fear . . . and when the instant was over, she slammed the door on the memory. If she was going to protect him, keep him safe, it had to be from herself as much as any external threat.

"Do you need me to remain here to supervise the forensic team?" she asked.

He shook his head, his hair gleaming even in the comparatively dull overhead light. "Finn did an excellent job, but I want us both checked out by our medics."

Conscious she had to return to Venice at full capacity, Zaira agreed, and thanks to Vasic's teleportation skills, was soon at a specialist Arrow medical facility with Aden. They were examined separately and the M-Psy in charge of her was able to ease some of the residual soreness in her head using his ability. He also ran a battery of tests to check her neural and psychic health after declaring that her abdominal wound had been expertly repaired.

"Treatment complete," the M-Psy said. "Your body suffered significant trauma and you need twenty-four hours of rest before going back on active duty." The slender male held Zaira's gaze. "That's not a suggestion. It's an order I'm putting on your file."

"Understood." Leaving the treatment room, she found Aden waiting for her outside. "I've been told to rest, but I need to return to Venice. Alejandro's already been sedated for over forty-eight hours, according to the report I've just had." That sedation had been very light, thanks to Ivy staying almost constantly with the damaged male, but Zaira wanted him out of it nonetheless. Many of the others in her care were also damaged, wouldn't have dealt well with her sudden absence.

Aden curled his hand around her upper arm, a sudden, passionate darkness in his eyes. "I have faith in your will. Fight for us."

Zaira's shields began to crumble. Breaking away from him, she shook her head and tried not to hear the screaming need inside her. "Your faith can't change genetics." Her instability was part of her DNA itself. "Your faith can't change the fact that I was born of monsters who were born of monsters. I can't erase the violence written in my blood. All I can do is cage it." Caught in that cage was the part of her that had made Aden feel pleasure.

For a single beautiful heartbeat, she had been someone whose touch meant pleasure. Someone who was wanted for a reason that had nothing to do with the fact she was a trained and experienced Arrow.

Thank you . . . For giving me you.

Aden would never know just how much that meant to her.

Those words would make the rest of her existence bearable.

Chapter 29

WORD SPREAD THROUGH the squad like wildfire: Aden and Zaira were back.

Blake told himself there was no cause for concern. As long as he was careful and didn't act on his urges again too soon, he could continue on exactly as he'd been doing.

The only change was that he'd have a partner, someone with whom he could share his work, someone who would admire his intelligence and cunning and cruelty.

That was what he'd do with his "resting" time—he'd finalize his choice of partner, groom his chosen one for the blood to come.

Chapter 30

THE FIRST THING Aden did after leaving the clinic was to get the implant in the hands of his tech people. He'd attempt to get hold of Ashaya Aleine later, but his next act was to make sure he was "caught" in public having a discussion with Vasic. The photograph hit Net feeds seconds later, putting paid to conspiracy theories about his capture and death, but the fact that those rumors had been leaked in the first place confirmed this wasn't about him—it was about defanging the squad.

Much as he wanted to take point on tracking their shadowy enemy, he had to assign the overall operation to Axl. As leader of the squad, he had to handle myriad other issues, including the fact that Pax Marshall was apparently attempting to poach young Psy meant for the squad—and in need of the psychic discipline only the squad could provide.

Then, two days after his return, he lost an Arrow.

Edward was one of the oldest of the active Arrows. An hour after his shift, the forty-six-year-old male put a laser pistol to his head and pressed the trigger. The empath to whom he was connected via the Honeycomb felt his sudden, violent, and total separation from the PsyNet. Shocked and heartbroken, she was hospitalized.

"We don't consciously feel emotions from the people we're connected to in the Honeycomb," Ivy told him in the hallway outside the empath's hospital room, her voice thick. "It's not that kind of a bond. But we do feel it when people die."

Aden hadn't realized that, suddenly understood exactly the burden borne by the Es. "I'm sorry."

A tight smile. "Most of the time the shock is minimal. It's part of the rhythm of the Honeycomb—some are born, some die." Releasing a breath as the two of them walked down the cool blue of the hallway, she said, "The unexpected deaths, though, they hurt. The accidents are bad, but the suicides are the worst."

"How many since the Honeycomb came into effect?"

"A statistically 'ordinary' number," Ivy replied, lines of strain around her mouth. "That in itself is a miracle after all the upheaval."

"Was the E able to sense anything from Edward at the moment of death?"

Expression sad, Ivy shook her head. "She did say he'd been difficult to bond with even on the shadow level needed for the Honeycomb. He said all the right things, did what she asked, but the bond she had with him was more brittle than any of her others." She turned on her heel. "I should get back to her. She's fragile right now."

Leaving Ivy to comfort the distraught empath, Aden tore apart Edward's life in an effort to find the reason for his suicide, Zaira by his side. "You're mourning him," she'd said bluntly when she appeared at Central Command. "You're not thinking rationally and need someone who can act as a sounding board."

"He was always stable," Aden said. "One of the foundation pieces of the squad and of the rebellion." As he went through Edward's personal belongings searching for a reason to explain the inexplicable for the hundredth time, he tried to understand and failed. "I didn't focus on him because I thought he was all right."

"Stop, Aden."

"I can't. He was one of mine and I didn't protect him." Edward had lived decades under Silence, survived decades under Ming LeBon's cruel control, only to break when there was hope on the horizon. "I didn't protect him, Zaira."

Zaira couldn't fight her instincts. Not here. Not with this

man. Going to him, she held his strong, beautiful face between her hands. "You're only one man," she reminded him.
"You can't protect us all."

Aden just looked at her, and she knew the answer: He was
their leader. The Arrows were his responsibility.

"No. I'm here." She couldn't walk with him into a new
way of life, but she could shoulder some of the weight of responsibility. "Tell me what you need." Breaking the physical
contact before she couldn't, before she went even closer
and drew his head down to her own, their lips touching, she
stepped back.

Aden shoved a hand through his hair in a rare physical
sign of internal agitation. "I've been through everything,
found nothing."

"The PsyNet. He could have created a psychic vault." They
were trained not to do that, as even the most intricately built
vaults could be penetrated, or might eventually degrade, leaking data into the Net. But—"Edward wasn't thinking clearly
at the end, could've broken operating protocol."

Jaw a hard line, Aden shook his head. "I've alerted a
PsyNet team to hunt for a psychic vault, but as far as I'm
concerned, Edward was thinking very clearly. He didn't de-
generate, didn't break down. He made a decision and carried
it through."

Zaira could see his point. From what they knew, Edward
had come home from his shift, taken a shower, dressed in a
fresh uniform, then sat down on his bed and fired the laser
pistol at an angle that meant he'd fall back onto the bed.

Making it easy for his body to be carried out and for the
blood to be cleaned up. Not a drop had fallen off the mattress.

"He was the perfect Arrow to the end," Aden said, and
she could see the brutal truth of it shredding him from the
inside out.

Unable to bear his pain, she looked at the metal trunk at
the bottom of the bed. It was where most Arrows kept their
belongings.

"I've searched that," Aden said, his voice rough.

"When I was first made an Arrow and given my own
quarters, I didn't trust that I wasn't being monitored." She
tried to lift up the trunk.

Aden bent down, helped her flip it onto its side. "You stored things below?"

"No. These particular trunks have a gap between the bottom and the floor—I added another panel to create a hidden compartment." Seeing the smooth wooden surface with its patina of age and marks at the edges, she nodded. "Edward did the same."

Aden passed her a knife from his boot and she eased the tip under one of the deepest marks.

The false bottom flipped out. Several notebooks fell to the floor.

Picking up one, Zaira opened it. Neat, tidy handwriting filled the pages. "This entry is about an assignment he was given to disrupt the technological advances of a certain human group." There was no emotion in the report, not even an opinion, just the unembellished details of the op, but the fact that Edward had felt the need to write it down was an answer in itself. As with Zaira's small, secret treasures, it had been an attempt to hold on to a piece of himself that wasn't supposed to exist.

Aden had been going through the other notebooks. "I have it," he said as the notebook in his hand fell open to a blank page. "This must contain his final entry."

The decision instinctive, Zaira took it from him. "I'll find it." Flipping to the page with the final lines of text, she absorbed them, looked up at Aden. His expression was carefully controlled. "Is there an answer?"

Zaira wanted to shield him from it, but there was no way to do so without blinding him to information he needed. She passed over the notebook in silence, the words already embedded in her brain.

I don't belong in this new world. Like an old and obsolete piece of machinery, it's time for me to be decommissioned.

Aden read the words three times and still they didn't make sense to him. "He was part of us," he said. "We even spoke about the new direction of the training—I wanted him to be one of the head teachers." Edward had never been violent, never caused a child harm, and in him, Aden had seen a man very similar to Walker Lauren. A man he respected.

"I don't think he ever came to Ivy and Vasic's home."

And, Aden realized, he hadn't been at Ivy and Vasic's wedding. He'd taken a duty shift so that younger Arrows could attend. "How did I miss this? That he was distancing himself from the squad?"

"You trusted him—he was a senior Arrow who had your ear anytime he wanted." Zaira took the notebook, went back to earlier entries. "There's nothing here except his normal notes. It's as if he made the decision the moment before death."

"Or he was thinking about it for a long period, but trusted no one with his thoughts." Aden gathered up all the other notebooks. He would read each and every one, try to understand. "I need to talk to all the senior Arrows."

Zaira held on to the final notebook when he would've taken it. "We'll read these together, Aden."

"Protecting me again?"

"Someone has to." He couldn't be trusted to do it himself.

Dark eyes met her own, the power in them a violent storm. "So fight for me," he said, the words passionate. "Fight for the squad. Be the partner I need, the partner I want."

Zaira had made her decision, knew it was the right one regardless of how brutally it hurt. But at that instant, she wondered who would protect the protector? Who would make sure Aden took a breath, laid down the weight for an hour or for a night? If she didn't bond with him, she couldn't be by his side on a regular basis, couldn't pull him back from the edge. He needed someone in that position. Someone tough enough to stand up to him and lethal enough to force him to rest if necessary.

And someone from whom he'd accept censure.

That particular short list had only two people on it and one of them was already bonded to another. That left Zaira . . . and the monstrous creature inside her.

Chapter 31

SEEING THE PHOTOGRAPH of the Arrow leader alive and well was unexpected, but his survival didn't have to equal the termination or suspension of their plans. The group had always known the Arrow wouldn't be an easy target.

It was time to move to plan B: sacrifice the data, go for a public kill.

The Arrow Squad had to die. For some inexplicable reason, this midlevel telepath and field medic was its nucleus; cut him out and the resulting fractures would mean the rest would be far easier to eliminate.

No squad.

No one to hunt the serial killers.

No one to keep unscrupulous corporates in line.

Perfect.

Chapter 32

OVER THE NEXT three days, Aden spoke one-on-one with every single senior Arrow in the squad—classified as Arrows who'd been active in the field for more than two decades. What he heard was troubling.

"I'm forty-five years old," a female Arrow named Irena said to him. "All I've ever known is Silence. All I've ever been is a killing machine." She stopped beside a tree with glossy green leaves in the underground park that abutted Central Command. "Emotion is my enemy and the discipline of the squad is all that keeps me sane."

The echo of Zaira's own reason for rejecting his proposal added another layer of ice to his veins. "The Honeycomb?"

Irena touched one of the leaves. "I wish I wasn't part of it." Dark hazel eyes met his as she dropped her fingers from the leaf and turned to face him. "I can feel it pressing against me, awakening things that shouldn't be awakened." A hand placed over her heart. "This organ is starting to wake, starting to have needs I can never fulfill. I don't have that capacity and I wonder if the need will one day drive me mad."

Again and again and again, he had the same conversation, discovered the same disturbing truth: the senior Arrows felt as if they had no place in the new squad. Each promised not to follow Edward into suicide, but only because that would leave him with a personnel shortage.

"I've told them we need their expertise, their experience, their strength," he said to Vasic as they sat on a sand dune in the desert to which Vasic had teleported them late on the third day. "I'm not sure they're hearing what I'm saying." He thought of what Irena had said. "They're having trouble hand-ling the emotions being nudged awake by the connection with the empaths—not *one* believes he or she can make it, even with you, Abbot, and Judd as examples."

"And Stefan," Vasic said. "He might not be an Arrow, but he is one of us."

"Yes." Aden knew that should he call, the Tk based on the deep-sea station Alaris would respond without question. "All four of you are powerful yet it doesn't seem to make a difference to the senior Arrows."

"They need to see you do it."

Aden wasn't ready to talk about that yet, not when the only woman he wanted by his side would only agree to stand there as a soldier—a woman who might only *be able* to stand there as a soldier. He'd been selfish in pushing her, he knew that. He also knew he'd probably do it again. Zaira was his own madness. "I'm not sure even that'll be enough," he said aloud. "We're all of a younger generation."

"Have you thought about using your parents?"

"My parents?" He was well aware that neither Zaira nor Vasic were fans of Marjorie and Naoshi.

"They're older than all the active senior Arrows and des-pite having lived in the outside world since their defection, surrounded by emotion, they've held themselves together," Vasic responded. "Put them in charge of the welfare of the older Arrows, the ones who are struggling."

"My parents aren't known for their kind hearts—and they survived in the outside world by sticking dogmatically to the tenets of Silence." No softness, no deviations from Arrow protocol. "That's not the life I want for my Arrows."

Vasic's black hair lifted in the warm desert breeze. "Yes, but it might be the life these Arrows need to live. In time, that may change—we just have to keep them with us long enough."

Aden considered Vasic's suggestion in silence, nodded slowly. "You're right." His parents might have any number of faults, but they also had a lifetime of experience that could help in this situation. They would know which tasks to assign to best keep the older Arrows stable, which mental exercises to teach. As important, the senior Arrows would listen because Marjorie and Naoshi had more than proven their mettle. "I wouldn't trust them to train younger Arrows, but they've always believed that Arrows who've put in their time deserve to retire in peace—regardless of their physical or mental state."

Aden couldn't see either of his parents treating the senior Arrows with anything other than respect, but he hadn't forgotten what Zaira had said of his father's comments about locking up Alejandro. Naoshi had likely deemed that an acceptable action because Alejandro was young, hadn't "earned" the care of the squad, but just in case—"One of us will have to keep a subtle eye on them, make sure they haven't become unforgiving of flaws."

"I'll take care of that," Vasic said. "But I'm certain it'll work—Ivy met your parents during the time you were missing and she said while they came across as abrasive, she also sensed a deep commitment to their fellow Arrows."

Aden was unsurprised. "I learned about loyalty from them." Only where he gave it to each individual Arrow and Arrow trainee, Marjorie's and Naoshi's loyalty was to the squad as a whole.

It was a subtle but vitally important difference that would forever divide them.

Vasic spoke again into the desert quiet. "The appointment will also clarify your parents' status in the squad now that we no longer have to maintain an external network."

That was what Marjorie and Naoshi had done while officially "dead"—acted as base command for all the different Arrow bolt-holes around the world, many of which they'd helped establish. Once Aden and his people got an at-risk Arrow out, Marjorie and Naoshi were the ones who'd set the defector up with a new life and teach that Arrow how to integrate into the world. A significant percentage, wanting to remain active as Arrows, had ended up in Venice under Zaira's command, but others had preferred or needed a quieter or more remote location.

The safe houses would stay in place and any Arrow who wanted to continue his or her life outside was welcome to do so, but the urgency and importance of the task was now over. Currently, Marjorie and Naoshi were at loose ends and struggling to understand the fact that Aden didn't intend to hand over the reins of the squad to them.

That he would never do, but their long service deserved a position where their status was clear cut and respected. "I'll talk to them."

"Why haven't you mentioned Zaira?" Vasic said without warning.

Aden looked at his friend's profile, Vasic's skin deep gold in the light of the setting sun. "Why should I?"

"Aden." Winter gray eyes met his. "I was with you when you first met her, and I was with you when you hacked the security systems to send her an e-mail. I know she means more to you than you've ever consciously acknowledged."

Aden thought of his and Zaira's time together in the aerie, and before that, of their fight to survive. The memories were burned into his soul. "You've never said anything before."

"I didn't understand who she was to you then." Reaching out to the little white dog who'd run along the top of the sand dune to sprawl huffing at his side, Vasic scratched his and Ivy's pet between the ears. "It took my love for Ivy to open my eyes."

A pause as they watched the last of the sun's rays fade.

"She's yours, Aden," Vasic said in the falling dark. "Always has been, always will be. And I'm fairly certain she considers you hers. Did you ever notice that the two of us were hardly ever in the same room together before my marriage? Zaira saw me as competition for you."

Aden thought of the feral fury with which Zaira had nearly attacked the RainFire woman, of the way the two of them had touched in the midnight hours, of the fact that she still wore his leather jacket, and gripped his wrist so hard he could feel his bones grinding into dust. "It's not enough," he managed to get out. "She believes her future lies in her past."

"And I believed my future held nothing but death."

Recovered from his exertions, Rabbit padded over to Aden and dropped a stick he'd brought from the orchard. Aden picked it up and threw it into the distance. Barking excitedly, the dog flew down the dune after the stick. "I've tried to reason with her. I've tried emotion."

Vasic propped his arm on one knee. "The only reason I lived long enough for Ivy to find me was that you were too stubborn to let me die. I don't need your stubbornness anymore—Zaira does."

Aden looked to his friend again as Rabbit began to run back with the stick. "I'll simply wear her down?"

A slight curve of Vasic's lips. "Some barriers need to be worn down." Eyes flicking down, he used his Tk to help Rabbit climb the sand dune.

Changing subjects, because thinking of Zaira made things hurt inside him that had been torn wide open when he touched Vasic's bond with Ivy, Aden threw the stick again for Rabbit. "Ashaya Aleine has agreed to work with our techs on the implant."

"You aren't worried about how she might use any data she uncovers?"

"Aleine has proven her principles, but the squad has officially hired her for the project. The contract specifies confidentiality." Aden didn't think the DarkRiver leopards, whom Aleine called packmates, would misuse the data, but he wasn't taking the risk.

"I can't work out how you managed that," Vasic said. "It's not as if Aleine isn't in demand."

"According to Aleine, I 'seduced' her with a glimpse of the implant." Aden had hoped the scientist wouldn't be able to resist, was glad to be proven right. "I need to talk to Walker."

Judd's brother had been Aden's teacher once, the only teacher who had ever truly seen him. The telepath had also helped Aden come up with the new curriculum for Arrow children, his answer to Aden's initial request a simple one that betrayed the powerful heart that beat in Walker's chest.

"Of course I'll help, Aden."

Walker might never have worn the badge of the squad, but he was one of them in a way Ming LeBon would never be. Walker understood loyalty, understood that even an Arrow's life had value.

"I can teleport you to him if you make contact—it's still relatively early in the afternoon in his region."

Aden made the call. Walker was in the middle of building a table with the children he supervised, but agreed to meet with Aden. "I'll see you at the church in three hours," he said. "That'll give me enough time to finish this and get down there."

Aden didn't know what connection the Laurens had with Father Xavier Perez, but his church was a known meeting point. Walker was waiting for them on the back steps when they arrived, his forearms braced on his thighs. Dressed in worn jeans and a simple white shirt with the sleeves rolled up to the elbows, his dark blond hair swept roughly back, he could've been any ordinary man. It was his pale green eyes that gave him away—intent and focused and strikingly intelligent.

Walker rose to his feet and joined Aden near the trees at the edge of the yard, Vasic 'porting away after a nod of greeting.

"You said you lost an Arrow," Walker said, his expression grim in the early evening light. "How?"

Aden told him, could see Walker taking it in. "I've accepted I have to lead from the front," he added, though he didn't yet have a solution as to how to get Zaira to accept his proposal. "But I'm younger by at least a decade from the ones at most risk. Seeing me make it won't be enough—and while my parents can keep them stable, I want more than a life in stasis for the senior Arrows."

Folding his arms, Walker leaned back against a tree. "For a long time, I saw myself as too damaged by Silence to ever be a good father, much less a good mate."

Yet Aden knew Walker was both. "How did you get past it?"

"I had to." A blunt response. "I had a daughter, a nephew, and a niece who needed me. I also had a brother who needed me, for all that he was an adult."

The wind riffled through Aden's hair as he stood there. "Judd was lucky to have you." Aden hadn't known it at the time, but unlike most siblings whose brothers or sisters were claimed by the Council for the squad, Walker had never lost touch with his brother—he'd kept Judd connected to the family unit, and in so doing, saved his soul.

"No, I was the lucky one." Walker straightened, the two

of them falling into an easy walk through the peaceful old graveyard behind and to the left of the church. "Marlee, Toby, Sienna, and Judd, they forced me to be a better man. The children expected me to know what to do in an unfamiliar environment, teach them how to live in it, and Judd expected me to care for the children's well-being so he could focus on their safety."

Walking through the neatly kept grass, Aden began to see what Walker was telling him; the other man was a teacher who never simply gave his students the information. They had to work for it, and in the process, learn. "I have to find a way to connect the old generation of Arrows with our most vulnerable." He clasped his hands behind his back. "I've been hesitant because many of the senior Arrows have very little flexibility in them—I don't want them doing inadvertent damage."

"I understand your worry." Bending down, Walker took a second to replace a bouquet that had been blown off a gravestone. "But being needed is a powerful driving force."

Aden thought of how he needed Zaira to need him, how it felt to be important to someone not because he was an Arrow but because he was Aden, and knew Walker was right. "Do you have any suggestions about how we can do this?" Aden wasn't arrogant, not when it came to his people. He'd take advice where he could get it and from Walker he'd listen to even the most outlandish suggestion.

"I wouldn't advise full integration all at once and you should regularly touch base with your parents to see how the older Arrows are handling any changes, but there's no harm in creating more opportunities for regular contact between adult Arrows and Arrow children. It can be as simple as having a senior Arrow teach a class of six-year-olds."

Aden knew no Arrow would disagree with that type of an educational request, so the mechanics were achievable. "I think," he said, considering the idea from all angles, "the classes would work better if done in partnership with a teacher more in sync with life beyond Silence."

Walker nodded. "One of the empaths, possibly, or even a non-Psy teacher."

Halting, Aden turned to face the telepath. "How can a

non-Psy teacher hope to understand children so violently powerful? He or she would have few defenses against a child's tantrum."

"Marlee's art teacher is a human," Walker told him. "She's elderly and frail and has no defenses against wolf claws or Marlee's psychic strength, yet she's kept a classroom in control for decades."

"Arrow children aren't used to non-Psy teachers," Aden said, his mind already working the possibilities. "There's also the security aspect—I can't risk exposing the children to those who might sell the information of their location and abilities." As shown by Zaira's childhood experiences and Pax Marshall's recent moves, some people would do anything to control such power.

"I can recommend some who can be trusted, including two from SnowDancer and one from DarkRiver who are on short-term contracts that'll end in the next few months." Walker stopped at the edge of the graveyard, beneath the spreading branches of a tree with leaves of a silvery green. "For now, I can help advise the people you already have."

Aden looked out at the peace of the graveyard and beyond to the trees, but his thoughts were far distant. "I want to make the squad a family." A place where even the outcasts could find hope. "Not just tied together by mutual need, but by bonds of emotion."

Walker put his hand on Aden's shoulder. "You will," he said. "You were an extraordinary boy and you've grown into a man as extraordinary."

The pride in Walker's words meant more to Aden than anything either one of his parents could have said. Because where Marjorie and Naoshi had abandoned him to further their cause, Walker Lauren had put his life on the line to come back into the Arrow training rooms one last time to give Aden the final telepathic lesson he needed to stay safe.

"Why did you come back after you were relieved of duty?" he asked as they started to walk again. "You risked everything." Walker had been transferred out to a more mainstream military school partway through Aden's elementary schooling, after the squad's leadership decided he wasn't a ruthless enough teacher for child Arrows. His covert

entry back into the training center would've been seen as a
breach of security, with the attendant fatal consequences.

"If I could have, I would've taken you with me," Walker
said. "That I couldn't do, but I could make sure you had the
tools to survive."

It didn't quite answer Aden's question, but he didn't push.

Then Walker added, "You're not my son, Aden, but that's
how I've always thought of you."

A stretching pain in Aden's heart that threatened to steal
his breath. Unable to speak, he simply nodded and knew it
was inadequate, but he also knew Walker would understand.
Walker had always understood him. "The squad will need
you more than ever now," he said at last. "Can the Snow-
Dancer alpha spare you?"

"I've spoken to him." Walker turned his face into the cool
wind. "I'm responsible for a group of children in Snow-
Dancer, too, and I intend to continue in that role, but I've
been taken off all other tasks so I can assist you." Finally, he
could help the boy he'd been forced to leave behind in a situation that would've crushed so many.

He'd never forgotten Aden, never not thought about him.
Small and with those wise eyes that were old beyond his
years, the boy had been better than all the darkness around
him. Now he was a leader struggling to guide his people out
of that same darkness and Walker would do everything in
his power to help him. "What about you?"

Aden looked at him with eyes that were even older than
when he'd been a child. "Me?"

"You speak only of the squad. What about your own needs?"
Aden had always focused on others, never on himself.

"I—" Aden paused, the hesitation unusual enough that
Walker turned to face him.

The younger man looked into the distance for several seconds before returning his attention to Walker. "It's selfish to
think of myself," he said at last and Walker had the sense he
was fighting an internal battle. "The squad's needs come
first."

Reflecting on his own family, on the pack, on what he'd
noted of their alpha, Walker said, "In the years since I joined
SnowDancer, I've learned that joy makes me a better father,

a better brother, a better uncle, and a better mate." He thought of his mate's smile, of the way Lara had of loving until it spilled over onto everyone in her vicinity . . . and how her love for him was a pulse in his heart. "The fact I'm happy colors my every interaction."

He clasped Aden's shoulder again, as he might with Toby. His nephew was a very different boy from the man Aden had become, but they were both his sons of the heart. "I'm not saying you're not a good leader, Aden. I'm saying taking time for yourself won't make you any less of a good leader, and the effect of your happiness will trickle down through the entire squad. Take what you need, what you're fighting not to need."

What he didn't say, because it was too heavy a burden for any man to bear, was that Aden was already a leader who was on his way to greatness. If he didn't lose his way, if he didn't break under the strain, he'd become a man who would be written of in history. To make it, he needed someone to walk with him, to hold him when things became too hard, and to fight for his right to his own happiness.

Aden needed love more than anyone Walker had ever met.

Chapter 33

EDWARD HAD DONE him a favor in committing suicide and sucking up Aden's attention, Blake thought as he skimmed another news article about his kill. It was a small mention, already gone from the headlines. That wouldn't last. He'd give them a second body, but not yet. Right now, his attention was on a different project.

He'd confirmed his choice of partner: Beatrice Gault, the teenager with the illusion gift paired with strong telepathy. Her specialization was an inbuilt ability to smash shields. She'd been signed over to the Arrow squad at age three, after she smashed her father's shields, causing brain damage so severe it had left him with a permanently paralyzed left side.

The experience had traumatized her, according to the PsyMed report he'd accessed, and she'd been a docile trainee from the start. It was noted in her training files that while she was an excellent soldier who would always follow orders, she did not do well on solo tasks.

Not suitable for command, had been the final determination.

In other words, she was a beautifully submissive personality, he thought, running his finger over her image.

Of average height, she had pale white skin over a fine-boned frame and eyes of brown. Her light brown hair she kept cropped tight to her skull. It gave her an appearance of waiflike youth. That could be very useful in gaining the trust of his targets.

She also had no special commendations on her file, no extra notes from instructors at all. Every other possibility he'd considered had at least one. Someone had taken notice of a special ability or an exemplary skill, or a negative aspect.

No one noticed Beatrice.

She did what she was supposed to do, she followed the rules, and when she went to bed, no one thought about her. He had run an experiment, casually mentioning Beatrice to two Arrows he knew had helped with her training. He'd said it was part of an evaluation to see if she was suitable for a live mission. Neither trainer had remembered her until he'd shown them her photo and file.

Even after that, they'd simply referred to their notes.

Beatrice was invisible. Her family had cut her off, and while the squad had taken her in, she was simply one cog in a machine. Having watched her, he knew she spent no extra time with any of her fellow trainees, had no one who might be considered a confidant or a friend.

He would become that person for her. It wouldn't take long. He'd studied psychology in an academic way in order to classify himself, so he knew she was a dependent personality who hadn't yet found a dominant to whom to give her absolute trust.

Aden didn't know about her. No one knew about her. She was perfect.

Chapter 34

AN HOUR AFTER his initial conversation with Walker, Aden called Vasic, Zaira, Cristabel, and Axl to a meeting around a table at Central Command, along with Amin and teleki-netic Nerida. He'd also asked Walker and Judd to attend. Judd had always known about Central Command, had kept their secret, and Walker had earned the loyalty of far more Arrows than Aden, his care of them as children something none who'd been in his classes had ever forgotten.

Judd and Walker were also the experts in Arrow integra-tion into a changeling pack—into a family akin to the kind of family Aden wanted to build from the cold ruins Ming and the Council had made of them.

He'd decided to leave Marjorie and Naoshi out of the dis-cussion until they had the basics hammered out—his parents weren't the best people to have in the room while discussing such a massive shift in Arrow life. He had, however, touched base with them and had their cautious agreement to the new senior Arrow-related duties he'd suggested.

Now, the others around the table listened to his proposal, took their time thinking about it.

Walker was the first to speak. "I don't agree with moving the children here."

Aden looked up. "Why? Central Command is safer than any other location." The fact that Arrow children had historically been taught and housed away from it was linked to their inability to keep the location a secret. Aden, however, wasn't concerned about that, not given the airtight security around Central Command.

"I'm not saying Central Command can't continue to exist," Walker said, "but it should function as the armored heart of a pack. A place where you can retreat to if necessary, hold off your enemies. There's no reason to live your life in a subterranean space."

Unexpectedly, it was forty-three-year-old Axl who said, "He's right." Eyes of deep blue met Aden's. "I don't know emotion, but I know that if you want plants to grow, you need light. Even the wolves from whom we acquired the artificial sunlight technology don't spend the majority of their time in their dens—their children grow up under the rays of a real sun, feel the chill of natural air."

Cris, who'd fully recovered from a recent gunshot injury, brought up a map on the table, tapped at the valley in which the training compound was located. Unlike when Aden, Zaira, and the other Arrows here had been children, all training was now centralized. The other facilities around the world had either been shut down or turned into bases of operations.

It was one of the few decisions made by Ming with which Aden agreed. Ming had done it because the children received far more one-on-one lessons with different active Arrows this way, and there were never days in which no one was available to take a session—meaning no days were "wasted."

Aden liked it because it meant the children had more of a chance to form long-term friendships. There was no risk they'd be separated, as he'd been separated from Zaira. She'd been so furiously angry with him for leaving her, but she'd come to see him one last time regardless. Forced to stay in strict position while waiting for his transport, he'd seen her hiding around the corner of a building, dark eyes flashing fire at him and a heavy scowl on her face.

"The squad owns acres and acres of land around the entire compound." Cris's clear voice broke into his memories, drew his attention to the map, though he already knew the location inside out. The squad's ownership spanned the entire valley and the jagged snowcapped mountains that bordered it on either end. Those mountains curved in on both sides, creating a natural barrier against any force on foot.

It was part of the reason Zaid Adelaja, the first Arrow, had chosen the location for the first training compound. As a result of over a century of quiet moves by the squad to gain control of all land in the vicinity, there were no other structures, roads, or even comm beacons for fifty miles in every direction beyond the mountains.

"I assume the evacuation protocols are up-to-date?" Judd asked while Walker scrolled through the valley specs.

Nerida was the one who replied. The Tk had previously assisted with valley security, but Aden had recently promoted her to the primary position, her predecessor having asked to retire to a quiet place in the sun. "We can clear the children within an hour of any threat notification," she said. "And the entire area is seeded with surface-to-air missiles and other security measures."

"It won't be enough if we intend to use the valley as our home base," Zaira said bluntly from her position directly across from Aden. "We may want to build a family, but if and when the information leaks, others will see it as a threat or a target."

It was an important point. No matter how much help Arrows had provided to the general population over the past months, they remained some of the most dangerous and feared individuals in the world. And fear could often turn people malicious as they sought to wipe out the cause of their fear. Aden was working on changing the world's perception of the squad but it would take time—and regardless, they would always protect their children.

After a short discussion, Nerida and Axl took charge of coming up with a new and even more aggressive security protocol.

Aden, meanwhile, would handle telling the children what was to happen, how their living arrangements would change. No longer would they be in antiseptic dorms—all children were to be assigned to a family unit headed by two Arrows, though, as per Walker's advice, the latter was to be a slow process. Under the plan, senior Arrows were to be treated as "uncles" and "aunts" with peripheral duties, rather than being in primary charge of the children, *unless* they requested otherwise and were judged ready for deeper contact and responsibility.

Vasic would start to connect with the youngest children, the ones who were least in control of their abilities but far more in touch with their emotions. His task was to be their point of contact, the one person they could go to without hesitation.

I'm not sure about this, Aden, the other man said.

I am. Vasic was one of the gentlest Arrows Aden knew, and he understood the vulnerable. He'd know how to calm their fears. *Bring Rabbit. Your pet is a better icebreaker than any words you could say.*

As for Walker, he and Cris would work together to assign compatible children and Arrows to one another, while Judd picked up most of Walker's duties back in SnowDancer. Zaira was to provide assistance where needed, including liaising with "damaged" or recently retired Arrows in Venice and elsewhere around the world who might want to relocate to the valley as teachers or to build families. While a number were dangerous and unstable, many were just worn out, might well thrive in this new environment where they weren't expected to be perfect soldiers.

The final member of the team, Amin, was placed in charge of organizing the new living spaces.

"The construction of the family units should be done by Arrows," Nerida pointed out. "It's the only way we can maintain security."

Amin shook his head, the dark, dark brown of his skin gleaming in the light. "We don't have the expertise."

"Amin's right," Aden said, fully aware of his people and their capabilities. "We were only able to build the extension to Vasic and Ivy's home because her father and several other community members oversaw the project."

"DarkRiver is in construction." Judd's voice. "I know you won't want an entire team in the valley, but they can construct the buildings elsewhere and Vasic, I, and the other teleporters can bring them in. Only the foundations would have to be laid."

"We should agree on the most efficient parameters for the houses," Amin began.

"They shouldn't all be identical and starkly functional," Walker interrupted. "Neither should you set them out in military-precise rows."

Nerida was the one who voiced the critical question. "Why?"

"Because you don't want the valley to look institutional." Walker's pale green eyes held each of theirs in turn. "You're creating a permanent home."

And a home, Aden thought, didn't need to be only efficient. He glanced at Amin. "We can ask DarkRiver's architects to personalize the homes in different ways." They were much better qualified for the task. "Focus on making sure we'll have the flexibility to accommodate diverse types of family groups—including those families that want to live together with others."

Getting Amin's nod, he turned to Vasic and Judd. "I need you two to speak to the other teleporters, make sure we have the capacity for the transfer."

"It will have to be done in pieces," Vasic said. "But we should be able to put the pieces together as long as Dark-River is willing to give us instructions."

Judd turned to Vasic. "I can't see them saying no. It's not like the squad's planning to go into construction."

"No." Arrows had other skills, skills that had a multitude of uses—and they didn't all have to do with death, not under Aden's watch.

"There's also Kaleb," Cris said, her next words as pragmatic as the neat little ponytail in which she usually wore her dark brown hair—and the lack of flash with which she handled a sniper rifle. "No point keeping him out since we all know he can go anywhere he wants."

Aden still wasn't sure about trusting the cardinal Tk, but Cris was right. They might as well use his abilities should he agree to assist. "Vasic—you or Judd touch base with Kaleb. Amin and I will speak to the DarkRiver alpha about the construction."

The rest of the meeting was taken up with the finer details of what would be a seismic shift in Arrow lives. *Zaira,* he said when she would've left with the others, *I need to speak to you.*

I've been away from Venice too long. Alejandro is unstable. Shifting her attention to Vasic, she asked the teleporter if he could give her a lift, was gone a second later.

Aden didn't stop her. If Zaira didn't want to do something, she wouldn't do it. She had to choose to come to him.

ZAIRA arrived in Venice knowing she was running away. "Thank you," she said to Vasic. "I believe Marjorie wanted to speak to you. Do you have a few minutes?"

At Vasic's nod, she directed him to Marjorie's location, then headed out to check on Alejandro. He wasn't in the compound, but, aware he didn't like to wander far, she did a sweep and found him standing beside a nearby canal. He wasn't alone.

A large man was gesticulating and poking Alejandro. That could've been lethal for the man in question if Zaira hadn't given Alejandro an order not to attack civilians who weren't a deadly threat. Because though his brain was damaged in certain ways, Alejandro retained all his offensive and defensive skills. He could kill most untrained individuals in a matter of seconds. As she came closer, she heard what the man was saying.

"I've seen you lumbering around. You're a big dumb lunk, aren't you?" Spittle flew out of the stranger's mouth, cruel laughter on his face. "You got any fucking brains at all?" The man continued to poke at Alejandro. "I told you this area is ours. No Psy scum allowed. Get lost or I'll show you the sharp end of my favorite knife."

Zaira could've ignored the insult to Psy, but never to one of her people. Especially not to someone who was deeply vulnerable on a level this bully of a man couldn't understand. Normally, she'd have threatened the man into retreat. Today, so soon after her disconnection from the Net, the rage not yet trapped in the abyss where it lived, the switch in her brain, the one that had been thrown when she was a child, it flipped again.

She saw her hand punch out, hit the male in the nose. That took considerable control—she could've killed him with a single hit. Instead, she just punched him again and swept his legs out from under him. Blood flew and he was on the ground, his bulk no defense against a fully trained Arrow.

No defense at all against Zaira in a rage.

At some point, her arm began to hurt and she was aware the man wasn't moving, but she couldn't stop. He'd belittled Alejandro, threatened to harm him in the future. Zaira had to put a stop to it right now. No one could be permitted to see her or her people as weak, because the weak got hurt and no one was ever again going to hurt her.

Zaira.

When Aden's voice sliced through her mind like a hot blade, she shrugged it off. He couldn't be here. She'd left him, left the man she wanted more than anything. But his strong hands were pulling her off her target, his hold not painful but resolute. She went to snap his wrist, couldn't make herself harm him. Changing direction, she twisted and kicked out in an effort to escape, get back to the man with a face smeared in red.

Arms clamping around her, Aden turned her forcefully away from the body. She caught a fleeting glimpse of another man. A tall one with winter gray eyes and dark hair. Some part of her said she knew who he was, but she couldn't process the thought right then, her mind hot red.

When the world shimmered around her, she screamed in untrammeled rage, conscious she was being teleported away. Then Aden was releasing her, the other man was gone, and they were alone in a moonlit desert, rolling sand dunes as far as the eye could see. Turning on Aden, she slammed herself into his body, taking him to the ground with her momentum. "He was mine!" she yelled, lifting her arm with the intent of plowing her bloodied and scraped fist into his face.

Instead of bringing up his forearm to block the blow, he placed his hands on her hips and just looked her in the eye, the quiet, intense power of him a hum in the air. She couldn't bring down her fist, couldn't complete the hit. Muscles straining as she held the position, she said, "I had him."

"Yes," Aden said, no horror in his tone. "Vasic tells me he's barely alive. He'll be in surgery for hours to reconstruct his face."

It felt as if her arm would break if she didn't bring it down.

Getting off this man she couldn't hurt, she rose to her feet, spun around to find something to fight, but everywhere she looked, there was only sand. It dissolved to nothing when she picked it up to throw, wasn't solid enough to pummel. Dropping to her knees, she screamed and screamed but the rage continued to boil in her until it consumed her, became her, became everything.

The arms that came around her were strong but didn't cage. Still she broke away, her hands gripping fistfuls of sand. The screams kept coming. They made her throat raw, stole the air in her lungs until there was no more sound and every muscle in her body ached, but the tension, it wouldn't leave her. She felt as if she'd shatter with a single wrong move, break apart from the fury inside her.

The madness had come.

ADEN tugged Zaira back against him when she went silent, a rigid figure on her knees in the sand. She didn't resist this time, but neither did she cooperate, her body stiff and her hands fisted. His own pulse was a drum, his fury for her a roar in his blood. "You're safe," he said, not sure what made him choose those words. "You're safe. I'm here."

Knowing the horrors of the mental landscape in which she might be trapped, he spoke to the nightmare. "You aren't locked in that cell anymore." Never again would anyone imprison her and he wouldn't allow the past to, either. "You live in the light."

She didn't respond, didn't say a word. It was as if she wasn't there anymore, as if she'd gone far away from this world where she'd been tortured and hurt and made to see herself as a monster.

No. "I won't let you go." He had no compunction in ripping his own shields wide open for her. "I need you."

Again, no verbal response, but when he eased her to the sand with him, she stretched out her legs. Keeping one arm under her neck and curving it around the front of her body, he put his other arm around her waist and held her tight against his own body so she'd remember this world, remember him. She was so still. Zaira was never still. There was too much fire inside her small form—and too much pain she'd never acknowledged.

It was pure chance he'd been there to stop her from killing the man who'd triggered her rage. Courtesy of Aden's mother making a request to speak to Aden, Vasic had just brought him in from Central Command when Alejandro had run into the compound. Aden had known immediately that something was seriously wrong even before Alejandro said, "Zaira isn't Zaira!"

The other man's words circled in Aden's skull now. Would the Zaira he knew come back to him? The Zaira who burned so bright even behind the strictures of Arrow discipline. The Zaira who saw parts of him no one else ever had. The Zaira who had always been his unspoken dream.

Or was she lost in a nightmare world formed of old horrors and older pain?

"Zaira," he said again, his breath making a curl at her ear waft gently before lying back down against her skin. "Stay here. Stay with me."

No answer.

Chapter 35

ADEN REFUSED TO give up. He couldn't, wouldn't take her back like this. Never would he put Zaira in a position where others might see her as weak or helpless.

He may as well carve out her heart.

"The first time Vasic teleported me to this desert," he said into the heartbreaking silence, "I didn't understand why he came to such places. All I saw was endless nothing." He slid one hand up and down her arm, wishing she wasn't in uniform, that he could touch her skin. "I think that was what Vasic saw at first, too. But by the time he brought me to it, he'd started to see how much existed here in the nothingness."

He pointed. "Look over there. See the grasses. I can't understand how they survive, much less the small insects you sometimes see. But there's life in this barren landscape and there's beauty." Taking a handful of sand, he allowed it to fall slowly through his fingers in front of her. "Even now, the moonlight hits the silica and the minerals within. In sunlight, it can be blinding, but I prefer it in the moonlight."

"I told you, you were never Silent." The words were a rasp of sound from a ravaged throat.

The hand crushing his own throat eased its grip. "That means I must be very, very good at shielding."

"Why won't you just admit I'm right? We both know it."

"Because then what would we argue about?" He closed both arms around her again, wanting to hold on forever—but Zaira couldn't be held. She'd have to come to him, have to choose him even after the horror and the nightmare and despite the very real fear that haunted her. He was selfish when it came to her, would ask it, but he'd never turn his back on her if she said no.

Zaira's name would always be written on his heart.

They lay there for a long time, watching the moon rise to its highest point over the sands, bathe them in silver. "Let me see your hands."

She lifted one, allowed him to cup it, examine the damage.

"You're badly bruised and cut up."

"I'll live." Dropping her hand back down, with his curled around it, she stared out at the moon, but her next words had nothing to do with the landscape. "They gave it names— antisocial personality disorder was one. I can't remember the others, but in the family, we always just referred to it as the madness. Like it was a sentient being out to hunt us."

"You're not mad."

"You can't make that true by saying it, Aden." Her head remained turned toward the moon, her profile fine and haunted by echoes of nightmare. "My family is one of those that was meant to be helped by Silence."

"Silence was flawed from the beginning."

"Yes." A deeper breath before she fell back into the quiet, shallow rhythm that barely seemed enough to keep her alive. "It clearly didn't restrain my parents, though it gave them the appearance of sanity. But it helped me."

"If I've never been Silent, then neither have you." Zaira's emotionless discipline wasn't something external that had been forced on her. It was an internal winter of the soul, one she'd chosen in childhood in order to survive.

Her hand moved under his as she flexed her fingers, fingers that had to be stiffening up. "I took pieces of Silence, used those pieces to build a cage to keep the rage and the insanity inside. The cage shattered in the RainFire aerie and I've been trying to rebuild it since. I'm failing."

Aden took the first clear breath he'd taken since leaving

RainFire. "You say you have the madness, but what I saw today was anger." He didn't know why she'd attacked the male but her raw fury had been unmistakable.

"I was totally out of control." Stark words. "If you hadn't pulled me off that man, I would've killed him."

"And if you didn't have anger inside you, you'd be in-human." He thought of the classified recordings he'd seen, recordings made by her family during her punishments for purposes of "monitoring the progress of the education pro-gram." It had been sadism, pure and simple. It was her father who was a Neve, but he'd clearly found his perfect partner in Zaira's mother. The two had enjoyed watching Zaira suffer. And she had suffered.

A small girl, fine boned and with dark eyes, dark hair, trying futilely to protect herself against belts and canes and whips.

In the later recordings, she'd simply curled into herself like a turtle inside its shell, taking the blows on her back and arms and legs. Until they'd forced her hands up above her head and beaten and beaten her as she spun suspended from a hook in the ceiling. Her blood had soaked her shift, splat-tered the walls.

And Aden, for the first time in his life, had understood rage. Even then, believing himself Silent, he'd understood rage. He'd been glad her parents were dead, that she'd beaten them to a pulp. If she hadn't, he would've gone out that day and done it himself. As it was, he had gone out and made sure no other Neve child was in the same situation. The warning he'd left for those who might attempt such horror in the future had stained the air with sick fear.

"Your anger is honest. It's real." He had to make her understand that it wasn't her fury at fault; it was her refusal to accept it. "Ivy says that the things we hold inside, the nightmares we stifle, have far more power than the things we expose to the light of day." He hadn't betrayed Zaira's trust by asking specifically about her, the question a general one, but he thought Ivy knew. She was an empath—she saw into hearts, even ones stunted from years of deprivation. "Accept your anger, Zaira, and you'll strip it of its power."

Zaira was quiet for a long time. "I don't believe you."

Aden realized at that instant that Zaira would believe his words only when he proved them true, and the only way he could prove them true was if she didn't retreat, as he could already feel her doing. "Don't go."

"I can't leave this desert until Vasic returns—though I will try to walk out eventually."

"Will you face me?"

Not an immediate response, but she did eventually turn.

"Don't go," he said again, bringing his hand up to lie against her face. "Don't step back from the world again. Don't leave me alone."

Dark eyes that hid so much. "I'll give my life for you." Fingers pressing to his lips when he would've spoken. "This is my peace." Her breath brushed his skin, so warm and alive even when she was shutting down in front of his eyes. "Let me live it. Let me be as normal as I can be."

Aden had spent his life fighting. For his Arrows, for the Net, for a better future . . . and for Zaira. He could've done so forever, but right then, he realized he couldn't when his battle would be at the expense of her sanity and her peace. He would not make her feel hounded, would not make her feel as if she wasn't good enough, as if she was too broken for him.

He would take her exactly as she was, because one thing was true, would always be true: "I'm yours." It was his turn to stop her words. "Just stay with me," he said. "In any way you want."

"You deserve better." Rough, broken words.

"There's no one better than you."

"I'll be the best soldier you ever have," she repeated in a shattered whisper.

"I know." It would have to be enough.

Chapter 36

BLAKE HAD BEGUN to "court" Beatrice. He'd started quietly by calling her into his office and commending her on her performance during a weapons drill. The truth was that she'd been average—not good, not bad. Acceptable. He'd praised her nevertheless and he thought he might have been the first person ever to do so.

The following day, he'd attended her hand-to-hand combat session, and spent time with her afterward, offering her personal tutelage. They'd spent two hours alone in an outdoor training area, and he'd been careful to encourage her, mimicking things he so often heard Cris saying to her students. The need for such approval was a weakness, but he'd chosen Beatrice because she was weak.

First he had to build her up, make her look to him for approval . . . then he had to break her down so she stopped thinking for herself and became his creature. That was why he'd berated her for a mistake toward the end of a session, after making sure he'd been nothing but encouraging and complimentary to that point. She'd all but crumpled inward. When he'd told her it was all right, that she could learn to correct her error, she'd agreed to another hour of instruction.

It wouldn't take long to break her to his will; she was already isolated and submissive, and he'd quickly become her "friend." He'd kill her without hesitation if she proved a mistake, but he didn't think it would come to that. Beatrice was hungry for approval, for attention. If she hadn't been such a well-behaved Arrow trainee, the trainers would've realized that she was fundamentally unsuited to the squad.

Then again, perhaps not. Beatrice needed to cling to something and the squad had given her the chance. He'd simply give her a far more individual opportunity. Once she was his, once she'd made the first cut, there'd be no going back. Satisfied with her progress to date, he was in the right frame of mind to receive a call from the individual who'd been so encouraging of his tendencies.

"Anyone in particular you'd like me to kill?" He knew the support he was receiving had to have a political motive, but it was working in his favor so he had no argument. "An intransigent business associate, perhaps."

"No. We can't be connected on any level." The speaker's voice was made unrecognizable by what had to be a simple scrambling program on their end. "I reached out to you because I don't agree with the direction the Net and, it appears, the Arrows are taking."

"Out of the goodness of your heart?" he said, pointedly using a human expression. "I'm touched. I was under the impression it had to do with undermining the fall of Silence." It had taken him time, but he was positive he knew the identity of his supporter—it had been a slipup during their last conversation that had given him the first clue and he'd taken that and dug.

He might be a psychopath but he was also a damn good Arrow.

"If that is my motive?"

"Silence or not, I have the same playground." The only difference was that now, his psychopathy would be considered an aberration; under Silence, his lack of empathy had been a coveted state of being.

Chapter 37

TWO DAYS AFTER her descent into unthinking and violent rage and Zaira could still feel the imprint of Aden's hand on her cheek, feel the warmth of it, the weight of it. She'd never seen him do that with any other Arrow, male or female, never seen him do that with anyone but her. She had, however, seen Vasic do it with Ivy Jane, and vice versa.

It was a touch of affection.

No one else had ever touched her in affection. "I told him he wasn't Silent," she muttered under her breath as she pulled her hair back into a neat knot at her nape.

She was dressing so formally because Aden had taken her at her word. If all she could be was a soldier, then he wanted that soldier beside him, wanted the squad to see a functioning pair at the top of their hierarchy, not simply a lone Arrow. Zaira knew he needed someone better but she couldn't walk away, her possessiveness toward him a deep pulse even below her shield of discipline.

Sealing the angular panel of her black coat, she walked out of her room in Venice and found Abbot waiting for her. The young Tk soon had her at Central Command.

"Abbot," she said before he could leave, "your relationship with your E—is it difficult, given your training?"

Abbot didn't shy at the personal question. "It was when we first met," he said. "But Jaya is an empath."

Zaira nodded, because what else was there to say? Empaths healed souls, healed hearts, even the most damaged and broken, and Abbot's E was more like Ivy Jane than the more delicate complement. Jaya had grit enough to love an Arrow.

"Thank you," she said to him.

Abbot left without further words, but she stayed in place in the underground green space where she'd asked him to bring her. An E would be perfect for Aden. Like Ivy, she would bring warmth and love into the lives of Aden's squad.

It *should* have been a halcyon image, but it didn't fit.

An E couldn't shield Aden, couldn't protect him from himself, couldn't physically take him down and tie him up so he'd rest. Aden would end up being the E's shield. He didn't need that added task.

What he needed, she thought as she walked into Central Command, was someone exactly like Zaira, only a little more sane. And there he was, speaking to Blake Stratton, an Arrow Zaira made it a point to avoid.

He makes my skin crawl.

Ivy had confessed that to her after Blake visited Ivy and Vasic's home. The E had felt guilty about her response because she'd vowed to welcome all Arrows, even the ones with terrible things in their past, but Zaira had told her her instincts were correct.

Blake was the worst type of Arrow, a man who actively sought blood and death. Zaira wasn't sure he'd make it under Aden's leadership, but she knew it was important to Aden to give every Arrow a chance. None of them were innocent, many scarred right down to the soul.

We all start with a clean slate today, he'd said in his squadwide briefing after officially dethroning Ming. *Whatever you were coerced into doing, or ordered to do, under our previous leadership lies in the past. You have the power to write your future.*

Zaira figured she had to give Blake that same chance, but it didn't mean she had to go near him. Standing back, she focused on Aden. As she'd expected, he was wearing a uniform identical to hers.

That wasn't right.

He might want the squad to see them as a functioning

pair, but at present, especially to the outside world, he was their leader, and the other races appreciated symbolism.

Catching Vasic's eye as soon as the teleporter walked into the large common area, she made telepathic contact. *I'd like to show you something.*

When he came over to join her by the glass wall that overlooked the underground green space, she showed him what she had in her hand. "What do you think of this?"

She'd never been friends with Vasic and she knew the distance came from her possessiveness toward Aden, but she respected him without question, would trust him at her back at any time—and he knew Aden as well as she did. He was also protective of Aden, and for that alone, she'd fought her primitive response and worked with him. Now he belonged to Ivy and was no threat to Zaira's need for Aden.

"Yes, you're right," Vasic said, his eyes on what lay on her palm. "It's exactly what he needs." Winter-frost eyes met her own. "How did you know to have it?"

"I had it made by a jeweler five years ago." She stared at the piece. "I don't know why. It made no sense then."

Vasic didn't push, didn't make her confront the fact that she'd had it created for Aden, because he was the only one who could ever wear it. Instead he said, "We both want the best for him."

Curling her fingers over her palm, she nodded. "He needs a keeper at times."

"He won't agree, but you're right." The teleporter's eyes went to the man they had in common. "We'll achieve more if we work together."

Zaira slanted him a glance. "You know I don't share well." She could say that to Vasic because he'd seen her as a violent, feral child, knew the primal base of her personality.

The winter frost glittered, but not with cold. "My mate tells me love is infinite. That Aden is my blood brother steals nothing from the fact that Ivy is my heart."

"I don't have that generosity of soul." She'd never learned it, knew only how to hold on jealously tight so that the things that mattered wouldn't be taken from her.

"Of course you do," Vasic said. "Alejandro is just one example of it. There is a reason every Arrow in Venice, even the most recalcitrant senior, would die for you." He left before she could reply, walking past Aden with a quiet word as Aden headed toward Zaira.

How's Blake? she asked, not lowering her guard until the other Arrow was out of the room.

Aden's expression gave nothing away but his mental voice was more open. *It's too soon to tell. He says all the right things, but it's impossible to know if he means any of it.*

The perfect Arrow demeanor, Zaira thought, could also be used as a wall behind which to hide. *You should put a watch on him.*

Amin keeps a subtle eye on him and he's noticed no outwardly aberrant behavior.

They both knew Blake was a good enough Arrow to fake compliance and discipline, but Zaira also understood that so was she; if she couldn't accept Blake being given a chance to redeem himself, then she couldn't accept that chance, either. It wasn't as if she had no blood on her hands.

"Ready?" Aden said aloud as he came to stand with his boots an inch from hers.

"No." Lifting her hands, she pinned the brooch she held to where the point of his jacket's angular front panel met his right shoulder. An arrow made of a titanium base, it had multiple black diamonds set into the bottom of the fletching.

The black gems were followed by blood-dark rubies, midnight sapphires, night green emeralds, and other dark gemstones, all the way back to black diamonds at the tip again. Look at it straight-on and the arrow appeared pure black, but that changed as soon as the light hit it. Then the colors could be seen in the black . . . as Aden had always seen beauty in her darkness, hope in every Arrow's soul.

Stepping back, her heart thunder, she said, "Now we're ready."

"Arrows don't stand out," he said, but he didn't remove the jeweled pin.

"You should." This was the first time they'd appear in public devoid of Kaleb Krychek's silver star. While the squad remained allied with the cardinal, they were no longer accepting any leadership but that from within their own ranks. "You're our public face."

He touched the arrow with careful fingertips. "Thank you. No one has ever given me anything so unique and beautiful."

His deep, quiet pleasure threatened to shatter the cage all over again. *Don't lose it,* she ordered brusquely. *It's one of a kind. Like you.*

And you, Zaira. Aden didn't close the final inches between them, but she felt as if he was touching her, holding her in place with the sheer, visceral power of his presence. *There is no one like you.*

He was right: she was a unique individual. But she was simply a person. Aden was something far bigger. He might not see it, but they all did. *Let's go.*

Moving as one to Vasic, the Tk having returned to the room after pulling on his own formal coat, they took position on either side of him.

He teleported them to the door outside the meeting room. "I'll be here during the meeting," Vasic said to them both. "I can get you out in a split second."

They all knew that if it came down to that, things would be beyond repair.

Heading inside without further words, Aden and Zaira took their places at the table. Kaleb Krychek was positioned next to Aden, while Nikita Duncan and Anthony Kyriakus sat across the table. Ivy Jane arrived seconds afterward, Vasic having brought in his mate last, so she'd have the protection of three Arrows.

She sat down beside Anthony.

"We all know why we're here," Nikita said as soon as Ivy was in her seat. "The interim Coalition has functioned as it should, but the attack on the Arrows makes it clear we need to show a stronger hand."

Krychek leaned back in his chair. "I won't allow a return to what the Council once was, Nikita." Ice-cold words.

Nikita didn't back down, the sharply cut edge of her glossy black hair swinging against the porcelain skin of her cheek as she spoke. "I understand we're to allow dissent in order to leach off tension in the populace, but it's gone too far if whoever took Aden and Zaira believes us vulnerable."

"I don't agree with Nikita," Anthony said, the two of them not looking at one another though they sat side by side. "But she's right in one sense. We are still seen as interim and that equals fragile and impeachable in certain minds. We have to nip that in the bud before it starts to make our task difficult—Pax Marshall is already making noises about having to comply with our mandates."

"Wait," Ivy said. "Pax is a businessman, right? Young, too."

"Twenty-four," Nikita supplied. "And he's taken control of the entire Marshall Group. He's ruthless and if we don't get him under control, he'll keep pushing."

Zaira touched Aden's mind. *Want me to disappear him down a dark hole?* She knew Aden had already had one run-in with Pax when Aden had warned the other man off attempting to recruit children who needed the training provided by the squad.

No. We don't execute people for being an aggravation.

Are you sure Krychek knows that? Zaira had the sense Kaleb thought more like her than like Aden.

Aden's eyes flicked to Kaleb. As if guessing the content of their telepathic discussion, the cardinal telepathed both of them. *Killing Pax would be an inconvenience. He's dangerous but he's also the most rational member of the family group—and as I said, we will not become the old Council.*

"Pax isn't the only one," Nikita said. "Jen Liu is making similar noises and the Chastains tend to follow where Liu leads."

Aden spoke aloud. "Regardless, the Arrows stand with Krychek—we don't wish to resurrect the old Council."

Ivy Jane leaned forward, her copper-colored eyes intent. "The fact is, the Net no longer supports the way previous Councils worked, even pre-Silence."

"Pre-Silence?" Nikita turned toward the younger woman. "They worked by consensus much of the time—the decision to undertake Silence took over a decade. Isn't that what you're proposing?"

Arms braced on the table, Ivy shook her head. "We can't afford to spend all that time in discussion. Not now, with the Net so fragile. We need strong decision-making—but we also need checks and balances." She held Nikita's gaze, her own unflinching. "The previous Councilors spent their time building their own wealth and power on the backs of the people they were supposed to rule. You can't do that anymore."

Nikita didn't back down. "Are you suggesting I become an altruist?"

"No, Nikita. I'm suggesting you decide whether you want to become a true leader, or if you want to be a politician."

That, I didn't expect, Zaira telepathed to Aden. *Ivy is so inherently gentle and yet she's going toe-to-toe with one of the most dangerous women in the Net.*

Yes, but Ivy is a leader now, too.

Of the empaths, hundreds of thousands of them. Key linchpins in holding the PsyNet together. *She knows how much power she holds,* Zaira said in approval. *I simply never expected to see her wield it.*

A telepathic knock on Zaira's mind at that instant. It was Ivy, her psychic presence as gentle as her physical one.

You two are going to back me, right?

Of course, Aden replied, as Zaira did the same. *The Es and the Arrows are a unit.*

Great, because Sascha's mom is one scary woman.

Even as she said that, Ivy was continuing to hold the eye contact with Nikita. Who finally said, "Issues of terminology aside, I have no desire to roll the Net back in time."

She loves Sascha, you know.

Zaira couldn't think of anything less apt to be true. *Nikita doesn't understand emotion any more than I do.*

I think you understand far more than you know—and so does she. Try to attack Sascha. You'll be dead before the day is out.

That's not love. It's protecting the family genetic legacy.

You're arguing emotion with an empath, Zaira. You know I'm going to win.

Emotion can blind.

Ivy's lips twitched, but she didn't reply, her attention on Nikita.

"Strength," Nikita said to the table at large, "doesn't have to be aggressive. It's about perception." An expressionless face, her grooming without flaw, and no sense of heart or emotion in her voice or gaze. "I might not be a leader but I *am* the best politician at this table, and I tell you that politics can win wars and this is a war."

Cardinal eyes unreadable, Kaleb said, "One thing the Net understands is power." His voice vibrated with it. "We do the broadcast."

"Anthony speaks," Aden said.

Nikita's response was surprising. "Agreed. Anthony is seen as the most . . . human. Having him appear to be leading the new Coalition will calm those who believe Krychek to be a dictator, while seeing the rest of us with Anthony will satisfy those who want to believe the old Council is as it was."

"I'll announce that the Coalition is now a permanent unit," Anthony said, the streaks of silver at the temples of his otherwise black hair giving him a distinguished air. "The addition of the empaths was the final step."

"I think we need someone else at the table," Ivy said unexpectedly. "Ida Mill."

"You want to bring the enemy to the table?" Krychek asked with a raised eyebrow. "Ida leads the anti-E brigade."

"Trouble happens when people don't believe they have a voice."

"Ida isn't ready to be convinced even by the clearest evidence," Kaleb responded, his tone hard. "She's a bigot who'll foster dissonance with her public disagreement with Coalition decisions."

Ivy looked troubled but nodded. "We can't afford that right now. But I still think the pro-Silence camp needs to feel like they have a real voice."

They didn't come to an agreement on that point, but all six of them stood side by side as they made the transmission through media channels and on the PsyNet declaring that, from this point on, the Ruling Coalition was no longer an interim agency but a permanent one. The membership was to remain stable until circumstances dictated the need for change.

Without being heavy-handed, Anthony made it clear that with Krychek, the Es, and the Arrows, as well as the F-Psy Anthony brought with him and the sprawling financial network controlled by Nikita, the Coalition was more than powerful enough to ensure its mandates were followed. He made no threats, spoke of no retaliation, but the message was crystal clear: the Ruling Coalition would permit dissent, but it would not allow anyone to destroy the hard-won stability of the Net.

Chapter 38

AFTER ALL THE work done to put their plans in place, this show of unrivaled strength was the last thing the group needed. Switching off the feed, the leader of the group—no matter if the others believed themselves equal—sent out a request for an urgent meeting.

Net stability could not be permitted to take root.

Chapter 39

THE SECTIONS FOR the first of the new buildings in the valley arrived faster than Zaira had expected and were put together at speed. The DarkRiver changelings had shared their expertise with a generosity Zaira wouldn't have understood if she hadn't spent that time in RainFire. It was about the children.

Changeling young were the packs' greatest weakness.

Yet Zaira knew she'd never use that knowledge to harm them. They were allies and they were becoming friends. Remi and Aden, in particular, had kept the lines of communication open.

"He says we're in remedial alpha school," Aden had told her a week earlier. "It's good to speak with someone who's facing many of the same challenges, though it may not appear that way on the surface."

The sane part of Zaira was glad for him that he was building another friendship, but the rage part of her was jealous as always . . . because she missed him. He had so many calls on his time, and though she was now his partner in this new life he wanted for the squad, it felt as if she'd barely seen him since the meeting ten days ago. And the aloneness, it was nibbling at her again though she was in the Net. This time, it wasn't isolation that haunted her; it was going to bed without Aden by her side. Her body had learned to crave him even after so short a time together.

Her hands curled into fists as she stood on a cliff that overlooked the valley lit by the orange-gold rays of the late afternoon sun, memories of her screaming madness in the desert a piercing echo that reverberated in her skull.

That's who I become when I step outside the box.

Accept your anger, Zaira, and you'll strip it of its power.

A crackle sounded from behind her, small feet crushing fallen leaves.

"You're not permitted up here," she said to the child who stood a short distance away.

The solemn boy with creamy skin pinked by time in the sun, his sandy brown hair neatly combed, and his uniform spotless, stayed in place.

"What's your name?"

"Tavish."

"How did you get up here?" It was a difficult hike even for an adult.

In answer, the boy raised a leaf off the ground without touching it. So, he was a telekinetic with teleportation abilities. No doubt he'd broken the psychic leash on those abilities, at least on some level, if he was here. While Zaira abhorred cages, she'd been forced to accept that some were an unfortunate necessity. Children didn't always understand why they shouldn't 'port somewhere.

And it wasn't always about making a fatal technical error and finding yourself in the middle of a city street in front of traffic that couldn't slow down in time or ending up buried in a house that had been crushed by an avalanche but still functioned as a visual lock. When Zaira was twelve, a boy Tavish's age had broken free and 'ported to his family home. He was shot dead by his much older brother, a telepath who'd barely survived the last time the Tk lost hold of his abilities.

After being in RainFire, being so close to the fragile forms of children, holding Jojo in her arms and feeling her small arms wrap around her, Zaira couldn't understand how an adult could so coldly execute a child, or how her own parents could've treated her with such brutality. It made her question if she had in fact inherited the madness as she'd always believed; if she had, wouldn't she be as cruel?

"Come here."

"I broke the rules," Tavish said after reaching her. "I'll be punished."

The words crashed into another memory.

No biting. Bad Jojo.

The little girl had displayed dejection at the memory of misbehavior, but her body and face had held none of the stoic endurance Zaira saw in Tavish. "You did break the rules," she said. "Explain to me why."

The child bit down on his wobbly lower lip, his Silence clearly imperfect despite his attitude. "You want to know why?"

"Yes. Why did you come up here when you know it's out of bounds?"

His eyes flickered, frown lines forming between them. "I wanted to see the houses from here. Aden told us we're going to live in them."

"Come stand next to me."

His steps were hesitant, his shoulders hunched in. Yet he came, though he could've 'ported away. Zaira didn't like that indication of how his spirit had already been so crushed, but those wounds would take time to heal. And they would, she vowed. Tavish and the other children had a chance, had hope.

Thinking of how her body, her spirit, had soaked in Aden's touch, how little Jojo had flowered under affectionate contact, she put a hand on Tavish's shoulder. He flinched and her rage at what had been done to him was a violent roar in her skull. Holding it inside because Tavish didn't need more violence, she pointed out the layout of the homes being built, how they connected to one another via the pathways being laid even now, and how the central area was to be left open as a gathering point.

There were no military straight rows, the houses set in small groupings instead, the pathways between them curving lines.

"No final decisions have been made on the individual elements in the communal space," she said, "but there will be a playground, along with trees to climb and provide shade."

Tavish's face lit from within before he shot her a scared look and stifled his innocent joy.

Zaira realized at that instant that she hated seeing fear on a child's face when he looked at her. How had her parents not felt the same?

"You must have control because you are a Tk," she said with a conscious effort at gentleness. As she could permanently damage or suffocate an opponent's brain, the harsh fact was that Tavish could break someone's spine with a thoughtless tantrum or an accidental slip.

His face fell, water gleaming in his eyes. "I know. My father said I was too dangerous to be around my sister." A hiccuping breath. "I didn't mean for the wood to hit her and hurt her. I was just practicing."

Zaira went down on her haunches. "I believe you," she said. "But I want to tell you that Aden has been speaking with Vasic, Abbot, and Judd." He'd also met with Stefan, a Tk who'd broken Silence not long after the first high-profile defections from the Net, but managed to keep it a secret. "They all say that control doesn't have to mean a complete lack of emotion. It means learning to be aware of the effect of strong emotions on your Tk so you can throttle it back before it slips the leash."

Seeing the wide-eyed and uncomprehending expression on Tavish's face, Zaira realized she was speaking at too high a level for his childish mind. She changed her approach, ran her hand over his hair. "It means you're allowed to be happy or excited." Allowed to be a child. "You must simply never forget your abilities—as a changeling cub can never forget his claws or teeth during play."

This time, the frown was deep. "I'll be punished for showing feelings."

"No, you won't." Never again would an Arrow child be hurt for simply being. "You will be punished for violating the boundaries, but only because those boundaries are there for your safety."

He flinched again, brownish hazel eyes stark and skin going white beneath his slight sunburn. "Oh."

And Zaira realized she had to answer Aden's question right now: How did you punish a psychically powerful child? Especially a child who, as yet, had no privileges in his life, and thus couldn't lose them? Yet to allow this infraction to go unpunished would set a bad precedent—Tavish needed these boundaries, needed rules to follow so he'd learn the necessary psychic and personal discipline.

It was the lack of such conscious discipline that had led to powerful Psy accidentally killing in the time prior to Silence. While the Protocol had been a mistake in many ways, in this the architects of Silence had been correct: psychic discipline *had* to be ingrained in childhood, until by the time the children reached adult age, they would temper their powers automatically.

Zaira had to get that across without further breaking this small boy's spirit.

"Your punishment is to be this," she said, knowing she was probably doing the wrong thing, but unwilling to leave him in painful suspense until someone better qualified had the time to handle the situation. "Go far enough back that you can no longer see the view, then sit down on the ground with your legs crossed."

Quickly accessing the boy's files by using the small organizer she had in her pocket, she saw he had consistently low grades in science subjects. "While you're sitting there, you have to write an extra paper on one of these three topics." She handed him the organizer to use, the three topics listed at the top of the open page. "I also want you to think about why you shouldn't have teleported out of bounds."

Giving her a dumbfounded look, Tavish bent his head to the organizer. It was a bare three minutes later that he looked up. "Can I ask a question?"

"Yes."

"Aren't you going to hurt me?"

The question made her rage roar red-hot. "The rules have altered," she said when she could breathe past it. "Pain isn't always the answer."

"Oh."

Fifteen minutes later, when Aden walked up to the clifftop and glanced at Tavish, who was frowning as he painstakingly wrote his essay, Zaira telepathed Aden an explanation of events. *Did I make a mistake?* Had she done damage when she wanted only to help?

No. Aden's gaze spoke to the seed of madness inside her, took away its loneliness. *You've given me the answer.*

I don't think extra homework is always going to work. It wouldn't have for me. At the start, she'd just have thrown down the organizer and stomped on it.

Aden came to stand beside her, the ankle-length leather coat he wore over a formal suit, blowing in the wind. *The answer is that each punishment must be tailored to the child. Tavish doesn't enjoy science and so it is a punishment. Another child may be changeling-like in enjoying outdoor exercise, so to be told to sit in a room inside during an exercise period will be sufficient. We're used to rules, but children aren't interchangeable and we can't treat them that way.*

Tavish looked up right then, saw Aden. His shoulders grew stiff, his Adam's apple bobbing as he swallowed. "I broke the rules," he confessed in a trembling whisper.

Aden crouched beside him. "I see Zaira has already meted out your penalty for that. Have you finished the paper?"

A shake of Tavish's head.

"You will." Pausing, Aden said, "Was the view worth the punishment?"

The boy took time to think about it before saying, "Yes. But only this time. I won't do it again."

"Good. Do you understand why we need to limit your teleportation right now?"

This time the nod was immediate. "I could go somewhere and not be able to get back. Or I could 'port myself off the cliff and not react fast enough to save my life."

"Then you understand."

As Zaira watched, Aden touched the back of the boy's head with a gentle strength that did things to her heart she didn't understand. "Finish your paper, so you can return to where you should be."

A tremulous hope in Tavish's expression, he bent his head to the organizer again.

ADEN and Zaira walked Tavish down together when he admitted he'd overstrained his psychic muscles and couldn't 'port back. The boy kept sending them furtive hazel-eyed glances from under his eyelashes, as if waiting for them to change their minds, but he didn't shake off Aden's hand when Aden ruffled his hair as they reached the compound.

"Go and get some more nutrition," Aden told the boy. "That trek and your 'port will have burned extra energy."

Tavish began to walk inside the training facility, stopped after only a few steps. It was obvious he was building his courage. Then he blurted out, "Do we really get to live in the houses?"

"Yes."

"You said we'd have families." A quaver in the question, the hope in Tavish's voice painful.

"Yes. Each child will be assigned to an adult Arrow or Arrows." Aden would slowly bring in non-Arrows to help balance the population, but the vetting process would take considerable time. At least one empath was already happy to settle in the valley—Abbot's Jaya. But as for the non-Es *and* those Es who didn't have such deep connections to the squad, none would be permitted in until they'd been cleared by both the squad's background checks and by an empathic panel.

Tavish's shoulders fell at Aden's answer. "Oh."

Not understanding the reason for his distress, Aden went across to him and, placing his hand on the boy's shoulder, crouched down in front of him again. "You don't wish to live with adult Arrows?"

"I'll follow the rules."

"Tavish." Aden put a hint of steel in his tone, aware from watching Remi that giving affection and protection was only one part of being alpha; the children also needed him to continue being the person who had the final word in any given situation. "You mustn't lie to me. Answer the question."

Muscles stiff under his hand, Tavish looked him in the eye and Aden saw the strength beneath the fear, knew this child hadn't been irrevocably broken. "The grown-ups hurt us."

Sensing Zaira going motionless beside him, Aden continued to maintain the eye contact. "The ones who hurt you won't be living with you." The known child-focused sadists in the squad had been erased from the world; Aden had never trusted them and he'd had no compunction in taking care of the matter himself.

Those men and women had been beyond redemption.

A few others, like Blake, were on probation because they'd never harmed a child, but had other dangerous and possibly indefensible tendencies. Some might even be murderous psychopaths, but Aden needed evidence before he made that call. If he acted without it, he'd be no better than Ming. Regardless, he'd permit no one on that list near the innocent.

The third group was the most problematic: good men and women who hadn't been strong enough to refuse to follow terrible orders. He had Ivy, Jaya, and his own senior people keeping a close watch on several, because now that Ming was gone and Silence had fallen, those men and women had begun to buckle under a crushing wave of guilt. Only two days earlier, Cris had stopped a suicide before it occurred and the Arrow in question was now in intensive counseling with an empath.

Tavish didn't need to know all of that. He needed to know only that he'd be safe.

"You'll be assigned to Arrows in the field." Arrows who, even if they'd taken a class or two, had never tortured or otherwise harmed the children. "Like me and Zaira and Vasic."

The boy's eyes grew bright. "Vasic? But he doesn't live here."

"Some children may train here and live elsewhere." Vasic's teleportation skills made location a nonissue and the security at the orchard was even more airtight now because of Ivy's position as president of the Empathic Collective. "Regardless, you're to live with those of us who do not hurt our children."

"But I'm not yours."

"Yes. You are."

Chapter 40

BEATRICE KNEW SHE wasn't a very good Arrow. She was just a disposable foot soldier, not one of the shining stars. She wasn't like Zaira, who was so strong and who needed no one. Beatrice fumbled things when she worked on her own; even her otherwise encouraging new trainer had made that clear.

"You're not skilled enough to work alone."

Those words had hurt her so much. She knew she wasn't supposed to have or to acknowledge emotions, but ever since the Honeycomb had come into effect, she'd found it near impossible to maintain the arctic calm within that was the Arrow way. No one had discovered her fractured Silence yet, but she was terrified she'd be disavowed when it happened.

Vasic and Abbot felt emotion, but they were important. The rules didn't apply to them. Ming had always said Beatrice and those like her had less value. He'd told her to her face that she should be ready to sacrifice herself if that sacrifice meant a more important Arrow would live.

Beatrice could do that, and even with her awakening emotions, she hadn't lost control of her abilities. Not even once. She'd been proud of that, so hearing Blake dismiss her competence as a solo operative had hurt even more. But then he'd said, "Partnerships can be valuable. You need a partner and I'm searching for one."

Never had she expected that such a senior, experienced Arrow would choose her for a partner. He'd even given her a choice. Of course she'd said yes. *No one* else had ever seen such potential in her.

Now she had to make sure she didn't screw up. She'd do everything he said, follow orders without hesitation. She'd be the perfect Arrow.

Chapter 41

THE DAY AFTER she'd met Tavish, Zaira put in time working on the construction in the valley. Venice was quiet at present and the Net in general had stabilized after recent disruptions. Much as it pained Zaira to admit it, Nikita had been right to insist on the public statement by the Ruling Coalition.

As for the hunt for the people behind Aden's and Zaira's abductions, that continued unabated. Both of them were in direct touch with the team tasked with following all possible leads, including those via property records. It turned out the bunker land was owned by a shell company that was owned by a shell company ad nauseam.

The final ownership led back to a five-year-old child who'd died fifty years earlier; but no Arrow had ever let a dead end stop him or her, and the hunt continued. Zaira didn't interfere with the investigation, aware she wasn't the best person to handle this kind of a back-end track—she did better with a physical target.

Instead, as she worked in the valley, she plotted how to get Aden to take a break from his duties as leader. He needed time to just be Aden, she thought . . . and remembered how he'd been in the bed in the aerie. He'd definitely not been thinking about his responsibilities then. The primal part of her stretched out at the memory of his arousal, at the remembered sensation of his hand clenching in her hair, and of how he'd felt so hard and hot under her.

Breasts swelling tight against her bra and pulse racing, Zaira could feel the rage that wasn't rage around Aden rising to the surface. Even two days earlier, she'd have fought to stifle it, but that was before she'd met Tavish, before she'd begun to question whether she had in fact inherited the madness, rather than simply being driven by a justified anger. If it was the latter, then there was the possibility she could leash her violent possessiveness and have the man who currently worked in her line of sight.

At some point during the past hour, several of the males had stripped off their T-shirts, sweat dripping down their backs. All were in Arrow shape, their bodies strong, but Zaira noticed only Aden. Sleek and muscled and beautiful as he maneuvered a heavy piece into place, she wanted to pet him.

His eyes caught hers as the thought passed through her head, and for an instant he looked incredibly young, the words he telepathed to her unexpectedly playful. *I'm never wearing a shirt again.*

She replied instinctively. *Good. I like the view.*

Forced to look away by his task, Aden nonetheless didn't break their telepathic connection. *Would you do what you did at the aerie? Touch me, kiss me, own me?*

You forgot the biting.

Anything you want, Zaira. I'm yours.

A shudder rippled through her at the passionate commitment in his tone, but a squadmate five feet to her left yelled for help with a falling wall right then, interrupting her sensual conversation with Aden. By the time she finished the assist and found Aden again, it was to see him in intense discussion with Cristabel and Walker.

No more time for play, she thought, disappointed. The latter should've worried her for what it betrayed about her discipline, but once again, she thought of Tavish and of how her parents had hurt her. She'd *never* do that to a child. Never. That cruelty was simply beyond her. So maybe, just maybe, she wasn't a monster and could be permitted to love Aden.

Returning to Venice after night had fallen over the canals,

that thought in mind, she'd just finished changing after her shower when Mica telepathed her. *We have intruders.*

Zaira had put the entire facility on alert as soon as she and Aden returned from the Smokies, the watch doubled and extra sensors laid down along the entire perimeter, including in the waters of the relevant canals. *How far?*

Three minutes till they cross the southwestern boundary line. Confirmation that it's two operatives, moving with stealth. A pause. *They have small packs. No visible weapons.*

Outside on the roof by this point and in a position to watch the boundary, she got down on her belly. *Did our scanners detect explosives?*

Negative.

Using the high-powered night-vision goggles she'd picked up, Zaira considered the pair. *Breathing masks,* she ordered, after weighing up all possibilities. *No one is to stop them.*

This couldn't be coincidence. Either Aden's and Zaira's rumored abductions had given someone else the courage to attack the Arrows or these saboteurs were connected to those who'd taken them. Zaira wasn't about to waste the opportunity to discover more.

Understood.

Zaira grabbed a mask for herself from a nearby storage locker as Mica initiated the telepathic tree that meant the order would hit every Arrow mind within the compound in fifteen seconds flat, then settled down to wait. It didn't take long. The saboteurs lobbed gas grenades into the compound before turning to make their escape.

Quickly ordering most of her team to remain behind to handle the gas, using countermeasures that'd ensure it wouldn't spread beyond the compound, Zaira and three others set off in shadow pursuit of the saboteurs. When the two—a male and a female, both in sleek black wetsuits—slipped into different canals, Zaira and Alejandro took the male, while the other team took the female.

Their target didn't come up out of the water.

Having long before prepared for such a threat to the compound, Zaira used the heat sensor built into her phone to track him, guessing either he'd had breathing equipment stored in an easily accessible part of the canal or he'd taken a short-acting tablet that boosted the oxygen in his blood, allowing a longer period of immersion.

Alejandro kept stealthy pace with her. While he wasn't cleared for solo missions any longer, his reflexes were flawless and she trusted him to watch her back. And, no matter what anyone else said, she thought part of the real Alejandro still remained, still had pride.

She would not crush that pride by consigning him to inconsequential tasks.

"Zaira." A whisper less than sound as their target disappeared from the sensors. "He must have an entrance below the waterline."

Zaira nodded, making note of the only possible building into which the target could've gone. Lapped by water and serviced by an overbridge, it was in neat but not elegant condition. A light came on in a room on the third floor above the waterline less than two minutes later, just as Zaira received a telepathic report from the other team.

Our target appears to have arrived at her personal living quarters. Entry was not observed, as it occurred below the waterline, but the silhouette seen in a room soon afterward matches the subject's shape and size.

Zaira told the second team to stay in position and go with the target if she made a move. *I'll organize for another team to relieve you at 0700 hours.*

Yes, sir.

Zaira and Alejandro stayed on watch until the same time, but their target seemed to have bedded down for the night. In the meantime, she'd already sent details of both locations to Aden, along with a request for more support. With the majority of the Venice contingent having relocated to the valley, she was running on a skeleton crew.

He was waiting for her when she handed over the watch to the relief team, and returned to her quarters.

"What did you find?" she asked, sitting on her bed to take off her boots after waving him into her room and going across to open the doors to her small and well-alarmed balcony.

"Both rented their apartments under false names, but we were able to use the photos on their IDs to trace their true identities." He leaned against her closed door. "They're not human or Psy but water changelings."

Zaira looked up. "Water breathers? That, I didn't predict." The water-based changelings tended to keep to themselves. Even other changelings claimed not to know much about the reclusive group. They certainly didn't pick fights—or hadn't.

Boots and socks off, she rose to get rid of her jacket while Aden remained against the other wall. He was once again wearing his ankle-length leather coat over a suit. The suit was black, the shirt the same color. She wanted him to take it all off so she could warm herself up against his skin.

"A number of the sea changelings do call Venice home," she said, forcing her mind back onto the right path. "I'll factor that into my new threat assessments."

"I've alerted our people in other water-edged or otherwise water-accessible areas to do the same."

Throwing aside her uniform jacket, she removed her weapons and set them carefully under her bed, right below where she slept. Access would take her less than two heartbeats. Roll off the bed, grab a weapon in the same move, shoot. Should the attack come via the door, she could roll under the bed to the other side and use the bed as a shield. Should it come via the balcony, she'd already be shielded by the bed's bulk.

"Any obvious red flags?"

Aden shook his head. "Both are living a vanilla life on the surface, working from home on building websites."

"Easy cover."

"We're tracing their clients, but as yet, they appear to be legitimate small businesses, so someone is doing the work. No military or other suspicious contacts who could've supplied them with poison gas bombs, but the woman is a chemist, could have the expertise to have made them."

"Even with that," Zaira said, "I'm guessing they're grunts. Low level and expendable. I'll keep them under surveillance—they may lead us to people with more authority if we allow their overseers to believe they remained undetected."

Aden nodded. "I'm working my contacts to arrange a meet with the alpha of water-based changelings and I've got people working on digging up more data about them. Either the entire group is in on it or they have two rogue members." He slid his hands into his coat pockets as she undid her tight braid and threw the hair tie on the small table where she kept wildflowers in a painted porcelain vase.

The delicately but brightly patterned vase was a direct violation of pre-Honeycomb rules. It had also been a gift from Aden. He'd given it to her a year ago, and it was one of her most precious treasures; he understood her desire for pretty and shiny things, had never judged her for it.

A sudden quiet between them.

"Did Ashaya Aleine get back to you?" she said quickly when he straightened in preparation for leaving.

A nod. "Soon after you left—she confirmed that it's a combination of the Alliance implant and the one she created; she also said that it's highly unstable. If we hadn't dug it out, it would've overloaded soon afterward, fail-safe switch or not."

The idea of Aden dead because someone wanted to play at being a scientific mastermind had Zaira's jaw going tight. "Is there any way we can protect ourselves against it?"

"No. I've asked Aleine to work on a possible defensive countermeasure, but the fact is, it's probable the only solution will turn out to be a different type of implant and even the Alliance implant is in its early days."

"I could live a lifetime without ever having something shoved into my brain again." And if it happened, she'd dig it right back out, no matter the consequences. "At least now we know whoever was behind this had the power and the contacts to get their hands on two experimental implants."

"Yes."

Another taut silence.

Aden began to turn toward the door. "I'll leave you to rest."

"Wait." She didn't want him to go, wanted his scent close and his presence within touching distance . . . and if she hadn't inherited her parents' madness, then . . . "I'm not ready for sleep. Would you like to stay for breakfast?"

Aden straightened. "I'll get the food while you shower."

• • •

ADEN returned with the food to find that Zaira was still in the shower. Carefully taking her vase off the side table to place it on the floor, he moved the table to in front of the bed and put the food on it.

Shrugging off his coat, he slung it over the back of the single chair in the room and placed that chair on the other side of the table. He'd just taken off his suit jacket and tie when the bathroom door opened. There was no steam. "You don't have to shower in ice-cold water," he said when she walked out in the simple black T-shirt and supple black pants that functioned as off-duty gear for most Arrows who weren't in civilian clothing for an operation. "That was only for training purposes."

"It was cool, not cold." Taking his jacket, the tie in one of the pockets, she hung it inside the closet built into the wall, then picked up his overcoat and did the same. "Why don't you wear your formal Arrow uniform to these meetings with the Forgotten and other groups? Blending in again?"

"In a way." He unbuttoned and folded up the sleeves of his black shirt. "A military uniform puts people on edge."

"How do you do it—appear harmless?"

"I've practiced."

Coming around the table, Zaira took a cross-legged position on her hard, narrow bed. She hadn't bought a fluffy comforter yet; the idea of it reminded her too much of her secret time with Aden, made her too angry with missing him. "Where are the nutrient drinks?" He had to have bought the other items on the table from a nearby café.

He tapped the glasses on either side, but when she reached for one, he picked up a slice of apple and held it out. "You like this."

Closing her fingers around the glass, she took a long drink. He didn't lower his hand. "Trying to break my will?" she asked.

"Never."

And because she knew he spoke the truth, she took the sweet, tart piece of fruit, bit into it. They didn't speak again until after they'd finished the meal in a silence that wasn't painful, wasn't alone. His breath, his scent, the competent, confident strength of his presence, filled the space.

"Have you slept?" she asked as he finished off his nutrient drink. His dress would've told her he'd been in meetings in other time zones, even if she hadn't been in touch with him about the saboteurs throughout the night.

He shook his head, his hair falling across his forehead. "I'll need to get at least five hours soon or I'll lose some alertness."

The needy, lonely, twisted part of her merged with the controlled Arrow at that instant, and they both wanted only one thing. "Stay."

He went motionless.

Uncrossing her legs, she got off the bed, braced for rejection. He'd seen her in the grip of the rage that was like madness, seen what she became. Maybe the time since that incident had made him realize just how bad of a bet she was in every possible way.

The half-insane girl inside her didn't hit out at him in a preemptive strike, simply curled into a hard knot in her gut. She was flinching, she thought, just like Tavish. Trying to make herself smaller so it wouldn't hurt so much. When she took hold of the table, he got up and helped her put it aside so that the bed was no longer blocked. Once that was done, she was aware of him waiting for her to speak again but she didn't have any words. So she just got into bed and faced the balcony.

If he wanted to leave, he could leave.

There was silence for a long minute, and then she heard clothing rustle, a belt move against fabric. The bed dipped behind her soon afterward. She lifted her head for his arm and saw he'd removed his shirt. He was hot against her, the arm he put around her waist muscled steel.

He wrapped his other arm around the front of her shoulders as he'd done in the aerie, enclosing her in protective warmth. And for the first time since she'd returned from Rain-Fire, she felt as if she could sleep again, no screaming aloneness in her skull, no crying deep in her soul from missing him.

A breath against her ear, his lips brushing her skin. "It's raining."

Her eyes went to the balcony doors and to the soft, misty

rain that had begun to fall. At that moment, it was as if they were back in the aerie, back in that precious, secret time when she could forget her twisted history.

"Sleep," she whispered. "I'll keep you safe."

He nudged his thigh between hers, their bodies utterly entwined. "How about we keep each other safe?"

She was the commander, her task to make sure no harm came to him, but she had the thought that right now they were just Aden and Zaira, and Aden was a man who would always want to protect his lover.

While they might not be lovers in the sexual sense, he was as entwined in her existence as their bodies were in this bed. Her heart, that twisted, scarred organ, felt things for him it felt for no one else.

Turning into his hold, her back to the threat of the open balcony doors, she closed her eyes and slept in the arms of the only person she had ever loved.

Chapter 42

BEATRICE FOLLOWED HER trainer down an alley that exited behind a human nightclub pulsating with noise far beyond the efficacy of the flimsy soundproofing. Sweat trickled down her spine and her pulse thudded, but she was determined not to make a mistake during her first live mission; she'd prove to Blake that he'd been right to take her as his partner.

"You remember the mission parameters?"

"Yes, sir." They were to incapacitate and acquire a specified human female. Brown haired and blue eyed, the female was twenty-three years of age. When Beatrice had dared ask why they were targeting a young human, Blake had answered her in an unexpected sign of respect.

"She's the child of a Human Alliance scientist who is in the process of developing a serum meant to neutralize Psy abilities. The Ruling Coalition has requested we interrogate her as she knows the pass codes of her father's highly secured systems. It'll allow us to download then erase all data before disposing of the male in what will appear to be a simple vehicular accident."

Beatrice had assumed the target must be very smart to have memorized all the codes, but as she saw the female stumble out of the club in high heels, a cigarette hanging from her fingers, she couldn't see any sign of that intellect. Not only were those shoes impractical to run in, the target, who apparently worked at the club, had a nightly habit of smoking at this time and this place, alone.

There was no light back here, no security cameras, no other traffic. The girl had to realize the data she had in her head made her a target. Why would she then not carry a weapon at least? Perhaps it had to do with intrafamily rebellion—Beatrice had been taught about that in her psych classes. Humans sometimes rebelled against their parents. It was a weakness that could be exploited both subtly and more directly.

Tonight, it was clearly to be the latter.

When she glanced at Blake, he gave a small nod.

The mission was a go.

Inhaling quietly, Beatrice stepped around the corner and toward the target. She'd dressed in civilian clothing for this mission, her dress as short and as sparkly as the girl's skirt. Beatrice liked the dress. It wasn't an Arrow thing to think, but she'd never had anything so pretty.

Her feet, of course, were in combat boots. An acceptable style choice, according to her research. That was good, because Beatrice wasn't sure she could've walked in high heels.

Catching sight of her, the target frowned. "Where'd you come from?"

"My boyfriend ditched me," Beatrice said, reciting the script she'd been given and mimicking the tone and intonation she'd seen in a movie clip; she'd found that clip herself, studied it in preparation for the mission. "Creep. He's screwing some girl in our car."

"Ugh." The target wasn't the least suspicious as Beatrice drew closer. "You want a cigare—" Her words ended in a choking sound, her eyes stunned as Beatrice incapacitated her with a single slamming hit to the throat with the side of her hand. Blake had made it clear no weapons or psychic abilities were to be used, this mission part of her equivalency exam in weaponless action.

Catching the target's heavier body as she fell, Beatrice pinched a nerve in her neck to ensure total unconsciousness. That done, she looked up, hopeful.

Coming out of the shadows, Blake said, "A near-perfect takedown." He lifted the target and threw her over his shoulder.

It was easy to move her without being seen. Blake had parked their vehicle in the deserted and overgrown lot next door, and they'd used a preexisting hole in the chain-link fence to get to this side. Three minutes after Beatrice had first seen the target, she was in the trunk of their vehicle as they drove to the interrogation center.

Chapter 43

ADEN SLEPT DEEPLY—or as deeply as any Arrow ever slept—and woke to find Zaira still in his arms, her hand over his heart.

She'd thrown her leg over his own sometime in their sleep, and his hand was spread on her lower back, under her T-shirt. Her skin was warm, softer than his own, her body relaxed. Not moving, he just drank her in. He didn't know why she'd asked him to stay, but he knew he'd have to be careful.

She was like a wild bird who'd finally decided a man could be trusted. One wrong move and she'd be gone, lost in the clouds before he had a chance to coax her back.

She stirred under his hand and he thought she must've woken, but then a small sound escaped her throat. It was tiny, as if she was fighting to hold it back, and it was a sound that did not belong in Zaira's throat. The sound of a trapped creature frantically trying to escape.

"Zaira."

She woke at once at the command in his voice. Her body stiffened a second later, and the instant after that, she was out of bed and standing beside it. He didn't take any counter-measures to stop her, simply rose to a seated position on the bed after she was out of it.

"You promised to keep me safe." A raw accusation that tore him to pieces.

As a child, Aden had once asked Vasic if he could travel through time as well as space. He'd never wanted that to be true as much as he did at this instant. He'd go back, kill her parents before they filled her head with nightmares. "I know," he said, admitting his culpability. "I'm sorry."

Her body rigid and her expression stark, she turned to the balcony doors. "Go."

Rising to his feet, he went to her instead and wrapped his arms around her, holding her unbending form. "I'm sorry," he said again, his jaw pressed to her temple. "I will fight every nightmare with you. Just let me in."

She stayed stiff for so long that he thought he'd lost her, but he wasn't about to surrender to the demons that haunted her, wasn't about to leave her alone when aloneness was her worst nightmare.

Making a keening noise in her throat, she turned without warning to beat at his shoulders with her fists. "I was fine before! Why did you wake me up?" Gritted-out words. "Why did you show me things I can't have!"

He bent, pressing his forehead to hers. "I'm yours. No matter what."

Huge, dark eyes, small, deadly fists on his shoulders . . . and a wild bird on the verge of flying away. "Don't go," he whispered, the words holding his heart. "Don't go. I need you to stay."

Aden. She crumpled into him, her arms locking around his waist.

There were no tears, no screams. Only harsh breaths and whispered horror about a nightmare that had once been real. His own muscles taut, he held her with painful fierceness, his wild bird who had chosen to come to him even in the darkest hour.

ARRIVING at Central Command sixty minutes later, having forced himself to release Zaira so she could return to her duties, Aden showered and changed into black cargo pants and a black T-shirt. He had no outside meetings today, intended to work in the valley, interact with the children.

An alpha was meant to be respected but not feared. Not by the innocent.

He never wanted to feel a child flinch from him as Tavish had done.

About to head out, he was halted by an incoming call from Judd. "Aden," Judd said before breaking off. "Give me a second."

In the background, Aden heard a childish voice, followed by Judd's deeper one. More children's voices followed before Judd spoke again. When the other man came back on the line, Aden said, "Where are you?"

"Watching over the pups. Their usual caretakers are having a meeting so we've been roped in." A warmth in the other Arrow's tone that Aden would've never predicted when Judd had still officially been part of the squad. "I was mediating a disagreement between three pups who wanted to play with the same ball."

"How did you mediate it?" It was a question with intent—if Aden's plans succeeded, Arrow children wouldn't be so perfectly behaved in the future. He needed to learn how to deal with these kinds of situations.

"I told them they'd have much more fun if they played a game between the three of them. Wolves are social by nature, so I didn't have to do much convincing." A short pause, the phone muffled again for a moment. "Okay, we can talk now. Drew's watching my group."

"Were you able to make contact with the leader of the water changelings?" The squad had kept a quiet eye on BlackSea the same way they kept an eye on any other group that might one day prove a threat, but they'd never been able to isolate BlackSea's leadership. What evidence they had pointed to a woman named Miane Levèque, but she was all but impossible to find if you didn't know where to look.

Vasic had once managed to teleport onto one of Black-Sea's floating cities after using a known water changeling's face as a lock. He'd 'ported back with a bullet lodged in the armor covering his shoulder and a wound on his temple where another bullet had grazed him. If he wasn't so fast, he'd have been dead soon after arrival.

Ming, in charge at the time, had decided not to waste any more manpower on a group that kept to itself, and the water-based changelings had ignored them in turn. Until the Venice incident.

Judd, on the other hand, was part of SnowDancer. The wolf pack was not only the biggest and most powerful pack in the country, it held that position even when worldwide packs were factored in. There was no way the wolves weren't aware of BlackSea on a deeper level, the reason Aden had reached out to SnowDancer via Judd.

Judd's next words confirmed his call had been the right one. "We'll be talking to them in a few hours. I can't tell you how it'll go—according to Riaz, who deals with BlackSea most often, the water changelings make SnowDancer look friendly."

Aden didn't ask if he could join the meeting. The wolves had barely begun to trust the Arrows, had gone that far only because they had Judd and the other Laurens in their midst. A group as reclusive as BlackSea would never agree to a face-to-face with Aden at this point. "I'm sending you everything we have to date," he said to Judd. "Tell BlackSea we don't want a war, but we'll give it to them if that's what they want."

Aden would allow no one to hurt his family.

JUDD slid away his phone and walked back into the sunshine of the newly green play area outside the den, the snow having melted away about ten days earlier. Drew was no longer watching over things. The other man had shifted and was currently buried under a pile of pups in wolf and human form, all intent on beating him in battle.

Judd wasn't the least surprised when a breakaway group came to attack him. He allowed himself to be taken to the earth, squirming bodies all over him until they pinned him down and howled victory.

Holding one of the smaller pups against his chest as he sat up after he was set free, he put the girl gently on the ground. She raced off to play with the ball again, while Drew, still in wolf form, shook himself as if setting his skin in place, then padded over to sit on the ground beside where Judd had taken a seat with his back against a large rock.

It was over fifteen minutes of comfortable silence later that Drew walked off to shift back into human form, returning dressed in his jeans and white T-shirt. While changelings saw nudity as a natural part of life, they weren't exhibitionists. Certain rules of behavior were scrupulously followed—by everyone but the smallest pups. Seeing a naked pup gleefully running through the den was a familiar and amusing sight.

"Your Arrow friends?" Drew retook his earlier position, his legs stretched out and face tilted up to drink in the sun, lake blue eyes closed. "They figure out who tried to take two of them out?"

Judd shook his head. "It's the changeling involvement I'm having trouble understanding." Drew already knew the facts of what had taken place; Judd had been clear with Aden that though he was more than prepared to help the squad, he wouldn't withhold information from his alpha and other senior packmates.

"Can't say I blame you." Drew opened his eyes, focused on the pups again. "Human and Psy was a weird enough combination, but all three?"

"It doesn't seem to fit the natural order of things." Except for rare pockets like in SnowDancer, where all three races had connected, their world was not a functioning triumvirate. "BlackSea in particular seems the least likely pack to be involved in a conspiracy."

"Yeah, they're pretty standoffish." Drew's laid-back voice was suddenly granite hard as he said, "We know every group has its bad apples, so it's probably not BlackSea as a whole."

Judd knew the other man was recalling the SnowDancer traitor who'd wanted to brutalize the woman who was now Judd's mate. "Brenna handled him," he reminded Drew. Both Drew and Riley were protective of their sister, sometimes forgot that she could take care of herself. "Where's Riley?"

A snort. "Mercy is, like, seventeen months pregnant. Where do you think?"

Mercy was more like six months along, but Judd got the point. "She's displaying more patience with his overprotectiveness than I would've expected." The DarkRiver sentinel had no tolerance for anyone "mollycoddling" her, as she'd put it. She was still on active duty, though on the advice of the pack healers—both SnowDancer and DarkRiver—she'd scaled back her physical exertion.

Judd might have been surprised at what she continued to do if he hadn't seen other soldiers do exactly the same. Changelings were physical beings and bed rest was only ever advised if there were medical complications. The majority of pregnant changeling women remained highly active almost to their due date.

"Love, Judd." A grin on Drew's face. "She's kinda crazy for my brother. Crazy enough not to throttle him when he invites himself along on her shifts."

Judd understood in a way he wouldn't have before he mated with Brenna. It was a knowledge he wanted for all his Arrow brethren, but it wasn't something he could teach—his squadmates had to experience the dawning wonder and beautiful agony of it themselves. They had to choose to step outside the Arrow black walls of their existence . . . or be lucky enough to find a man or a woman who cared enough to batter down those walls.

"I haven't actually seen Mercy recently," he said, his mind on the woman who'd smashed through his own defenses and claimed him. "Brenna was asking how she was."

"Aside from the belly, she looks and acts exactly like the same old Mercy." Drew's grin grew wider. "Riley swears she popped out overnight—word from the healers is that she might not go all the way to nine months."

Judd came to attention. "You're not concerned?" Premature births could be very dangerous even with all the medical technology at the world's disposal.

"We get more multiple births than the other races," Drew reminded him, "so a lot more babies end up preterm. The healers are used to handling it, and the babies are usually much healthier than Psy or human babies born prematurely."

"Psy preterm babies are the most at risk."

A slap on the back. "Good thing any pups you and Bren have will have changeling blood."

Judd tried imagining Brenna with child . . . and succeeded. There was no block now, no fear of what kind of a father he might be. One day, when they were both ready, he would hold his and Brenna's child. For now, he'd help watch over both SnowDancer's and the squad's young. "I'm nearly afraid to ask how you know so much about gestation and birth," he said to Drew.

"Because I have a brother who's been barred from the infirmary in both packs unless he's bleeding or Mercy's giving birth." Drew's shoulders shook, the wolf in his eyes. "He's chewed the ear off both Lara and Tamsyn."

"I understand his worry." As far as anyone knew, this was the first time a leopard changeling and a wolf changeling had conceived together.

Drew's expression turned solemn. "Yeah. I think everyone does—which is also why Mercy is being so weirdly nice." A suspicious edge to his tone, as if he expected his brother's mate to turn into a hissing, bad-tempered cat at any instant. "She says she can feel the pupcubs and they're as happy as pie, but since Riley can't feel what she does . . ."

A ball came rolling their way on the heels of Drew's words and Judd used his telekinesis to throw it back. Where that would've once made the kids look on in awe, now they just raced after the ball. He'd become normal to them, part of the landscape of adults they trusted without thought. Aden, he thought, was attempting to create the same for children who'd never known kindness at adult hands.

Judd had been one of those children until Walker hauled him back into the family. Now he was a man who'd fight for the innocent and the vulnerable at Aden's side. Because no child should ever grow up surrounded by coldness and fear.

Chapter 44

EIGHT HOURS AFTER waking in Aden's arms, Zaira went to the valley to speak to Nerida about more soldiers to add to the rotation on watch over the saboteurs. Even with the two extra people Nerida had already sent in, Zaira's crew was stretched—she didn't want them burning out, especially since they had to be prepared to strike should a higher-level target or targets present themselves.

She was heading into the main complex when she ran into a teenage trainee.

"I'm sorry, sir." The girl snapped into an at-attention pose.

"Not your fault," Zaira replied and was about to walk on when she realized she'd never seen this trainee at any of the sessions she led. "What's your name?"

"Beatrice Gault." The girl swallowed.

"Why haven't you attended the senior martial arts sessions?"

"I have, sir. In the back row."

Zaira stared at Beatrice's face, trying to remember. In the end, all she got was a vague recollection of a trainee who'd been wholly unmemorable. Beatrice had made no mistakes, needed no correction, but she'd also not been the best of the best. "I'll see you tomorrow." Zaira would be taking the session again.

"Yes, sir."

Walking into the building, she told Nerida her needs and the other woman said she'd organize the extra personnel. "Do you want Arrows who've worked or lived in Venice previously?"

"If you can spare them, yes," Zaira said, aware that her city had unique pitfalls newcomers might not understand.

Nerida scanned current placements and operations assignments on her organizer. "I may have to throw in one or two who haven't had experience there."

"That should be fine. I'll partner each newcomer with someone familiar with Venice." Leaving Nerida, she went to head out to catch her teleport back to Venice, hesitated.

After a moment's thought, she turned and made her way to the room where she knew Walker and Cris were going over personnel files and holding interviews so they could match up children with compatible adult Arrows. Flexibility was to be built in, in case of serious clashes, but the squad had to start somewhere.

Cris looked up as soon as Zaira entered, tawny brown eyes pinning her in place as the experienced Arrow had so often done when Zaira was one of her trainees. "Zaira—I thought you were dealing with the situation in Venice."

"I am." Zaira hesitated again because this wasn't her area of expertise . . . but something about Beatrice had triggered an echo in her. "Are you assigning the older teenagers and those in their early twenties to family groups?"

Cris gave her a considering look at what had to be an unexpected question coming from her. "Our focus is on the children," she said. "However, we are placing teenagers up to age sixteen. Anyone older will in all probability prefer independent accommodations."

"That doesn't mean they don't need families." Zaira had always had Aden. It had been enough to keep her sane, remind her she had value beyond being a cog in the Arrow machine.

Zaira's instincts said Beatrice might have no one who reminded her of the same.

Leaning back, Walker Lauren frowned. "You're right. Children return to a healthy family unit throughout their lives." He ran a hand through his hair before nodding. "We need to make sure every Arrow has a home to return to, regardless of age."

Zaira should've left then, her point made, but she couldn't forget Beatrice's voice—so flat and with an edge of defeat, as if she was used to not being remembered. Zaira knew what it was like to feel so alone, to feel that no one in the world knew of her existence. Sometimes, while she'd been trapped in the cell created by her parents, she'd screamed and screamed just to see if anyone would come.

No one ever had.

"Assign Beatrice Gault to me," she said.

Walker looked at her, careful and with the same intense quietness to him that was such an indelible part of Aden. "All right," he said at last, as if she'd passed some silent test. "The smallest children take priority, so it may take up to seventy-two hours for the assignment to be made. We'll have to speak to her first."

"Understood." Leaving the room, she reached for Aden's mind.

Her breath caught.

He'd left their private telepathic pathway open as if in invitation and as she slipped in, it felt like coming home. The rage wanted to curl around him like a wild pet, affectionate and sure of its welcome. Never had he rejected her. Never. Her emotions for him a primal pulse within her, she said, *It wasn't your fault.*

He'd accepted blame for her nightmares, but she was the one who carried darkness in her blood, not Aden. Somehow, he'd survived his childhood and come through Arrow training with his spirit intact. Not only intact but strong enough, generous enough, to embrace each and every broken soul in his care. *Thank you for holding me.*

Come find me so I can do it again.

She'd realized this morning that there was no going back. The idea of sleeping without him, of not having his mind open to her own, it hurt more than anything had ever before hurt in her life. If there was a chance she hadn't inherited the madness, that she could control her rages, then Zaira wasn't going to be a coward.

She would do this. After all, she belonged to him, always had. There was only one thing she needed before she could surrender to her craving to possess the extraordinary man who saw the shadows of her and found them beautiful. *Don't let me become a monster, Aden,* she said. *If I go mad, promise me you'll give the execution order.* She wouldn't ask him to do the actual execution himself; he cared about her, would be destroyed by it. *Don't let me become my parents' shadow mirror.*

You won't, Aden said as his face came into view, the two of them having been walking toward each other from opposite ends of the valley compound.

His faith in her made her soar, but she was too pragmatic, too aware of what lay beneath the thin shell of control. *I need the promise.*

No. A hard jaw, an unwavering expression.

Zaira had a raw moment of insight, of understanding. Giving the order would break him, too. Aden was incapable of harming her—and that knowledge, it made her heart ache. She'd thought the organ too stunted to feel with such passionate agony. But it did.

Because this beautiful, powerful, incredible man saw her as precious.

As if she was his shiny, sparkling treasure. One he'd permit no one to take from him . . . not even her. "You are a stubborn man," she said, her voice husky.

"Only about things that matter."

He kept giving her more gifts, kept making her heart struggle to beat and giving strength to the tiny flame of hope inside her, the one that whispered she wasn't insane, just a little broken. That was okay. Vasic was a little broken and Ivy loved him. Aden had broken pieces inside and they fit into the astonishing tapestry of him.

Most of all, her lover wasn't scared of imperfection. "I'll wait for you in Venice," she said, brushing her fingers over his as another Arrow called out to him and her teleport spotted her. "Don't be late."

"I won't."

They separated but the telepathic pathway between them, it remained open until the teleport took her far out of range.

Chapter 45

BLAKE COULD FEEL his need building again.

He was having to go slowly with the human female. Beatrice had questioned him as to why the interrogation center was an abandoned warehouse and not an Arrow facility, and he'd had to pull rank to shut her down. She'd obeyed, of course, but he couldn't risk pushing her too far too soon. Beatrice was a long-term plan, one that required patience. If he could corrupt her, he'd have someone with whom to share his finest moments.

With that end result in mind, he'd allowed her to take the lead in the interrogation.

His prey wasn't a scientist's daughter and knew nothing of any codes; it was amusing to watch Beatrice attempt to get the data out of her, but so far, his apprentice hadn't done any real damage. That would change in two days, when he took over after her "failure." Blood would flow, sweet and wet, as his victim screamed, but right now, he had to satiate his urges elsewhere.

Having made sure his schedule was open for at least three hours today, he scanned the semilit pathway between two streets filled with restaurants. Humans and changelings were so often stupid; they believed that walking in pairs would save them. He'd never taken two bef—

His eyes locked in on a couple heading toward him.

Not human.

Not changeling.

Psy.

He could tell because they looked nervous to be holding hands, as if not yet sure of the fall of Silence. As he watched, the man floated a rose to the woman using what must be very minor Tk if he'd been allowed to remain a civilian. The woman clasped the flower to her chest.

Blake wanted to crush them for their stupidity, but he'd never previously taken Psy victims on his own. His prior Psy targets had been Ming-sanctioned. As such, Ming had created a solid shield around those minds so that their death agonies wouldn't alert the Net and draw unwelcome attention.

If he took these two, it would be without the benefit of that shield. Either one could shout out a telepathic scream, so he'd have to do it fast, as with that boy on the beach. An interesting challenge, he thought, his decision made. He waited until they moved just past his hiding place in a shallow recess in the wall, was a heartbeat away from striking when a mind knocked on his on the PsyNet.

Nerida.

Throttling his urges, because ignoring the Arrow in charge of security assignments wasn't an option if he wanted to remain undiscovered, he stayed where he was and the stupid Psy couple with their sickeningly weak bodies walked past and into the night.

Forty-eight hours, he promised himself as he stepped out onto the psychic plane to speak to Nerida. Forty-eight hours and not only would he be able to assuage his need, he'd own Beatrice in the doing. Because it wasn't Blake who'd take the victim's life. No, he'd save that pleasure for Beatrice.

Once she did that, she'd be his.

Chapter 46

ELEVEN HOURS AFTER his phone call with Aden, Judd was at the San Francisco waterfront with Hawke and Riaz. Lucas and his senior sentinel, Nathan, met them at the Embarcadero warehouse both packs used for meetings with BlackSea.

It was SnowDancer that had taken point during the initial negotiations with BlackSea, since the water-based changelings had reached out directly to the wolves. The DarkRiver leopards, their closest allies, had agreed to remain in the background, though the lines of communication between the two packs had stayed open throughout. Prior to the final alliance, however, all three alphas had met face-to-face, because SnowDancer would not ally with anyone who did not also ally and deal with DarkRiver and vice versa.

The two packs had a blood bond that went deeper than any relationship they had with another pack. While neither alpha would admit it, Judd had the sense that the packs were becoming one while remaining distinct and separate. They were two branches of a powerful family, a truth that would be sealed the day Mercy gave birth.

"No seacraft spotted," Lucas told them as they stepped out of the back of the warehouse and onto the private pier protected from prying eyes by high fences on either side. "We did sense a disturbance in the water a few minutes out. They're on their way."

Hawke folded his arms, pale blue eyes narrowed. "Since when can you sense disturbances in the water, cat?"

"Since we placed sensors in a deep perimeter into the bay, wolf." Lucas's own eyes glinted panther green in the quickly falling darkness. "Seemed smart if we're going to have water changelings coming in and out on a regular basis. Wouldn't want to miss an invading force."

"So little trust."

"Exactly the same amount as you."

Both alphas grinned. Because an alliance was one thing. True trust took years to form. And a blood bond such as that between SnowDancer and DarkRiver was so rare that most other changeling packs couldn't believe it was real. Especially given that both were predatory packs.

Respect, Judd thought, was the bedrock of that relationship.

The water stirred in front of them at that moment, a woman in a sleek black wetsuit rising out of it, her eyes a translucent hazel uptilted a tiny bit at the corners and her black hair slicked to her skull. Two others rose with her, men Judd tagged as Malachai and Griffin from his premeeting briefing by Riaz.

Malachai dwarfed Miane's five-foot-five or five-foot-six height, his shoulders broad and his body muscular. Griffin, by contrast, wasn't much taller than Miane, but he moved the same way Judd had seen the most dangerous DarkRiver cats move. Light on his feet, his muscles fluid.

The two males were wearing only wetsuit pants, their chests bare, while Miane Levèque's suit appeared to have no zippers or other fastenings that Judd could see now that she'd hauled herself out of the water and onto the pier.

No one had moved forward to offer help. In time, the BlackSea alpha might accept Lucas's or Hawke's assistance in such a situation, but that would take a friendship that hadn't yet formed. Until then, like any alpha, Miane Levèque would not appreciate any such courtesy—would, in fact, see it as an insult.

"Welcome to DarkRiver territory," Lucas said, as Miane made eye contact with him and Hawke in turn. Her eyes were no longer a human hazel, but an intense, endless black that echoed the deepest part of the ocean. So pure was the onyx of her irises that it made it appear as if she had no pupils.

Stefan had once described the silken darkness of the depths to Judd. Living on Alaris gave the other Tk a unique perspective on the world. Judd wondered if Miane Levêque swam that deep, looked in through the portholes of the deep-sea station financed in large part by BlackSea.

"Thank you for the welcome." Miane inclined her head in a regal move. "We tried not to damage any of your sensors."

Lucas's lips kicked up at what was very much an alpha comment, challenge and amusement entwined. "I appreciate it." A nod back toward the warehouse. "Would you like to come inside? My packmates can bring in towels."

"We do not mind being wet." Miane's expression remained cool. "My people and I have investigated the members of BlackSea involved in the attempt against the Psy squad you term allies."

The Arrows weren't yet full allies, but Judd appreciated that neither Hawke nor Lucas had made that distinction when asking for information. He knew it had to do with family: the Laurens were packmates, the Arrows their family, and thus by extension, due some measure of loyalty so long as they didn't act against either pack.

"And?" The silver-gold of Hawke's hair caught the fading light, the strands afire. "Find anything useful?"

Miane Levêque nodded at Malachai. The large male, who was standing with his hands clasped in front of him, spoke without moving an inch out of position. "Jim fell away from BlackSea eight months ago. Though he remains a technical member, paying a percentage of his income into the pack fund so that he can access BlackSea's resources, he hasn't attended any Gatherings in that time frame and, as far as I can ascertain, has broken contact with all his compatriots but three.

"Those three," the sea changeling continued, "are scattered over remote parts of the world, so his connection with them is distant. None have heard from him in the past two months."

Lucas slid his hands into the pockets of the black pants he

wore with a dark green shirt open at the collar. "He's turned loner?"

Miane Levèque was the one who answered. "Many sea-based changelings are loners by nature, or tight with only a small family unit. Prior to eight months ago, Jim was part of a pod of ten."

"His pod doesn't know why he went his own way," Malachai said, following on so flawlessly from Miane that Judd wondered at their relationship. It wouldn't be the first alpha-lieutenant pair he'd heard of since becoming part of SnowDancer.

"Olivia's story is nearly identical," Miane said in that cool voice that was almost Psy but for the icy anger Judd could sense in her words. "She fell away from her peer group around the same time and made it clear she wanted no contact."

"She even ignored her siblings' messages and attempts to find her." Malachai paused, and only when Miane nodded slightly did he add, "She had a mate, and a child who would now be two. The mate's body was found six months ago—it was almost all bone and we know his identity only because of DNA. The child remains missing. Her name is Persephone."

The BlackSea lieutenant's words made Judd's gut tighten. He saw the same concern and anger on the faces around him. If sea changelings mated like the wolves or the leopards, then it was for life. The death of a mate could shatter the one who remained and, in this case, perhaps lead her to make dangerous and unstable decisions.

Malachai's next words, however, seemed to point to a far more sinister truth.

"You were right to assume these events are connected to the disappearances that led us to seek an alliance with you," the BlackSea lieutenant said into the tense quiet. "Jim and Olivia were two of those who vanished—we didn't know their location until you sent us the data."

Judd had been briefed by Riaz on why the sea change-lings had decided to change their isolationist policy. Part of it had to do with the changing political climate, but the most important driver was that a number of their pack—such as it was—had vanished without a trace. Because of BlackSea's unusual structure, it had taken time for Miane to realize what was happening. BlackSea wasn't anywhere near the biggest pack in the world, but it was the only one that had members worldwide; those members were scattered across great bodies of water, including lakes and the largest rivers in the world.

Also affecting the record was the fact that many of the sea-based changelings swam alone, only meeting up with others of their kind once a year. In some cases, as with Olivia and her mate, couples had disappeared, meaning the one person who might have reported the disappearance had also been taken. At last count, at least twenty-seven members had been confirmed as missing.

"Given what you now know of Jim's and Olivia's actions," Hawke said, "is it possible your missing went voluntarily?" His voice held the undertone of a growl, but it wasn't a threat, simply an indication his wolf was very much present and listening.

Miane's changeling eyes didn't reflect light like those of terrestrial changelings, instead seemed to suck it in. "No," she said immediately. "The missing are all solitary by nature but they have intense ties to others despite the fact that they may only have met up once or twice a year. One confirmed missing member was half of a pair, would have never left his mate haunting the sea, searching for him."

Judd tried to imagine being away from Brenna for so long, only seeing her after long stretches, couldn't. It made him understand why the water-based changelings had stayed separate and alone for so long—it must be frustrating to not be understood, to have outsiders constantly finding fault with a life most simply could not comprehend.

"We want a chance to talk to both Jim and Olivia," Miane said. "They will not be able to lie to me."

Hawke glanced at Judd.

He stepped forward. "The squad wants to keep them under surveillance, as they may lead the Arrows to a bigger player—and, I'm guessing, to the people behind these vanishings."

Miane Levèque's cold black eyes held his. "We'll be patient. But they are my people."

Judd wasn't about to be intimidated, but he could understand her response. "The squad has little interest in them beyond the contacts either might make." His phone vibrated at that instant, in the pattern he'd assigned Aden. "Excuse me. I have to take this."

Aware of the others continuing to talk as he put the phone to his ear, he listened to what Aden had to say, felt his blood ice. "I'll pass on the news. BlackSea will want to come to Venice."

"Vasic is happy to complete a 'port if requested."

Hanging up without further words, Judd returned to the meeting. When he caught Hawke's eye, the alpha leaned closer. Dropping his voice to the subvocal level that he couldn't actually hear himself, Judd passed on the news. Hawke's features grew hard. "Miane," he said, interrupting the other alpha midsentence, "your man is dead."

The BlackSea alpha went eerily motionless. "The Arrows?"

"No," Judd responded. "Jim jumped off his balcony onto the street. The Arrows on watch went immediately to his assistance, but his neck was broken." Since the balcony wasn't that high off the street, the working conclusion was that the other man had either landed wrong or been dead when he was thrown over the edge. At this point, however—"There's no evidence of outside involvement, though the squad will be performing an autopsy to check for signs of psychic coercion."

"Tell your friends to treat him with respect."

"Aden has offered a teleport should you request it."

"No. We'll make our own way there." Returning her attention to Lucas and Hawke, she said, "I must leave. We'll talk further after I discover why a bright young man is dead and another member of my pack is suspected of a terrorist act while her daughter remains among the missing."

The three sea changelings disappeared into the water seconds later, no bubbles coming up to betray their presence as they swam their way out.

"I think," Judd said slowly, "you should seed sensors even deeper out."

Lucas crouched at the edge of the plascrete, looking at the water that kept its secrets. "Yes. These allies are a little too quiet to trust just yet."

ZAIRA looked around Jim Savua's small apartment. It was anonymous, the furniture the kind of hard-wearing and inexpensive pieces a landlord might use to furnish a place. Zaira was no expert, but she'd learned how to judge such things as part of her Arrow training. A person's surroundings could tell you a great deal about that individual.

What this apartment told her was that the man hadn't lived here long. When he had, it had been a place to sleep, nothing else. His clothes still lay in his suitcase and his cooler held no food, though there were a couple of take-out containers in the trash. Also in the trash were multiple disposable injectors.

Like long-use injectors, these could be placed against the skin or pulse point, depending on the drug involved, and the drug punched painlessly into the bloodstream. The only difference was that they were much cheaper and sold by the box. While disposable injectors did have legitimate medical uses, they were also popular with recreational drug users.

"Did his body show signs of long-term drug abuse?" she asked Blake Stratton, who'd been on watch with his partner at the time of the incident. She hadn't been pleased to discover his presence. Nerida had made a last-minute substitution when the squadmate Zaira had cleared for the op broke a femur quite badly. The other woman should've contacted her, but hadn't—a mistake Zaira would make sure Nerida knew not to make again.

She didn't trust Blake, did not want him in her city.

When he came to stand beside her, the tiny hairs on her neck and arms rose in primal warning. "It was difficult to tell with the damage caused by the cobblestones, as well as the blood," he said. "But I did notice he had scars from what appeared to be healed scratch marks, and his skin was yellowish, in the way that occurs with users of Halcyon."

Halcyon was the street name for a highly addictive substance that worked on all three races, though on Psy, it had a tendency to lead very quickly to psychosis. It did also cause some users to scratch their skin bloody. Breaking away to make a call to the pathologist, she asked him to do a complete drug profile.

"Thank you," she said to Blake afterward. "Your shift is complete. Return to Central Command and check in."

The other Arrow left without comment, but she didn't turn

her back until he was gone. About to return to her survey of the apartment, she glimpsed Yuri coming toward her. He was one of the people she'd chosen, a forty-seven-year-old Arrow who'd been with her in Venice since the start. Pragmatic and reliable, he wasn't flashy in his abilities or even in the way he carried himself, but she knew if she asked Yuri to do something, it would get done and get done well.

Zaira, we may have a problem.

Chapter 47

SINCE, OTHER THAN Yuri, the room held only her and two trusted forensic people, the fact that he'd used telepathy was a sign of something serious. *What is it?*

I was on watch with Blake when this happened. I was on the street side, Blake on the other side so we could cover all exits.

Zaira didn't need him to spell it out. *Do you think he pushed the dead male?*

I don't know. Yuri put his hands behind his back. *I know we considered that the victim might've been thrown dead over the balcony, but from my perspective, it appeared as if he jumped. However, he could've been trying to get away from a threat inside the room.*

Alert to the fact that her strong dislike of Blake could color her viewpoint, she said, *See if you can find any surveillance images from street cameras.*

I'll do it now. A pause. *I apologize. I should've kept him in my sights.*

Zaira's eyes met Yuri's and she saw in them the same deep unease she felt when it came to Blake. *If it was him, we'll make sure he doesn't have a chance to do it again.*

A nod of agreement.

As the older Arrow walked away, Zaira considered whether to pass on Yuri's suspicions to Aden and decided he had to know. If the squad had a traitor in their midst, he had to be rooted out.

She called in a quick report once she was out on the street alone. "We need to watch him."

"I'll make sure of it. He's down to run combat sessions over the next three days, so he'll be under the eye of a number of senior people."

Zaira wanted to smash Blake's mind open, uncover the truth, but she knew it wouldn't be that easy. "He's too well trained to break under interrogation, but he is arrogant enough to lead us to his handlers if he's somehow part of a larger conspiracy." They both knew that even if he had caused Jim to die, Blake might simply have been acting on his own distasteful urges.

"Yes. What about the woman?"

"Safe and alive, though she is acting erratically." Zaira was aware that if they showed their hand, they'd lose all hope of tracking the woman back to a handler, but they also wouldn't have anything if she was dead. "I say we bring her in."

"Do it," Aden said. "Judd's also just passed on the information that Olivia Coletti has a child aged two. Look for any signs of her."

That data immediately affirmed Zaira's decision to act. She did not want a vulnerable child in the hands of a Halcyon user. Giving the order to the team watching Olivia, she walked back to the compound through the early morning streets. It was only four thirty; even the bakers didn't appear to be up yet.

She wasn't surprised to see Aden heading out of the laboratory hidden in one wing of the compound. "Pathologist find anything definitive?"

"No signs of a struggle, no mind-control lesions on the brain. Tox screen is pending but he's certain it'll confirm Halcyon—the body shows all the outward signs of long-term use." He walked into the courtyard with her to wait for the second target to be brought in. "If Blake is working against us, he's renounced his status as an Arrow."

Zaira knew how much loyalty meant to Aden, how seriously he took it, so she could guess his reaction to any betrayal. "Blake fit Ming's regime. Yours asks too much of a man who's only ever cared for his own skin."

Aden glanced at her. "Did he hurt you?" Ice-cold words.

She shook her head. "The look in his eyes reminds me of the look in my parents' eyes." Psychopathic and self-involved, not an ounce of empathy. "I want him to be a traitor so I can kill him."

"That's why we have to have proof."

Zaira nodded reluctantly, knowing Blake wasn't the only Arrow with a problematic past and personality. To go after him without proof would splinter the trust that held the squad together. "This conspiracy," she said, leaning against the wall, vines growing up the weathered plascrete on either side. "Why target one of the most lethal groups in the world? What is the payoff in having the squad out for vengeance?"

"I don't have an answer yet." Aden leaned beside her, his own arms folded. "We might get some indication when the BlackSea alpha arrives."

As she listened to what he knew so far, she was hyperconscious of the fact that his arm was touching her shoulder, that his uniform pants and plain black tee showcased the muscular strength of his body, that he smelled good enough to lick.

Pushing off the wall without warning, she walked around the corner and into a small alcove hidden from the world by a heavy mass of overhanging vines as well as its position tucked in between two buildings.

"Zaira." Aden followed her. "What—"

Slamming him against the wall, she pressed her lips to the strong, powerful beat of the pulse in his neck. Since she was already falling into the abyss, her control shredded, why deny herself the pleasure that was the flip side of the nightmare memories she could no longer stifle?

He shuddered, one hand sliding up to curve over the back of her neck. And then their mouths were meeting and it was wild and undisciplined, wet and hot, and she stopped thinking, the rage in her drugged into a haze of want focused on this beautiful man whose hunger for her seemed as feral as hers for him.

Sir, we're almost at the compound.

She dug her nails into Aden's shoulders, the raw need inside her threatening to turn her blind and deaf to all other concerns.

"The woman is about to arrive," she rasped out, giving a tele-pathic order at the same time. *Take her to room 7A.*

Twisting her so that she ended up with her back against the wall as the last words left her mouth, Aden kissed her again, his hard body pressed to her own and his hair tumbled from her fingers. One hand came up to cradle her jaw as he ran his tongue over her lips and took and took until she couldn't breathe, and that was absolutely fine because he was doing things to her that made pleasure singe her nerve endings.

Sir, the target is in place in room 7A.

The rage that wasn't rage with Aden went to shove aside that interruption, but her Arrow training kicked in at the last instant. *I'll be there soon,* she replied and forced herself to break the kiss. *Aden.*

Chest rising and falling in harsh breaths and pupils dilated, Aden watched her mouth as if he'd devour her all over again.

Zaira was fine with being devoured. *Fine.* "I'm meant to be the out-of-control one," she whispered.

He shot her a look that made her burn, made her realize just how much he kept contained beneath his calm, stable skin. It felt as if he'd shown her a secret, shown her a small madness within himself. She couldn't stop herself. She pressed close, claimed another kiss, was claimed, that strong hand on her jaw and his body crushing her to the wall.

And Zaira realized that some prisons could equal pleasure, not pain.

WHEN they entered room 7A, it was to discover Olivia Coletti was neither blindfolded nor gagged, but she wasn't struggling, her dark blonde hair hanging limp on either side of her badly scarred face as she sat motionless in a chair. Her dazed brown eyes and the yellowish tinge to her other-wise pale skin tone—pale to the point of translucence—explained her lax state.

"Halcyon," Zaira said, knowing this woman would give them nothing. She was too zoned out. First they'd have to dry her out. Though chances of intel were low even after she was sober—Halcyon also had one major side effect: it affected long-term memory.

She did make an attempt, got nothing except for one single word.

"Persephone," Olivia said, her eyes staring out into nothing. *"Persephone."*

The tone of Olivia's voice disturbed Zaira. *The child may be a hostage,* she said to Aden. *Even if not, her situation can't be good.* If the little girl was even alive.

Aden nodded. *We'll get Olivia into detox, but I'll grant access to the BlackSea alpha when she arrives—depending on Olivia's place in changeling hierarchy, she may feel compelled to answer her alpha's questions.*

Look at the scars on her face. To Zaira, they looked like healed cuts. *If those aren't from a previous injury, then it might not only be Halcyon that's keeping her silent.*

Aden's response told Zaira he was following her train of thought. *We'll make sure the medics assess her for further signs of torture.*

Giving the order for Olivia to be taken to an Arrow medical facility, Zaira spoke to Mica, who'd led the team that had brought the woman in, and asked if they'd discovered anything in her apartment. The answer was expected: "Nothing but a four-day cache of disposable drug injectors preloaded with what must be Halcyon—though I'm having it tested to confirm—and some clothing."

Zaira released her lieutenant to his duties and walked back outside with Aden. "I didn't get a chance to tell you earlier"—because she'd decided to pounce on him instead—"but it looks like both Jim and Olivia simply took a water taxi into Venice a week ago. We're working on backtracking further, but my instincts say we'll find no paper trail that leads back to anything substantial." This entire conspiracy was too well organized.

"Update me if there are any developments." Ordinary enough words, but his eyes took her back to their stolen kisses, her body humming at the proximity to his. "I have to return to the compound, but I'll be back soon . . . and we can finish our earlier conversation."

Her heart slammed against her rib cage.

Chapter 48

BEATRICE STARED AT the target she'd taken as part of her first live mission, nausea churning in her gut and threatening to erupt from her throat. The girl was crying again, begging to be released. Beatrice had given her water and some food, so she wasn't emaciated, but her face was thinner, her eyes red.

"I don't think she knows anything," she dared whisper to Blake. "I've used every viable interrogation technique."

Blake backhanded her. Hard.

She fell to the floor, stayed there when he came to straddle her body and wrench back her head with a grip in her hair. Blood trickled from her nose, her entire face a throbbing pulse. "You used only the nonviolent methods," he said, his voice toneless and cold. "You've failed the test."

Her eyes burned. "No, please." If she lost him, she'd have nothing and no one.

"Stop sniveling and get up. I'm going to show you how a real interrogation is done."

Rising to her feet, she wiped away the blood and tears and followed him to stand beside the girl, who looked at her with scared eyes. "Please help me," she begged. "Please."

Blake grabbed the girl's jaw in a punishing hold. "There is no help here." Taking a hunting knife, he cut a deep line over her left breast while muffling her screams with his palm.

Blood blackened her thin red top, but he'd cut with care to

cause pain without doing a debilitating injury. Beatrice's stomach lurched nonetheless and she would've stumbled back if Blake hadn't raised his head and said, "This is how you get answers." Removing his hand from over the woman's mouth when her scream died to snuffles, he held the knife, point down, over her abdomen. "Your father is a scientist, is he not?"

The woman nodded frantically. "Yes, yes! He is!"

"And he's creating a serum to neutralize Psy abilities."

"Yes!"

"Good, we're finally getting somewhere." Turning, he held the blade handle out toward Beatrice. "Get the rest of the information."

Chapter 49

IT WAS AFTERNOON in Venice by the time Zaira was able to go off shift, and though she'd been up for well over twenty-four hours, she went to bed with a deep sense of frustration at how little she'd unearthed about the conspiracy targeting the Arrows.

The pathologist *had* just confirmed that Jim's brain, while showing signs of Halcyon damage, wasn't the Swiss cheese that scans showed his female partner's to be. Even after a full detox, Olivia might never salvage large blocks of memory. Jim, on the other hand, might well have made a total recovery.

According to the pathologist, the male may have been "one of the lucky few who have a kind of natural protection against long-term Halcyon damage."

"Which is why he had to die," she said to Aden when he joined her in her room ten minutes after her own return. "If it was Blake, he was very careful about it."

"No luck with surveillance feeds from security and street cameras?" Sitting on the bed, he took off his boots and socks.

She shook her head and, having already changed, stood in front of the closed door and indulged her need by watching him. Boots set aside, socks beside them, he rose and removed his belt to drop it by the boots. "Beggars belief to think this situation is unconnected to our abductions."

"Agreed. Two different entities suddenly after the squad?

I don't buy it." Zaira blew out a breath and watched him strip off his T-shirt. "How are things in the valley?"

"On track." He stretched, rubbing the back of his neck, his body flexing.

Breath catching in her throat, she clenched her stomach. "How do we do this? What are the rules?"

"We make the rules." He closed the distance between them, crowding her up against the door in a way she'd permit no one else. With Aden it felt as if she was basking in sunshine, her body turning molten.

Running her hands up his sides, she shivered when he dipped his head to kiss her throat. On the PsyNet, her shields began to fall, but she'd built fail-safe after fail-safe since RainFire. No one would know her emotions, know that he was her greatest weakness.

She held his head against her, craving the contact, the sensations he aroused in a body that, before him, had never understood it had the capacity for such pleasure. But as her mind began to haze, she felt the hard thrust of his erection against her abdomen. "Do you want full sexual contact?" Zaira wasn't sure if she could trust even Aden to invade her body in that way.

Aden lifted his head, palms braced on either side of her shoulders. "Sexual penetration is the final step. Many more precede it."

"How do you know?"

"There are manuals."

"Manuals?" She gripped fistfuls of his hair. "I want to read them."

"If you get in bed," he said, his lips against hers, "I'll download them to your organizer."

"Blackmail?"

"Negotiation."

The rage in her wanted to curl around him. "These better be worth it," she said, sliding into bed as he found the slimline device on a small shelf by the door and came to join her, his body sleek and strong and healthy, his olive-toned skin warm.

Tapping the screen, he brought up files from his own account, then lay down on his back beside her, holding up the organizer so they could both see the screen. "This bed needs to be bigger," he said, and lifted one arm so she could use it as a pillow.

She turned into his body so that she was on her side and he wrapped his arm around her. It made her feel precious again. Worth protecting. "As long as you don't go far, we can get a bigger bed."

That *look* again, the one that said an inferno blazed below the calm waters of him. "Vasic passed on this package of data," he said, his voice rough. "It apparently originated with Judd, but Vasic's added to it, as did Stefan."

I'M happy you need it had been Vasic's only comment when Aden raised the subject of physical bonding.

"That's ridiculous," Zaira said suddenly, her eyes on the screen. "The pulse point of the wrist cannot be an erogenous zone. It's just like any other part of the arm."

Aden's body grew taut. Placing the organizer beside him, he picked up her hand and bent it slightly back to expose the delicate skin above her pulse. He didn't touch it with his mouth as the literature had suggested. Instead, he used a fingertip to map the tracery of fine veins beneath the skin. "Your skin is softer than mine," he said. "Did you know that?"

"Yes." Warm breath against him, her eyes trained on what he was doing to her wrist. "I like the way you feel against me."

His body grew impossibly harder at her confession, but he continued to trace her veins with a fingertip. It was difficult to hold his concentration, especially with Zaira's unfettered breasts pressed against his side, the thin barrier of her black tee no impediment to feeling the lushness of her. The fact that her nipples were hard ratcheted up his primal response.

Long conditioned to suppress all sexual desire, his penis was now very definitely receiving signals from the rest of him and it liked those signals despite the almost painful intensity of the sensation.

Bringing Zaira's wrist closer as his erection throbbed, he licked out very gently over the pulse point, then blew on it.

Her pulse skipped, fingers curling into her palm. "Perhaps the manual writers do know something," she admitted.

Instead of releasing her, he put his lips to her skin, licked out again. She tasted of Zaira, of power contained in a small form, of ice and of steel. Blowing on her skin once more, he released her. She didn't pull away, allowing her hand to fall on his chest, over the racing beat of his heart.

Her fingers curved, her nails grazing his skin.

It was too much provocation.

He had her under him before he consciously processed what he was about to do. Halting with his weight braced above her, he looked at her face, into her eyes. "If you ever want me to stop, just say."

"Why would I do that when I can just break one of your ribs instead?"

And Aden found he knew how to smile after all, his lips tugging up at the corners. "That'll work, too."

A small fist mock-punched him in the abdomen. "I wouldn't hurt you." Thunder in her gaze.

"You are so beautiful." The words came out raw.

Freezing, she looked up at him for a long, long time. "You mean it," she whispered. "You really do."

He didn't understand why she'd even question that, but he didn't have time for a discussion. Not today. Bending his head, he kissed her. She opened for him immediately, one of her legs curling over his hip in a distinctively possessive act. Reaching down, he pulled up her other leg until she was locked around him, her arms wrapped around his neck as she held him to her.

"Mine," she said on a kiss.

The single word branded him to the soul. "Yes."

When he allowed her to feel the weight of his lower body, she slid one of her hands through his hair to grip at it. He groaned at the tug of sensation, at the sign that his wild, dangerous lover was with him every step of the way. Pushing up her tee, he drank in the silken feel of her skin, shaped her rib cage. *How can you be so small and so strong?*

Her answer was to bite down on his lip. Not hard enough to hurt or to draw blood. Just enough to send an electrical current directly to his erection. Shuddering, he shifted his hand to close it over the warm globe of her breast.

She jerked, nails digging into his nape. "Don't stop."

The husky order sliced like a scalpel through any control he might've retained. Raising his head to look at her face as he touched her, Aden saw her eyes flutter shut and his entire body turned into one big pulse. Giving Zaira pleasure was an intoxication, her trust in him a drug. With no one else would she allow herself to be this vulnerable—that knowledge alone was enough to drive him to the edge.

When the scrape of his thumb over her nipple elicited a throaty moan, he knew he should file the response away for later retrieval and future use, but his brain wasn't functioning too well. All he wanted to do was taste her, touch her, devour her.

Lowering his head on the roar of need, one hand under her back to arch her up toward him, he sucked at her nipple. Zaira twisted under him, her legs sliding over his body, but she didn't push him away. Continuing to lick and suck at her, he drank in the small sounds she made and suddenly understood that he had a deeply primitive core that gloried in his ability to give his lover what she needed.

"What—" Zaira sucked in a breath as he switched to her neglected breast. "What should I do?" A gasp. "For you?"

Drunk on her, Aden didn't reply.

Shuddering as he grazed his teeth over her breast, she said, "Do you want me to take off my top?"

Aden had to stop, tense every one of his muscles, his penis ready to explode. "Yes," he finally gritted out.

Reaching down, she tugged off the soft fabric. He didn't see what she did with it, his eyes on her naked upper body. She appeared even more delicate this way, the skin of her breasts pale and already marked by his caresses. Closing his hand over the flushed flesh of one breast, he bent his head to the other, not yet done with his self-imposed task.

The sound that came from her was a shocked combination of pleasure and sweet need, her arousal damp and hot in the air.

It turned Aden into a creature of pure want. He took Zaira's mouth in harsh demand. Arms and legs locking around him again, she met him kiss for kiss, their bodies rocking instinctively against one another and their breathing choppy. He drank her up and demanded more, his greed for her voracious.

• • •

ZAIRA didn't know how to process this much pleasure, this much sensation, but neither did she want to stop. Especially when Aden was so totally out of control. She'd always thought he was beautiful, but seeing him like this, his cheekbones flushed and his hair falling around his face as he gorged on her, she had no words to describe the way he affected her.

"Yes," she said.

Eyes jet black and glittering with need, he shook his head, as if to clear it for thought. "Yes?"

"Full sexual contact," she whispered, running her fingers over his kiss-swollen lips. "I want it." Even in the midst of such unadulterated pleasure, part of her knew this was a moment out of time. If she was lucky, the madness might not live in her blood, but that didn't alter her nature, didn't alter her feral possessiveness where Aden was concerned.

A possessiveness that in itself was like insanity.

"Zaira." His body trembled from the vicious control he'd managed to assert over himself. "Are you sure?"

"Yes." She wanted every part of him she could hold, at least for these hours where she was sane and rational and not a monster—because she wasn't sure she could hang on to her reason as she spiraled further and further into emotion. Further and further into the extraordinary, deadly, powerful man who was her lover. "I want you." Drawing him closer, she pressed her mouth to his.

Kissing was a wonderful, *wonderful* thing. She loved being able to taste him, loved being able to feel his breath as the perspiration-damp heat of his body rubbed against hers. It was so intimate, more intimate than anything but his mind open to her own. She slid hers open just enough for him and he swept inside to deepen the already intense intimacy of the contact.

Afraid time was running out, that she wouldn't get to experience the entirety of this sexual inferno with him, she moved her hands to his waistband and undid the button, lowered the zip. He cooperated, kicking off his pants, but one of his hands still cradled her jaw and neck, the other on her breast as he continued to kiss her as if he couldn't get enough.

Zaira. Zaira. Zaira.

Something fell dully to the floor as his mind burned with her name, and she realized it must be the organizer with the manuals. She should've probably read those so she'd know what she was doing, but all she wanted to do was touch Aden. Rubbing against him, she made a frustrated sound. *Aden.*

He didn't ask her what she wanted, just lifted off her, hooked his fingers into the sides of her pants and panties and pulled. His breath caught as she was exposed and he paused with her clothing halfway down her thighs, but she twisted to remind him she wanted to be naked.

Jaw clenched, he got the items off. When he would've come back down, she touched her toes to his briefs, her leg bent. Getting the hint, he got off the bed and stripped off the briefs before returning to his position over her. She barely glimpsed him. *I wanted to admire you.*

ZAIRA'S words almost ripped away what infinitesimal control Aden had managed to claw back so he could be certain she was ready. *Later,* he said, one of his hands on the side of her face as he held her in place for another kiss. This one was raw, deep, almost rough, but she didn't push him away. Wrapping her legs around him instead, she arched into him.

Wet heat slid over his cock, her arousal unhidden.

His heart slammed against his ribs.

Then she began to kiss his shoulders, his neck, and he knew he was one more caress away from losing it. Running his hand down her side, he insinuated it between their bodies in an effort to distract her—and pleasure her. "I have to make sure you're ready." That part of the manual he'd memorized; if Zaira was giving him the gift of her trust, he would do nothing to abuse it.

She moaned at the first brush of his rough-skinned fingertips. "I am ready." Nails digging into his shoulders, she writhed under him. "But . . . Aden . . . what . . ."

Sweat broke out over his body at the now wordless gasps

that spilled from her mouth as he stroked his fingers through her liquid-soft folds to find her clitoris and rub. His fingers were wet with her, the lubrication both easing his way and driving him crazy. When he moved his hand lower, to nudge at the entrance to her body, she bit him on the arm.

"No?" he asked, his muscles so tense it felt as if they would snap.

Why did you stop?

Her response made his penis jump. Sliding one finger into her in a slow, relentless push that made her moan, he pressed his thumb against her clitoris at the same time. "Like this?"

Hips moving against him, she scored his back with her nails. He fisted his free hand against the bed at the silent answer and moved his finger in and out of her while caressing her clitoris in a ragged motion that echoed his harsh breathing.

Zaira didn't seem to mind, her body squeezing tight around his finger less than half a minute later. Biting down on the back of her own fist to muffle her scream, she melted around him. He was at once deeply, unashamedly proud of giving her such extreme pleasure, and on the verge of breaking.

Withdrawing his finger from her body as he called on every ounce of his Arrow training to hold on to his splintered control, he cupped her damp heat and sought her mouth for a kiss. She opened for him, her hands tight in his hair as she claimed him in return.

Licking her tongue over his before she broke the kiss, she raised her eyelashes. "Now," she said, and shifted her body so that his penis nudged at her wet heat.

Aden's brain short-circuited.

ZAIRA could feel Aden's ragged control in the painful tension of his muscles, but he still found the willpower to say, "You're certain?" His voice was hoarse, the hand he'd placed once more on the side of her face tender.

Her body spasmed on emptiness even as her heart, that battered, twisted organ, ached. "Yes."

He didn't ask again, just gripped her under the hip with one strong hand and pushed the tip of his erection into her passion-swollen entrance.

"*Aden.*"

Sliding his other hand under her neck to hold it gently but with unmistakable possessiveness, he said, "This'll hurt."

Kissing him again in answer, she spoke to him mind to mind. *I choose this pain,* she said. *I choose you.*

Zaira. Her name held so much passion, so much emotion she almost couldn't bear it.

Except it filled her up to overflowing . . . and then Aden filled her. It was slow and hard and deep and it took her breath away. A tear rolled down her face and it had nothing to do with pain, everything to do with the emotions that clawed her heart. Wrapping her arms around Aden's neck, she pressed her cheek to his.

Zaira, are you—

Don't stop, she whispered. *Don't stop.*

Stroking his hand over her thigh, he pulled back, then pushed in again, even slower this time. It felt . . . Zaira's body arched, her mind splintered. But she wasn't lost. Aden was there around her, with her.

It's always been you.

His voice, his words penetrated the cascade of sensation taking her over and it was too much. Too beautiful. Too precious. Too wonderful. Skin threatening to burst, she held on to him as tight as she could and she hoped she had the will to fight the rage and the broken need that lived in her, with or without the madness.

For him, she'd fight. For Aden. Always, for Aden.

Chapter 50

BEATRICE LAY CURLED up in bed, her body hurting from the beating Blake had given her as punishment for her failure. She hadn't been able to use the knife on the target, had thrown up instead; she deserved the penalty he'd meted out.

"You are a pathetic excuse for an Arrow." He'd spit on her after the beating. "I'm not sure you deserve a second chance, but I'll give it to you in two days. Be ready to do what needs to be done or you'll be demoted back to a worthless piece of trash no one sees, much less considers for a partnership."

She'd promised him she'd be ready, but her body shook at the idea of carving a living being with a blade. She'd been taught how to in classes under Ming LeBon, been shown exactly how much pain and damage a body and mind could bear before it broke, but it was easier when practicing on corpses.

Real people bled. Real people cried and screamed.

Slapping her hands over her ears, she rocked, knowing she had to get this under control or she'd lose the only person who cared anything about her, the only person who would miss her if she was gone. "I can do it," she whispered. "I can do it. I can make him proud."

Chapter 51

MIANE LEVÈQUE ARRIVED in Venice at ten p.m. the same day. She came to the compound dressed in a sleek red dress paired with black heels, her hair in a flawless twist at the back of her head and her face made up with artful precision. Her lips were a bold red that echoed her dress.

It is as much armor as our clothing, Zaira telepathed to Aden when they met the BlackSea contingent of three in the courtyard surrounded by the weathered and vine-covered dual-level buildings of the compound.

Yes, Aden responded.

The two of them had caught five hours of sleep when scouts alerted them to the presence of the BlackSea team in a Venice hotel. The water-based changelings had made their presence obvious only after they got into Venice without setting off a single alarm, even though the squad had been watching out for them. Zaira was certain the show of stealth had been a deliberate display that warned the squad to take them seriously.

"Jim Savua's body is in a refrigerated lab space within," Aden said, taking the lead.

"Olivia?" Miane asked, holding Aden's gaze with an unblinking black stare that made the tiny hairs on Zaira's arms rise; she had the distinct sense that while the BlackSea alpha appeared human right then, she wasn't, not fully.

"Olivia Coletti is in detox." Aden didn't look away from that unnerving gaze. "She's said her daughter's name but nothing else."

Miane's expression didn't change but her eyes became even colder. "I want to see her." It was an order.

"The squad has no reason to trust you," Aden said flatly, and Zaira realized he was responding as another alpha, one who was making it plain that Miane Levèque was a guest in his territory with no rights to demand anything.

A changeling alpha would respect nothing less.

"If she comes to harm in your care, it will be considered a hostile act."

"Her brain is fried on Halcyon—she did the harm herself."

Zaira caught the slight change in Miane's features, identified it as surprise. The BlackSea alpha hadn't expected drugs to be in the mix.

Stance becoming less aggressive, she said, "I would request a chance to talk to Olivia." This time, the words were polite. "She may speak to me when she wouldn't to you."

Aden held her gaze before giving a small nod. "We'll permit the visitation, but you'll be observed."

"Please make certain the observer isn't in close proximity. She needs to scent her pack, no one else."

"Understood."

"Jim?"

"This way."

Aden led the BlackSea alpha and her two guards to the lab. With the Venice compound clearly compromised, there was no reason to maintain secrecy. Those Arrows who wanted and had earned a life out of the spotlight had already relocated to other covert squad properties. Most had chosen the valley.

This compound would soon cease to exist.

Inside the lab, Miane Levèque stepped close to Jim Savua's thin but still muscled body in silence and took his hand. His brown skin was dull and yellowed against the healthy glow of hers, his face bearing the ravages of Halcyon. A haunting humming sound came from Miane's throat a second later, the purity of it sinking into Zaira's bones and surging through her blood.

Reaching out to touch her fingers to the male's closed eyelids after what was clearly a song of sorrow, the BlackSea alpha turned to the pathologist. "The drug use is confirmed?" she asked and though her tone was even, it held the roughness of grief.

"Beyond any doubt."

"Thank you." She turned to Aden, a wet gleam in her eyes.

The sign of vulnerability surprised Zaira . . . except Miane Levèque wasn't vulnerable even at that instant. Her strength pulsed under her skin, her sadness stealing nothing from the anger that burned in her gaze.

An alpha mourning a lost packmate and unafraid to show her emotions.

"If the squad has no objections," she said, "we will take our packmate to the sea that was his home."

Aden looked to the pathologist. "Release the body."

Walking out with the BlackSea alpha after she ordered one of her guards to arrange the transport, Aden held out a blindfold. "If you wish to see Olivia, there are certain conditions. Including the fact that you alone will be taken to where she's being held."

A sudden stiffness in the spine of the tall, wide-shouldered male in a black suit who shadowed Miane. He leaned down to speak in her ear, his voice so quiet that Zaira picked up nothing. The BlackSea alpha angled her head to respond and her voice, too, was subvocal. One thing was clear, however. The two were having an argument.

He doesn't want her to go alone and he's determined to push the point, Zaira 'pathed to Aden. *Certainly no cipher.*

Aden glanced at her. *A strong alpha isn't scared by the strength of those around him or her, Commander.*

Zaira resisted the temptation to touch him, though it was difficult when he was once again making her heart ache. *Who do you think will win this argument?*

I wouldn't bet against either.

Miane Levèque turned back to them. "Will transporting Olivia here do her harm?"

"Yes," Aden replied. "She's currently hooked up to drip meds and in a special medical bed that monitors her vitals."

The BlackSea alpha held out her hand for the blindfold, gave it to the guard who'd argued with her, the one who was most probably her lieutenant. Jaw clenched, he nonetheless wrapped it around her eyes and tied it securely, his expression making it clear that if anything happened to his alpha, he would rip them all to shreds with his bare hands.

Zaira decided she liked him.

Abbot had been on standby for this contingency and now appeared to teleport Miane Levèque to the facility, along with Zaira. Aden remained in Venice with Miane's guards, a deliberate decision on his part—he wanted to make sure he was on hand should BlackSea have brought more reinforcements.

At present, the squad had no way of knowing whether or not the water-based changelings had acted against the squad as a group, or whether Jim and Olivia had broken away for reasons of their own.

Guiding the alpha to the correct room with a touch of her fingertips against Miane's upper arm, Zaira ushered her inside. "You may remove your blindfold once I shut the door." The room was a generic infirmary room, with no windows and nothing else that would betray its location.

"Thank you."

Zaira pulled the door shut, authorizing a computronic lock before removing herself from the vicinity and using her organizer to connect to the feed from the room. Having already pulled down the blindfold, Miane Levèque let it hang around her neck as she closed the distance from the door to the bed.

Reaching Olivia, who had her eyes closed, Miane put her hands on either side of the woman's face and leaned in so close that her breath mingled with Olivia's. Her lips moved, the words inaudible.

Zaira increased the volume levels to maximum and barely caught, ". . . you home. I am here."

A promise, she surmised.

"Wake."

This time, it was an order, in the same alpha tone Zaira had heard Remi use in RainFire, the same tone Aden could put in his own voice.

Olivia's eyes fluttered open. The clarity of the feed

allowed Zaira to see that her gaze was dull, but it sharpened quickly. "Miane." The single word came out a sob.

Stroking back Olivia's hair, Miane leaned in to kiss her on both cheeks. "Shh, I have you."

Raising one thin arm, her skin still bearing the yellowish tint of Halcyon, Olivia grabbed at her alpha's wrist. "Persephone. They have Persephone."

"Who?" Miane asked, the harsh anger of her echoing the emotions in Zaira's heart at the thought of a vulnerable child in the hands of the enemy.

Olivia shook her head, her face crumpling. Her eyes phased out at the same time, going dull and staring out into nothing.

"Olivia." Miane's voice was alpha again, her packmate's name imbued with command.

A sucked-in breath as Olivia struggled to focus. She came back enough to say. "E-mail. They sent photos of our baby." Sobbing took her over. "Killed Cary. They killed him, said they'd kill our baby, too, if I . . ."

This time when she phased out, she didn't come back, the Halcyon damage yet too deep. Instead of leaving, Miane Levèque kicked off her high-heeled shoes and got into bed with her distressed packmate, holding her close and murmuring things too soft for the microphones to pick up.

It took fifteen minutes for Olivia to fall asleep again.

Leaving her with another kiss, the BlackSea alpha pulled up the blindfold.

ADEN took Zaira's report telepathically when she returned, glanced at Miane Levèque afterward. "Are you aware of your packmate's e-mail address?"

"Malachai is just retrieving it." Miane's face was all hard angles, her eyes pieces of jet. "Olivia was too affected by the ravages of Halcyon to lie. Someone used her daughter as leverage to get her to commit these acts."

I agree with her, Zaira said, remembering the anguished pain in Olivia's voice. *Olivia's medical readings also indicated extreme distress.*

"We've cooperated with you far beyond what anyone could

expect," Aden said when Malachai spoke quietly into his alpha's ear. "We're also willing to assist you in retrieving the child, but for that, we need the data from your packmate's e-mail."

"The enemy of my enemy . . . ?" Raising an eyebrow, Miane glanced at the phone Malachai had just handed her.

Rage burned in those black eyes.

Turning the phone toward Aden without a word, she waited as Aden and Zaira scanned the image.

Zaira's own rage roared to the surface at the photograph of a small, teary-eyed girl clinging desperately to a rag doll with red hair. Her dress was dirty and her surroundings barren, the bed on which she sat nothing but a cot without a mattress. The doll's hair, of what appeared to be thick red wool, obscured over half of Persephone's face, but there was no hiding the thinness of that face, or of her body. It was clear she hadn't been given enough food or any real care.

They've put her in a cage. The insane little girl inside Zaira had her lifting her head to meet Miane Levèque's eyes. "I will find her for you, bring her home."

The alpha's dangerous expression didn't alter as she said, "I'll accept any help. I know Psy have teleporters who can use people's faces as anchors. Can you teleport to her?"

"I'm telepathing the image through to a teleporter to verify," Aden replied.

Vasic? Zaira asked.

Yes. If he can't get to someone, no one can. Jaw a hard line, he was quiet for a minute before shaking his head. "He can't get a lock—her face is too obscured and the room too generic. Do you have a better photograph of her?"

"We'll find one," Miane said, and after a short conversation with Malachai, showed them four other images on the phone. "Can your teleporter go to any of these people? They're all missing, too, and it's possible they're being held in the same location as Persephone."

Zaira waited for Vasic's response once Aden sent through the request, her stomach tense.

"No," Aden said at last. "Either their features have changed in a substantial way—or they're dead."

Miane's anger was black ice. "Olivia wasn't scarred when she disappeared," she said. "Would that kind of a change destabilize a teleport lock?"

Aden nodded. "When it's that extensive, yes."

"The depth and degree of Jim Savua's Halcyon scars would've had the same effect," Zaira said, wondering if Jim's reaction to the drug had in fact given his and Olivia's captors the idea of destroying their victims' faces just in case BlackSea gained access to a teleporter like Vasic. "Persephone was likely left alone only because by the time the people behind this began to scar their prisoners, her face had already changed naturally."

Anger crackled in the air and it wasn't all coming from the changeling side.

"It appears your enemy has thought of every angle," Aden said into the tense quiet. "However, if you have any other missing packmates you want our teleporters to try to find, we're willing to make the attempt. A single mistake on their end could break things wide open for both the squad and BlackSea."

Miane inclined her head in regal acceptance of the offer. "Malachai will send you more photos, and we will share the information about Olivia's e-mail account so you can track from your end while we do it from ours." Her chilly gaze, which had gone to her lieutenant, shifted back to Aden. "We did not attack you and have no desire to make an enemy of you."

A strand of her hair escaping to slide against her face, she added, "You should also know that Jim was no drug addict. He lost two family members to a drug that was created by a sea changeling"—a tightening of her lips—"and that affects our biochemistry specifically. It turned him adamantly against drugs."

"It could also be argued that he had a genetic predisposition to addiction."

"Do you know your people?" A blunt question.

"I get your point."

"Olivia, too, was strong and healthy, with no tendencies toward mind-altering substances."

"Could she have built the poison bombs?"

"Yes. She's a chemist, a very good one."

Stepping out into a patch of moonlight, Aden said, "It appears your packmates were forcibly addicted to keep them on a short leash. Olivia was likely addicted after building the bombs—or the components at least."

Yes, Zaira thought, that made sense. Olivia's captors had used Persephone as the leash at first, but had wanted further control when they sent Olivia out into the world. In all probability, she'd come to the end of her expertise, and was thus rendered expendable. Now, so would her daughter be.

Screaming anger howling in her skull, Zaira knew there was a good chance Persephone was already dead, killed when her mother outlived her usefulness, but until she knew for certain, she would consider the child alive and a hostage.

"I would not sacrifice my people this way," Miane said in answer to the unasked question in the air. "I would not degrade them."

Zaira believed her. There was something undeniably ruthless about Miane, but her grief was real, as was her fury.

"The e-mail details." Malachai passed over a slip of paper.

Zaira immediately saw why he'd been able to get into his packmate's account so easily.

The password was "Persephone."

Looking up with her own fury a firestorm inside her, she said, "No child should ever be put in a cage."

"It appears we understand one another." Reaching into a hidden pocket, Miane retrieved a black card engraved with her name and contact details and gave it to Zaira. "Should you need to get in touch with me. Now, we must hunt."

It looks like you have made a political ally, Aden said as Miane and her guards left.

Zaira held the card so Aden could see it, too. *I think she sensed that we are very similar in certain ways.*

"You should take her up on her offer."

"For political purposes?"

"No, out of friendship. If nothing else, you will have a conversation with a woman rumored to be a mako shark in changeling form—though I'm not so certain she's anything so explicable."

Zaira slid away the card. "Friendship." She'd never con- sidered the concept in relation to anyone but Aden, certainly never with anyone outside the squad. But she'd already broken countless rules. Why not this one, too?

Chapter 52

DEVRAJ SANTOS WAS on the phone with one of Aden's people, hammering out details of the training protocol they were creating for the fiercely strong and unique psychic abilities now appearing in the Forgotten population, when Aubry ran into his office. Dev took one look at the urgency on his normally laid-back vice director's face and cut the conversation short.

"What is it?" he asked Aubry.

"There's just been a kidnapping attempt against five of our children."

Dev's anger was an arctic thing. The Forgotten had been through this once before, would rise up in bloody war to stop a second wave of innocent death. "The ones with Snow-Dancer and DarkRiver?" The two packs had offered safe harbor for gifted Forgotten children who needed to grow into their strength away from covetous eyes.

"Safe." Aubry flipped an organizer toward him, his Texan drawl having turned clipped and hard. "These five are too young to relocate, were playing together in a small park when a fucking assault force came after them."

Taking the organizer, Dev flipped through the images from the scene. "Injuries?"

"Kids are scared but safe. All three of the parents who were shooting the breeze while the kids played are down with severe wounds." His hand tightened, tendons pushing up against the deep brown of his skin. "The adults confirmed the attackers were Psy, and that they had a symbol on their uniforms that traces back to the Marshall family."

"How are the children safe if this was an assault force?"

"Luck," Aubry said, voice grim. "Tag and Tiara were armed and close enough to respond to the telepathic cries for help. Otherwise, we'd be looking at dead parents and abducted children."

In spite of his anger, Dev could see what Aubry couldn't, blinded as the other man was by the terror and pain he'd witnessed at the site. "Why would the team wear identifiable gear, Aubry?" It went against every tenet of black ops. "Especially that of a prominent family?"

"Stupidity? Arrogance?" Aubry ran both hands over his clean-shaven skull, his eyes glittering. "Tiara and Tag shot a couple of them, so we've got blood at least, even if they all escaped. Fucking cowards."

Dev walked out with Aubry, heading to go see the injured and the scared, but his mind continued to pick holes in the believability of the scenario. Yes, a number of Psy had proven they'd cross any lines to obtain power and Dev's people were starting to display some very unusual ones, but the Marshall family was a business empire, not a military one.

"Don't forget," Katya said to him that night as they stood on the balcony of their apartment in a soaring high-rise. "The 'Marshall' part of their name comes from Marshall Hyde. The family changed its surname to his first name when he first rose to power in the Council. Ruthless is their nature."

"But the Marshalls are smart." The family group was a significant force in the financial world. "This wasn't smart— if I know their identity, I can launch a retaliatory attack."

Katya nodded slowly, the wind pasting strands of her fine blonde hair to his shirtsleeve. She'd grown it out until it now reached the middle of her back, and every so often, she'd smile at him and hand him a brush in memory of the time when he'd carefully untangled her hair though they'd been strangers to one another.

"Yes," she murmured. "The Marshalls never pick fights unless they know they'll win."

Sliding his arm around her, he tucked her to his side. "My gut tells me that, no matter what, there was always meant to be at least one survivor who could point us toward the Marshalls."

A frown of concentration on his wife's face, her skin gilded gold by the sun she'd been getting as she helped play babysitter to a friend's young and active children while the friend and her husband took a long-overdue honeymoon. "Maybe the Forgotten and the Marshalls have a common enemy," she said at last. "Could be you're supposed to get angry and eliminate them."

Dev ran his fingers desultorily over her nape, satisfaction uncurling in his gut when her eyes closed, a sigh of pleasure escaping her throat. "It's also possible the family was arrogant enough to think they didn't need subterfuge, that it'd be an easy snatch."

"How do we find out which?"

"Pax Marshall and I are going to have a conversation." Pax might have a rep as a stone-cold bastard, but if he was behind this, he had no idea who he was baiting.

Chapter 53

FRUSTRATED BY THE inability of their tech people to trace the e-mails Olivia had received back to an identifiable source—even more so after Vasic confirmed he couldn't lock on to any of the people BlackSea had tagged as missing—Zaira went to speak to the team she'd charged with pinning down Olivia's life prior to the moment when she'd been captured.

"The trail goes dead in Milan," Mica told her, after running through the data they had to date. "It's as if she appeared out of nowhere a month ago."

"Or out of a holding facility." Pulling up the photograph of Persephone, she examined the child in detail, fighting her anger to think clearly. "She's not thin enough to suggest she's been mistreated a long time."

Mica nodded. "Mother and daughter held together until the mother was dropped off in Milan?"

"Yes, I think so." Zaira stared at the image of the little girl who clutched at her doll and could feel her fear, her confusion at what she'd have seen as abandonment. "Focus on Milan. Use facial recognition software. Unless she was teleported in, which in itself will tell us something, she will have used transportation at some point."

Leaving Mica to organize the detail-oriented task, she

realized that hovering would achieve nothing. She'd already sent search algorithms out into the PsyNet in case Persephone's abduction had been mentioned there, and she'd touched base with Miane Levèque to see if the water-based changelings had any further data.

The answer was no, though Miane intended to return the next day to speak to Olivia again, once the medication had had a chance to further clear her system.

In the interim, Zaira needed to do something to burn off her anger and she owed the teenagers in the valley a martial arts lesson. She'd canceled it the day before, part of the fallout from the attempted attack on the compound, but it was important she fulfill her commitment today—because Persephone wasn't the only child about whom Zaira was concerned.

Beatrice remained on her mind.

She made sure to make eye contact with the seventeen-year-old once the class assembled under the valley sunlight. The brown-haired girl had taken position on the periphery of the back row and couldn't seem to hold the contact.

Not pushing the issue, Zaira took the class through the advanced training session. For the first time, she didn't only correct mistakes, she made sure to offer praise for tasks well done. That didn't come naturally to her, but she was learning along with her students. The teenagers didn't react to her change in tactics as openly as the much younger Tavish had, but they lingered after the session to speak to her in a way they'd never before done—like flowers parched of sunlight, then given just a ray.

A single act of kindness, she thought again, could change a life.

"Beatrice," she said when she saw the girl about to break away. "Stay. I want to speak to you."

"Yes, sir."

Finishing her conversations with the other trainees without rushing them, Zaira went over to the teenager. "Walk with me."

Zaira led the compliant girl toward the trees beyond the training area. It was a significant distance but Zaira didn't push the speed. The gentle pace was good for Beatrice, would further stretch out her muscles. Only once they were far enough from the compound that no one could overhear them, did she say, "Who beat you?"

The teenager froze, her eyes skating away as her skin paled. "No one."

"Beatrice, I can tell by the way you move, the way you moved during training." She well remembered how her own muscles had felt after a beating, how every movement had become agony. Beatrice was past that first excruciating stage and into the aching stiffness. "Who beat you?"

The girl stood mute, her eyes huge.

"You feel loyalty?"

A nod. "He has been . . . kind to me."

"He may simply need an education in our new protocols." Zaira stifled her instinctive and aggressive protective response because she knew not all the older teachers fully understood the changes in the squad. "Physical torture of any kind is now unacceptable—that means we won't torture him, either."

Zaira would also make sure she didn't go near him, because if she did, she'd smash his bones to dust. "He'll simply be retrained."

Beatrice squeezed one of her hands with the other.

"You are now part of my family," Zaira said. "As such, I have responsibility for your well-being."

"Wh-what?"

Zaira realized Walker and Cristabel must not have had a chance to interview Beatrice yet. However, given Beatrice's physical state, any further delay was no longer an option. "You are now part of my family unit," she reiterated. "That means you are mine to care for. Mine and Aden's."

A tremor went through Beatrice's body. "Why?" she whispered. "I'm not special. Not like you or Aden."

Zaira touched her hand to Beatrice's cheek in a conscious gesture of affection. "We're all special to the people who are our own."

The girl's body began to shake. "I—I—"

Zaira hauled her into an embrace, acting on the instincts of the feral, broken survivor she'd once been. She was careful of the girl's injuries, but her hold was in no way tentative. That wasn't what Beatrice needed. "There's no cause for fear. I'm capable of killing almost every other Arrow in the compound." Sometimes a bigger nightmare was the only thing that kept other nightmares at bay. "Those I can't kill, Aden and I can together. *No one* can hurt you."

Gripping at her with desperate hands, Beatrice whispered, "I failed my mission."

"What mission?" Beatrice wasn't yet authorized for live missions, so if her trainer had taken her on one, he'd broken fundamental Arrow protocol.

"To get the scientist's daughter to speak and tell us the codes."

Zaira was aware of most of the major operations in progress, but had heard nothing of this. Connecting with Aden on their private and familiar telepathic pathway, she said, *Is there a mission in progress to do with a scientist and the retrieval of codes of some kind?*

No.

"Beatrice." Zaira gently tugged up the girl's head so she could look her in the eye. "This mission was not sanctioned."

Beatrice's face went bone white, her already unsteady breathing turning jagged and shallow.

"Don't be afraid." Zaira held the girl's face in her hands as she reinforced her earlier reassurance. "You've done nothing wrong."

"I hurt her." It was a shaken whisper, her shoulders hunched in. "But I didn't use the knife like he asked. I promise."

"I believe you." Zaira continued to look into Beatrice's eyes. "The error was your trainer's. You're not authorized for wet work." She used blunt words to reach Beatrice's Arrow training. "You know that."

"He said I was special." It was a lost sound.

"You are. You've come through the fall of Silence with the capacity to handle emotion without losing control of your abilities." No one had made a note in Beatrice's file about the latter, and it was the *lack* that Zaira had noticed. Because almost every other student had a note about disintegrating conditioning leading to psychic mistakes.

"You can show your peers the way, teach them how to stay disciplined even with emotion in their lives." Zaira herself might have been able to learn from the younger woman had it only been about power and emotion, but Zaira's problems resulted from the way she'd been treated as a child, the scars affecting her every action.

Beatrice's lower lip trembled. "I'm sorry."

"It's all right." Zaira kept her hands on the girl's face, thinking of how much such a touch would've meant to her as a lonely and abused little girl. "What's his name?"

Chapter 54

BLAKE WAS INTELLIGENT and he was trained. He was also starting to have doubts about Beatrice's suitability as a partner so he made sure to keep tabs on her. The instant he saw Zaira take her aside, he had a decision to make and he made it quickly. There was a chance Zaira was simply talking to Beatrice about training issues, but there was also a chance the girl would break, and if she did, he'd be dead within minutes.

Then there was the fact that Yuri had been watching him. He'd counted on the squad's belief in loyalty to shield him from suspicion in the death of the would-be terrorist, but it looked like he'd miscalculated. He'd only done the favor to create a marker with an individual with certain advantageous resources.

Now it was time to collect.

Stepping inside the office he was cleared to use when he came in to run sessions, he tapped a junior telepath who had enough Tk to be useful. Even if they were already suspicious of him, the alert would've gone out to senior personnel, not junior. The Tk appeared in seconds, confirming his belief. When Blake asked for a 'port into New York, the younger male hesitated. "Sir, that's at the end of my range."

"Aden has authorized it. You'll catch a jet back home."

"Yes, sir."

Once in New York, he didn't waste time killing the boy. Instead, he gave a short nod and blended into the bustling metropolis. His PsyNet trail was already secure; the squad couldn't hunt him on that level.

He was free.

Chapter 55

THE HUMAN FEMALE Blake had kidnapped was unconscious when Vasic led a team to rescue her. "She'll live," the teleporter told Zaira and Aden afterward, the three of them standing near one of the new houses in the valley. "A cut across one breast, psychological torture, but no permanent physical damage, though she would've died from lack of water within the next day."

"He wanted Beatrice to kill her." Zaira's voice vibrated with withheld fury.

Aden brushed his fingers over hers as they stood side by side. "He'll pay for what he did."

Glancing to his left and down before looking back up, Vasic said, "None of the teleporters in the squad can get to him. Blake was well trained in telepathic cloaking."

It took Aden a second to realize his friend had looked automatically toward where his gauntlet had been on his left forearm before the amputation. *You miss the gauntlet,* he said telepathically while he considered how to track down the rogue and murderous Arrow. It wasn't only that Blake was a threat to innocent people—he could do major damage to the squad's reputation, which would feed back into the Arrows' ability to live their lives.

Winter gray eyes met his. *I became used to having easy, immediate access to various systems.* He took out a small organizer. *I'll adapt.* A pause before he said, "I have the details of Blake's office in the valley and his quarters at Central Command. I'll check out Command first, since he spent more time there." He teleported out.

Able to sense Zaira's frustration, Aden closed his hand around her own. "We'll find him. He's well trained, but he's being hunted by the entire squad." It was rare for Arrows to hunt their own, but when they did, the pursuit was relentless. "He won't have time to catch a breath, much less do damage."

Fingers curling around his own, Zaira gritted her teeth. "I want to be part of the team hunting him. Right now, Persephone is out of my reach but I can do something productive about Blake."

"The operation is already under Amin's command, and you have visitors in Venice to keep an eye on." BlackSea had a dangerous advantage in the watery city.

"I just feel like we're losing the battle against evil." She leaned her body against his on those words, and at that instant, Aden realized they had any number of eyes on them. Arrows and children.

Weaving his fingers through her own, he looked down into her face. "You saved two lives today. Evil didn't win there." *And it won't win in our fight to be together.*

The fire flickered in her gaze. Raising her hand, she laid her fingers against his jaw.

A public claim. A declaration of intent.

PAX Marshall was arrogant but he wasn't stupid. His vehicle was an armor-plated tank. Safe in most circumstances. Except against a man who had the growing ability to control metal and machines.

Waiting until Pax was on a quiet road outside of the Marshall estate in Vermont, Dev pulled over behind him, focused on the other vehicle's engine . . . and Pax's car stopped moving.

He could see the Psy male attempting to reboot the onboard computer as Dev got out, walked to his car, and knocked on his window.

Pax looked at him with cool blue eyes, a weapon no doubt

in his hand, but he opened the door and got out. "Is this how you usually arrange a meeting?" he asked as he buttoned his dark blue suit jacket, his hands as elegant as his features and the cut of his blond hair.

"A necessity." Dev kept his hands in the open as Pax had done.

Pax's upper-class English accent was clipped as he said, "The necessity being?"

Dev told him, watching his face for any indication of guilt or otherwise, but Pax Marshall had the expressionless face down to an art. "I see," the other man said. "You realize I'm not lacking in intelligence. Why would I send in a black ops team emblazoned with our well-known emblem?"

"Precisely because you're smart—smart enough to run a double bluff." Dev had done his research, knew that the reason Pax was CEO of the Marshall Group despite his youth was that he had a way of doing the unexpected, leaving his competitors stunned and off balance.

"Then it appears we are at an impasse."

"Guess so." He couldn't get a read on Pax, but he knew one thing. "If it wasn't you, I suggest you track down the perpetrators, or the next time, your plane might be the vehicle that stops moving." Dev couldn't actually affect objects that distant or large yet, but Pax had no need to know that.

"Do you have the DNA profiles of the ones who left behind blood?"

Dev handed them over.

Two hours after he and Pax parted ways, word came that all the men on that list, plus two others, had been found shot point-blank in the back of the head. Pax sent him a short message not long afterward: *They were not ours and they knew nothing beyond the strict parameters of their mission, which was to abduct the children and leave behind a witness. Contractors should really take care when choosing clients. Your children are safe.*

Dev took everything the other man said with a grain of salt. The double-bluff possibility still applied; from everything Dev knew, Pax Marshall was ruthless enough to kill his own people to make a point.

. . .

ZAIRA spent the remaining daylight hours making sure she knew the exact locations of every water-based changeling in Venice. The task was complicated by the fact that they didn't exactly stand out or call attention to themselves, but thanks to the groundwork laid by Arrows since the squad began, she had back-end access to a number of very secure databases. She also had a network of informants in the city.

She'd started putting that network in place the instant she was assigned the Venice command. Marjorie and Naoshi had always assumed they'd be in command when Venice went active, but logistically, they couldn't run Venice as a fully functioning base of Arrow operations *and* maintain the complex system of safe houses around the world. The latter was a task at which they were expert and that no one else could do. That, at least, was what Aden had told them—and it was all categorically true. Marjorie and Naoshi had long ago proven their exceptional ability to settle at-risk Arrows into safe new lives.

What Aden didn't point out was that his parents, despite their undisputable skill and position as initiators of the rebellion, were, in many ways, stuck in the past and in the old way of doing things. In contrast, Zaira, like many other Arrows who'd come of age with Aden, understood that while fear was a weapon, even better was information—and not just from Psy sources.

It was that kind of a commander Aden had needed in Venice.

After she kept her word and paid the first few scared informants as promised, others had started to pass over pieces of data. According to one of her long-term and more talkative informants, word on the street was that "the scary Psy chick is all about business—don't mess with her and she'll treat you square. Cross her and maybe you find your ass floating in a canal one dark night."

As far as street reps went, Zaira was pleased with hers.

In the end, she calculated she'd identified eighty-five to ninety percent of the water changelings in the city. The remainder had to have come in via no known transport options, never registered to receive any services, and drawn zero notice. Miane Levèque and her guards failed only on the last factor—and Zaira knew that had been on purpose.

The BlackSea alpha had wanted to make her presence felt.

Now, as Zaira pulled herself onto the balcony outside the hotel room where Miane Levèque slept tonight, she didn't for an instant forget that the other woman was a deadly predator.

The lock on the balcony door was more secure than she'd expected, but Zaira had always been good at getting into places. Waiting in silence for ten minutes until she was certain no one was moving in the room beyond, the night hushed around her, she slipped inside. Her eyes already adjusted to the darkness, she saw that she was in an elegant living area. No one else breathed in the room.

She knew that there was, however, a guard on the door directly outside.

Zaira had checked the hallway before she came in this way. Conscious of the acute hearing possessed by so many changelings, she made her way to the bedroom door in absolute quiet and listened. No movement.

Slipping inside, she saw Miane's form beneath the sheets in the large bed. Most people would have believed her asleep. "Your body is too tense."

The BlackSea alpha's hand reached out to turn on a bedside lamp. Its glow was soft rather than cutting, but Zaira was prepared regardless. She'd narrowed her eyes so as not to be overwhelmed by a sudden change from dark to light.

"Really?" Miane said. "I thought I'd controlled the tension."

"Enough to fool the majority of people." Zaira leaned against the wall by the door, arms folded. "You don't need the gun you've got in your other hand. If I wanted to kill you, you'd be dead."

"Are you sure?" The other woman sat up, the sheet sliding away to reveal a slip in a pale color Zaira thought might be called champagne. Her eyes held Zaira's and they weren't black as they'd been during their initial meeting, but a lighter shade.

"Yes," she said, as Miane got out of bed and, placing the

gun on the bedside table, pulled on the robe that had been
thrown over a nearby chair. That robe matched the slip. "I'm
an assassin. You're well trained and dangerous, but you don't
expect me to come up behind you and snap your spine."

"You'd have to get that close to me first."

"I could've done it two hours ago, while you were visiting
the elderly human who lives in the neighboring district."

Miane went preternaturally still. "You followed me."

"Of course." Zaira wasn't about to allow a threat to
wander freely around her city. "The human is a relative?
Your features are distinctive."

"My grandmother," Miane said, and Zaira knew she'd
only shared that because it was something Zaira could easily
discover on her own. "Would you like a coffee?"

Zaira stepped aside to let the BlackSea alpha pass into the
other room, careful to follow at a pace that allowed her eyes
to adjust to the much brighter light Miane had flicked on.
"No coffee for me."

Waiting while the other woman prepared one for herself,
she wasn't surprised when the door opened, the big male
named Malachai in the doorway. His eyes went to Zaira,
grew hard. "Miane?"

"I'm fine, Mal. Zaira decided to drop by for a visit."

"Next time, use the door," Malachai said, his voice holding the distinct edge of a growl.

Zaira kept her silence and wondered what sea creature
growled. Or perhaps that was the human part of Malachai.

Laughing softly, Miane shook her head. "Think of her as
another me. I'm sure you'll understand her much better."

Expression unchanged, Malachai met the crystalline
clarity of Miane's hazel eyes, something silent passing between them before he withdrew. "I don't normally have
guards," the BlackSea leader told Zaira. "However, with the
rash of disappearances"—her mouth tightened—"the lieutenants are edgy."

Zaira wondered how the other woman had accurately
guessed her thought processes. "You don't feel their presence is a comment on your abilities and skills?"

"No. I wouldn't be BlackSea's First—its alpha—if they
doubted my strength." Coffee prepared, she took a seat on

one of the sofas, gestured for Zaira to take the one opposite. "I'm glad you decided to take me up on my invitation."

"Why did you offer it?"

"Partly because the Arrows would be a good ally to have." She held the cup balanced on one knee, cold fury in her next words. "If the bastards who've taken my people hadn't thought to disfigure them, your teleporters could've brought them all home by now."

"I'd have made the same decision in your shoes." Done whatever it took to protect her family.

"But," Miane added, "I also did it because you're the first woman I've ever met who reminds me of me."

"You live an emotion-rich life." While Zaira had spent most of hers in chilling Silence.

Miane drank some of her coffee. "BlackSea is unique. Some of us are very similar to other changelings in our inter-actions, while others are loners in a way even the feline changelings would struggle to understand. Our emotions are sometimes not what you would expect."

Zaira thought about the squad, about how many walked alone even while part of a group. "I think you'll find more Arrows who understand you."

"Perhaps." Eyes gone obsidian, the other woman said, "BlackSea doesn't trust easily and it's clear Arrows don't either, but here we must. Someone is hunting my people and yours." A grimness to her tone. "I've sent word across Black-Sea about little Persephone. It'll take time to get to those who live in the very deep, or in the most distant places on this Earth, but of the hundreds of confirmations I've received so far, none have caught any glimpse of her."

In the ensuing hours, the two of them went over theories and possibilities and split tasks so they wouldn't waste time following leads in areas that weren't their strengths. Zaira wouldn't normally have made such an arrangement with a relative stranger, and she knew neither would Miane, but the alpha's anger over Persephone's fate was visceral and it spoke to the same in Zaira.

"I am angry for and worried about all those who've been taken," Miane said at one point, her bones sharp against her skin. "But to imprison a child? That is against every rule of engagement. It would cost them *nothing* to release a child so young. That they haven't makes them monsters who deserve no mercy."

Gut instinct told Zaira that Miane could be trusted on this point; she and the BlackSea alpha were very much on the same page. If she was wrong, she'd deal with it after the girl was located. Until then, the Arrows and BlackSea would have a temporary working alliance.

It was well past midnight by the time they finished.

"Aden," Miane said as she made herself a second cup of coffee. "He belongs to you, yes?"

"Yes." He'd given himself to her and she would not release him from that promise. Not even if she failed in her bid to live this new existence. That was why she'd asked Vasic to make sure she was eliminated should she become a deadly threat either as a result of the madness—because there remained a chance it lived in her genes, a pitiless intruder who could strike at any time—or because of her violent possessiveness.

The teleporter had looked at her with those wintery eyes, said, "He'll never forgive me. Or you."

"But he'll be safe." What Zaira feared more than anything was that the madness would make her turn on Aden. "Will you do it?"

"Only if his life is under imminent threat."

Zaira had to be satisfied with that and hope Vasic never had to fulfill his promise. If he did, Aden *wouldn't* forgive it; he'd lose his closest friend as well as his lover in one savage blow. Zaira would've asked someone else but Vasic was the only one she trusted to watch out for Aden's interests above all else.

Evil didn't win there. And it won't win in our fight to be together.

No, it won't, Zaira vowed, but part of her knew that the choice might be wrenched out of her hands, rage swamping her in black fog that drowned out all reason.

Chapter 56

ANTHONY LISTENED TO what his daughter was telling him and knew he had to act. "How many?"

"At least twenty-five," Faith responded, her voice high-pitched and her words running together. She'd called him directly after an intense unsolicited vision, was clearly still feeling the aftereffects.

Stopping her when she would've spoken again, he said, "Are you alone?" He understood that her bond with her jaguar changeling mate gave her a way to leach off dangerous psychic energy, but foreseers needed someone with them after the most powerful visions. It was one of the reasons why F-Psy had always been and would always be part of a tight clan group.

Even when Anthony had believed Faith had to be isolated for her own good, he'd made sure she always had medical oversight.

"No," she replied. "I was with Mercy when it happened. She's here."

Identifying the named woman as a DarkRiver sentinel, Anthony didn't reach for his other line to contact Vaughn. He and Faith's mate had come to an understanding over the two and a half years the couple had been mated and Anthony didn't have any compunction against making contact should Faith be at risk.

"Father," Faith said, her voice breaking, "you have to stop him. He's going to kill them all."

"I'll take care of it."

Considering his options after hanging up, he moved to a screen at one end of the room and called Ming LeBon. The former Councilor's face filled the screen moments later, the birthmark on the left side of his face a dark red that would've drawn the eye if Anthony hadn't already been familiar with Ming's pigmentation.

"Anthony," Ming said. "What can I do for you?"

"I've had a disturbing prediction hit my desk."

"Clearly this prediction involves me."

"It does." Anthony put his hands behind his back. "You will apparently kill an entire human family group within the next forty-eight hours, including all the infants."

"I see. What's your interest in this family group?"

Anthony didn't know the family involved—to her panic and horror, Faith hadn't been able to identify them, her vision focused on Ming. "None," he said. "My only interest is the fact that you will realize only after the killing is over that your reconnaissance data was wrong—you will make a very dangerous mistake." He paused to let that sink in.

"According to the F-Psy who had the vision, you will execute the patriarch last, on the theory that watching his family being tortured will cause him to talk." Stripping the human's mind would be faster, but that often destroyed parts of the brain—and Ming, Anthony knew, was an expert in torture. "What you discover is that he never had any knowledge of whatever it is you suspect."

Ming held his gaze without blinking. "I appreciate the call."

"There's more," Anthony continued. "The murders will start a chain reaction that'll lead to weeks of riots in your region. It appears images of the victims' bodies will be leaked with your name attached to the violence, calling your leadership of the region into question."

"I see."

"Will you be spilling innocent blood, Ming?"

"I'll make my decision after reviewing all the facts."

After he signed off, Anthony input all the identifiable

elements of Faith's vision and set his computers to searching on the slight chance that he might trace the family and be able to warn them. If they died, Faith would blame herself. That horrified guilt was the reason so many foreseers had switched voluntarily to business-only predictions at the dawn of Silence. The weight could crush, the pain could devour.

Anthony had never wanted that for his child.

MING rarely second-guessed himself. The last time he'd done so, it had been in his handling of the Arrows. He'd made a serious mistake there. The operation scheduled to take place in another twelve hours, on the other hand, hadn't raised any red flags. He hadn't even planned to be there—the fact that Anthony's foreseer had connected it to him without his physical presence made it near certain the foreseer in question was Faith NightStar.

And Faith NightStar was never wrong.

Accessing the file once more, he checked the data. The patriarch of this family group was maneuvering for political power in Ming's region, had already made connections with a number of powerful supporters. That wasn't what made him worth killing—Ming could crush political climbers without bloodshed.

The thing that had pushed Ming to give the interrogation and assassination order was that the patriarch appeared to have access to information that came from inside Ming's headquarters, which meant Ming had a leak he needed to plug. However, according to Faith NightStar, his people would torture and execute the man's entire family and still not discover the identity of the leak.

The other possibility was that Anthony was lying and twisting the facts to suit his own agenda—except Anthony had never shown any interest in Ming's region. The NightStar patriarch was tightly focused on his foreseers, the family empire and reach such that he didn't need to make land grabs.

Closing the file, he walked out of his office and down to the underground bunker that housed his data analysts. "I want you to mine down for information on Kurevni," he

ordered. "Get me hard links to where and how he gained
access to classified data." The previous run had been thorough as per the standard protocols under his command, and
as everything appeared to line up as expected, Ming hadn't
seen the need to go any deeper.

"Yes, sir. How far?"

"Exhaust all possibilities." He would put the action on
hold until he had absolute confirmation. Ignoring a warning
from Faith NightStar was not a decision to be made lightly.

Chapter 57

MORE THAN FORTY-EIGHT hours after the initial attack on the compound in Venice, the search for both Blake and the abducted child continued unabated. It would've been easy for Aden to focus on those two ops and forget his larger vision for the squad, but he knew there would always be another mission, another mess to clean up, another predator to stop.

Aden could not—would not—allow that harsh truth to destroy the future he was trying to build. Neither would he allow Zaira to be consumed by the darkness that so often swirled around Arrows.

Which was why he'd called Remi the previous day and made a request. Now he looked out on a scene he would've deemed impossible prior to his and Zaira's abductions. In front of him was a lush green landscape under a bright mountain sun that bore little resemblance to the rain-lashed terrain of three and a half weeks before.

That wasn't the surprise.

It was the fact that little Jojo was currently earnestly explaining the concept of "catch" to an Arrow child a year older than her. That child kept looking to Aden for permission, until he stepped in and, hunkering down beside the boy, said, "Throw to me, Jojo."

Giving a happy smile, Jojo threw. When Aden caught it,

she clapped her hands for him. He threw it gently back, and when she successfully caught it—after a little wobble—he put his hands together for her. The next time Jojo threw to the Arrow child, the boy tried to catch, but his coordination wasn't good at the unfamiliar task and he dropped it.

Jojo laughed. "Pip oops!"

Looking uncertain, Pip picked up the ball and threw. This time, Jojo fumbled it. "Oops!" she cried with a big smile that made it clear she didn't mind at all. "Jojo oops!"

Aden saw Pip relax as the boy began to understand that there was no right or wrong here, no test. Rising to his feet once he was sure the two were happy playing together, he looked across to where Zaira was watching over another group. She'd already been "tackle hugged" by Jojo, as Remi had laughingly called it.

Aden wasn't the one who'd remembered to buy a gift of candy for all the children to share. That had been Zaira. And she'd snuck in a special piece for Jojo, who'd giggled and eaten it then and there.

All systems go?

Looking up from where she leaned lazily against a large rock, she shot him a faux salute. *I say we let Jojo run this op—she already knows everyone.*

Perhaps she'll one day be an alpha.

I'd put money on it.

"Here, kitten." Remi rolled the ball back toward Jojo when it went too far.

"Thank you for agreeing to this," Aden said to the alpha after the children returned to their play, the two of them standing under a soaring tree with wide sheltering branches. "I didn't expect it."

He'd made the request regardless—because having spent so much time in the valley of late, he'd realized that Arrow children didn't know how to play. Even with explicit permission, they waited to be told what to do because that was the first phase of the training process—rote learning. Independent thought wasn't encouraged until much later.

Remi shrugged. "Not like you and Zaira hadn't already been in the area, and they're just cubs."

Aden knew that to the leopard alpha, that designation

included the Arrow children as well. "You should be careful. There are those who'll use your weakness where children are concerned against you."

Throwing back his head, Remi laughed with abandoned joy. "Like it's a big fucking secret how much our cubs mean to us." A grin. "Same as yours do to you, it seems, so heed your own warning, my friend."

Aden had caught sight of several Arrow children pausing to watch Remi laugh, watched them return to their play after furtive glances at him, as if to check it was still okay. "I concede the point," he said to the amused alpha, while continuing to keep a psychic eye on the children within his shields.

This was a test group of ten. He had three in his shields, Vasic had three, and, as the strongest telepath, Zaira had four. The reason was to protect the changeling cubs in case of an inadvertent psychic loss of control. So far, the Arrow children were on their best behavior, but if these "playdates"—as Remi called them—carried on on a regular basis, childish fights were inevitable.

The extra shielding would both protect against any psychic damage and give the squad an insight into which children required more one-on-one psychic training to help them harness their strength in a safe way. Because, while Silence had fallen, some of its lessons remained viable: violent psychic abilities were dangerous and could ruin the life not just of the victim, but of the child who'd caused the injuries or death.

Part of Aden's duty was to keep young Arrows and those around them safe until the children had the skill and control to do so themselves. Flexible external shielding that wasn't hard and painful, but stretched to give a child room if he or she needed it, would work in the interim.

"They're quick," Remi said, nodding at the kids. "It won't take long before they're scrambling all over your valley."

Aden hadn't shared the location of the valley with Remi, not because he didn't trust the alpha, but because the information would make anyone who possessed it a target. He had, however, spoken to the alpha about the setup, asked if Remi had any suggestions when it came to creating community areas.

In the end, it turned out that Aden's instincts had led him in the correct direction. "Would you be willing to permit interaction between juveniles as well?" he asked the other man.

"Sure, with the right safeguards—but you gotta be ready to deal with teenage romance."

Aden didn't immediately reply, his mind having to quickly regroup. "Not an issue I'd considered."

"Figured that." Remi's grin was slyly feline. "We're talking teenage hormones, Aden. Leopard changelings of a certain age get to be very tactile and your teens are going to be experiencing freedom after a lifetime of deprivation." A raised eyebrow. "Pretty combustible mix. There'll be definite sneaking off into the trees so make sure your kids get the birds and bees talk if they haven't already."

Aden knew he could stop potential sneaking off with a simple order, but that defeated the purpose of teaching Arrow young how to have lives beyond a certain rigid existence. He thought of what he and Zaira might have done had they had the freedom to act on the visceral tug between them, knew it was a rite of passage he needed to allow the teens in the squad.

"We'll have to agree on rules of behavior," he said to Remi. "My juveniles will do better with them."

"It's a good idea all around. Liable to be misunderstandings and hurt feelings otherwise."

The alpha smiled and rubbed the hair of a cub who came over to lean against his leg, as if needing a rest, only picking up the thread of their conversation once the little boy had run back into the play. "As an example—teenage changeling tries something on a skittish Psy, gets rebuffed, changeling will back off totally. That's part of our rules, so your kids will then have to make the move."

Aden wasn't sure Arrow teens would make any such moves, no matter how deep their need. "I'll get more counselors assigned specifically to the juveniles."

"Shit, Aden, these are teenagers. No matter how hard we work to prepare them, it'll be a culture shock on both sides."

"Some shocks are necessary." The teens would figure things out once they had successful examples in the group . . . then he realized they already had an example. Sienna Lauren was a viciously powerful cardinal Psy mated to an alpha wolf. She was also young enough that the teenagers would find her relatable. The only question was if the girl who'd once been forced to be Ming LeBon's protégé would want to return to the Psy in any way.

WHEN told of the squad's request, Sienna made her decision in a heartbeat. "I want to do this," she said to the wolf-eyed man who held her heart. "Those kids are me not that many years ago." Lost and without hope. "I want to show them that we aren't just our abilities, that we can have lives, fall in love, explore the world if we want."

Hawke thrust a hand through the silver-gold of his hair as they walked through the corridors of the den. "I had a feeling you'd say that."

"You're worried."

"Ming was connected to the squad for one hell of a long time." His jaw grew tight at the name of the former Councilor. "We both know he wants you dead if he can't possess you."

"All the information we have says the squad has broken away from him."

"I'll only be happy once the bastard is dead," Hawke growled.

Sienna knew he was intensely frustrated that they couldn't move against Ming, but for better or worse, the ex-Councilor was currently the biggest stabilizing force in a large part of Europe. Because of the innocents who'd be harmed in the chaos that would ensue should Ming be taken summarily out of the equation, Hawke had agreed to hold off on the op to eliminate the man he hated for what Ming had done to Sienna.

Her mate was a good man, a man she hadn't dared dream of before she ended up in SnowDancer.

Wanting to kiss him until she couldn't breathe, she slipped her arm through his and turned her thoughts to how they could make the situation with the Arrows work. "I can meet the teens in the compound set up for E trainees." Situated on the border between DarkRiver and SnowDancer lands, the compound had intricate security protocols. "I'm sure the squad won't quibble about that when they're the ones who made the request."

Wolf looking out of his eyes, Hawke cupped the side of her face. "Anyone lays a finger on you, I will shred them." It was a promise.

"Ditto." She tugged him into a kiss. Fire sparked along their bond, and when the kiss broke he raised an eyebrow. "Reminding me you're dangerous?"

Kissing him again, she pressed her hands against the wide wall of his chest. God, he was a beautiful, sexy man, and he was hers. "Can't have Your Alphaness seeing me as weak."

He snorted. "I haven't been taken in by you since you were a damn juvenile with a smart mouth and a big attitude."

"I love you, too."

Cheeks creasing, he wrapped his arm around her shoulders and they continued to walk. "I'll organize a security detail for you. You can't watch your own back."

Sienna didn't argue; she wanted to believe in what Judd told her Aden was trying to do—create a squad that didn't just use up the gifted and dangerous, but provided a haven, a home for them. But she couldn't forget that the squad had been born in darkness, and that Ming had dug himself into it for decades. Remnants of those loyal to him or to his policies might yet remain and it would take only one to end the joy she'd found in this new life. "Here's my stop," she said in front of the door to the communal room utilized by the junior soldiers.

Sienna could have requested a jump straight to senior— not because she was Hawke's mate, but because of her abilities and proven strength in a fight—but she liked developing with her age group. Being a senior wasn't just about fighting strength or skill; she still had a lot to learn.

Kissing her again, to the wolf whistle of another soldier who was walking in, Hawke squeezed her hip before lightly biting her lower lip. "Go drive Drew crazy."

Sienna laughed and entered the session. Grabbing a seat next to Riordan on the comfortable and slightly ragged sofa as they waited for everyone else to come in, she found herself telling him what she'd been asked to do by the squad.

"So you're going to be the Loooooove Guru?" His dark eyes sparkled.

Narrowing her own eyes, she sat up and pointed at him. "Just for that, you're coming with me next time." The first time, she'd go alone, talk to them on a level only Psy who'd been through Silence could understand.

"Hey!" A scowl. "Hawke's your guy. Ask him."

"They need to see functioning Psy–non-Psy friendships as well." Sienna sank back into the sofa. "I'll ask Evie or Kit, too, as we continue the sessions."

Riordan shook his head and hooked his arm around her neck. "I must really like you, Sienna Lauren. You do realize that's time I could be spending with Noelle?"

"Ask her to come along," Sienna said, wondering if Hawke would agree to host one of the "contact" sessions in SnowDancer territory. She knew the RainFire alpha had already agreed, but, according to Hawke, RainFire had very few juveniles and teens in comparison to SnowDancer.

If the DarkRiver cats came on board as well, along with some of the nonpack human teens her packmates knew through school or other friendships, it could be a true kaleidoscope of the world. Maybe she was thinking too far ahead, but what if she could help make it happen? The teens of today would grow up into adults in a matter of a few years—and those adults would have friendships scattered across the races.

Their world might eventually become a true, functioning triumvirate.

PSYNET BEACON

Rumors are swirling in the Net about Aden Kai and his qualifications as the leader of the Arrow Squad. Sources that appear to be close to the squad have repeatedly stated that Aden is nothing but a low- to mid-level telepath and field medic. There is speculation that he is nothing but a stalking horse for the true leader of the squad.

The *Beacon* has reached out for confirmation from the squad, but they have maintained their silence, as per their operating protocol.

PSYNET BEACON: LIVE NETSTREAM

It may be a good covert maneuver, but I cannot respect a leader who hides behind weaker members of his group.

Anonymous
(Papeete)

Aden Kai is a skilled fighter, as witnessed by those of us at the infection outbreaks where he was part of the team that protected us. The fact that he may only be a low-Gradient Psy takes nothing away from those skills; leadership isn't only about power.

G. Smith
(New York)

The squad has never answered to the public and never will, but surely they must understand that this makes them appear weak?

T. Tzak
(Karachi)

This new post-Silence PsyNet is nowhere near as strong as it was under the past regime.

Anonymous
(Fez)

Even if Aden Kai is a shield for the true leader, he does not appear to have the strength associated with the squad. Is it possible that the squad is no longer created of the elite and that, in fact, it is nothing more than a simple black ops team?

J. Jeram
(Grozny)

Chapter 58

ADEN WAS CONSIDERING the *Beacon* report Vasic had brought to his attention when he received a comm call not from Hawke Snow, but from Lucas Hunter. "Hawke's going to touch base with you later," the leopard alpha said. "I wanted to talk to you about this idea of yours."

Realizing the two alphas must've discussed it with one another, Aden said, "What's DarkRiver's interest in this?"

Lucas's green eyes were suddenly not human anymore. "I have a cub who is as much Psy as she is changeling. It'd be nice if she grew up around children of both races."

It was a motive Aden could believe. "Would you agree to a contact session?" The RainFire pack was small, had a limited number of cubs. Enough for the test ten, but a larger group would overwhelm them. Aden had intended to rotate the Arrow children, though it wasn't his first choice—such a tactic would interrupt friendships in progress, such as that between Pip and Jojo.

If DarkRiver or SnowDancer agreed to his plan, however, children could be put into different groups that interacted together over a long period. It would create more well-rounded Arrows as well as forging bonds that crisscrossed the country. Aden wanted those bonds for the children under his care, wanted them to witness the different lives they could choose to live.

Being an Arrow didn't have to equal a sentence of isolation and aloneness.

"Yes, DarkRiver will do it," Lucas said, the decision one he'd clearly already made. "I'll speak to Remi to see how RainFire is handling things; I'll give you a call in the next day or so."

"Thank you," Aden said, aware this was a big step for the insular changelings. Lucas had couched it in terms of the benefits to his own child, but Aden knew that the changelings had once again thought of all children—Arrow "cubs" included. It was their weakness and, oddly, their strength.

"Wait." Lucas frowned as Aden went to end the communication. "You know a Psy family called Liu?"

"The Liu Group is one of the strongest in the Net." Aden had been in contact with the matriarch a number of times since he took over leadership of the squad. "I can make the introduction if you want to talk business."

Lucas shook his head, his shoulder-length black hair sliding forward before he tied it roughly back at his nape. "They've been fucking with us," he said bluntly. "Small things, but it's irritating."

"An example?"

"We're currently building new infrastructure for one of our media companies—they bought out the entire supply of a particular necessary component, putting us off schedule by two months." The leopard alpha scowled. "I'd understand if Liu needed the component, but they have no use for it. Just like they don't for the microbrewery they just bought out."

"A microbrewery?" That didn't fit into any of the Liu Group's business interests. "Is it highly profitable?"

"It was a small family operation and profitable at that level. Now it's just sitting there, nothing in production." Lucas's frown deepened. "Two changeling-owned clubs used that brewery almost exclusively to supply their patrons. You see what I'm talking about? It's like they're playing a game, probably because we won a couple of recent contracts for which Liu also put in a bid."

"That doesn't sound like Jen Liu." The family matriarch was ruthless and would continue to be a thorn in the Ruling Coalition's side, but she didn't waste money or energy. "I'll speak to her. This may be a junior member of the family who's let power go to his or her head."

"Appreciate it," Lucas said before signing off with a small nod.

Contacting Jen Liu immediately, Aden raised the question. She called him back after forty-five minutes with a very strange report. "It appears we have been doing the things alleged by the DarkRiver alpha. However, we have no record of anyone ever giving the orders to action the incidents."

"Could a junior have circumvented your decision-making process?"

"Highly improbable, though I've asked my deputy to investigate." Her expression was faultlessly Silent, but Aden had the feeling the green-eyed, silver-haired telepath was annoyed. "I'd like to speak to Lucas Hunter and see if we can come to an accommodation. I currently have people tracking the supply chain to see where the parts may have gone—" She paused, her head angled, as if listening to another voice.

"The parts have been located," she said a second later. "They were delivered to a family warehouse, and since the documentation was in order, the warehouse manager simply put them on the shelves." The matriarch's expression grew even more icy. "Someone is playing games, and those games may have an impact on our business activities."

Aden knew the changeling sector was a lucrative one that had long been closed to Psy. With the fall of Silence and with other changes in the world, that door was now partially ajar. Aden wouldn't put it past another family group to scuttle the Liu Group's reputation with changelings in an effort to win contracts.

"I'm sending you Lucas's contact details." That done, he said, "Have you had any other similar experiences?" It could be simply petty business politics, but Aden never assumed anything.

"My family hasn't, but Kalani Chastain mentioned that a human business association recently filed legal papers that delayed a crucial project."

"It sounds like an ordinary dispute."

"Yes, until the other side didn't turn up to any of the hearings. The judge threw out the filing but the damage was done."

The hairs on his nape prickling, Aden contacted Chastain

as soon as he and Jen Liu finished speaking. The barely twenty-nine-year-old head of the family assumed the Ruling Coalition was taking her to task for the delay in what was a Coalition-funded comm station upgrade, and had no hesitation in giving him the full details.

Since he didn't have a contact within the human association in question, he asked Zaira to get in touch with Bo. The Arrows and the Human Alliance had a cautiously "friendly" association that boiled down to "don't step on my toes and I won't step on yours."

Making the contact, Zaira called back. "He's checking, will get back to you within the next hour."

Every cell in Aden's body seemed to awaken at the sound of her voice. "Did Miane have any further success with Olivia?" he asked, conscious the BlackSea alpha was currently running everything from a base in Venice while she did what she could to help her packmate heal.

"No, but Persephone was alive as of ten minutes ago." Zaira's voice turned edgy, hard. "A new e-mail came into Olivia's account, warning her against talking. Persephone was holding a printout of the most recent *Beacon* update, complete with a date and time stamp. And her captors didn't forget to obscure her face enough to make it useless for a teleport lock."

Aden's own anger was a razored thing—he would never forget those recordings of Zaira in that cell of a room, and the idea of another child undergoing the same made him want to do cold, deadly violence. "That implies Olivia does know something."

"The Halcyon may have done its job there; her memory is shot. Persephone's abductors will realize soon that Olivia didn't give us anything."

Because if she had, Aden thought, the squad would've moved. "Stay on it," he said. "They won't risk harming the child until they're dead certain Olivia is contained." The breathing room was minuscule, but it might be enough to save a tiny and vulnerable life.

"Amin tells me Blake is like a rat in a hole," Aden said, knowing she wanted to be kept up-to-date on that hunt. "The team doesn't have him yet, but they know he's trapped in New York." There had been no new murders that bore the rogue Arrow's signature, likely because of the unremitting pressure created by the squad's tracking teams.

"Good." An icy response, followed by the unexpected. "I miss you. You've addicted me to you."

He felt his lips curve again, the smile starting in his heart and spreading outward. Like the children, he, too, had discovered there was more to life than being an Arrow or even the leader of the squad. And he'd discovered it with his deadliest commander. "Success."

No laughter, but her final words were a caress. "See you in bed."

"Every night." At present, that was the only time they were together—Blake, Persephone, the constant rumors in the Net, the integration of adult Arrows into family units with Arrow children, it all required care and attention.

But the rest periods, those were theirs. Even if it was a bare five hours, Aden made sure the squad knew he was offline except for major emergencies. Fully accepting his mantle as second in command, Vasic had stepped in to take the calls that would normally be routed to Aden.

It was the favorite part of his entire day.

Bo Knight contacted him fifteen minutes after that thought passed through his head. "The association in question categorically denies ever filing those papers."

"Interesting."

"Isn't it?"

"An individual or a group attempting to pit Psy against human?"

"I'd say that, except I had a very similar conversation with one of SnowDancer's lieutenants not long ago." Bo's tone was terse. "We were apparently buying land out from under changeling packs—except we weren't."

Aden's prickling instincts went on full alert. "Do you know of any other incidents?"

"No. But I'm going to look into it."

"As will I." Subtle and insidious, someone was playing what appeared to be a very patient game of chess.

Chapter 59

IT HAD TAKEN Ming's data analysts fourteen hours to complete the deep background on the Kurevni situation. They'd run into a number of dead ends, as could be expected from a man who was attempting to subvert Ming through a spy inside Ming's own camp.

"Then," the senior analyst said, "we discovered this." He laid a piece of paper in front of Ming.

It was a list; specifically, step-by-step instructions on how to set up a post office box no one would ever trace back to Kurevni. "When did he receive this?"

"Seven months ago. It came from an anonymous account," the analyst added, anticipating Ming's next question.

"You have the location and number of the P.O. box?"

"Yes, it wasn't difficult once we knew the time frame and the steps Kurevni would've taken to open it. I sent one of our people to covertly empty the box." He held out a sealed envelope. "This was the only thing inside."

Ming saw it bore the postmark of a major metropolitan city, but the postage had been paid in cash, the inked stamp generic. "Untraceable?"

"Yes, sir. The postage could've been purchased at any corner store."

Slitting open the envelope, Ming used the tips of his fingers to retrieve the piece of paper within. It held complete and confidential details of Ming's plans for an undeveloped piece of land. Below that were a number of suggestions as to how Kurevni could leverage the information to build his profile.

"We processed the envelope. No DNA or prints." The analyst took the letter and envelope from Ming. "I'll get the letter tested, too, as well as the sealed parts of the envelope."

"Do it quickly," Ming said, though he didn't expect any useful results; the puppet master behind this was very clever, clever enough that he—or she—had almost manipulated Ming straight into a trap that, according to Faith NightStar, would've equaled his downfall.

Dismissing the analyst, he ordered his personal black ops team to retrieve Kurevni and bring him to Ming's subterranean office. Soon the man was before him, sweating copiously despite the cool temperature in the office, runnels of perspiration flowing down his temples and his pale blue office shirt bearing large wet patches under the arms.

The smell of fear was pungent.

When Ming took a seat in the chair across from him, nothing but a few inches of uncarpeted plascrete floor between them, the other man found his voice. "You can't do this. I'm a well-known figure."

"I don't intend to kill you, Mr. Kurevni." Ming found him pathetic; this, he thought, was what the Psy would become without Silence. Weak and easily crushed. "Neither will I torture you," he added, "since it's clear you know nothing." Kurevni was simply a puppet.

"However"—he leaned in so close that Kurevni had nowhere to go—"I strongly suggest you stop taking advice from anonymous sources who would like me to do exactly that, not simply to yourself, but to your family."

"Wh-what?"

"You are being led like a goat to the slaughter." One perfectly placed to take center stage in the destruction of Ming LeBon. "Much of the data you've been fed is confidential." Not high level, but high enough that Ming did unquestionably have a mole in the ranks. "I planned to torture your entire family, including your newest grandchild, in order to make you give up the name of your source." He calmly and carefully detailed the methods his operatives would've used. "As you can see, my people excel at prolonging pain."

"I don't know!" Kurevni said, his face having gone from fever-flushed red to a sick, pasty shade of white. "I swear it. It was all through a post office box."

Ming leaned back. "Convince me."

Voice ragged and eyes wet, Kurevni began to talk, but he had pitifully little to tell. "I swear," he said again when Ming didn't respond. "I just thought you had a discontented staff member."

"Perhaps," Ming said in a deliberately toneless way, "it's time to rethink your friendships with unknown sources." He glanced at a guard. "Take him home."

Kurevni's mouth fell open. "Aren't you afraid I'll talk about this?"

Ming looked into Kurevni's fear-chilled eyes. "You're free to talk, but make funeral arrangements for your entire family beforehand and ask their forgiveness for the agony in which they'll spend their final hours. The infant won't understand, but I know emotional beings are sentimental about such things."

Kurevni threw up over the side of his chair. Trembling when he raised his head, he said, "I'll drop out of politics on my return home."

"On the contrary, I strongly insist you stay. Competition is good." The appearance of it made the populace feel as if they had a voice, a choice, and that, in turn, kept them docile. "Of course, should I find you in possession of confidential information from my camp again, the Kurevni line will cease to exist."

Broken now, Kurevni looked to Ming for instruction. "Do you want me to shut down the post office box?"

"No, leave it open." The anonymous source might yet make a mistake. "Clear it as per usual, but open nothing. Call the number you'll be given and one of my men will retrieve it."

"I'll do whatever you say. Just please don't hurt my family."

Ming watched the other man leave. That situation was resolved, but it left him with another issue. He now owed Anthony Kyriakus. Ming didn't like owing anyone anything. At present, there was nothing he could do about this particular debt, but what he could do was use the details of this incident to open a line of communication with the Arrows. It was the squad's task to keep watch on events that could deleteriously affect the Psy, and riots in Ming's territory would've caused countless casualties as well as triggering serious financial repercussions.

If he did it carefully enough, he could start to rebuild the bridges he'd burned. Having the Arrows back as his personal death squad would make him powerful enough to take on even Kaleb Krychek. And owning Vasic as his pet teleporter would make eliminating Sienna Lauren a far easier project.

Aden would have to die, of course. Ming didn't understand how a midlevel Tp and field medic had ended up with the leadership of the squad, but as long as Aden lived, Ming's leadership would be under threat.

To defer suspicion, he'd wait a suitable period after he retook control, and he'd be careful to make it look like an accident.

Decision made, he returned to his office and initiated the comm link. "Aden," he said when the Arrow leader answered. "I have certain information you might find useful."

Chapter 60

ADEN WAS TRYING to put the puzzle pieces together when Zaira walked unexpectedly into his Central Command office the next morning. Running his hand down her back simply because he wanted to make contact, he said, "Venice?"

"Nothing to report." To his surprise, she rose on her toes to brush her lips over his jaw before turning her attention to the comm panel he was using as a work screen. "Why are you staring at random pieces of data?"

He went through each of the data points for her. "It appears to be an orchestrated campaign to sow seeds of mistrust between various groups." It couldn't be simple chance; the incidents all bore a similar cunning signature.

"Clever," Zaira said. "Why waste money and resources on a military attack when you can break alliances or poison the air before the alliances ever form? Push it a bit more and irritation turns to aggravation, then to serious conflict. And while your opponents fight among themselves, wasting their own resources and manpower, the puppet master becomes the most powerful by default."

That was why Zaira was one of his commanders. Not just because of her lethal abilities, but because her mind saw patterns where even he had trouble. The motive she'd ascribed to this series of events was not only plausible, it explained why the targets spanned all three races.

"Is that admiration I hear?"

Zaira nodded. "Doesn't mean I agree with it—but the concept is smart, especially how they're capitalizing on old fault lines and fragile new business overtures." She tapped the data point Bo had provided about his people's recent land conflict with the changelings. "Humans and changelings have always been a loose coupling, mostly because Silence separated out the Psy. Create a fracture there, too, and you end up with three isolated races."

"At which point," Aden said, "you start creating infighting in each group." He frowned, split the screen to bring up a *Beacon* article from a few days before. It was small and he'd noticed it only because of the names mentioned, but now . . .

It appears the former Councilors are no longer keeping to their rumored "gentleman's agreement" to stay out of each other's businesses. The Duncan Corporation has just underbid Scott Enterprises on an airjet contract. At a bare fifty million, the contract is minor relative to the turnover of both companies, but it is notable given the identities of the parties involved.

Zaira watched in silence as he contacted Nikita Duncan. Her response to his request for business data was frosty, but when he indicated this might be a larger issue that could impact all her business enterprises, as well as the markets themselves, she confirmed his suspicions.

Hanging up, he told Zaira what he'd learned. "Nikita and Shoshanna were never allies, but they don't undercut one another since that would drive down prices overall. Nikita did put in a bid for the contract, but it was a deliberately high one."

Nikita hadn't spelled it out, but Aden knew the reason for the Duncan bid was to make the other party feel as if they had a viable second choice. Not ethical, but Nikita wasn't exactly white as snow. "She says the error was introduced at Shoshanna's end. Someone in Shoshanna's camp forwarded an impossibly high bid rather than the correct one."

"So we've got people embedded within the trusted circles of major players." Zaira's eyes gleamed. "Someone really smart and really patient put this entire operation together.

Their only mistake is the timing." She leaned into him. "A year ago, the connections between various groups were far more amorphous. Lucas Hunter and Jen Liu, for example, might never have made contact."

Wrapping his arm around her waist, he turned her body to face his. "Regardless, this has to be working on some level, particularly with smaller groups who would never connect their problems to a larger conspiracy."

Zaira thrust her hands into his hair without warning, gripped at it, and pulled him down till his lips were a bare inch from hers. "It's had a taste of you," she whispered. "The rage inside me. Now it wants to gorge."

EVERY time he was near, his scent would get into her lungs . . . No, that wasn't true. He didn't have to be near. She'd come here, to his office in this underground place she preferred to avoid, because she hadn't seen him for six hours and had started to hurt inside her chest from missing him.

"Take me," he said, his dark eyes filled with so many things she didn't understand.

"You're already mine." It came out instinctively, from that primal, possessive core at the heart of her nature.

He pressed his forehead to hers, not fighting her hold. "I know, but do you?" His hair fell over his forehead to brush hers. "Deep inside, do you know?"

She didn't understand his question, and the frustration made her pull at his hair. "Stop talking in circles."

"A psychic bond," he said, his mind touching hers.

She wanted to open so badly to him. "If you do that, I won't ever let you go." If the physical connection had sealed them together, this would turn that seal into an unbreakable glue. "Even my death won't free you." The psychic scars would be irreparable.

"Whether we bond or not, your loss would change me forever." A quiet voice that held so much power it vibrated with it. "You are written indelibly on my soul, Zaira. Nothing will ever alter what you are to me."

Her rib cage seemed to compress her lungs, the pain sharp.

No one but Aden had ever treated her as if she had that much value, that much worth.

Sliding down her shields, she found his were already open for her. The connection was deeper than a private telepathic pathway; it was the kind of contact two operatives might make so they could work as a seamless unit. The difference was that this connection was fully open on his end. No barriers. No shields. No secrets.

She could've gone in and taken everything, drunk in every second of his life. Greedy though she was, she didn't do that—the rage creature inside her liked the gifts of himself that he gave her. It wouldn't mean the same if she took advantage and stole him. And this . . . the intimacy made her shudder. There was no aloneness now, not even a whisper of it, Aden's strong, distinctive presence a silent partner she could carry with her.

Unlike a simple telepathic bond, this one wouldn't snap once she was out of range. Their minds were tangled together now, as tangled as their limbs when they were alone behind the closed doors to her Venice room. With the tangling came a sense of satisfaction that quieted the possessiveness that clawed at her always, her desire to keep him for herself no longer a monster she had to fight.

"Will you stay?" she asked, though the feral thing in her soul hissed at her not to speak the question, not to give him any reason to second-guess his decision to be with her.

"Have I ever left?"

"No." Not since the instant she'd woken in that infirmary to find the boy with the quiet eyes and the quiet feet at her bedside. "My mind is a dark place." She shied away from opening herself up to him as he'd done for her. The twisted girl inside her adored him, didn't want him to see the horror of her.

"Show me when you're ready," Aden said, his words intensified by the echo inside her mind, the sense of him wrapped around her.

Zaira wasn't sure she'd ever be ready.

Closing the final inch of distance between them, she pressed her lips to his. He angled his head to create a better fit and then they were kissing. The intimacy made a hot, tight fist form in her abdomen, the rage stretching out inside her like one of the big cats she'd seen in RainFire.

When Aden shifted closer, running one hand around her waist to spread it low on her back, the fist grew tighter. His hand was big, warm, and she wanted to feel it on her bare skin. She didn't realize she'd telepathed the request to him until he tugged up the back of her uniform top and managed to slide his hand underneath despite the fine armored vest that she wore over the black long-sleeved top.

The rough warmth of his hand against her skin was a pleasurable shock, one that was rapidly becoming familiar.

Shivering, she wrapped her arms around his neck and held him to her as she tasted him until her head spun and the rage was molten in her blood. His hand moved slightly on her skin, just enough to make her shiver again as he opened his mouth over hers to deepen the kiss. Her nipples rubbed against her bra, her skin stretched tight over her entire body.

It felt as if she was losing herself in him, but that was all right. After all, he'd given himself to her.

The knock penetrated only in that it might be a threat to Aden. Breaking the kiss, she released him to turn and focus her mind beyond the door. The psychic signature on the other side was easy to identify. "It's Nerida."

Aden pressed his lips to the curve of her neck from behind. "She's my ride to New York. I'm heading to see Dev."

That explained his civilian clothing. "Your security team?"

"I can't be seen with a security team," Aden replied, his hand on the panel that would open the door. "That defeats the whole purpose of the squad's reputation, especially with the *Beacon* publishing rumors about my suitability as squad leader." Authorizing the door to open, he nodded at Nerida.

I'll come with you, Zaira said, not angry at the *Beacon* article because she knew full well it was idiotic and that Aden would have a plan to handle the subtle attack on the squad.

Now, he looked at her.

As your . . . She paused, at a loss. *I will never be a girlfriend.*

Aden thought again of laughter, and that he might be capable of it. *We can discuss terms later.*

Stepping out with Nerida, he asked if she was fine transporting them both. Unlike Vasic, Nerida wasn't a teleporter by birth, but a Tk who had teleport abilities. As such, her range, while wide, was more limited than Vasic's. Increasing the number of passengers further narrowed that range, as did any other duties she may have completed recently that required a psychic burn.

"No problem," she said.

'Porting them to the basement of a refurbished hotel that was shuttered while it waited for the final planning permits, Nerida left for her next task. Depending on the timing, Aden and Zaira would most likely catch a high-speed jet back, making the final part of the trip back to Central Command in one of the vehicles they kept garaged near the closest jetports.

"You want to spend some time here on Blake's trail?" Zaira asked as they walked out of the hotel via a basement exit. "We can hit the locations that have already been searched."

It was a standard technique: when caught in a trap, you returned to the place your hunters thought they'd cleared. "That's a—" Aden's instincts suddenly went on high alert, his subconscious picking up something his conscious mind hadn't yet worked out.

"Aden! Get down!"

The bullet buzzed over his head a split second after Zaira's cry. He'd dropped to the pavement, palms flat on the plascrete and legs stretched out, the instant she spoke. An Arrow did not ask his partner to clarify a warning, trained to know that a single nanosecond of delay could equal death.

That lesson had just saved his life.

Zaira was moving past him within two heartbeats, her legs covering the ground at lethal speed. Following on her heels, Aden pinpointed her target—a slender male holding a weapon at his side.

"Down!" Aden yelled at a passerby who hadn't already hit the ground.

The assassin turned and shot again midrun, but Zaira had judged his movement and dodged it, as did Aden. The bullet slammed home in a tree. That was the last shot the male made. Zaira slammed him to the ground the next instant, his face hitting the pavement with such force that blood spurted out, his nose clearly smashed in.

Aden saw Zaira's expression, realized she'd fallen into the blind protective rage that would leave the assassin dead in seconds.

Zaira. Secondary threat.

As she jerked around to neutralize the imagined threat, he was already contacting Vasic. His friend appeared a second later, his boots, jeans, and dirt-stained T-shirt telling Aden he'd probably been helping Ivy with the gardens the empath was creating in the valley.

Zaira turned back right then, her focus on the unconscious male once more. "He tried to hurt you." The words were calm—if Aden hadn't known her, he'd never have perceived the ice-cold fury inside her.

Vasic 'ported them both to a desert cloaked in night just as Zaira's body tensed for a deadly attack. *I'll take care of the assassin,* Vasic said. *Call me when you need to return.*

Then he was gone.

Aden went to touch Zaira, help her calm down . . . and she turned on him. Her eyes dull and blank, her face set, she slammed out with a fist, followed it with a kick. He blocked her moves, but made no offensive ones of his own. *Zaira,* he said telepathically and verbally. "Zaira, it's Aden."

Her hand-to-hand combat skills were deadly. Aden could hold his own against her only because he was bigger and stronger. It usually gave him just enough of an edge that they were evenly matched, but he realized at that instant that he'd never fought against a Zaira in an unthinking rage.

She was a fury, a whirling storm.

He took a blow on the jaw, a second in the neck, a third on the cheek.

Realizing she wasn't hearing him, Aden focused on getting her down with as little damage as possible. It meant taking a number of further blows himself, but the one thing Aden would not do was hurt Zaira. He'd made that promise to her long ago, would never break it. Instead, he used his greater bulk against her, slamming his body into hers as she lifted up on one leg to deliver a roundhouse kick.

Unbalanced, she fell, and he saw her knee begin to bend

the wrong way. He flipped her so she wouldn't fall wrong and twist or tear her tendons. His action had the unintended side effect of throwing her harder against the ground, the air rushing out of her. He came down over her before she could recover, clamping his hands on her wrists and using the weight of his lower body to pin her down.

"Zaira!"

Muscles tense enough to snap, she tried to throw him off. He crushed her to the sand while gripping her wrists, but not so hard that he'd leave bruises. "Zaira, it's Aden," he repeated.

No recognition in her eyes, on her face, her mind a closed door.

Chapter 61

ZAIRA, IT'S ADEN.

The words sank through the black fog, disappeared. But they came again and again and again, until she could no longer disregard them, until the fog around her mind started to lift enough that she could understand the meaning behind the words.

Aden.

She knew that name, knew the face of the man leaning over her, knew that silky black hair that fell over his eyes and shone blue-black in the moonlight . . . knew those lips that bore a cut that dripped blood, knew that cheek with its spreading bruise. "You're bleeding." The words were hoarse and hesitant, as if she was speaking a language she didn't know.

When she tugged at her wrist, he opened one hand enough that she could slip her wrist out. Raising her hand to his face, she wiped away the blood. "I did this." The fog had almost totally burned off, leaving her with the blinding light of knowledge. "I hurt you." Hurt the one person she'd promised to always protect.

"I wouldn't be much of an Arrow if I couldn't take a few blows."

He was trying to make her feel better. But the hollowness in her, it went soul deep. "I hurt you." No longer caught in the madness, she remembered why this had all begun. "I was angry because he wanted to hurt you, then I did it for him." She'd also almost lost control on a public street, could've permanently damaged the image and reputation of the squad. "I came a second away from exposing the monster that lives in me, in giving those who hate the squad a reason to exterminate us."

Her eyes burned, her throat grew rough, the pressure inside her building and building. Twisting to the side under Aden's body, she tugged her other wrist free and wrapped her arms around herself, trying to hold together the fragmenting pieces of her.

Aden wouldn't allow her to hide. Shifting to lie beside her, his face looking into hers, he brushed back her hair. "I'm fine. And what the public saw was a hard, fast takedown that'll only reinforce our reputation as dangerous adversaries."

Her eyes went to the cut, the bruise. "Don't you understand, Aden? I can't remember." The blows, the kicks, nothing but the pitch-black of violent rage. "I thought I'd escaped, but this makes it clear that I *did* inherit the madness." The insanity and violence was in her blood, in her genetics. "Those impulses are built into my neural pathways."

Aden, his beautiful, bruised face looking into her own, his jaw so stubborn. "I don't believe in predestination. We make our own destinies."

She wanted to believe him, but she also knew the truth. "There's a reason why our race was desperate enough to accept Silence, accept a truth that was a lie. I'm part of that reason." It was nothing he could alter. "I can't risk a life beyond the strictures of harsh discipline." Somehow, she had to leash the rage again, lock in the insane girl inside her, and once more become the cold-eyed Arrow nothing . . . and no one, could touch.

Zaira wasn't certain she could, that she hadn't come too far, but if she didn't, then who would protect Aden?

"Is that what you want for Tavish?" A pitiless question. "For Pip and the other children?"

"They're young," she began. "They can—"

"No." He gripped the side of her face. "If what you say is right, if we inherit the worst of our genetic lines, then they can't. One day, they'll be here, in this moment, and their lives will end in a hard black box created of rules of behavior that allow no freedom. Is that what you want?"

"What I want doesn't matter!" It never had. "Madness exists! It's always existed, especially among our race." The Psy had disproportionately high rates of insanity and mental illness, the dark flip side of their extraordinary gifts.

"If you're mad, then I will walk with you into the darkness," Aden said, his grip tightening on the side of her face. "Don't you *choose* to leave me, Zaira. Don't you do that."

Her heart, that stunted organ that he'd given new life, hurt at the pain she sensed in him. Wrenching away from him because she couldn't bear it, she sat up with her arms wrapped around her knees and she stared out into the vastness of the desert. And she thought of the hope in Tavish's eyes, of the little girl who'd held her hand after the RainFire playdate and asked if she was permitted to have a doll now.

Their dreams, their hopes, they were chains holding her to the here and the now, refusing to allow any retreat.

And the biggest, strongest cord?

It was Aden.

The man who sat beside her. The man she had hurt. The man who'd allowed her to hurt him. "Why don't you ever fight back when I lose control?"

"Because you've been beaten enough. Never again."

It made her heart flinch, the way he said that, the potent emotion in his tone that she wanted to hoard and wrap around herself. "How do I fight, Aden?" she whispered, her shoulders slumping as the twisted rage creature inside her soul curled up into a fetal ball. "How do I fight something bred into my bones? I don't want to become a monster, to lose myself."

"With blind faith." He gripped the wrist of one hand with the other. "And with love." Raw words. "Don't let one setback drive you back into a cage." He took a shuddering breath. "I won't stop you if you believe this is your only hope of survival, but if there's even a ghost of a chance otherwise, then *fight*, Zaira. Fight for us. Fight for the children who will one day be us. Fight for the little girl you once were, the one whose spirit never flew away, no matter the horror."

Zaira thought of the beatings, the deprivation, the blood in her mouth when she'd bitten her tongue as she tried to stifle her screams. She thought of a family where serial killers begot serial killers and where parents could treat a child worse than they would a stray animal. And she thought of the man who wanted her to fight the evil that had birthed her.

It was too much. Something just broke inside her.

This time, she didn't scream. Her body shook as wet trails leaked out of her eyes. "What's happening?" she gasped, panicked.

Aden's arms locked around her. "You're crying," he said, his own voice rough.

"I don't cry," she said through the wrenching pain of it, that strange, hot water blurring her vision.

"Maybe it's time." One hand in her hair, his other arm steel around her, he pressed his cheek to hers. "I'm here." Always.

And those horrible, hot tears, they broke the banks and swamped her in a violent deluge.

ADEN didn't know how long Zaira cried. All he knew was that the tears were leaching the poison from her system, the rage and the hurt that she'd kept inside for so long that they'd become toxic to her very breath. She cried until she had no tears left, and then she cried dry tears so hard that he worried she'd cause herself physical injury.

But he didn't tell her to stop, didn't tell her to hush.

Night turned to dawn in the desert, the air chilly, and still she didn't speak. Instead, she lay in his arms as he stroked her hair, and every so often she'd cry again. It broke his heart into a million pieces each and every time. In the twenty-one years he'd known her, Zaira had never cried. Not once.

These tears were a release.

Beyond them . . . beyond them might lie their future, or a loneliness made more terrible by the beauty of what had passed between them in the past weeks. If he lost her to the nightmare, if she chose to go back into the cage of endless discipline and no emotional connections, he wouldn't recover.

He'd function, he'd do what was necessary, but those wounds would bleed always.

The knock on his mind on the PsyNet came an hour after Zaira fell asleep in his arms, exhausted and wrung dry. It was Vasic. "Aden," he said once Aden opened his mind on the sprawling psychic network and stepped out to speak to his best friend. "Nikita Duncan's been shot."

Aden knew that was important, but he also knew that the most important thing in the entire world right now lay in his arms. "Can you handle it?"

"Yes. Do you need a 'port back?"

Aden didn't want even that slight interruption, but the desert sun would soon be high and he wanted Zaira to sleep. "Can you get us back to Zaira's Venice room?" He sent his friend an image of the room.

The moment of disorientation was immediate, their landing on the bed whisper soft. "A remote teleport over that much distance?" Aden looked at Vasic's mind on the PsyNet, the silver brightness of it entangled with sparks of color that spoke of Ivy. "You've become stronger."

"I've been exploring my abilities—it seemed to me that a born teleporter should be able to do far more than simply rapid 'ports or short-distance remotes." Vasic's mind pulsed with lightning sparks. "I'll feed you all data I find about Nikita." A pause. "Rest, Aden. You've earned it."

Dropping out of the PsyNet, Aden gently pulled a blanket over both himself and Zaira without bothering to remove her boots or his own—he didn't want to risk waking her. As he closed his eyes, he could feel her breath against his skin, her pulse steady under his hand, and it was exactly where he was meant to be. Leaving his mind wide open to her own so she wouldn't wake alone on any level, he allowed sleep to sweep him under.

VASIC had always stood in the shadows behind Aden. He'd never seen it as a lesser position—the two of them had their strengths and Aden's was in front, his leadership not a mantle he put on, but one integrated into every part of his self. Vasic, by contrast, functioned best as a lieutenant who had Aden's back. Politics wasn't his strong suit and neither was conversation.

That didn't mean he couldn't step temporarily into Aden's shoes, especially when his friend was battling to save a relationship that was the only private, personal, selfish thing in his life. Aden had given everything to the squad—it was time they stood for him and gave back.

So Vasic gave orders designed to make sure neither Aden nor Zaira would be disturbed. Mica in Venice was more than competent enough to cover for Zaira for now, while Nerida, Cristabel, and Axl could handle operations in the valley, and Amin had charge of the Blake team. Anything else was to be directed to Vasic. He'd decide whether or not it was an emergency that warranted disturbing Aden.

Arriving in Nikita's high-rise office in San Francisco a bare five minutes after his conversation with his best friend, he found she'd been shot while standing in front of the plate-glass window that looked out over the glittering city. She'd have been dead except for the fact that the glass in her building was all heavily reinforced. It had slowed the momentum of the bullet to the extent that when the projectile hit Nikita's forehead, it only penetrated skin and bruised bone before falling to the carpet.

The shattering glass, however, had moved too fast for her to avoid. It had sliced her arms and upper body, including a jagged cut to her abdomen and one to her throat that had sprayed the walls in blood. Nikita's aide, Sophia Russo, had heard the shot and run inside. Seeing the carnage, she'd ordered a young and relatively weak Tk on the Duncan team to teleport Nikita to the nearest hospital.

That happened to be a public one with an experienced M-Psy on duty who'd begun work on Nikita right there in the parking lot that was the only location lock in the young Tk's mental files. An hour later, Nikita was still in surgery.

"The bullet is the same type as that used by the assassin who tried to hit Aden," Vasic told Krychek, who'd also arrived on the scene. Vasic had picked up the bullet only after recording the blood-splattered site so Aden could see the scene exactly as it had been.

"Is the assassin talking?" Krychek asked. "If not, I can intervene."

The squad had telepaths of their own who could break shields, but it hadn't been necessary in this case. "He's talking.

He knows nothing." Vasic had asked Axl to confirm that with a telepathic scan—at 9.7 on the Gradient, there were few untrained individuals who could hide their secrets from Axl.

The shooter was lucky he was Psy; he'd been able to consciously lower his shields so Axl could do the scan without causing harm to his brain. Any other race and Axl may have had to force it, causing permanent damage. "He was hired to make the hit and paid an exorbitant deposit to offset the risk involved in targeting an Arrow."

"A contract killer?" Krychek looked at the shattered glass streaked with Nikita's blood. "An intelligent enemy."

"Yes." The fewer people in the inner circle, the fewer people who could leak data. "The more we learn, the more it confirms we're not dealing with another fanatical group like Pure Psy—this is far more strategic." Vasic knew Aden had shared his theory, of a shadowy puppet master intent on fostering disorder, with all of the Ruling Coalition so that they could head off possible clashes between different groups. He'd also told the changeling alphas with whom he had contact, as well as informing Bo.

"Aden and Nikita," Krychek said, "have only one common denominator."

"The Ruling Coalition."

"The sudden rumors about Aden's competence have to be part of a fallback plan."

Vasic shook his head as he hunkered down to examine the way the glass had shattered. "I think it was part of the assassination plot itself—what better way to prove Aden's lack of power than by shooting him in broad daylight?" Everything about the attempts on Aden's life indicated a motive beyond his death, and that motive was to demoralize and humiliate the squad.

Someone did not want the Arrows around to disturb or stop their future plans.

Krychek's cardinal eyes scanned the blood on the walls. "Will Aden respond to the rumors?"

"The squad doesn't publicly explain itself." Vasic knew Aden would answer the allegations when the time was right, but not by stripping the shield of distance and dark secrecy that kept the squad's vulnerable safe.

Rising to his feet, he looked to Max Shannon, Nikita's security chief having just returned to the office. "News?"

Face set in brutally hard lines, Max said, "Shooter was in a room in the high-rise directly across, as I suspected. I found the actual tenant bound and gagged in the bathroom." The human male, who'd been a cop before he agreed to work for Nikita, put his hands on his hips.

"The tenant said he woke from sleep to find a masked female holding a gun to his head; she told him he'd be fine if he didn't fight." His eyes took in both Vasic and Kaleb, and though Max was, on the surface, the least powerful individual in the room, Vasic knew it would be a mistake to treat him that way.

The former cop not only worked for Nikita, Vasic had cause to know that Max had challenged her decisions on more than one occasion and won. Not many people could make that claim when it came to one of the most ruthless women in the world. Oddly, that fact increased Vasic's respect for both parties involved—Max, for remaining clear-eyed even in the face of Nikita's immense power, and Nikita for being unafraid to give a position of trust to someone who wasn't a yes-man.

Vasic's instincts told him that Max's wife, Sophia, was cut from the same cloth as her husband. Yet Nikita had made the ex-Justice Psy her most senior aide. Neither appointment made sense to those who saw Nikita only as a power-hungry bitch who'd eat her own young to get to the top and to stay there.

Those people seemed to have forgotten the child Nikita did have, the one she'd raised successfully to adulthood despite the fact that the child had been born into an environment hostile to her very existence. And according to Ivy, Nikita would coldly execute anyone who so much as lifted a finger against Sascha.

"I've ordered a forensic team to go over the apartment used by the shooter," Max added. "I'm not expecting them to find anything—this shouts professional hit to me." Folding his arms over his white shirt, he nodded at Kaleb. "If this is about targeting members of the Ruling Coalition, you should be the primary target."

Vasic agreed with Max; Krychek was unquestionably the strongest Psy in the Net.

"Yet I haven't been under threat." Kaleb walked around the bloodied glass to meet Vasic and Max in the center of the room. "Anthony and Ivy?"

"Safe." Vasic had made sure Ivy was always protected, while Anthony had been in the NightStar compound for the past three days to attend internal family meetings.

"Could Ming and Shoshanna be behind this?" Max asked with a raised eyebrow. "Those two suffered a serious demotion with the fall of Silence."

"If we accept that today's assassination attempts were part of the same large conspiracy," Vasic said, "then Shoshanna appears to have been targeted by this group. Anthony's said it's possible Ming was, too, but it could be a smokescreen to hide his involvement. The same with Shoshanna."

"Both will probably have airtight alibis," Max replied dryly. "I'm fairly sure certain people lie as a matter of principle."

"Of course." Kaleb's smile was arctic. "I'll check in on them anyway."

Vasic didn't trust Krychek, likely never would. Not as he trusted Ivy or Aden or even Zaira. However, he'd come to understand certain things about Kaleb that permitted them to work together—like the fact that the deadly cardinal was devoted to the woman with whom he was bonded. And Sahara was deeply connected to the empaths, called many friends. Any destabilization in the PsyNet would impact those empaths, and that would feed back to Sahara.

So in this circumstance, he could trust Krychek. "Thank you."

Nodding, the cardinal telekinetic left.

"Nikita?" Vasic asked Max as he prepared to 'port out.

"No news yet." Lines around his mouth, the other man said, "Sophie's alerted Sascha. Nikita's tough, but the damage was catastrophic." He shook his head. "I'm not sure Sascha will get a chance to say good-bye."

Chapter 62

ZAIRA WOKE WITH the subconscious awareness that she hadn't slept much. An hour or two at most. It was discomfort that had woken her—her eyes were gritty and her throat felt lined with sandpaper. What didn't hurt were the arms that held her close, warm and strong and intensely protective.

Aden.

Lying quiescent against him, she fought the urge to move, get something for her throat. Then Aden's hand slid up to that very place, curling gently around it. The warmth was soft, barely noticeable, but her pain eased almost immediately. "I always forget you have actual M abilities."

Jaw rubbing over her hair, he continued to work. "Is that better?"

"Yes." She turned in his arms, her eyes on the closed balcony doors, beyond which Venice lay cloaked in night. The world was hushed, not even the lap of the canal water breaking the veil. "I don't like crying."

Pressing his lips to her temple, Aden said, "You needed to cry."

Zaira rubbed the spot over her heart. "I feel hollow inside, like I've been wrung dry." For the first time in an eternity, she felt as if she could think without the echoes of nightmare. "Do you think it's permanent?" Not waiting for an answer because she knew the answer and it wasn't something she wanted to face at this instant when she could have been any other normal woman, she turned back into him. "Let me see your lip, your cheek."

Aden bent his head, allowed her to examine him.

She made sure her touch was delicate, the kisses she placed over his bruises soft. "I'm sorry."

"Apology accepted," he said, as if he knew how important it was to her that he do that, that he acknowledge she'd done something wrong and needed to apologize. She couldn't bear it if he simply expected her to lose control and harm him.

Pressing her lips to his throat, she drew in the taste of him, the scent of him. "The PsyNet is buzzing. I can feel it." Yet she didn't open to the news feeds, didn't want the interruption. "Do you need to be somewhere?"

"No." He held her face to his throat, his skin rippling in response to her kiss. "I'm right where I'm meant to be."

The hollowness inside her filled with other, brighter things. With how he made her feel so important and so worth his time, his touch. The sensation was strange and part of her was scared of the lightness of it. The girl she'd been looked on wide-eyed, not sure who she'd become if she wasn't full of a tight knot of rage that colored her every interaction and choice . . . but she didn't fight it.

Blind faith. And love.

Undoing the buttons on his white shirt, she pushed it off his shoulders. He shrugged it off, but when she undid his belt, her knuckles brushing the hard ridges of his abdomen, he said, "I have a gift I planned to give you on our return from New York."

The tortured and scared girl inside her dared step a little closer to the surface, her hope mingling with the adult woman's desire. "Where is it?" she asked, kissing her way across his chest as she did so.

"Right pants pocket."

Sliding her hand into it, she suddenly frowned. "Why aren't you wearing my gift?"

"I attached it to the lapel of my suit jacket."

Zaira remembered seeing that jacket hung on the back of his office door; he'd clearly forgotten to put it on before Nerida teleported them out. "I have it." She removed her hand from his pocket and turned again to the balcony side to look at her gift in the faint light coming in from sources outside.

It sparkled.

Pretty and delicate, it was a ring made of either white gold or platinum, the central stone a rectangular-shaped ruby with faceted sides. Diamonds dotted the band. The avaricious, possessive heart of her wanted it at once. "I can keep it?"

Rising up behind her, he took her left hand and, tugging the ring from her grasp—to her scowl—slid it onto the finger next to the smallest one. "If you wear it on this finger."

Lines formed between her eyebrows. Raising her hand to the light, she said, "What does it matter?" The answer came to her as the ruby glinted in the night. "Ivy wears her wedding band on this finger."

"Yes." A kiss on her jaw that made her want to stretch out and surrender her body to him. "It means you belong to me. The ruby is for your fire, the diamonds for the strength of your spirit, the platinum for the sleek beauty of you in combat."

Her fingers curled into a fist as the light, bright sensations inside her continued to expand regardless of the other, darker thing that lived in her and that didn't want to give up its real estate. Shifting over onto her back and trying not to think about the latter, she ran the fingers of her other hand down his jaw and over his chest. "Vasic wears a ring, too."

Aden's lips curved slightly, his eyes lighting up. "You'll have to ask me to marry you to get me to wear a ring. The brooch will have to do in the interim."

Zaira had never, not in a million years, believed she might one day get married. That was for other, better, less broken people. But now Aden had put the thought in her head and it was so astonishing that she didn't know what to say. So she kissed him, sliding her ringed hand to behind his neck to hold him close as she put up ferociously protective shields around the fragile new hope in her heart.

Because the rage? It wasn't gone. Already she could feel it pooling in her belly again, the clarity of her earlier thoughts altering with its presence and the lightness inside her entangled with threads of a heavy, bloody darkness. *Aden, I'm not fixed,* she said, the words holding despair.

You were never broken. There's nothing to fix.

Tears fell again from her eyes, were mingled in their kiss. She wished she could believe him, believe her quiet boy who had become a powerful man, but where Aden had a faith that had taken the squad from the pitch-black of a subterranean existence to the sunlight of the valley, Zaira had always had blunt pragmatism. She knew even blind faith and the greatest love couldn't change a miswired brain.

Chapter 63

SILVER MERCANT WAS loyal to her family.

It was at the core of every Mercant, that familial loyalty. "Politicians and kingmakers come and go but family is forever" had long been the family motto. That didn't mean Mercants didn't know how to be loyal to others, too. According to Silver's grandmother, once, long ago, the Mercants had been the loyal knights of a king. Many had died in battle to save that king, until only a lone Mercant knight was left and the king's enemies were slain.

"That was when we were given land on which to rebuild our family."

Silver didn't know if that was truth or old family legend, the time of kings so far in the distant past that she couldn't imagine it. What she did know was that the gene for loyalty— if there was one—ran strong in her family line. So strong that once they gave their loyalty, it would take a cataclysm to break that bond. It was why they didn't offer their allegiance lightly.

Kaleb Krychek had, however, earned it.

Not only had he kept his word in his dealings with the Mercants, Silver had watched him over a number of years and come to understand that Kaleb didn't turn on those who'd given him their loyalty, even when the people in question broke or got hurt or were otherwise unable to perform their duties. He treated his people as if they had worth beyond temporary usefulness. She was in no doubt that he'd chosen her as his aide because she was a Mercant, but she also knew that had she proven bad at her job, she'd have been demoted without hesitation.

Instead, she'd been promoted to a position of sprawling responsibility, her task to act as the liaison between all three races in emergency situations. Her contacts—effectively Mercant contacts—had spread out across the world as a result of that promotion and had led to a decision that had never before been made in the past three generations.

Kaleb Krychek was now considered a Mercant.

Whether or not he was ever told of that decision remained Grandmother Mercant's decision, but from this point forward, he'd be treated as a member of the family unit. They'd already given him their loyalty, but now, no matter how bad the situation, they would never abandon him, would fight for him and with him to the death. Family always stuck together. It was why the Mercants had survived where others had fallen.

"Sir," she said, walking through the open doorway of his Moscow office an hour after Nikita Duncan was shot.

He wasn't at his desk, but at the shelves on the far right wall, pulling out a hard-copy volume. She didn't understand why he kept those volumes when he had a direct link to the PsyNet, but even lethally disciplined cardinals had their peccadilloes. "Silver," he said. "Have you heard anything about Shoshanna or Ming on the grapevine?"

"Nothing beyond the obvious—financial maneuvers and political games to consolidate power."

Moving away from the bookshelf, he said, "You wanted to speak to me."

"The matriarch of my family has recalled something that happened eight months ago that might have some bearing on today's events."

"Nikita's shooting?"

Silver inclined her head in the affirmative. "The matriarch was approached via anonymous channels and invited to join a small group of 'visionaries' who would nudge the world in the right direction."

"Did Ena Mercant say yes?"

"Of course." The Mercants liked information, and the best way to get information was to be in the thick of things. "But she was never again contacted. Her belief is that my connection to you was deemed too high a risk factor."

"A pity," Kaleb said, cardinal eyes thoughtful. "If she is approached again, please let her know I have no argument with her joining the group."

"The matriarch wouldn't take kindly to being given permission." Kaleb was now family, and as such, he had to understand family.

"Ah." Kaleb folded his arms. "In that case, ignore that last request. I appreciate the information."

"Would you like me to see what I can dig up on Shoshanna and Ming?"

"Yes. It's always better to be armed before heading into battle."

That, too, was why Kaleb fit into the Mercant family: he wasn't only powerful but mercilessly intelligent. "I'll begin now." Before leaving, she said, "Has there been an update on Nikita's condition?"

Kaleb shook his head. "She remains in surgery. Tell Ena the Net may undergo a power shift if Nikita dies—and if the position does open up, there's no one better placed to step in."

"I agree, but grandmother doesn't like the spotlight, and I believe she appreciates Nikita." Silver had always thought it was because the two women were both at peace with their ruthless natures, and both as viciously loyal to their young. "I will, however, pass on the information." The Net was already in turmoil after the shooting—Nikita's death would disrupt things on the meta-level.

If the worst happened, the Mercants would make sure they were ready to ride the storm tides.

HAVING raced to San Francisco from Yosemite with Lucas at the wheel, Sascha ran into the hospital wing to find security blocking her way. They moved aside the instant they recognized her, and when she pushed through the doors with Lucas by her side, she saw Sophia Russo walking toward her.

"Sophie," she said to the woman who'd become Nikita's right hand despite the fact that the ex J-Psy was in no way Silent.

Thanks to Sophia's husband Max's friendship with a member of DarkRiver, Sascha had come to know Sophia well, and to like her even more. This time, she'd thought, her mother had chosen someone both strong and loyal.

"The surgeons have the bleeding under control," Sophia told her, coming forward to take Sascha's hands in her own. Fine black gloves covered her skin to negate the possibility of skin contact, Sophia's shields problematic as a result of the work she'd done scanning the minds of the vilest criminals. "They're hopeful."

Sascha held those words to her heart. "I never imagined I'd be here," she said to her mate when Sophia went to get a glass of water. "I never thought my mother could get hurt, she's so strong and ruthless."

It wasn't until some time after her defection from the PsyNet that Sascha had begun to understand that Nikita wasn't as one-dimensional in her pursuit of power as Sascha had once believed. This past year, she'd consciously looked at Nikita's history and realized that, while her mother had always liked power, she'd gone into hyperdrive twenty-nine and a half years ago.

After the birth of a cardinal E daughter who needed every protection her mother could provide.

It was Nikita who'd sent her the book that gave her some idea of the scope of her empathic abilities. And it was Nikita who'd made sure Sascha survived to adulthood in a world hostile to empaths. Nikita wasn't "good," would probably never be good, but she'd been as much of a mother to Sascha as she could be, given her own experiences and the state of the world while Sascha was growing up.

Lucas cuddled her close, his touch, his scent, the warmth of his body her own personal anchor. "One thing I know about your mom, kitten. She's as tough as an old wolf. I figure she's probably snarling at the surgeons right now."

Surprised into a wet laugh, Sascha looked up when the doors opened again. She wasn't entirely surprised to see the man on the other side. Her mother and Anthony Kyriakus had always spoken more than Nikita did with most other Psy.

Sascha had never picked up a deeper emotional tie, but then, they both had titanium-strong shields. And both had come of age in Silence.

"Your mother," Anthony said, "is she stable?"

"They've controlled the bleeding but she's still in surgery."

Not saying anything further, the head of PsyClan Night-Star took a standing position not far from the doors, his hands behind his back and his patrician face set in expressionless lines. Yet Sascha was certain there was emotion within. His mere presence here confirmed it. That emotion wasn't directed at only Nikita, either. This powerful and apparently Silent man hadn't ever given up on his daughter, for one. Faith had left the PsyNet, but unlike Sascha, she'd never been cut off from her family unit. Anthony had kept her safe.

The same way Nikita had protected Sascha as a child. Nikita's tactics hadn't been maternal, hadn't been gentle, but they had kept Sascha safe.

Don't ever be anything but perfect, Sascha. This is the result of failure.

Nikita had taken Sascha to a rehabilitation center as a child, shown her the mindless husks of those who'd been psychically brainwiped. As a warning, it had been stark and merciless—and it had stuck. It was fear that had spurred Sascha to build intricate shields nothing could penetrate. "I love her, Lucas," she whispered. "I think she did the best she could, given her own life experience."

"It's all right, kitten. You're permitted to love her."

"She's not a good person." Nikita had done terrible things, things that could never be forgiven.

Lucas's hand curved over the side of her face and into her hair. "You can love someone while being aware of their flaws." He shook his head, his green eyes suddenly panther-bright. "I hate that word, but it's the only one that comes to mind."

She knew the reason for his aversion to the word *flaw*. For so long, it had been used to describe Sascha—she'd used it to describe herself. "I can't forgive her the horrible things she's done . . . but I still love her."

Sophia returned just as the doors to the operating suite opened.

"Councilor Duncan's surgery was successful," the white-haired surgeon said, using Nikita's former title. "She's currently being moved to a recovery room."

Sascha's heart thudded. "I'd like to see her."

"We have to wait for her to wake. I've given her the pre-arranged psychic command passed on to me by her personal medic."

"How long will the healing process take?" Sascha knew her mother; Nikita would hate being laid up, though she might not put it in those emotional terms.

"Because of the depth and nature of her injuries, we made the decision not to use fast-healing techniques. It'll allow for a complete and more stable recovery, but it will take some time."

Sascha thanked the surgeon for the information, then waited while he went to check on the state of Nikita's consciousness. It was a half hour later that a nurse came to fetch Sascha. About to enter through the doors to the surgical ward, she paused and glanced over her shoulder at Anthony. *I'll tell her you're here,* she said after a polite telepathic knock. *You'll wait?* It seemed important that he do that, that he not leave.

Yes.

Lucas walked into the surgical ward with her, checking Nikita's room for threats before allowing her to step in. Closing his hand over hers when she would've gone in, he tugged her close. "Don't feel guilty for loving her." His own love for Sascha pulsed through the mating bond. "At this instant, she's simply your mother and you're her cub. That's a bond that's difficult to break."

Turning her head to kiss his palm, Sascha took a deep, shaky breath and walked in.

GROGGY from the aftereffects of the deep sleep into which she'd put herself during the surgery, the pain from her wounds requiring her conscious attention to manage, it took Nikita's eyes a full minute to zero in on the woman walking toward her. She didn't, however, need the visual cue. She'd known who was at the door the instant it opened.

Sascha. The only child she had ever borne. The cardinal who everyone had told Nikita was flawed, but who she'd known was a power who could not be allowed to come into her own. To do so would equal her death. So she'd crushed her child, and in so doing, saved her life and forever lost her.

"Mother." Sascha closed her hand over Nikita's, her fingers warm.

The contact was jolting. Nikita rarely touched anyone, and she hadn't touched Sascha in years. It was the way she'd been brought up to be, until nothing could alter the foundation of her nature. "Why are you here?" The words came out a croak.

Sascha didn't let go, didn't step back. "I wanted to see that you were all right."

"Not safe." Nikita had done everything in her power to disassociate herself from Sascha, to convince the world her child meant nothing to her, but Sascha's presence here could negate all her careful groundwork. "Find you." As soon as the words left her mouth, she knew she'd betrayed too much, her brain yet sluggish.

Sascha's hand tightened on hers. "I'm an empath, Mother," she said softly. "I understand."

Nikita met the white stars on black that was Sascha's cardinal gaze and allowed herself to live fully in this moment when her daughter was with her and Nikita didn't have to pretend she didn't matter. "You are well?"

"Yes." Sascha's lips curved shakily. "The baby's in good health, too—getting bigger every day. More mischievous, too. Yesterday, she smooshed her hand right into a chocolate mud cake after I turned my back for a minute. Had chocolate frosting all over her face." A laugh that made her eyes fill with sparks of color. "Her mother's daughter."

No one could say that about Sascha. Where Nikita was hard, Sascha was gentle. Where Nikita's conscience was a fluid thing that had led her to make decisions that ended lives and destroyed careers, Sascha would sacrifice her own life before harming another being. And where Nikita had shoved her child out into the darkness, Sascha would hold on tight to hers no matter what.

"Does your child look like a Duncan?" Nikita had seen

visuals captured by photographers she'd contracted, but they were all from a distance.

Sascha nodded. "And a Hunter. She's the best of both me and my mate." A pause. "Would you like to meet her? I can bring her."

"No. Not safe." Nikita drew her hand away. "Go."

Instead, Sascha touched her hand to her hair. "I'm glad you're okay, Mother." Leaving when Nikita said nothing, she closed the door behind her.

Expecting it to stay that way for a considerable period, she found it opening again within the span of two minutes, the man who entered familiar. Nikita felt her body stiffen. She was used to speaking to Anthony as an equal. Right now, she was vulnerable, weak. "Is there a problem the Coalition needs to handle?" she asked in an effort to gain the upper hand.

Anthony halted beside the bed. "No." He scanned her with cool brown eyes that had always seemed to see right through her. "You're in significant pain. Why are you conscious?"

"Do you really expect me to allow myself to be unconscious in an unfamiliar environment?" The only reason she'd put herself under during the surgery was that she knew Sophia and Max would make certain she had guards throughout. Those two might argue with her more often than they agreed, but they would also never stab her in the back.

Max and Sophia had integrity stamped on each and every cell in their bodies.

The trade-off of having to accommodate their viewpoints in her decisions, even when the accommodation equaled less profit or power, was worth it. Because there were very, very few people Nikita could trust in this world. She wasn't about to discard two who had agreed to work with her on the proviso that they would immediately sever their contracts should she act against their conscience.

Who knew, after long enough under their influence, she might even become an honorable person. Like the man who stood looking down at her. Anthony was ruthless, but she knew he had never crossed the lines she had. He protected where she destroyed.

"I'll make sure you're safe," he said, voice hard. "Go under."

Other than Max and Sophia, Nikita didn't trust anyone to watch her back. Well, except for Sascha—her child didn't have the killer gene. Anthony did. "Pain is nothing."

"If I wanted to kill you," he said, "all I'd have to do right now is rupture your healing wounds. You're too weak to stop me."

Nikita wanted to disagree, knew she was wrong. "Why did Sophia allow you in here?"

Anthony just looked at her.

Turning her head, Nikita stared at the wall . . . and then she closed her eyes and put herself under, where the pain didn't stab at her.

Chapter 64

ZAIRA WENT TO see Ivy ten hours after the tears that had broken things inside her. Aden had stayed with her throughout, only leaving to go to New York an hour past. Blake remained in the city, but Amin's team was having trouble pinning him down and he wanted Aden's input on their strategy.

The one good thing was that Amin was dead certain Blake hadn't committed any further murders, too focused on keeping himself alive. Meanwhile, BlackSea had left Venice, taking Olivia with them; Aden had authorized her release when medical scans showed the woman had neural damage to her memory centers. Distraught, she remembered her child, but she had no other useful information.

And that child, to Zaira's intense frustration and anger, remained among the missing. Miane hadn't said anything and neither had Zaira when she farewelled the BlackSea alpha, but they both knew Persephone's time was running out at a critical pace, if she was even still alive.

"I *need* to find her," Zaira said to Ivy as she helped the E . . . helped her friend put together a secondary trellis for her berries. "The idea of her caged that way, to die without ever seeing daylight again." She shook her head. *"No."*

Ivy's face was somber. "You're doing everything you can," she said. "Vasic's kept me up-to-date with the search efforts—I know you have data crawlers in the Net and on-line, and that the word has gone out among all Arrow contacts worldwide."

"It might not be enough." The renewed rage inside Zaira was rigid and tight and red. "These people are *smart*, Ivy. It's like they watched Pure Psy and other groups implode and learned from their mistakes."

"A cold mind behind it all?"

"Subzero. Aden says that doesn't rule out the other races—simply because they were never Silent doesn't mean they can't be evil or calculating. The person at the top of the food chain could be Psy or human or changeling."

"Yes, that's true." Ivy was quiet for a minute as she hammered in a nail. "I can sense a certain level of emotion at all times and I've passed humans and changelings on the street and just felt like shivering." She did so now, as if in sensory memory. "Bad people are bad people, full stop."

Ivy's words touched too deeply at Zaira's own fears. "I need to know if I'm bad inside," she forced herself to say as she took the hammer from Ivy, her ruby ring sparkling in the light.

Features set in a dark frown, Ivy tightened the printed cotton scarf she was using to keep her hair off her face. "Of course you're not," she began, her voice getting that fierce tone it always did when she was about to launch into a defense of Arrows. Ivy didn't think the squad should forget what it had done under Ming and pretend it had no blood on its hands, but she also believed that since this was the first time all of them had ever had a chance to make a free choice, that choice should be what defined them.

"No, I'm talking about—" Zaira shook her head, started again. "I cried," she said and because it was too hard to go on right then, covered her pause by hammering in a nail to strengthen the supports. "I haven't cried since I was three years old and I decided crying didn't help anything."

"So you just stopped?" Ivy held the support brace in place as Zaira pounded in a second nail.

Putting down the hammer, Zaira tested the brace to make sure it would hold. "Yes."

"You were one tough little girl."

Zaira helped Ivy lift up the trellis and get it into position, the posts going into the holes Vasic had already dug for them. "I had no choice." Crying weakened her and she couldn't afford to be weak. "Why are you building this anyway?" she muttered as the two of them fought to get the posts exactly in place. "Vasic could've pushed all these nails in within a minute, got the trellis positioned in less time."

"Doing orchard maintenance helps me think, clears my head."

"Martial arts does the same for me." She glanced around. "Where's your shadow?" She'd become used to Ivy's small white dog.

"Vasic took him to the valley," Ivy said with a smile. "He's great with the children." Posts finally in position, she asked Zaira to hold up the trellis while she poured in the fast-acting eco-plascrete that would set it in place.

"Tears are a release," the empath said as she worked. "Think of it as your body flushing emotional toxins."

"Aden said that, too."

"How do you feel now, after the tears?" Ivy finished one post, moved to the second.

"As if I'm walking on thin ice and could crash through at any moment, but I can do my job." She turned her eyes to the orchard, the trees bright with new green leaves. "Aden needs me to be strong, to be sane."

Rising to her feet, Ivy said, "Aden just needs you." A soft statement potent with empathic power. "He's always been so alone, Zaira, deep inside where even Vasic couldn't reach."

"It's the responsibility." He carried an impossible amount on his shoulders, had done so since he was a child. "Have you ever met his parents?"

"Only once."

"They're relentless," Zaira said. "Nothing matters but the squad. Nothing." Not even their son. "They taught Aden it was his responsibility to lead the rebellion and then they *left* him." Just abandoned him for their cause. "He was a child." Zaira's rage burned.

Reaching over, Ivy touched her fingers to Zaira's cheek. "I can take some of your anger away temporarily, but the truth is that it's a part of you. You have to learn to manage it."

"Can it be done?" Zaira looked into Ivy's coppery eyes,

knowing Ivy was too honest to be able to hide her true reaction. "Or am I insane?" All this time, she hadn't asked the question because she thought she knew the answer, and it wasn't one she wanted to know. Now she had to fight this enemy and, to do so, she needed to know its face.

"I have to read you," Ivy said, voice gentle.

Bracing herself, Zaira nodded. There was, however, no feeling of intrusion even as Ivy's eyes turned obsidian in a display of quiet power, the black streaming with sparks of color Zaira might not have expected if she hadn't seen the eyes and minds of other empaths. The PsyNet was already "infected." Rather than being the stark black-and-white landscape it had been for so long, it was now a black sea webbed with fine gold strands, the space in between glittering with stubborn glints of color.

"It's not working," Ivy said at last, rubbing her fingers over her temples. "Your shields are significant and, I think, instinctive on such a deep level that asking you to force them down will only hurt you." Eyes still an obsidian shimmering with color, she held Zaira's gaze. "What I can tell you is that I get no sense of 'wrongness' from you, for lack of a better word. I've always sensed that with the mentally ill."

Zaira wanted to cling to that, but while she might not be insane in the truest sense of the word, her violent, uncontrollable rages were so close as not to matter. Her pathological possessiveness toward Aden was less of a monster now that he'd chosen to be psychically connected to her, but the rage was as powerful as ever. "Can you teach me how to handle my anger?"

Ivy closed her hand over Zaira's, the empathic warmth of her soaking into Zaira's cells. "We'll do it together," she said, the words a promise. "I have faith that the girl who chose to stop crying at three years of age has the will to conquer this demon."

Blind faith. And love.

ADEN returned to the valley after spending several hours in New York. Say what you would about Blake, the man was one hell of an Arrow as far as his skills went—he was trapped, but he wasn't giving up. Frustrated by the lack of success in hauling the murderous bastard in, Aden wanted to find Zaira, talk the entire op over with her, but she'd made it clear she wanted time alone, and she'd be the first to tell him that their needs didn't trump the needs of Arrow young.

"Cubs need to see their alpha," Remi had told him. "It's about family, about feeling safe."

So though his soul hungered for Zaira, he changed into casual gear and walked through the valley, taking in the completed houses and the ones still going up. The air was cool but not cold, and though the very young were already asleep, older children sat studying by windows and he saw a hesitant game of football in progress in the open green space.

"Sir." They stopped when he neared.

"Go on," he said, and when they seemed stiff and unsure, he thought of that phone call with Judd, of cubs and adults and alphas. "Do you have room for a new player?"

Their astonishment was so great it penetrated fairly strong Silence training. "You, sir?" asked the girl who seemed the oldest.

"Yes. What are the rules?"

He played with them for an hour, aware of the gathering crowd of other teens and adult Arrows—including his mother, who'd moved into the valley with his father. But not the one person for whom he watched. His gut was in a knot. He knew there was a chance Zaira might never return to him. When he'd left her to head to New York, she'd been distant, curled into herself, and her mind, it hadn't connected with his.

Even now, it was empty inside his skull, her fire missing.

"Goal!"

Ruffling the hair of the boy who'd scored, Aden said, "I think you all need to get to bed."

An immediate chorus of "Yes, sir"s but no stiffness now. These children were still reachable. That didn't mean they didn't bear wounds, but with the right care, those wounds would heal.

"We didn't bring you up to be the leader of the squad so you could waste time playing with children."

Looking into his mother's face, Aden said, "You didn't

bring me up at all." A blunt truth. "As for how I choose to lead the squad, that decision is mine." He knew Marjorie and Naoshi had expected to guide their son where they wanted him to go, had been stunned to realize one day that he'd grown both independent and away from them.

Despite it all, he did respect them. Without his parents, there would've been no rebellion.

"Are you planning to respond to the *Beacon* article?" Lights glowed in the windows of the homes around them, but his mother's eyes were dark.

"In my own way and when it's time."

"You should eliminate the *Beacon* editor. That'll get the message across."

"Mother, that is the old way." Aden didn't intend to bring up the next generation to think violence alone was the answer. "We're going to work smarter."

"You should listen to those of us who've lived longer, seen more."

"And are stuck in prehistoric times?" came a familiar voice, a familiar mind sliding into his. *Sorry I'm late. Bo wanted to talk, see if we had any updates on the attempts to foster conflict between various parties.*

Staggered by the cool rush of relief that she'd chosen to come to him regardless of the fears of madness that haunted her, he put his arm around her shoulders, saw his mother's eyes go to their connection. But when Marjorie spoke, it was to say, "Venice?"

"Empty. Everyone has been relocated and all movable property will soon be gone." Zaira slid her own arm around his waist. "My opinion is that we keep ownership but rent it out. In the future, younger members of the squad could use it as a covert home base should they need one in that part of the world."

"The other rentals would provide good cover." Marjorie nodded before turning to Aden.

The fact that she had large, thickly lashed eyes set in a delicate face gave her an appearance of almost doll-like fragility.

It was a premeditated lie. Marjorie Kai was as pitiless an Arrow as Aden knew.

"You're far weaker in psychic ability than we intended," she said to him. "See that the weakness doesn't extend to your leadership."

Aden held Zaira back when she would've lunged at Marjorie as his mother shifted on her heel to walk away. "I've heard it a million times," he reminded her. "It ceased to have any effect while I was still in my early teens." Even as defectors, his parents had found ways to get messages to him—those messages had always been focused on how he could best serve the rebellion "despite" his "substandard rating on the Gradient."

Zaira scowled up at him. "Why don't you just tell her exactly how strong you are?"

"I like to imagine the look on her face the day she finds out."

"She'll probably take joint credit for it with your father."

A smile filled his veins. "True." *Will you stay?*

Where else would I go? With that sharp comment, she began to walk to the simple cabin-style home that had been assigned to them in the valley. DarkRiver's architects had taken their ideas and requests and come up with an overall design plan that suited the people who'd be using the buildings. Even the larger houses, meant for bigger families, carried through the warm, natural style that allowed for plenty of open space and light.

"I came by earlier, spoke to Beatrice," Zaira said.

"How is the girl?"

"Healing slowly—Abbot's E is helping her. I asked if she wanted to move in with us, since we have the spare room, but another Arrow her age reached out to her in the aftermath of the Blake situation and the two are happy bunking together with three other year mates."

"As long as she knows the offer is open." Lights began snapping off around them, though more than a few adults remained up. "Blake's still in the wind but Amin's keeping up the pressure. We will get him. And Krychek's uncovered nothing that points to any of our obvious suspects being behind the conspiracy, but he's planning to make some personal visits, too."

"Nikita?" Zaira asked as they reached their cabin.

"Alive." Walking inside, he shut the door and, in the darkness, hauled her close, kissing his way down her face to find her lips.

"Aden," she murmured, just as rain hit the windows. "I've made a decision."

"What?"

"If we have to deal with the bad things anyway, then we should get to indulge in the good as much as we want." She pushed up his T-shirt. "Take this off."

He had no hesitation in obeying. Throwing the soft cotton aside, he helped her strip off her uniform. The instant she was naked, he put his hands, his mouth on her. She protested. "You're still half—"

Stealing her words with a kiss, he wrapped his arms just below her ribs and hitched up. She moved fluidly with him, locking her legs around his waist and her arms around his neck. He held her in position as he walked forward until her back gently hit the wall. Bracing her against it, he placed one palm flat on the wall, his other on the sleek muscle of her thigh.

The feel of her acted like nitroglycerine in his blood, setting off a sensory explosion that made his heart thump and his skin heat. At that instant, with the rain cocooning them from the world and the squad in good hands for the next few hours, he could be just a man, just Aden. And Aden wanted to sink into the dangerous, fascinating Arrow in his arms.

Over and over and over again.

"I like this," Zaira said definitively before running her hands down his chest, then back up to curl one possessively over his nape.

Wanting more contact, he moved his body forward, changing position to brace his forearm above her head. It pressed his chest into her breasts; so close, he saw her pupils dilate as her nipples hardened against him, felt her pulse begin to race. "I see definite benefits to it." Moving his hand from her thigh to one plump breast, he squeezed and molded as he dipped his head and put his mouth on her throat.

Zaira moaned and, sleek and strong, tightened her grip around his waist. Her skin was delicate under his mouth, under his teeth, tasted of the ice and steel of her. Hungry, ravenous, he kissed his way up her throat and along her jaw to her mouth. She met him kiss for kiss, hot and wild under his hands, a lover who turned his control to ashes. There was no leash when he was with Zaira, no shield, no barrier.

She wouldn't permit it and he didn't want those walls between them.

Caressing his hand down her side and over the dip of her waist, he stroked between her legs from below. Liquid honey on his fingertips, his lungs protesting as he fought to breathe. But the air was full of pheromones, full of the lush, erotic scent of her desire; with every inhale came another raw wave of sexual heat in his blood.

She shivered at that instant and bit him gently on the neck. He lost his rhythm, had to go still and concentrate to rediscover it . . . just as she bit him again in that exact spot. "You're derailing my plan," he told her, his voice rough.

"Good." A demanding kiss. "Take off your pants and I'll stop."

"Liar."

A gleam in her eyes that he thought might be inner laughter. "Take them off anyway."

"I'll have to let you go to get rid of my boots."

She insinuated her hands between their bodies to undo his belt, then got busy on the button of his black cargo pants. "You're an Arrow—figure out a way to do it without letting me go."

Stomach clenching as her fingers brushed the ridge of his erection, he accepted the challenge and got to work. It took several minutes, especially since Zaira was determined to distract him—and since she was naked and beautiful and in a sexually playful mood, she had a distinct advantage.

Not that Aden would ever complain about being seduced by Zaira.

Finally succeeding in kicking off his boots and remaining clothing, he crushed her body to the wall, his rock-hard penis pressed against her abdomen. "I win."

Meltingly wet under his fingers, she nibbled at his lower lip and moved her body against his, her skin rubbing over his pulsing erection. "I think I win, too."

Aden slid his hand under her head and gripped her hair to hold her in place so he could watch her as he stroked his fingers through her honey-slick folds. Zaira made a husky sound deep in her throat, her pleasure a primal aphrodisiac that caused his penis to throb. Gritting his teeth to hold back the orgasm building inside him, he gripped her under the thighs and, shifting her higher up the wall, thrust into her in a single deep stroke after an instant of eye contact that told him what he needed to know.

She was with him, wanted this.

A short, high sound escaping her mouth, she dug her nails into his shoulders. "Aden," she said breathlessly. *"Aden."*

Slamming both hands palms down on either side of her head as the sound of his name on her lips further eroded his control, Aden used the leverage to pull back as much as he could, given her grip on him, before sinking deep into her once again in another hard thrust. She was wet, tight heat around his cock and silken, lithe warmth around his body.

"My Zaira," he said, his voice so rough the words were almost unrecognizable.

But she understood, her eyes going soft in a way Aden knew only he would ever see. Then he moved again and again and her back arched, her body bathing him in renewed heat as her orgasm rushed over her. He held off his own pleasure long enough to watch her splinter, and then he surrendered to the roar of need.

Barely able to stand afterward, he stumbled to the bed and got them both on it.

There were whispers after that, followed later by the soft rasp of skin on skin, and the mingled breaths of two people who didn't want to be anywhere but with one another.

Chapter 65

SHOSHANNA SCOTT HAD been all but off the grid since before the fall of Silence and of the Council, but Kaleb knew exactly where she was. He always knew the locations of all the dangerous players in the Net—Shoshanna might not be as psychically powerful as him, but she had a politically lethal mind.

Visual locked, he teleported to outside her London home the day after the attempt on Nikita's life. The building had originally been owned by Henry Scott but he'd transferred it into his and Shoshanna's joint ownership two years prior to his death—a subtle but telling sign of their relationship at the time. Shoshanna had been the definite alpha member of the pair until Henry's sudden tendencies toward violence. The rest of Henry's estate had gone to his family group, another mark of Shoshanna's intelligence. Taking on an entire family was bad business.

Doing up the button on the jacket of his black suit jacket, the shirt below it the same shade, he walked up to the door. He could've as easily teleported to right beside Shoshanna, but he had political intelligence of his own. The door opened in front of him, a uniformed member of staff inviting him inside. Walking down the corridor with its marble-inlaid floor, he was shown directly to Shoshanna's study. A slender brunette, she was standing by a table on which were spread a number of hard-copy maps of ancient London.

"Have you ever studied the layout of the city?" she said as he walked in, the cool white of her fingers tracing the route of the river Thames. "It's an interesting project to occupy the mind."

And a great way to keep people from focusing on what Shoshanna was up to in her self-imposed exile. "I didn't realize you had an appreciation for history."

She looked up, ice blue eyes meeting his. "It is from history that we learn lessons about the future, is it not?"

He inclined his head, wondering exactly what she'd learned from Henry's doomed association with Pure Psy. Enough to mastermind a worldwide conspiracy? Or perhaps simply be a part of it.

"So." She came around the table. "How can I help you?"

"You've retreated from public life. I came to see if you were sick."

Shoshanna's smile was cold, a false image she'd perfected as had he. "I've decided there's far more profit in focusing on my business interests. Politics can be deadly—a fact Henry learned too late."

"A wise move." He looked around the room. It was filled with bookshelves, leather-bound books lined up in neat rows on the gleaming wood of the shelves. But, unlike Kaleb's own library, it didn't look like any of the books had been read. He thought it was a set, meant to put non-Psy at ease. "Are your businesses performing well?"

"I'm sure you're well aware how they're performing."

He was. Shoshanna had ridden out the fall of Silence and, even factoring in the contract she'd lost to Nikita, she was now in a very healthy position. Silver had somehow managed to get her hands on the specific numbers, so he knew *exactly* how well Shoshanna was doing. "So you've dropped out of political life on a permanent basis?"

"Much safer that way." She glanced at an incoming call code on the large comm screen on the wall to the right, ignored it in favor of returning her attention to him. "I'm a survivor, Kaleb. Post-Silence, the PsyNet is looking for a kind of governance I can't provide. What I can do is leverage my contacts to place Scott Enterprises in the top tier before other businesses find their feet."

Her logic was faultless, but his instincts told him she was hiding something. It could be anything from black market trades to industrial espionage to involvement in this conspiracy. He'd keep a careful watch on her. Even the most meticulous planners eventually made mistakes.

Leaving after another minute of conversation where no information was exchanged, he next checked in on Ming. The other man was heavily occupied with keeping Europe stable, his focus absolute from all appearances, but he was also a master strategist.

Silver's sources had come up empty on Ming but for a vague rumor that he'd threatened a political rival named Kurevni. Since the man in question was still running against Ming, that appeared to be a false claim. Unless, of course, Ming had put Kurevni in place for reasons of his own—which he was fully capable of doing.

However, that was standard operating procedure for many powers in the Net. Kaleb was far more interested in seeing what his instincts told him about the likelihood of Ming being a part of the conspiracy. Their conversation was brief and pointed. He left with the distinct impression that Ming hadn't given up on reclaiming the Arrows.

That motivation could explain the attempts against Aden's life and reputation, but it didn't explain everything else. Ming was all about order, not chaos. However the idea that all the suspicious events were unconnected, that different players were responsible for different elements, seemed improbable. Still, he wouldn't discard it.

The fall of Silence had rattled more than one cage.

Ming wants you dead, he messaged Aden. *I'm sure that's not news, but you should be aware his intent remains strong.*

Aden responded within a minute. *Is he our puppet master?*

Unknown. Too many variables in play. It might be time for Kaleb's alter ego to do some covert digging.

Before that, he spoke to the heads of two powerful families and, while they both said all the right things, Kaleb's instincts went on high alert. "Both Marshall and Rao are up to something," he said to Sahara when he returned home.

"Why did you focus on them in the first place?"

"Rao remains a power player in Southeast Asia, but the

family suffered significant losses as a result of the fall of Silence—and those losses may continue." It made the Rao family prime candidates for discontent. "Pax Marshall, in contrast, has kept the ship steady, but he shows all the signs of being a man who wants the kind of power you can only get at the Council—or Coalition—level." Kaleb smiled and, because this was Sahara with him, it was real. "He reminds me of me in certain ways." The only difference was that Pax's goals might be in opposition to Kaleb's. "Ambition and pitiless will."

"And I know exactly how dangerous you can be." Sahara rose on tiptoe to kiss him, her hands braced on his shoulders. "We can't ignore the other races, either, especially given how cleverly humans and changelings have been targeted by this conspiracy." A frown forming over the dark blue of her eyes. "The Psy civil war, followed by the fall of Silence, destabilized the financial world in general, but the nimble businesses are surviving. A number of non-Psy businesses are actually doing better."

"Yes." It would be in the latter's interests to undermine the stability fostered by the Ruling Coalition. "There're too many suspects. We're going to need further data to unearth the linchpins." Putting his hands on her hips, he said, "It appears the Ghost is about to come out of retirement."

Sahara's lips curved. "I've always found the Ghost mysterious and deliciously sexy."

Kaleb kissed her, her smile sunlight in the dark, twisted places inside him.

Chapter 66

"NOW THAT YOU and Zaira are a unit, Ivy and I can step out of the media spotlight," Vasic said to Aden as the two of them put together another cabin the day following Aden's return from New York.

Amin's latest report stated that Blake had been corralled to within a five-block perimeter. It was now a matter of pinning him down. As for the conspiracy and the race to find Persephone, Zaira had already set multiple data-gathering operations in progress, and Aden had spoken to a number of sources earlier in the day.

Everything that could be was in play.

The afternoon belonged to the valley and to his Arrows. Difficult as the decision was for Aden to make, given how deeply Persephone's imprisonment reminded him of Zaira's childhood, he couldn't ignore all the other children in his care. Each and every one was just as vulnerable—ignoring them now would undo all progress to date. These children expected betrayal, expected rejection.

Aden would not put another scar on their hearts.

Zaira had agreed with him, saying she'd prefer to work in the valley than go around in circles getting angrier and angrier at the lack of any viable leads.

"It's not that easy," he said in response to Vasic's statement, part of him still thinking about Persephone and considering if they'd left any stone unturned in their search for the innocent little girl. Losing her to the monsters would devastate Zaira.

The idea of a child dying in a cage was her personal nightmare.

Jaw muscles tense, he returned to his conversation with Vasic. "Ivy makes you far more accessible to the public at large."

"While Zaira is seen as a threat," Vasic said, going down to pet Rabbit when the dog dropped a piece of wood at his feet in an attempt to be helpful. "Devoted to keeping you safe, but a threat nonetheless." He looked up at Aden from his crouched position, his eyes no longer remote and cold as they'd once been. "That's good. Your mate should be a blade in her own right."

Yes, she was a blade. Dangerous and devoted and passionate.

Aden.

Turning at her voice in his mind, he saw her walking toward him. He wiped the sweat off his brow using the back of his hand, his T-shirt sticking to his body, and waited for her to reach him. He liked watching her move, whether it was in combat or in life. She was so fluid, so light on her feet, her body all curves that belied the lethal focus in her eyes.

She'd changed out of her Arrow uniform after leaving the empty Venice compound under Mica's watch, was dressed in old brown cargo pants and a white T-shirt that had streaks of dirt on it from the work she'd been doing helping Ivy and the children with the garden plots. He'd heard Ivy's laugh ripple out more than once, the two women clearly having become closer friends than he'd realized. Because, while Zaira didn't laugh, she'd been involved in conversation with Ivy every time he glanced over.

Reaching him, she stopped with her boots touching his and a starkness in her eyes. "I need you." *The memories are haunting me.*

Not stopping to think about it, he gathered her against him, her own arms coming around him in a steely grip. Stroking his hand over her hair, he spoke softly to her. "Are your PsyNet shields holding?" He knew it was important to her that her emotions remain private from the world. If she needed it, he could wrap his own around hers temporarily.

A nod against him. "I just needed you." Her hand fisted in his T-shirt. "Ivy says craving such contact isn't a weakness, that we've all been starved of it all our lives."

"Yes." He ran his hand down her back, allowed her to sense his own need through their psychic connection. It wasn't a true bond, not with Zaira's mind shut to his except for a narrow pathway, but it was enough to wet his parched soul. If that was all she could ever give him, it would hurt him deep within, but he'd never blame her for it.

Zaira had had her ability to trust ground into dust long before they'd met. Yet despite everything, she'd stayed, was fighting for him and the life they could have together. He knew she'd spoken to Ivy, intended to continue working with the empath to find a way to handle the rage that kept stealing her reason without warning. It would've been so much easier and safer for her to have backed off, but she had immense courage, his Zaira.

And she loved him in every way she could.

Today, she drew away after another five minutes of silent togetherness. Touching his unshaven jaw in an unexpected caress, she went back to Ivy and the children. Aden was aware of multiple Arrows watching her and him in turn, but he returned to his task without saying anything. He couldn't teach or train his brethren for this aspect of life—each Arrow had to come to his or her own conclusions and decisions on the matter, though if one approached him, he would share everything that wasn't private.

A few minutes later, he became aware of another presence at his side.

Looking down, he found a child staring up at him. She had dirt on her T-shirt, too, her pale blonde hair scraped back into a ponytail and her feet in child-sized boots.

"Where's your helmet?" All the children had been taught that if they came near the ongoing work sites, they were to wear helmets.

Huge blue eyes blinked rapidly before she rubbed away a speck of dirt that was hanging off one lash. "I forgot."

"Aden."

Catching the small helmet Vasic threw him, having 'ported it in during the conversation, Aden handed it to the child who he now knew was named Carolina. He hadn't had to access the records for that data—Zaira had telepathed the name to him a second ago, because regardless of how Zaira saw herself, children saw her as safe.

To her befuddlement, Arrow children gravitated toward her just like little Jojo had done in RainFire; they wanted to be around her when she was near. So she took care of them in her pragmatic and deeply honest fashion. Aden thought the children saw the same thing he did—that Zaira's heart was as pure as theirs.

"Here," he said, reaching down to clip the strap under Carolina's chin.

She frowned at him, her conditioning having clearly been nascent at best when Silence fell and the training protocols were changed to teach psychic and emotional discipline *without* erasing or sacrificing the ability to experience emotions.

"Where's your helmet?" she asked suddenly.

Aden had taken it off earlier, now put it back on. "You're right. I should wear it."

Nodding, she continued to stare at him, a child of approximately six with lines between her eyebrows.

"Is there something you need, Carolina?"

Her smile was glorious. "You know my name!"

"Zaira told me."

"I like Zaira. She's not mean." Smile fading, Carolina continued to stare at him.

He hunkered down in front of her so she didn't have to crane her neck. "What is it?" he asked, certain she wanted something.

She shuffled closer and beckoned him with one hand. When he placed his ear next to her mouth, she whispered, "Can I have a hug, too?"

It felt like a kick to the heart, the shakily spoken words. Closing one arm around her, he rose to his feet, her weight so light, so fragile that he couldn't wrap his mind around how anyone could've ever imagined that torturing a child was an acceptable thing. "You can have a hug anytime you want."

Eyes bright and wet, she locked thin, dirt-streaked arms tight around his neck. Placing his free hand against her back to hold her to him, this tiny girl with her breakable bones and her breakable heart, he saw that Zaira and Ivy had both stopped working to look his way.

Ivy's mind touched his. *Just hold her, Aden. She'll be okay.*

Following her advice, he decided to walk around and inspect the other homes in progress. His men and women took in his small burden but didn't comment, instead giving him short updates on their particular projects. Slowly, Carolina raised her head from his tear-wet neck and started to look around.

When Cris said, "Come here, Caro. You can help sweep the floor clear of the building dust," the little girl let Cris pull her gently from Aden's hold and put her on her feet.

Wiping Carolina's face with a cloth she'd found from somewhere, Cris gave the child a small brush and a dustpan and led her into the newly finished home. *I'll watch over her, Aden. Zaira says you'll have more company soon.*

Cris was right.

Two minutes after he returned to his position working beside Vasic, he found himself talking to a thirteen-year-old boy who didn't make physical contact, but who stayed with him for over an hour while younger children came by and tugged on his hand or simply raised their arms. The older teens kept their distance but they looked on, taking in the changes in the squad.

It didn't surprise him in the least when some of the children went straight to Vasic, Cris, and the others, including a Zaira who didn't blink an eye at being asked for affectionate contact. Watching her seat a little boy in her lap while she showed him a blooming flower, he realized she'd changed on a far deeper level than he'd understood.

This Zaira wouldn't only take care of a child's practical needs, wouldn't only protect. She'd make sure his or her spirit was also nurtured. *It's not so hard,* she said to him out of the blue. *They don't lie and hide what they need and I can follow instructions and requests.*

Aden felt a smile curve his lips. He didn't hide it, didn't

show his men and women and the children an impassive face. *Except when the instructions are given by me.*

Of course. You need to be challenged on a daily basis.

Tiny, soft fingers touched his lips in wonder, the child he currently held starting to smile, too. As with Carolina, tears streaked many of the small faces in the valley that day, but smiles soon took them over, hope an incandescent and innocent flame in their eyes. And as the children attached themselves to certain Arrows for reasons of their own—including more than one surprising choice—that flame started to flicker in spurts and startled sparks in the eyes of adult Arrows, too.

It felt as if the entire valley was coming awake.

He looked toward Zaira. *Your courage started this.* She'd come to him in front of everyone, exposing her need, and in so doing, showed the children it was all right. *Your fire lives in them now.*

Her mind swirled around his, as if in a psychic kiss.

Chapter 67

THEY HAD TURNED him into prey.

Sweating, his heart thudding, Blake hid in the narrow space behind an overflowing Dumpster. The stench made his stomach churn, the physical response a reminder of how badly he'd fallen. How badly they'd made him fall. They'd made him an animal scrabbling for scraps and a place to rest.

The hunger to kill was furious in him now, his blood boiling.

Worse was the physical gnawing in his gut that urged him to look in the trash for food.

No. He would not stoop to that. Especially not when he had a better option.

It was time to call in his marker.

Waiting until Amin's team had passed, missing his shielded mind by mere inches at most, he pulled out his phone and called his contact. "I need an extraction." It was then that he realized not all of the stink was from the Dumpster; he was filthy.

The person on the other end took time to reply. "Who is this?"

"No games," Blake gritted out. "You know exactly who I am and I know exactly who you are." He paused to let that sink in. "You made a mistake, exposed yourself." It had been a small error, a single slip of the tongue, but that was all he'd needed.

"I'll make sure not to make personal contact next time."

"You do that. Now I need a fucking extraction."

"You're an Arrow. Act like one."

"I also have the entire squad out for my blood. *Get me out*."

A pause on the other end before the other party said, "I can organize it in another twenty-four hours. It's too hot right now—my sources tell me the city is crawling with Arrows and with Krychek's people."

"I won't survive twenty-four hours."

"You can take a kill," was the cool response. "Do it. Calm down so you can think."

He thought of the amount of attention, the heat, and knew it would be irrational to act now, but the need was violent. And his contact was counting on that, counting on him being stupid. "Twelve hours," he said. "Or I might decide to talk."

"Don't threaten me." A rustling sound. "Be at the following location in exactly twelve hours." The person on the other end of the line gave him the coordinates.

Hanging up after agreeing, he crawled out of his hiding place, flipped up the hood of his sweatshirt, and headed toward the one hidey-hole the squad hadn't yet found and that Blake had kept in reserve. The small apartment had belonged to a man he'd killed years before. He'd made sure the taxes were paid, as was the rent, and since no one had ever come looking for the dead man, it wasn't likely anyone would do so now.

The only problem was that the building was a busy one. Too many eyes, too many witnesses. That, however, didn't matter now. All he had to do was slide in without attracting any notice, and stay down for twelve hours.

After that, he'd be free once again.

Chapter 68

IT WAS TAMAR who found the smoking gun the next morning. The financially savvy twenty-four-year-old woman whom Aden had saved from an execution order, and who'd been working for him long before the Arrows rebelled against Ming, said, "The money for the apartments where the two saboteurs were found came from a shell corporation, but I was able to strip away the layers to get a name."

That name was Hashri Smith.

It wasn't difficult to trace the man, given the information Tamar had uncovered. He proved to be a midlevel human businessman based in Singapore. Portly, with a thick head of black hair and round brown eyes that gave him a permanently startled air, he ran an import-export business that appeared to be fully legitimate. Nothing in his background said he had the kind of contacts or interests that would lead to an attack against Arrows.

He was, however, making frantic calls to a disconnected comm number night after night. During the day, he constantly mopped up perspiration using a handkerchief, his brown-skinned face haggard. Surveillance images taken from his own security cameras showed him jumping at shadows, as if he expected to be assassinated at any instant.

"He's been cut from the fold," Aden predicted before he made the executive decision to have Smith brought quietly in. Normally, he'd have waited, watched, but his instincts told him that would be a pointless delay—and if there was even a slim chance the human male knew Persephone's whereabouts or fate, Aden couldn't justify even a short wait.

Vasic went in and grabbed Smith while he was sleeping, the teleport made so swiftly that only someone who'd been inside the target's bedroom and awake at the time would've noticed it. Since Smith slept in a separate bedroom from his wife, there was no witness.

Vasic seated the male in a room deep in Central Command that was a pure black cube. He and Zaira kept watch as Aden talked to Smith; though none of them believed the now shivering man was dangerous, it would be stupid to be complacent.

"You know who I am?" Aden asked Smith after taking a seat in the chair across from him.

Dressed in white-striped red flannel pajamas, the whites of his eyes visible and his hands tightly locked together, Smith jerked his head up and down. "Arrow," he croaked out.

"Would you like a glass of water?"

Another jerk.

I'll get it, he telepathed to Vasic and Zaira before walking out to do exactly that. *I need him to trust me.*

Why? Zaira's blunt tone. *Rip the truth from his mind. Olivia was brought in five days ago. Two or three more days at most and her daughter's captors will realize Olivia's memories were permanently damaged.*

Do you really believe this man is anything but the lowest level of pawn?

Folding her arms as Aden returned to the room, Zaira focused a hard stare on Smith. The man visibly wilted. *Damn it,* she muttered. *He's the worst excuse for a terrorist I've ever seen.*

Giving Smith the water, Aden sat in patient silence while the other man glugged it down.

Smith handed the glass back with a hand that trembled. "Th-thank you."

Aden placed the glass on the floor beside his chair. "Do you know why you're here?"

Smith's eyes shifted left then right, his hands twisting in

his lap. When he shook his head, Aden spoke very quietly. "Hashri, I can scan your mind, pick out anything I need to know. I can strip you of every one of your secrets."

The man's Adam's apple bobbed, his breathing turning ragged.

"But I won't," Aden continued. "That would make me no better than the murderers we hunt." It was a decision Aden had made with the fall of Silence. "However," he said when the businessman looked hopeful, "my personal moral choice isn't stronger than my loyalty to the squad. I will do whatever is necessary to protect my men and women and, in this case, an innocent child."

"I don't know anything," Smith blurted out, tears streaking out of his eyes. "I really don't."

Aden knew no further persuasion would be needed. As Zaira had realized, Smith wasn't a criminal mastermind—he was a bit player who'd been given just enough power to feel useful and not question his masters. "Tell me how and when this all began."

"Um." Smith wiped his face with his knuckles, his expression eager to please. "Eight months ago, I received a letter—an actual, printed letter—asking if I'd like to be part of a networking group designed to connect business owners together in a mutually beneficial way. It said I'd been chosen because of my innovative advertising techniques."

Smith swallowed convulsively again. "My business wasn't doing so well, so I thought, why not? I figured I might find someone who could maybe help me get a few more contracts."

Eight months ago, Vasic said inside his mind. *Same timeline as the BlackSea abductions and months before the fall of Silence.*

The cracks had begun to appear to anyone who was paying careful attention. Aden had noticed, known those cracks were permanent. *Psy or non-Psy alike could've read the signs.*

"Did you keep the letter?" he asked the pajama-clad man in front of him.

He shook his head. "Later, they told me to get rid of it."

Aden decided to follow up on that instruction later. "What did you do after deciding to join the group?"

"I RSVP'd to the number included in the letter and got a recorded message saying I'd soon be sent another letter with further details." Smith looked up, the whites of his eyes now red with burst blood vessels. "I don't know why I'm here." His voice was a plea. "I just did a favor for a friend."

"Finish your story." Aden made no threat, his tone even, but Smith trembled.

"A week after that first contact, I received another letter. It listed the names of three other businesspeople in my area who were interested in the networking opportunity. We contacted one another, got together. I figured one would be the person who'd started the group in the first place, but no one copped to it." Smith shrugged. "I didn't really worry too much about it—the others were good people and we made an agreement to help each other where we could."

"Your business improved," Aden guessed.

"Yeah." A shaky smile. "I suddenly started getting more contracts. Nothing huge, but enough to bring me out of the red. When I was sent a third letter four months later saying that the organization that had brought us all together and ensured our prosperity would like a favor in return, I called back on the number provided and left a message saying yes. I figured I owed them."

"What occurred?" Aden said when the other man paused and looked to him as if for further instruction.

"I got a letter thanking me for my assistance and asking me to pay for a couple of apartments. But first, I had to follow instructions to set up a shell corporation and all that." Smith sighed and seemed to slump in his chair. "Soon as I saw the shell corporation stuff I knew something was hinky, so I ignored it . . . and my contracts started falling away." Shoulders shaking, he began to cry. "I have kids, a wife. I can't go bankrupt. I did what they asked."

"Where did you get the money for the rents?" Smith had paid for a full year in advance, and Venice rentals weren't cheap. If there had been a money transfer, Tamar might be able to track it.

"I was overpaid a couple, maybe three times on invoices, and since the letter said the money would be provided, I figured out quick that the extra was for the rent."

Aden had already made sure Tamar had full access to Smith's files. Now he questioned the older man in detail about the specific contracts that had brought him the money, and telepathically alerted Tamar to push those forensic investigations to priority status. "Did you ever hear from your benefactors again?"

Smith shook his head. "When I heard about what happened in Venice—about the suicide—and I realized it was from one of the rentals, I called the number I had, but it was disconnected. I talked to the others in the group to see if anyone else had an e-mail or something, but the others had the same number."

And had no doubt been asked to do small tasks of their own. It turned out Smith knew the basic gist of those tasks, but Aden would get the details from the others. When he did a few hours later, he saw why Hashri Smith and his associates continued to breathe. All knew only a minuscule detail at best, and none of those details led to anything but dead ends.

Also interesting was that all four reported a gradual downturn in business over the past two months. Used up and discarded, Aden thought. Nevertheless, he released the terrified businesspeople with the coda that should they be contacted again, they were to alert the squad. "I don't believe they'll be contacted," he told his team of senior Arrows late that afternoon. "Smith and his cohorts played their roles and have now been written out."

Their opponent was not only smart and sly but ruthless and calculating. If it was a human or changeling, they had to have high-level Psy support or the ability to hack into secure Psy databases. Aden's bet was on the former—all the conflict-causing "tricks" to date that had to do with the Psy had been too well designed and targeted to have been thought up by an outsider.

It had to be someone who had deep knowledge of the PsyNet and the politics within it.

He said as much to Zaira as they took an hour out to de-stress with hand-to-hand combat in a quiet corner of the valley. Spinning out with a kick that tapped his ribs without causing harm, she said, "Your instincts are usually right on things like this."

Avoiding a blow that would've connected with her jaw if he hadn't pulled it, she tried to get in under his guard, got a shoulder tap for her trouble. "Clever."

"I wouldn't want you to think me easy prey."

Zaira knew that was ludicrous. "Never . . . unless it's in bed."

Molten heat in his gaze. "What shall we try tonight?"

She sent him an image.

Barely avoiding what would've been a mock-killing blow, he shot her an image in answer. She stumbled, then narrowed her eyes. *If you ever want me to do that, you have to do what I suggested.*

Deal.

She pointed an accusatory finger. *You wanted both anyway.* The faint smile on his face gave him away.

So did I, she admitted before she went at him, no playing now.

He held his own, both of them breathing hard by the time they called a halt. "Where are you headed?"

"Miane called," Zaira said, the break over and her mind on a little girl who probably didn't understand why she was locked up, why her mommy hadn't come for her. "Olivia's memory wasn't as shot as we initially thought—she remembers being with her daughter, so they were both held at the same place."

It eased some of the raw fury in Zaira to have it confirmed that at least Persephone hadn't been alone the entire time she and her mother had been held captive. "I've been invited to one of BlackSea's floating cities to sit down with Olivia and Miane to see if we can narrow down the location."

Aden ran a hand through his hair. "The alpha wants an Arrow in the mix."

Nodding, Zaira said, "She knows we have access and contacts closed to BlackSea." And vice versa. "I better get going. The meet is in fifteen and I need to shower—Vasic's offered to do the transport."

"Have they promised not to shoot him this time?"

The darkness inside Zaira flickered with what might have been laughter. "According to Miane, as long as he doesn't return uninvited, he'll leave without holes in his body."

Aden suddenly frowned. "Did Vasic attempt to lock on to Persephone's face using the extra photographs Miane was able to locate?"

"Yes." Over and over. "But the images were all from months before her abduction. Children grow too fast." Vasic couldn't lock on to the one-year-old girl because she no longer existed.

"But if Olivia's memories are coming back," Aden said, "then she may have an image inside her head. See if you can get that out."

Zaira nodded. "I will." The only problem was that Olivia was changeling, with the attendant natural shields. "I have to go." Sliding her hand over Aden's cheek, she pressed her lips to his, the kiss soft. A promise to return and a gift she took with her as she walked once more into the darkness, the rage inside her black lava that became blood in her veins as she sat down in front of a broken woman whose mate was dead and whose baby was in the hands of monsters.

"They'll kill her," Olivia whispered, rocking back and forth in a room inside a city that moved with the sway of the waves. "They'll kill my poor, sweet girl. Mama's here, Mama's here, that's what I always told her after they took us to that place. Mama's here." Sobs rocked her frame, horror in her eyes as she looked up. "Where is she?" She grabbed at Zaira's hand. "Where's my baby?"

Chapter 69

BLAKE WASN'T AN idiot; he understood he was a threat. That was why he came three hours early to the rendezvous location and set up a hidden surveillance post. The individual who arrived at the spot at the exact time they'd agreed upon immediately eliminated his concerns.

Walking out onto the pathway hidden in a mostly forgotten part of Central Park, he said, "I didn't expect you to turn up yourself." Their being seen together could bring down his reluctant ally's entire house of cards.

"When something needs to be done, it's better to do it yourself." A glance at a sleek silver timepiece that, until then, had been hidden under the battered gray sleeve of the hooded sweatshirt that his "savior" wore with the hood pulled up, mirrored sunglasses obscuring a highly recognizable face. "You're ready?"

"Yes." Amin's team was breathing down his neck. Blake had known, walking into the park, that if he had to walk back out, he was dead. "I'm pretty sure the squad's surrounded the park within a one-block radius."

"No matter." Hands shoved into the sweatshirt's large front pocket in the way of young humans and changelings, his ally began to move. "I have a vehicle parked in a bay used by maintenance crews. It has the city markings and we can take it directly to the heliport."

Planning and intelligence, Blake thought. Perhaps a little too much planning. "I'll drive." He wasn't about to be driven to the slaughter.

"Suit yourself."

"You realize I could be an asset?"

"Of course I do. Why else would I be here?"

Because he'd threatened blackmail. Blake didn't speak the words aloud and, well aware he was with someone as dangerous as an Arrow, watched for guns, for injectors, for lethal backup. The one thing he didn't watch for was his own arrogance. He thought he was safe behind the wheel of the vehicle. He never felt the toxin that entered through the skin of his palms when he put them on the steering wheel.

Leaving him in the stolen city truck, the other party got out on sneakered feet. It took three minutes to walk to a well-trafficked part of the park and blend into a group of youths who eventually flowed out onto the streets. A pity to discard the Arrow but he'd proven himself an unstable threat; with him dead, there was no risk of premature exposure.

The next stage of the plan could be put safely into operation.

Chapter 70

WHEN AMIN CALLED in the discovery of Blake's body, Aden went to collect it himself. The cause of death was simple enough to determine, as was the fact that he'd been murdered.

"No surveillance feeds anywhere in the vicinity," Amin told him, and though his dark face was impassive, Aden could guess at his frustration. "I have him two blocks from this location, but no glimpse of any other viable suspect."

Leaving a team behind to go back over Blake's entire trail in case he'd left behind a fail-safe data cache, Aden took Blake home, and that night, he was laid to rest in the simple graveyard situated at the foot of the mountains on one end of the valley.

"When Blake did what he did," Aden said, "he surrendered his status as an Arrow. Many of you have asked me why I brought him back." He looked around at his gathered brethren, Zaira's hand tight around his. She, too, had asked, and when he'd told her why, she'd nodded in solemn acceptance.

"He is here because, for all his mistakes and the horrific acts he perpetrated, he was family," Aden told the others now. "Just because he went rogue and we had to hunt him with a view to execution doesn't mean he was excised from the family. He was no longer an Arrow, but he remained part of us." Those words, he spoke for all the Arrows around them, young and old. Every child from age thirteen onward was present.

It was important they understand that this family was forever.

Even Beatrice had chosen to attend. Zaira had spoken to the girl ahead of time and her other hand was currently linked with Beatrice's. *She's fine,* Zaira told him when he touched her mind with the question. *Your words mean more to her than what Blake did. She's been hurt before, but she's never been certain of belonging anywhere.*

That was exactly why Aden was doing this, not just for Beatrice, but for all his people. Squeezing Zaira's hand, he continued to speak. "We can abhor the actions Blake took without cutting him from the family tree," he said, wanting to make sure no one had any doubts about the point he was making on this dark night veiled with starlight, the mountains shadowy sentinels around them.

"We can consider him a murderous threat to society and a traitor to the oaths that bind us together as Arrows, without attempting to erase the fact that he was one of us. He wasn't a good man but he *was* an Arrow. He watched my back and yours for many years." Blake hadn't been all evil all the time. "We do not erase those who were our own. We do not forget. He existed. For better or worse, he was one of us."

Stepping back, he watched as the memorial was put in place, Blake's ashes buried in a biodegradable container that meant he would eventually become part of the earth. The small memorial set into the ground with his name on it would remain, however, and it would be kept clean and free of debris by a rotation of Arrows and older trainees.

For many years, there had been no memorials, Arrows passing and gone without leaving a sign. Aden had begun the memorials behind Ming's back. The day he'd finally ousted the other man, he'd ordered a larger memorial that listed the names of all the Arrows who had come and gone from the formation of the squad, starting with Zaid Adelaja.

Each had existed. Each had a claim to the family of Arrows.

Warm, strong fingers flexed against his palm, curled even tighter around it. He let Zaira's fire warm him as they committed Blake's soul to whatever lay beyond.

• • •

WITH Blake dead, and his incipient reign of terror ended, the squad and Aden had one less thing on their plates, but that didn't mean much.

"Olivia tried so hard," Zaira told him that night as they got ready to catch the five hours of sleep that was the minimum on which they could function at full capacity. "I could see her trying to squeeze her memories dry. She even offered to let me smash her shields even though it might cause permanent brain damage or death."

Zaira rubbed her face. "She was hysterical by the time we finally left." Eyes bleak, she put her head against Aden's shoulder. "Vasic 'ported to every location he could think of from Olivia's scattered memories, but she didn't see anything specific enough." Her arms slid around his rib cage, her hands closing over his shoulders from the back as she held on to him. "If we don't find Persephone, I think Olivia will find a way to commit suicide."

Aden wanted to promise her it wouldn't come to that, but they'd both seen too much evil to believe in fairy tales. "We're fighting for Persephone," he said instead. "And if her mother, drug addicted and abused, is strong enough to retain some memories, then the child will also be strong."

Zaira nodded. "I just hope we make it in time."

They fell asleep tangled in one another and woke to their duties.

First, the technical specifics of Blake's death remained under investigation—the neurotoxin had been quickly identified, but, while not common, it was readily enough available that no one supplier could be pinpointed.

"Given Blake's disruptive activities and mode of death," Aden said to Vasic that afternoon, "it's possible he was either inadvertently or consciously working for the people who've been trying to undermine the squad. The fact that it's highly likely he caused Jim Savua's death further ties it all together into a single conspiracy."

His back to a dark green fir that echoed the others around them, Vasic flexed the robotic arm that was Samuel Rain's latest attempt at a functional prosthetic. "This thing creaks."

"So it's a no?"

"I'll give it another three hours." Stretching out the fingers, he froze midflex. "Or maybe not." He teleported out and was back within a minute, sans arm. "The entire thing froze up."

"Samuel won't be happy."

"He threw the last one into a deep hole, then had me 'port in and retrieve it after he calmed down." Vasic pinned up his sleeve as the wind riffled through his hair. "As for Blake, the fact that he was taken out so cleanly, with minimal fuss, fits our enemy's MO." Vasic's eyes tracked Sienna Lauren's small movements as she sat on a tree stump in the distance, Arrow teenagers on similar makeshift seats around her.

The cardinal X, her distinctive dark red hair currently pulled into a ponytail, had requested they all leave, giving the teenagers freedom to ask the questions they wanted to without fear of oversight. Aden hadn't been able to agree to that for security reasons, and he knew the changelings hadn't either, but they'd all withdrawn out of view and out of hearing range.

Like Aden and Vasic, the leopards and wolves were scattered in the trees surrounding the compound deep in pack territory, a compound normally used for the training of empaths. "I would've bet money Hawke Snow would rebuff my request." The wolf alpha was viciously protective of his pack.

"If Ming hadn't claimed Sienna as his protégé, she'd have ended up in the squad," Vasic said. "And Hawke is mated to her—a man does many things for love."

Yes, Aden thought, he did. "Do you think she's sharing a manual? I'm not sure the squad is ready for such well-armed teenagers."

Vasic glanced at him, a faint curve to his mouth. "I'm glad to see you've found laughter."

Aden didn't smile, but his friend was right. No matter his and Zaira's duties, they continued to manage to find each other, managed to rest skin to skin. The intimacy of having his deadly commander fall asleep in his arms was blinding and perfect. "Being with her . . . it makes everything else bearable." Her fire lit up his life.

"Yes," was all Vasic said, his next words about someone else altogether. "Alejandro has adapted surprisingly well to the valley."

"The children love him because he'll play a simple game with them for hours with no sign of impatience."

"Did Zaira order him to do that?"

"No. Her only order was that he not cause harm to the children." Zaira didn't like controlling Alejandro, but she'd taken on the task because without it, the brain-damaged Arrow would be confused and dangerous. "He simply walked out of his cabin one day and joined in a game. Added to the fact that he made the independent decision to get me during the incident in Venice, there's cautious optimism among the medics that his brain may have started rewiring itself."

"The chances of a full recovery?"

"Nil." The drug had done too much damage to Alejandro's brain. "But if he stays on this trajectory, he could eventually have a life that requires very little supervision." The latter would take longer to achieve with Alejandro than it would with a civilian because of the male's deadly training. "For now, he appears content living in the cabin next to ours, and doing tasks within the compound. Nerida has him on the security detail to protect the children and it's an assignment that suits him."

In the clearing under the sunlight, an Arrow teen leaned forward, face more animated than Aden had ever seen it. It bolstered Aden's view that this had been the right decision, the time he'd carved from his schedule to arrange it more than worthwhile. Even though she was now twenty, Sienna Lauren could reach these teenagers in a way he and other adult Arrows couldn't. "Did you talk to Judd?" he asked, thinking of another member of the Lauren family.

Vasic nodded. "SnowDancer's had three more reports of dissension-causing events." He telepathed the details to Aden. "Hawke and Lucas are handling it, keeping the changeling groups calm."

"Bo is doing the same with the Alliance." Krychek, meanwhile, was speaking to the heads of powerful Psy family groups in order to alert them to the situation.

All of them were aware that the very people they were warning might be involved in the conspiracy.

There was no help for that, not at this stage. They had to work on the theory that most people weren't involved—not a theory without cause, given how well the people behind the conspiracy had managed to contain all data. That simply wasn't possible with a larger group. It had to be a small, intelligent cohort.

"It's piecemeal, though," Aden continued, thinking about his and their allies' efforts to foster calm. "Things will fall through the cracks." Creating conflict that caused bitter divisions. "We need a better system to communicate data between all three races, as well as mediate disputes."

"Silver Mercant's network?"

"A good start, but it's targeted at first responders rather than the leadership." And the agreed-upon operating protocols applied only to emergency situations. "We need a system in place that equals day-to-day communication so even an organized enemy can't pit us against one another with a little fancy maneuvering."

Vasic bent down to pick up a pinecone, rising with it in his hand. "Set it up."

It was exactly what Zaira had said when he'd mentioned the topic a while back, but Aden wasn't ready to change his focus from the squad to the world. But even as he thought that, part of him knew that if the squad was to become an integrated piece of the fabric of the world, it couldn't remain separate.

POLITICS reared its head two hours later, Nikita Duncan adamant that the members of the Ruling Coalition have a very public meeting. She'd discharged herself from the hospital against medical advice because it was her belief that people—and not just Psy alone—needed to see them alive and well and handling their responsibilities. It would put paid to the surge of rumors that called the Coalition's unity and strength into question and nip any others in the bud.

Rather than making a formal appearance, Nikita had suggested they do a walk-through of one of the New York neighborhoods that had suffered the worst casualties when the infection in the Net went viral. She was certain that she could maintain the facade of health for that long.

"You'll be asking us to kiss babies next."

Aden agreed with Krychek's cool comment. "Such a

walk-through will appear false when it comes to those of us who aren't politicians," he pointed out. "Better if we advise the residents we're coming in and will be available to answer questions in a central location."

Krychek's eyes met his, the two of them standing side by side in the valley because Krychek had come to help teleport in materials for more homes. "Are you actually planning to allow the populace to question you?"

"No. And neither should you." The Ruling Coalition didn't need to become a regular political body, not yet. The PsyNet was too fragile at present; people needed to believe that its leadership was unassailable. "Our simple presence will be enough." A sign of the power that backed the Coalition. "Ivy, Nikita, and Anthony are seen as more approachable—Ivy, in particular—and can be the ones who speak, unless they have objections."

"Yes, fine, but your option leaves us wide open to threats," Nikita said via the mobile comm in Aden's hand, her face thinner than it should be and dark shadows under her eyes.

"Hiding allows the enemy to win." Anthony Kyriakus's tone was resolute, and though he was disagreeing with Nikita, he was also currently standing right by her chair, in what appeared to be a study in her private apartments. "We must show our enemies—and our people—that we aren't afraid and can't be intimidated."

"I agree with Anthony," Ivy said from one side of the split screen. "My Es tell me people are edgy, scared. I can feel it, too." She rubbed a fist over her heart. "Seeing us all out in force, unafraid, will go a long way toward easing the fears fostered by the spate of rumors and speculation."

Kaleb glanced at Aden, the sunlight making the white sparks in his cardinal eyes appear golden. "Can you set up security measures? This could be our chance to catch the people targeting members of the Coalition."

"I'll take care of it." Aden had already discussed such a move with the cardinal Tk and knew Krychek was right; this would be the perfect opportunity to put it in play. "If you second a small squad of your people to me, I can make sure our security strategy is fully integrated."

PSYNET BEACON

Rumors continue to swirl in the Net about the efficacy of the Ruling Coalition. Nikita Duncan is no longer in the hospital, but she has not been seen in public since the shooting.

Aden Kai, too, has disappeared from public view, perhaps as a result of questions about his capabilities—or lack of them—to lead the squad. However, it is possible that he is simply involved in covert work, as per the Arrow mandate. Regardless of his location, he must understand that the squad is under fire and he has to respond.

The *Beacon* has contacted the squad and is currently awaiting their answer.

PSYNET BEACON: LIVE NETSTREAM

Quite frankly, I'd lose respect for the squad if they did make a public statement. Even so, it's worrying to realize that the people we rely on to protect us might be just as weak as any other man or woman in the street.

Anonymous
(Tauranga)

Are we sure Nikita Duncan is even still alive?

H. Dwyer
(Dublin)

Kaleb Krychek should simply take over and execute anyone who doesn't want to follow the rules.

C. Tsang
(N'Djamena)

It feels as if we're going backward instead of forward. With the fall of Silence came hope for a better world, but now chaos lives on the doorstep.

V. T. Jose
(Ushuaia)

Chapter 71

LESS THAN TWO hours after the meeting with the other members of the Ruling Coalition, and well before the planned announcement of the Coalition's availability to the public, Aden and Zaira went into the proposed neighborhood. It was just past five in New York, the sunlight warm. Sixty minutes after their arrival and initial reconnaissance, they mapped out the security strategy from their concealed position on a rooftop.

"Any security will have to be subtle," he said to Zaira. "The whole point of this exercise is to calm the populace, not put them on edge."

"We should check out the parameters of the park the Coalition intends to use, see if there are any areas we need to sweep for hidden devices beforehand." A pause. "It would be much safer if the meeting was indoors."

"And much less effective."

"Don't get dead."

"I wouldn't dare."

Feeling her mind curl around him, Aden made his way down to the small neighborhood park with her. The two of them were dressed in civilian clothing—jeans and a white shirt for him, over which he'd thrown on the leather jacket Zaira had lent back to him. She wore a soft pink V-neck sweater borrowed from Ivy over her own black pants. It made them appear the couple they were, and meant they blended in with the people around them, though Aden could tell he was being recognized.

Three or four people nodded at him, but didn't interrupt. An elderly man, however, came over. "You're the Arrow," he said, leaning heavily on a cane. "I heard you were captured, dead, or in hiding."

"As you can see," Aden replied, "I'm alive and well." He also planned on a small demonstration of his power later that night in order to quash the claims of him being too weak to lead the squad.

The time for secrets was over.

Now his men and women needed him to be a bogeyman bigger than any other.

"Stupid rumors." A huffed-out breath from the elderly man. "Can't afford to have you die—the whole thing would collapse."

Leaving the man sitting on a wooden bench, he and Zaira did a sweep of the park while appearing to do nothing but stroll, his left hand loosely linked with her right. It was why she'd accompanied him rather than any of the other members of the squad—the tabloids were already starting to hint at a relationship between them, so her presence wouldn't be remarked upon except in that context.

They kept their senses on alert the entire forty minutes it took them to map out the park. It was highly likely the enemy had some kind of base in New York. It explained how they'd been able to organize the previous attempt on Aden's life so soon after his arrival in Manhattan. If they were so bold as to make a second attempt, Aden and Zaira would be ready.

At present, though, the only people nearby were families taking advantage of the gentle early evening sunlight, and other people out for a stroll. When a small girl accidentally kicked her ball over to Aden, he kicked it back to her. She waved at him in thanks and kicked it on to her father.

A ray of sunlight hit her tight bronze curls just as Aden felt his senses prickle. *Zaira.*

I feel it.

They turned as one to look behind them, but there was no

assassin, nothing but ordinary people involved in their own affairs. Aden scanned visually and telepathically, picked up a faint hint of deadly intent, but it wasn't close. Then his eye caught a glint high up on a building. Even as he processed that information, his visual cortex was cataloguing other glints.

And he realized the enemy had mobilized the heavy artillery this time.

A target with big impact and with a low threat ratio away from other, stronger members of the squad: that was likely to have been the calculation when Aden was chosen to die.

Killing him would destroy the Arrows and strike a blow to the Ruling Coalition at the same time. As a bonus, it would rip away the shield of fear and mystique that protected the most vulnerable members of the squad. After all, shooting Aden in full view of so many witnesses would prove his lack of strength. Not only that, but if some of the witnesses were also murdered, it would indict the squad as being ineffective protectors against the monsters.

Aden had made it his mission in life to appear weak. It was what had allowed him to rise to a position of leadership within the squad right under Ming LeBon's nose. But at that instant, as he prepared for countless sniper rifles to fire, all directed at him and Zaira and the innocent people around them, he knew the time had come for him to show his true colors. No small demonstration as he'd planned to orchestrate later tonight.

This was going to be a big one.

"Get down!" he called out in a voice that was calm but brooked no disobedience . . . then he reached for power as he'd never before reached. Always prior to this, he'd asked only a little, been given it with no questions asked from the five men and women who knew what and who he was.

Today, he squeezed Zaira's hand and he took everything. She went to her knees beside him as he channeled her ability through himself, but no matter that he'd stripped her of her psychic weapons, she made no effort to close that channel, to block him. Neither did Vasic, Axl, Amin, or Cris. Their power blasted through his psychic veins in a single split second. In the next, it became far greater than the sum of its parts.

Because Aden wasn't a simple telepath. He was a mirror.

Hidden deep in his mind, behind the shields Walker Lauren had taught him to build, was a lens that reflected and multiplied the power he could channel from others. At that instant, he was stronger than a cardinal, the strength of five powerful Arrows merged by his mind into a roar of pure energy.

His telepathy expanded exponentially, until he could scan the entire city, but he didn't seek to target the minds of the shooters. They were too distant and he couldn't guarantee he'd locate each and every one. There were too many innocent lives at stake to chance a mistake. Shoving out his right hand, his left still locked with Zaira's, he thrust out his power just as the bullets began to hit.

ZAIRA sucked in a breath as she saw a bullet heading directly toward them, readying her weakened body to push Aden out of the way. But the bullet seemed to slam into something before she could move and it just fell to the ground like a bird stunned by flying into an unexpected obstacle. Blinking, she stared as it happened again and again . . . and finally she caught a glimpse of the barrier. It was like an oil shimmer on a wet road, visible only in patches of light and color.

A soap bubble as strong as titanium. Stronger.

Looking up at the man who was holding that shield unlike any she'd ever seen, she sucked in another breath. Aden's hair was blowing back in a breeze that existed only around him, his eyes an impossible reflective silver and his right hand held palm out as he stopped those bullets dead. She was weak because he was pulling power from her, but in the shadow of his power, she felt no sense of weakness, of being in a situation she couldn't escape.

A second later, she watched in astonishment as he flicked his hand and the bullets stopped hitting the ground. Instead, the soap bubble became a mirror that echoed his eyes and the bullets pinged back along the direct flight paths on which they'd arrived.

Around her, the people who'd hit the ground at Aden's order gasped and stared as bullet after bullet reversed trajectory, heading straight back toward the shooters at a speed that only the fittest and fastest would survive. Many wouldn't—eyes to the scopes where they were set up at apartment windows, they wouldn't be able to imagine a bullet reversing course. And so they would die.

The bullets stopped coming moments later. Some of the snipers had to be dead. Others had likely missed death by a heartbeat and would be racing to get away. Her telepathic strength was faint with Aden having locked her into his personal network, but it was enough to reach the high-rises and the cardinal mind she needed.

The rats are running, she said to Kaleb Krychek, having snapped out a warning to him the instant before Aden initiated the highest level of the psychic protocol the six of them had agreed to when Aden was only twenty-one and Zaira twenty. She'd known Vasic wouldn't be able to respond as fast as usual, not with the teleporter forming one point of the five-pointed star that was the engine for Aden's extraordinary ability, but Krychek was as swift a teleporter.

All she'd said was, *New York!* It had been enough.

I have two dead, two contained, Krychek responded. *One more in progress.*

Leaving him to the hunt, she got to her feet and placed her free hand on Aden's jaw. *The situation is under control,* she said mind to mind. *You can drop the shield.*

It took him a minute, the tension leaving his body muscle by muscle until the breeze stopped, the mirror sliding down to fade into the ground. His eyes, however, remained that eerie reflective shade she'd never before seen. "Casualties?"

"None here." She gasped as her own power returned to her in a storm surge. Her hand clenched on his, her breath hitched. When it was over, she found she had *more* power than she'd possessed before Aden initiated the transfer. It filled her to the brim, until it felt as if her fingertips were overflowing with it.

The mirror, she thought, looking into silver eyes that still surged with echoes of power. The mirror had made her power *more,* made it brutal. She'd known the mirror's effect since the day Aden first told her about it, but never had she experienced it to this degree. Power that strained at her skin, her eyes flowing obsidian from the force of it. Aden could literally protect the entire valley, even if he had access to only midlevel Psy. Give him a full squad of lethally powerful Arrows . . . The idea of it was breathtaking.

Not only because of what he, himself, could do, but what he could create in the Arrows themselves. He gave back more than he took, and in so doing, he could create a turbocharged army. He'd be an unstoppable force if not for one simple and inevitable side effect, and even that wasn't enough to negate the fury of his gift.

"Krychek just told me that he's found two dead shooters so far," she said, stifling her fascination with the true depth of his ability for now. "He also has two others contained."

There was no more time to speak after that. People swarmed Aden, wanting to say thank you, to state their astonishment over his display of power, and to tell him that they'd never had any doubts about the Arrows.

PSYNET BEACON: BREAKING NEWS

Many in the Net have recently questioned the abilities and qualifications of the enigmatic man who leads the Arrow Squad. Rumors reported in the *Beacon* itself stated that Aden Kai was nothing but a figurehead, a field medic who played the leader so as to protect the squad's true leadership.

Today's display has put those rumors and speculations to rest in an incontrovertible fashion: Aden Kai isn't only powerful, he is a *power*. There is no longer any doubt as to why he is the leader of the squad, and why he has a seat on the Ruling Coalition.

PSYNET BEACON: LIVE NETSTREAM

I've watched the footage captured by nearby security cameras and civilian phones multiple times, and I still can't believe what I'm watching. Aden Kai's abilities are unparalleled. Does anyone have a label for his designation?

B. Baker
(New Orleans)

Spectacular!

V. Ting
(Cape Town)

Aden Kai today proved that not only is the squad made up of the elite, it is made up of men and women with designations unknown to the general population, as it should be for a covert squad.

I feel safe in the Net and in our future.

L. Layton
(Cambridge)

I am breaking squad protocol in stating this, but it needs stating: Aden is not our leader because of his abilities.

He is our leader because he understands each and every member of his squad and pushes us to our very best.

He is our leader because he goes first against every threat, no matter the risk.

He is our leader because we know that should we fall in battle, he will not leave us behind. He understands the code of soldiers as the Council never did.

He is our leader because he has never forgotten that he is an Arrow. He may sit on the Ruling Coalition, but he is no politician and he is no Councilor. He is an Arrow and he will always be an Arrow.

A member of the Arrow Squad
(Location Error: Unable to Be Determined)

Chapter 72

KRYCHEK HAD TELEPORTED the captured snipers into a solid concrete bunker for which he'd sent Vasic the teleport visual. Aden's best friend telepathed him from the valley, a location so distant that Vasic normally wouldn't have the range. *Those experiments we did didn't prepare me for this.*

I only really needed you and Zaira, Aden said, having realized that after the fact. *The mirror has matured, needs less fuel.*

I don't think the others will complain. Vasic appeared beside him in a quiet corner of the park, Aden and Zaira having finally extricated themselves from the astonished and grateful civilians. "Cris's and Axl's telepathic ranges have also expanded significantly, while Amin just teleported home."

That was a surprise. Amin's Tk was a bare 3 on the Gradient—his primary ability was a variant form of telepathy. "Make sure they all monitor their energy levels. I don't think the rebound effect will be simple tiredness this time." Always before, anyone he'd drawn from had experienced tiredness after the boost faded, but he'd never drawn this much power or fed such a tremendous amount back.

"No," Vasic agreed. "We're all going to crash, but judging from past experiments, we should have three or four hours at least."

That risk was why Aden was so careful about when and

how he used the mirror. He always had to consider the future effect—the squad couldn't afford to have six of its senior Arrows out of commission or dangerously tired at the same time. "See if you can do some quiet shuffling of duties so that when the crash hits, people are less likely to notice."

"Amin's due for a break anyway," Vasic said, already making notes on an organizer. "I'll roster him and Cris off, since she's been going nonstop for the past month. Everyone expects you and Zaira to rest together now, so that only leaves Axl and me, and Axl has a habit of disappearing into the Net. No one will comment if he does it again, and I can just say I'm going to be with Samuel Rain for the duration and out of touch while he tries an experimental prosthetic."

"Good." Turning to Zaira, her hand still locked in his and her eyes ink black, Aden ignored any watchers and drew her into a kiss, needing her on a level he'd never needed anyone else. "You're okay?"

"Deliciously power drunk but my mind is clear." She rubbed her cheek against his, his private and deadly commander who'd just allowed him to make a public claim that allowed no room for interpretation. "We'll talk more later. Go do what you need to do. I'll take care of things here."

Leaving her to head the team sweeping through the highrises used by the snipers in search of dead or injured shooters Kaleb may have missed in his initial search, Aden went with Vasic. Once at the bunker, he found two of the snipers were uninjured except for a scratch on one, while a third had a tourniquet around his upper arm that had been inexpertly tied.

A body lay in the corner.

When Aden looked at Krychek, the cardinal Tk said, "He suicided rather than cooperate. His brethren are far more pragmatic."

One of the snipers snorted, his white skin bearing a raw red scrape on one cheek, possibly from when he'd jerked out of the way to avoid a bullet. "It was a contract job. No way I'm going down for it. Ask me what you want to know."

The two other snipers weren't as chatty, but seemed cooperative enough.

"When were you told to move?" Aden asked.

All three stated they'd been contracted two days earlier and instructed to wait in Manhattan for further directions. The men had initially been told the hit would likely take place near the Shine building, and as a result, all three had spent the time scoping out the best lines of sight toward Shine.

"Then the order comes that we have to hit you in the park," stated the sniper who had a spiderweb tattoo on his left hand, the blue-black ink dark against his light brown skin. "I had to haul ass, get myself in position. Ended up having to incapacitate a tenant, when I prefer to find sites without witnesses."

His own telepathic reach enormous right now, Aden let Zaira know to search for bound or injured inhabitants of the buildings the snipers had used. "Were you told to work together?"

"No," said the man with the tourniquet around his upper arm, his features echoing Aden's own ethnic makeup. "At least I wasn't—but today, when I got the order to move, it said others would also be gunning for you and I was to ignore it and follow the mission parameters."

The other two snipers confirmed his story.

Despite the fact that the shooters had initially been directed at Shine, Aden was certain Devraj Santos had no involvement in the assassination attempts. The more likely scenario was that someone had been watching Aden, keeping track of his movements. While he'd been careful, he'd never hidden his visits to talk to Santos and it was the one location where the enemy could be certain to locate him.

It meant the enemy might not in fact have a base in New York.

"Who hired you?" Krychek asked as Aden processed both the patient nature of the setup, and the implications in terms of the money involved. Keeping so many snipers on the payroll and idle for two days wouldn't have been cheap.

Whoever this was—individual or group—they had significant cash flow.

"All anonymous, via wire transfers," said the most talkative assassin. "Same as usual. Only difference is I had to wait for their signal and be in Manhattan." Another shrug. "Got paid to wait so why the fuck not?"

"Was I the only target or were there others?" Aden asked.

Counting the dead and the badly injured one Zaira had just located, the count was at seven snipers overall so far. Too many even for an Arrow.

"I was paid for you," said the tattooed sniper, "but they paid extra if I'd agree to do as much collateral damage as possible."

The other two said the same, admitted they'd been told to aim specifically for families and children. It confirmed Aden's suspicions on the motive behind the public attacks: to create panic and fear when the world had just barely begun to recover from the horrors of the infection, as well as the civil war in the Net.

"You are threats." The chill in Kaleb's eyes communicated itself to the snipers, who all went deathly still. "You also have no viable data. We have no reason to keep you alive."

The three men were silent for a moment, no doubt calculating odds and percentages, as snipers were trained to do.

One or more of these men could be part of the larger organization, Aden said to both Vasic and Kaleb. *The only way to know for certain will be to tear through their minds.*

Two are Psy, Krychek responded. *I've tested their shields and they're solid—I can break them, of course, but there's a high chance I'll kill them in the process. The one so eager to speak is a changeling, with their impressive natural shielding.*

Which meant that breaking his shields would most probably cause brain damage or death. Aden had no compunction meting out harsh treatment to men who made their living killing others, especially ones who'd admitted they would've murdered children, but smashing shields often produced only limited data. Better to see if they could break them down first.

"You can have the numbers of my bank accounts," one of the snipers said into the silence. "Trace the money back to where it came from."

Which would very likely be an anonymous account, Aden thought. However, it provided another avenue of investigation. He took the information the men rattled off, passed it on to Tamar.

Further questioning revealed nothing, and, as expected,

the Psy snipers balked at being asked to voluntarily lower their shields.

At which point, Kaleb teleported out, as did Aden and Vasic, leaving the three men in a featureless underground bunker none could escape. The two Psy weren't telekinetics—while Kaleb and Aden questioned the snipers, Vasic had traced their identities using DNA scans, found one was a low-level telepath, the other a midlevel psychometric.

So far below the earth, their basic telepathy wouldn't work, but Aden had deliberately left their minds unfettered on the PsyNet in an apparent oversight, though in truth, he'd already assigned two Arrows to monitor any PsyNet activity. It was also why he and Kaleb hadn't revisited the idea of smashing their shields. He wanted to see who the men would attempt to reach and whether they had direct access to those behind the conspiracy.

His gut told him the chance of that was low; these men would now be discarded as Hashri Smith had been. Pawns, all of them. "Whoever is running this conspiracy is cold-blooded but it appears they have nothing against using fanatics," he said to Krychek as he, the cardinal, and Vasic stood on the cliff overlooking the valley.

The sniper who had suicided had traced back to Pure Psy. Not such a huge surprise. Because while the squad and Krychek's forces had picked up or eliminated all the major players, there were a scattering of minor ones floating around.

Kaleb looked down at the valley. "The dregs of Pure Psy are just fodder They're rootless, looking for someone to tell them what to do. Easy pickings."

Vasic stepped right to the cliff edge. "I think it's now undeniable that we're not looking for an individual but a group. There's too much coordination, too many worldwide events, and their data spans all three races."

Which meant that to cut this off at the root, they'd first have to find all the branches.

KALEB had known for some time that Aden was no medic. Or not *just* a medic—because the Arrow was fully trained and capable as a field medic. But what he'd seen today was incomprehensible. "According to the data I hacked, all his tests come back to a 4.3 telepath and 3.2 M," he said to Sahara when he returned to Moscow.

"I can't work out how he created that reflective shield." Kaleb could deflect bullets and missiles, but not return them to their locations with the precision Aden had displayed unless he was focusing specifically on a particular shot.

"It really looked like a mirror in the recordings." Sahara smoothed his iron gray tie, Kaleb having been in a meeting with Jen Liu when Zaira Neve contacted him. He'd teleported out without explanation, conscious Zaira would never telepath him unless it was a major emergency. Factoring in the possibility the Arrows might be under attack and he could end up being unable to avoid a bullet if he teleported in too close, he hadn't locked in on their faces but made the call to come in near the park around which he knew the two were running a security check.

As it was, he hadn't needed to speak to them to figure out what was going on. "How did he do it?" he said. Moving back from Sahara, he tossed her several small items from his desk, including a piece of lapis lazuli she must've been playing with absently as she worked on a report requested by the Es. "Throw them at me at the same time."

She rolled her eyes but did as asked. Kaleb had no problem freezing the objects in the air, but he couldn't reverse their trajectories all at once on their original flight paths—the objects all arrowed toward a central point. "He must be a telekinetic of some kind." Except Tks could never keep their abilities under wraps—telekinesis had a way of making itself felt, especially telekinesis that vicious.

Plucking the items from the air, her bracelet making a gentle sound as the charms swung against one another, Sahara put them back on the desk. "Does it matter if you know the details?"

When he just looked at her, she laughed. "Right, of course it matters. You like to know everything."

"I like to know the variables in play—and all possible threats." He'd never disregarded Aden as others had; instead of basing his calculations about Aden's level of power only on the Arrow's official strength, Kaleb had considered the deep loyalty Aden seemed to engender in his men and women. The events today made it clear even that might have been an underestimation. "Aden could be a significant problem."

"He's focused on his own people," Sahara reminded him, tugging him into the kitchen. "I have a feeling even if you handed him control of the PsyNet on a silver platter, he wouldn't take it."

"The irony is that if I had to hand off power for whatever reason, he's the only one of the Ruling Coalition I'd trust to take the Net in the right direction." Like the empaths, Aden had a core of honor that Kaleb had never developed.

Making a nutrient drink, Sahara passed it to him. "I would've thought you'd say Ivy."

"Ivy Jane is an empath," he said after drinking down half a glass. "She skews too much toward emotion." Whereas Aden understood that the Net couldn't totally discard the emotional discipline that had held it together for more than a hundred years.

Sahara nodded slowly. "Anthony?"

"He's connected to Nikita." While Kaleb could work with Nikita, he'd never trust her. "I can't predict how that connection will alter his viewpoints."

"I don't know." Sahara leaned with her elbows on the counter. "I have a feeling if change is to happen, it'll occur in the other direction—Anthony Kyriakus does not budge from where he stands."

"Neither," Kaleb pointed out, "does Nikita Duncan."

"Immovable force meets irresistible object?" Her eyes sparkled. "I wish I could be a fly on that wall."

"Perhaps I'll 'port us there in the depths of the night." Finishing off the drink as Sahara laughed, he put down the glass and decided that he didn't need to eliminate Aden from the equation. Sahara was right—the Arrow didn't want to rule the world. He wanted only to make it safer for those under his command.

That was a goal Kaleb could understand and appreciate.

Walking around the counter, he drew Sahara into his arms and took her laughing mouth with his own in a kiss that held his devotion. The drive to protect that which mattered was the core of everything—without it, he would be a nightmare and the Arrows pure darkness.

Chapter 73

THE CONSCIOUSLY DRAMATIC and bloody massacre had been meant to be a public declaration of the squad's weakness, one that would spread fear throughout the world, for if the bogeymen of the Net weren't safe, who was? But it had ended up a confirmation of Aden's—thus the squad's—power.

The catastrophic failure eliminated the group's success with the Nikita Duncan strike. The world had already forgotten that in the face of Aden Kai's impossible display. The only way to salvage anything from the situation was to kill him once and for all. No theatrics, no public spectacle, just a simple hit that proved the squad's mortality.

If he'd been a valuable target before, he was even more so now: take down a man of such immense power and the shock wave would shatter the foundations of the world. And in the meantime, they'd go after his people. Not as much impact to kill an unknown Arrow, but kill two or three, and suddenly, the world would take notice.

Chapter 74

THE CRASH HAPPENED exactly five hours after Aden had used the mirror. Because of Vasic's groundwork, it went like clockwork. For Aden and Zaira the crash coincided with the time of their normal sleep shift, so they just locked the cabin door and, stripping off, fell into bed, their minds and abilities shutting down.

Nerida and Yuri, who Aden trusted deeply and who he'd intended to tell about the mirror in any case, knew what was up and to cover for the six who were down. As it was, all was calm until seven hours later, by which time he and Zaira had come naturally awake.

"Six-and-a-half-hour recovery period," Zaira said on waking, her eyes still drowsy. "Makes you a lethal threat, Aden Kai."

Stretching out his arm, he placed his palm on her abdomen as she stretched. "Your telepathy?"

A disappointed look. "Back to normal. So if you ever turbocharged an army, you'd have supersoldiers for five hours. Hmm . . . that's still not bad. Especially if you only turboed half, leaving the other half to cover for the six and a half hours until you woke back up and could restart the cycle."

Aden raised an eyebrow as he stroked his hand up to her rib cage. "Who are we invading?"

"I like to plan ahead." Zaira was raising her hand to his

cheek when her phone went off. Answering it, she jerked up into a sitting position. "Persephone is alive," she said after a short, intense conversation. "Miane says another e-mail just downloaded into Olivia's account."

A psychic knock came on Aden's mind right then, the squad's tech surveillance team having seen the same message.

Having sat up, he curled his arm around Zaira as she brought up that message. It was another image of the forlorn and scared little girl; once again she held a printout of the latest *Beacon* update to verify time and date—and once again, her face was obscured enough to make it impossible to 'port directly to her.

The message below was cold: *Do not attempt to track the child. Do it and we will cut her into small pieces which we will send to you by mail. Any rescue attempt or perceived attempt by BlackSea will equal her death.*

Jawbones grinding against one another, he put Zaira's phone on the small table she'd brought from her Venice room and that now sat to one side of their bed. "They don't know we're working with BlackSea."

"Exactly." Rage vibrated in her own voice, but it was frigid. "Miane's people can't risk being caught—they'll continue to work behind the scenes in the search to find Persephone and the other missing members of their pack, but they need our help for live actions." She turned to face him. "I don't have any other pressing mission briefs. I want to focus on this."

Aden didn't even have to think about it. "Do it," he said, not only because no child should have to suffer such hell, but because Zaira needed to save this one child as she hadn't been able to save herself. "Use whatever resources you need."

Hands fisted, Zaira gave a small, frustrated scream. "The thing is—I don't know where to go," she said, her voice taut. "None of my search bots on the PsyNet or Internet have turned up anything."

None of Aden's sources had unearthed anything, either. "I'll speak to Krychek, see if the NetMind or—" He froze, his mind shining a thin beam of light on a near-forgotten piece of data. "Hashri Smith's business associates," he said. "The woman."

Zaira sat up on her knees, her hair wild around her shoulders. "She was asked to wire a bribe to an official in Denver six months ago in order to expedite certain building permits—but the owners of those buildings are all ordinary people." She shoved back her hair. "Deep background, telepathic scans, none of it points to any kind of involvement in the conspiracy."

Having already pulled up the report on an organizer, Aden scrolled down. "Secondary report confirms the first. We're keeping an eye on them, but so far, it looks like someone did them a favor for no discernible reason. The e-mails we were able to retrieve show them expressing surprised delight at the swiftness of the permits."

Zaira blew out a breath and, getting out of bed, began to pace. Since she was dressed in only a pair of black panties, the sight was distracting despite the serious nature of their discussion, but Aden didn't tell her to put on clothes. He was an Arrow, not an idiot.

"Why offer a bribe to expedite permits that provide you with no advantage?" Zaira frowned, turned on her heel, and continued to pace. "It's not like the contracts with Smith and the others. These people have no idea they were done a favor and no reason to believe anyone who claims to have facilitated it."

Aden tapped the organizer on his knee, the whole situation niggling at him. "That's exactly it. The people running this op aren't stupid—their every action has been well thought out, planned. I can't believe they'd waste several thousand dollars on creating a pointless dead end."

Jumping on the bed, Zaira grabbed the organizer, then made a frustrated sound. "I don't know how to find the data I need!"

Aden gave in to temptation and, wrapping his arms around her, dropped a kiss to the tip of one bare breast. "I'll wake Tamar. Put on some clothes."

Fingers weaving through his hair, Zaira pressed her lips to his temple. "After we find Persephone," she whispered, "we'll take a whole night just for us."

"Deal."

Tamar was rubbing her eyes when she walked into the restricted underground part of the main training complex, the natural tight curls of her hair looking as if she'd stuck a finger into an electrical socket, and her clothing yellow pajamas with white stars on them that had Axl taking a long look as he came in at the same time.

Then his eyes dipped to the pink sheepskin boots into which Tamar had shoved her feet.

"Civilian," Tamar said before he could make a comment. "Civilian who has had only four hours of sleep because she's obsessed with ripping apart all these shell companies upon shell companies."

Axl ran his eyes up and down again. "How exactly did you pass for Silent? Was the examiner blind and psychically deaf?"

Tamar made a face at him. "Go on and take your vitamins, Battle-Ax. No creaky old men needed here." Stomping into tech central on the insult, the entire room lined with banks of computers, she sat down in front of the central core and proved that her brain was functioning at full capacity. "What do you need?"

Zaira braced her hand on Tamar's desk while Aden took a minute to touch base with Axl, no doubt checking on his physical and psychic status. "Can you dig up all building permits that bear the signature of the official who received the bribe?" she asked Tamar.

"Sure." The younger woman began to work. "It'll be hundreds if not thousands. Time frame will narrow it."

"Month on either side of the bribe," Zaira said after a moment's thought. "We can go wider if this doesn't pan out."

"Or if it does." Aden's quiet words had her looking up. "If he can be bribed once . . ."

Zaira nodded, watched Tamar work. *Creaky old man?* she telepathed when Tamar paused to allow the computer to run the search algorithm she'd just input.

Heat bloomed under the silken ebony of the other woman's skin. *He always makes me feel like a child with dirt on my face.* Her fingers raced over the old-fashioned physical keyboard she preferred over a projected one. "Got it. Main screen."

Setting aside her curiosity about the way Axl, who so rarely spoke to anyone, had spoken to the young civilian analyst, Zaira went toward the main screen, now filled with a comprehensive list of roughly two hundred permits. "Strike out the properties we've already checked, and those linked to anyone in the Ruling Coalition." Not that she trusted them all, but there was no reason for anyone in power to destabilize the Net.

That still left around a hundred and fifty permits.

"How about the ones related to places like restaurants or other public locations?" Tamar suggested.

"Yes, do it." She could go back to those later, double-check.

This cut took them under the seventy-five mark.

"The majority look to be small residential dwellings," Aden said, scanning the list. "We can't disregard them, not with how easy it would be to turn a basement into a dungeon, but let's put those ones in a separate group, see what's left over."

Fifteen permits.

Seven had to do with a single comm station. It turned out to belong in part to SnowDancer, the rest owned by another changeling pack. "I think it's fairly safe to disregard that," Zaira said.

"Agreed." Aden's body brushed hers, the living warmth of him welcome. "There's zero chance Hawke Snow doesn't have trusted people working at that station—nothing this big could go on under their noses."

The other eight took more time to break down.

Two were warehouses that appeared likely at first glance, but further digging showed that both had burned down a year ago, the permits for a slightly different rebuild currently in progress. Their locations meant no underground facility was possible.

The third was related to a lab that processed medical specimens and wanted to extend its fumigation and air-conditioning systems. The fourth and fifth involved adding sanitary facilities to the lowest level of a midrise building in a city fringe location. The sixth had to do with the renovation of a store in the main shopping district. The seventh linked to major repair work in a high-rise that had structural issues, while the eighth was a brand-new apartment building to be constructed on a large lot.

"The lab and the midrise," Zaira said and Tamar threw up

records on both properties. "Because why risk applying for a permit anyway? It has to do with something they couldn't hide or that might attract unwanted attention from the authorities. Plumbing, electrical work, digging for new vents or pipes."

Aden's features were grim as he went through all the data they had. "The others are also in difficult locations—too many security cameras, too much foot traffic."

Pulling back her hair, Zaira secured it with a hair tie she'd had around her wrist. "I'm taking a team and checking out the top possibilities now—I'm going to call in two teleport-capable Tks to transport us." Speed was of the essence. Persephone's captors might not kill her, but tonight, Miane had shared something else with Zaira, a secret so big it was tightly, *tightly* guarded.

When young, she told Aden, having informed Miane he'd have to know, *water-based changelings have been known to die after extended periods of not being permitted to shift, and Olivia has no memory of water during her captivity.*

Though the Halcyon damage means her memory is suspect, she does remember vividly that it hurt to shift once she was in Venice—and Miane says that only happens after a prolonged period of forced abstinence from shifting.

Every muscle in Aden's body went rigid. *The child has likely not been given the chance to shift since her abduction eight months earlier.*

Zaira swallowed the rage in her throat. *Miane says children who've died previously—after being caught inland in drought zones in past centuries, their parents unable to get them to other suitable water sources in time—lasted seven months at most. Persephone's living on borrowed time. Her heart will simply give out soon.*

"Go," Aden said, after hauling her close for a hard kiss. "I'll work with Tamar, coordinate other teams to check out the secondary possibilities."

"Make sure they don't betray their presence," Zaira said, though she knew her squadmates were all trained to be shadows. "And ask Krychek to assist." She didn't trust the cardinal, but she'd noticed one thing during the times he was in the valley—Kaleb wasn't cruel to children.

The fact that he'd grown up under the aegis of a serial

killer—a truth Zaira only knew because Aden had obtained certain highly restricted files—could've pointed in either direction as to his own inclinations if not for his relationship with Sahara. Ivy and the other Es loved Krychek's mate; thus, Zaira surmised that the woman wasn't tainted by evil. Which meant Krychek, deadly though he was, wasn't a murderous psychopath.

Aden touched his hand to one side of her face. "I'll call in every resource."

Chest tight, Zaira hugged him fiercely before walking out on her way to the midrise that struck her as the most likely location. It was isolated, it had a large basement area, and the ownership records were murky at best. Arriving with her team while the area was yet cloaked in the heavy gray of predawn, she spent precious time on reconnaissance. The sheer number of hidden security cameras told her they were on to something.

"Blind the cameras," she told Mica.

"I can give you five minutes," he said, already hooked into the system to feed it a loop. "Three, two, one, go."

Zaira and her team infiltrated the building on silent feet, ghosts in the gray. One half went up, the other down. Zaira was in the latter group, and when she ghosted down the steps into the basement, a single glance was enough to tell her they were too late.

The building had been in use until recently. Food wrappers lay in the small trash bins in two corners, while the layer of dust on everything was fine. When she pushed open the only door down there, it was to discover a room with the utilitarian and commonplace gray walls she'd seen in the first image of Persephone.

Below the bed with its dirty brown blanket lay a red-haired rag doll.

"NONE of the other locations show any signs of involvement in the conspiracy," Aden told Zaira when she returned to the valley after confirming the lab was exactly what it seemed. "They must've cleared the midrise when we brought in Smith and the others."

The timeline fit with the debris they'd found, the amount of dust on the floor and the shelves. "Damn it!" Infuriated, she went to throw something . . . and realized she was holding the little girl's doll.

Hand trembling, she placed it gently on the table beside her and Aden's bed. And though the rage threatened to push her to angry blindness, she took a minute to breathe, just breathe, as Ivy was teaching her, and when she opened her eyes, it was to see Aden's beautiful face in her sight. "What do we do now?"

"We keep going back and forward through the permits," he said. "It's our one solid lead and we will mine it down to the bone if that's what it takes."

Zaira shuddered, nodded.

"First, though, you have to eat." Tugging her outside, Aden drew her to one of several outdoor tables set with nutrient drinks as well as other foodstuffs.

A number of children were already at those tables, smiled when Zaira slipped into a seat. "Here, Zaira," Tavish said from across the table. "This bread is nice."

Heart aching with too much emotion, she took the offering. "Thank you." *Aden, I don't know if I can handle this.* Handle their innocence while knowing that somewhere out there, another child as innocent was being slowly suffocated to death.

Aden's hand closed over her shoulder. *Yes, you can. You've always been stronger than you know, with a wild and fiery spirit.*

A small hand curled into Zaira's at that instant, a tiny girl with big green eyes in a face that reminded Zaira of her own, looking up. "Can I sit here?" she whispered.

"Yes." Her voice came out rough, almost harsh, but the child smiled and scrambled onto the bench seat beside her.

A single instant of kindness, she thought again, her heart breaking. *How do we save them all, Aden?*

One at a time.

Chapter 75

WHILE ZAIRA AND a number of other teams continued to mobilize to find Persephone, Aden watched over the children and the Arrows in the valley. Interview requests kept being made on air and on the PsyNet by media sources desperate to talk to him, but Aden had no intention of appearing on any screen or answering any questions.

The squad had to maintain a fine balance between not being so "other" that they became terrors people wanted to kill and being so visible that the other major powers considered them a threat.

Better to be the shadow who had a face, but a face you saw rarely and mostly when the shadow saved you from harm. His deliberate lack of public appearances would also ease the minds of those who might've believed the Arrows would make a bid for total power in the Net.

And his place was here, holding together a family that had as many damaged adults as it had innocent children. There were, however, some hopeful signs. From the start of the relocation of the squad's "heart" to the valley, Aden had made it clear that regardless of their geographical assignments, each member of the squad had a confirmed space in a home here. Aden had been surprised—in a good way—at how many of the long-range scouts had begun to return to the valley in the time between assignments.

Jaya and Ivy, the two Es most involved with the valley, had begun to drop a quiet word in his ear when they felt a scout wasn't ready to leave:

"His heart is too hurt."

"She's tired."

"They need to heal."

Aden had found ways to delay assignments by juggling squad members. It was easier now that so many of the older or "broken" Arrows had come out of hiding, and because his men and women weren't being wasted on Ming's personal vendettas. As for the training sessions with their young, those continued—sometimes a lesson was tough, but it was never brutal.

When Aden found Carolina sobbing behind one of the cabins that afternoon, he didn't hesitate to scoop her up in his arms and rock her until she sniffled and told him what was wrong. "I can't make my mind do what the teacher says." Her lower lip shook. "I tried hard, Aden. I really tried."

"You don't have to do it all at once," Aden told her, making a mental note to have a talk with the teacher involved. Walker was doing an incredible job of educating them in how to handle the increasing emotionality of their charges but not all had adapted well. He knew they, too, were trying and that it would take time. What gave him hope was that not one had asked for a transfer.

Rubbing away her tears with small fists, Carolina said, "Really?" A quiver of hope. "I won't get in trouble?"

Aden sat down with her in his arms, his back against the cabin wall. "The reason you need to learn to control your mind is that you're a Gradient 9.3 Tp showing signs of being a natural combat telepath."

Carolina's family had signed her over to the squad when she was three. She'd hurt herself by stepping onto a piece of broken glass. In her pain and panic, she'd broadcast so loudly that she'd incapacitated every individual within her home. Like a gun going off near a changeling's ears, it had made them psychically deaf. Two younger members had ended up unconscious, one with what they'd initially thought was permanent brain damage. "Your strength means you can do a lot of harm with your mind if you're not careful."

Big eyes looking into his, solemn and sad. "I could hurt my friends?"

He didn't want her to feel only those emotions when it came to her ability. "Yes, but if you learn control, you can also do amazing things to help people."

A thoughtful silence. "Do you think I can learn?"

"I think you're very smart and might one day be as strong and as disciplined as Zaira." Pressing a kiss to the top of her head when she beamed at him, he set her on her feet again. "Go on and join your friends." Arrow children were allowed to have friends now, but they were also always closely supervised. The fact was that their abilities were lethal, a truth none of them could afford to forget. But where before the protections had suffocated, they were now a simple safety net the children appeared to find comforting.

Taking another minute of quiet, he located Zaira's mind on the PsyNet. She was so contained, her light shielded from prying eyes, but that didn't matter, not so long as she trusted him with it. "Any news?" he asked.

"We found what might be another bolt-hole, but it doesn't appear to have ever been used. Mica's seeded it with electronic bugs, so we'll hear the instant anyone returns." Her mind reached out to his along their conscious bond. "We're about to investigate the final three locations on our current list—I should be back in the valley by nightfall."

"Persephone couldn't have a better champion," he said, knowing that if he heard any reports of the child's body being found, he'd make damn sure Zaira never laid eyes on the heartbreaking discovery. It would break her. "I'll see you tonight—I'm heading out soon to pick up a new recruit."

That recruit was a two-year-old child who'd broken his mother's arm during a telekinetic tantrum that had taken place in a large and busy shopping mall three hours earlier. The woman didn't want to give up her son, but she needed help. Aden intended to offer it; whether or not the mother and child could move into the valley would depend on if the deep background check he'd initiated on the mother and her family showed any traitorous tendencies.

He was cutting through a sunlit city park on his way back from the assessment, his thoughts on how best to help the traumatized child, when he discovered that their hidden enemy hadn't given up, had simply been waiting for an opportunity.

His instincts said the loving mother he'd just left hadn't betrayed him, though the squad would no doubt debrief her to make certain. More than likely, the enemy had started to keep track of all rumors or reports of powerful or dangerous children, aware that, sooner or later, the squad would respond. Perhaps they'd intended to hit any Arrow who came to assess the child. It was pure luck that the Arrow in question was Aden.

And three hours was plenty enough time to get an operative in place.

This time, there were no theatrics, no complicated setup, nothing to warn him so he could strike out with his abilities. He felt the danger only at the last instant, the bullet whining through the air behind him.

He was shot.

He had a feeling the projectile had been meant to hit his skull, take him out in a single split second, but he'd listened to his instincts and moved at the last moment. The bullet entered through the back of his neck and punched out the front. He knew it missed his spinal cord because he still had functionality in his arms and legs, but from the blood spraying out, it had hit a major artery.

Drawing very slightly on Vasic's telekinesis because he didn't want to weaken his friend—who was currently with Zaira's team—he clamped a hand over the gushing wound and, managing to stay on his feet, projected a shield that stopped the second bullet. *I'm hit,* he telepathed to Abbot; the Tk had been waiting for him at the end of the park so they could do a discreet 'port back to the valley.

His attacker took off at high speed.

Abbot 'ported in, took one look at Aden, and didn't bother to give chase. Placing his hand on Aden's shoulder, the other man took him directly inside a medical facility maintained by the squad. Aden's knees buckled on arrival, the blood loss critical. But even then, his mind, it tried to reach out to the one person for whom he was the first priority, the one person who was his own.

Except they weren't truly bonded and with his blood pumping out with each beat of his heart . . . she was too far.

ZAIRA felt the faint whisper of Aden's psychic touch just as they cleared the final property on their list, but when she responded, she felt only blankness. Nothingness. Ice infiltrated her veins. Grabbing Vasic's arm, she said, "Aden—go to Aden!"

The two of them found themselves in a white corridor splattered with blood a heartbeat later, two nurses and a doctor working on the man who lay on the floor, his skin pale and his white shirt saturated with red where it hadn't been cut away by the medical personnel. "No." It was a keening whisper.

Dropping to her knees, she found his bloodied hand, gripped it. "No." *You don't get to go. You don't get to leave me alone.*

There was no answer from the one person who had never let her down.

"We need to get him into the OR!" The doctor looked up. "Vasic, teleport him in."

That quickly, Aden's touch was gone from her hand, the medics 'ported away with him. Kneeling on the floor staring at the red on her palm, Zaira felt the rage inside her rise in a murderous wave. She got slowly to her feet, and by the time Vasic returned, she was heading toward Abbot, the younger Tk standing shell-shocked in the hallway.

"I need to get Judd," Vasic said. "He may be able to do what the medics can't."

Zaira heard him through the rage. She didn't know Judd well, had believed him another Tk. Clearly, he was something more. Vasic was gone on the next breath, and all she wanted to do was annihilate the person who had hurt Aden.

VASIC couldn't teleport to Judd, not with the way the other man's shields were structured, so he did the next best thing: got himself to SnowDancer territory, then called Judd. "Aden's hit. Dying."

Judd asked for a telepathic visual and, using it, teleported himself to Vasic's side, his face set in harsh lines. "What can I do?"

Taking him back to the operating room, Vasic watched the Tk-Cell move in to attempt to repair the damage to Aden's artery and veins. It was so severe the medics couldn't plug the hole—Vasic had heard one doctor use the word "shredded," and from what Vasic had seen, the bullet had been designed to cause maximum damage.

Judd might not be able to do much, either, his ability to move the cells of the body a slow and careful process that might not beat the ticking clock on Aden's life. But each time the monitor beeped, it meant Aden was alive.

Vasic listened to that monitor for too long.

By the time he realized he hadn't told Zaira what was happening and went back out into the corridor, she was gone.

PSYNET BEACON: BREAKING NEWS

Aden Kai has been shot. Unconfirmed reports are coming in from those who witnessed the shooting. All state it was a killing hit.

"His jugular was torn wide open, or more likely his carotid, maybe both," one witness stated. "Look at all the blood on the grass. It just gushed out."

"No one can survive that," said a medic who was on his way to a shift at a nearby clinic at the time of the shooting. "He's dead."

The *Beacon* is attempting to make contact with the squad for verification.

Chapter 76

ABBOT HADN'T WANTED to leave Zaira alone in the leafy and sunshine-laden park where Aden had been shot, but she gave him no choice. "You need to cover Aden's security shift in the valley. Go."

The younger Arrow hesitated, his sea blue eyes scanning the people who'd drawn back from the center of the scene at their arrival. "You're not safe here alone."

That was what she was counting on. "I'm giving you a direct order."

"Yes, sir."

Staring at the blood on the grass after he left, Zaira crouched down to touch her fingers to it. It was still wet, the speed of events fast enough that the inevitable gawkers hadn't stepped close enough to contaminate the scene. Driven by rage, her first thought had been to track the shooter, but then she'd realized there was an easier way. If this individual had shot Aden in broad daylight, then he or she was brazen enough to try again. A second public attack on an Arrow would cement the conspirators' point that no one was safe.

So she'd give them an easy target.

Only Zaira didn't play by the same rules as Aden. She didn't only do surface telepathic scans as she waited while ostensibly checking the evidence; she went as deep as she possibly could without causing damage or alerting her targets. Part of her was still thinking, still able to remember that if she smashed the shields of blameless people, it would undo all the work Aden had done to place the Arrows in a position where the public didn't fear them so much that they sought to hunt them out of existence.

We can protect ourselves, but what of the Carolinas, the Tavishes, and the other children we don't even know about yet? If people start to fear Arrows, it's a short step to start eliminating those who might grow up into Arrows.

Aden's words. Words she could still hear through the roar of rage. As she could feel her small breakfast companion's heartbeat as she sat so vulnerable and happy beside her. As she could hear the hope in Pip's voice when he asked her when he could go play with Jojo again.

She would keep the innocents safe. She couldn't promise the same for the guilty.

A few people dared come closer as she worked, including a man who said, "Is Aden Kai all right? We were some distance away so we couldn't help, but we saw the shooter."

"He's fine." No matter what, Aden needed to remain invincible in the minds of the public. "Can you describe the shooter?"

"A runner. Male, I'm fairly certain. I'm sorry, that's all I saw."

The witness was human, his shields paper-thin.

Her deep scan of his mind told her he wasn't lying. So she scanned the next person and the next and the next, frustrated only by the changelings' tough natural shields and by those Psy who had good enough shielding that her intrusion would be noted.

Those people she evaluated visually.

Two were mothers with very young children in prams, the third an elderly woman who walked with the aid of a cane. She felt confident in eliminating them from the suspect pool, though she took mental snapshots of their faces so she could trace their identities should it become necessary.

Every other individual who came within her proximity was subjected to a deep scan that told her all their secrets, all their nightmares. She didn't care about any of it, discarding all data that didn't relate directly to Aden and the attempts on his life.

He wouldn't agree with her choice, would say she was violating people. Zaira didn't care. Not when he was lying bleeding in a hospital bed. Not when his mind had disconnected from her own as his psychic abilities shut down. Not when his blood still glistened on the grass in front of her.

Eyes burning with what she told herself was pure rage, she hit on another changeling mind. This one was a healthy adult male in running clothes. That alone didn't make him guilty; there were a number of runners milling around, the park having a well-utilized track. Because she couldn't use her telepathy to clear him, she watched him with her peripheral vision while she used a small scanner she'd grabbed off a medical tray as a prop, as if she was gathering data from the scene.

The truth was that the tool was meant for DNA scans and loaded with the profiles of those in the squad; all it flashed was Aden's name, his blood painting the grass. The rage boiled hotter with each iteration of his name, each reminder that he'd been hurt, might be dying.

When she continued in her apparent work without doing anything flashy or interesting, the crowd began to disperse, until only a white-haired human couple and the changeling runner were left. She didn't discard the elderly pair until a deep scan showed them as having no ulterior motives. The changeling made no aggressive moves, but she stayed within his reach, within shooting distance.

Her patience was rewarded five minutes later as he slid his hand surreptitiously to the back of his shorts. By the time he brought out a sleek gun complete with silencer, she was already moving. Her body slammed his to the ground as his finger touched the trigger, the shot thudding into a nearby sculpture. The human pair screamed while the shooter grunted and tried to punch her in the face, but Zaira had calculated his muscle mass and strength in the time he'd watched her, had already devised countermeasures against his greater strength.

She was also powered by rage.

Avoiding the blow, she smashed a single fist down at the precise angle to do maximum damage.

Blood spurted. His eyes altering from human blue to a slitted black, he swiped at her with a clawed hand. She flipped out of reach and deliberately waited until he was almost upright to kick out with one booted foot and dislocate his knee. He crumpled to a sideways position on his knees with a scream of fury, this changeling who had shot the only person who had ever loved her.

Not giving him time to recover, she kicked again, smashing his jaw.

Another kick, this one to his ribs. She deliberately avoided his head, not wanting him unconscious, wanting him to feel this, feel the cold rage that drove her. She saw others join the human couple, saw phones turned in her direction as people recorded the violence, but that didn't stop her. Today, Aden wasn't there to stop her, either, his solid, stable presence missing from her mind.

The aloneness howled, the rage creature wanting blood, wanting to brutalize this man who might have stolen Aden from her forever.

Taking the shooter to the ground once more with another well-aimed kick, where he lay on his back and struggled to breathe through his broken nose and shattered jaw, his face smeared red, she stepped on one thick wrist so he couldn't get her with his claws, and when he lifted his other hand to slice at her, kicked out with her boot at an angle that would've broken a Psy male's bones.

Changeling bones were tougher, so the bone didn't break, but she did enough damage that his hand didn't seem to work as it should. When he scrabbled at her, there was no power in it, his claws not even penetrating the tough fabric of her uniform pants.

He was totally at her mercy.

When she glimpsed his form begin to shimmer, she said, "Don't shift." Her own gun in her hand, pointed directly at him. "You do and I'll shoot directly into the shift." She didn't know exactly what that would do, but she had a feeling it would be fatal. "It'll be interesting to see if the pieces of you that end up scattered all over this park will be from your human or your animal form."

The man's body solidified, the threat clearly finding its mark.

She thought about how to torture him and a hundred different methods popped into her mind. Sliding away her gun and lifting the foot not on his wrist—which she'd slowly crushed and which had to be causing him agony, she placed it very carefully on his sternum and met his gaze. The torture was psychological this time.

She had no intention of crushing his ribs into his internal organs. To do so would equal too quick a death. But he believed she did, terror a slick sheen over his eyes. Giving him just enough time to truly fear her, she took her foot off his sternum and went down on her haunches without removing the boot she had on his mangled wrist.

Then, dropping her voice into a range that would be inaudible to their audience but which this changeling would hear, she said, "You have two choices. To die quickly or to die slowly and in intense agony. If you choose the latter, it doesn't matter if you later beg me for mercy. I won't have mercy. I don't know how. I was trained that way."

She saw from his expression that he believed her.

Speaking through the blood that had bubbled down to his mouth, he said, "Quick." His voice was slurred as a result of the damage she'd done to his jaw.

"It doesn't work that way," she said, grinding her boot into his broken wrist without doing anything other than slightly shifting her weight.

A scream erupted from his throat, causing their silent audience to flinch. Waiting until he'd settled, she said, "Tell me what you know." She didn't elaborate—there was no need for it. And this one had to know something. His hit had been too up close and personal with too high a risk of capture. He was either a leftover Pure Psy fanatic or part of the conspiracy.

Instinct told her it was the latter. He hadn't intended to become a martyr; his plan was to escape. And there was the fact that the squad had picked up certain scuttlebutt in the dark highways of the world—seemed like the contract killers were turning down major pay packets at any whisper a

hit might involve an Arrow. Too many of their fellow killers
had been eliminated or taken hostage for the money to be
worth it.

And even those who still believed in Pure Psy were looking askance at recent events. The latest whispers tagged by
the squad said the fanatics had started to mistrust their new
ally when it was only the Pure Psy people who seemed to be
dying—without any observable change in the status of Silence in the Net.

The honeymoon was over in those quarters.

As a result, the conspiracy had likely run out of disposable bodies and been forced to use some of its own. "Talk,"
she reiterated coldly when he didn't say anything.

"They'll kill me."

"So you choose a slow death." Retrieving a blade from
her boot, she had the point at his eyeball with such speed that
he blinked, not realizing the blade was so sharp it would split
his eyelid.

When it did, blood dripping into his eye, he said, "No."

"Then *talk.*" She bent closer, always keeping an eye on
his limbs. His shattered jaw meant he couldn't bite her, but
she didn't disregard that, either.

As it was, he knew he was beaten, saw living death in her
eyes. He spoke in a near-subvocal murmur and though his
words were a touch garbled, she understood it all. And she
knew he'd given her everything he had on the wider conspiracy, his fear of her too pungent to allow for a bluff. But
she had one more question to ask him. "There's a changeling
child. About two years old. Her name is Persephone."

His throat moved, Adam's apple prominent. "She's dead,"
he whispered.

The rage in Zaira wanted to stab the blade into his eyeball. "You saw the body?"

A shake of his head. "I helped move her to a new holding
area, and after, I was told she died in the night." A touch of
horror in his expression. "I never agreed with keeping the kid."

But he hadn't helped the small, vulnerable girl, which
made him just as culpable. "Tell me the location of the new
holding area, and any other locations you know."

He gave her three addresses.

"Quick," he said at the end, his breathing strained and pupils hugely dilated. "You promised quick."

Zaira let the tip of the blade touch his eyeball. "I lied." She wanted to torture him until he begged for her to end it. The fact that they were in public didn't matter. The fact that people would see her as a monster didn't matter. Icy rage had morphed into a red-hot murderous anger that shoved at her to rip him limb from limb. Smash in his skull as she had her parents'. Erase his face.

Sunlight glinted on the ring on her finger as she went to wrench back her captive's head with a grip in his hair.

If you didn't have anger inside you, you'd be inhuman.
I refuse to accept that my Arrows are frozen in amber.
I have faith in your will. Fight for us.

The memory of Aden's voice, his absolute faith in her, halted her when she would've punctured the changeling's eyeball in the first act of brutalization. The rage monster in her hesitated.

Don't go. Don't leave me alone.
I have faith that the girl who chose to stop crying at three years of age has the will to conquer this demon.
I like you. You're nice.
Aden just needs you.
There is a reason every Arrow in Venice, even the most recalcitrant senior, would die for you.
Blind faith. And love.
Breathe, Zaira. Take a minute and just breathe.

Remembering Ivy's lesson through her fury, she focused on the ruby on her finger, the ring that Aden had given her because *he* wanted to keep *her*, and took a breath. Another.

Aden loved her.

All those other voices were of people who liked her, too, who thought she had value as a person. If she did this, if she surrendered to evil, she'd lose them all. Persephone would die. And if Aden survived, he'd wake to find himself alone because the rage would've swallowed Zaira whole: she'd promised him he'd never be alone, that she'd always be with him . . . that she'd be his partner.

You aren't locked in that cell anymore. You live in the light.

Aden was gone from her mind and it hurt. It *hurt.* But he'd marked her regardless, and she clung to the echo of him, holding him possessively tight. *Don't you go,* she said along the dead telepathic connection she kept trying to force open. *Don't you leave me. I'll become a monster if you do.* It was a threat that held endless need. *I can only be human if you're there to teach me.*

No answer, but the rage creature inside her was leashed. Looking down, she found herself facing a gaze full of terror, one eye red with blood that had dripped from his split eyelid. She'd broken him, obtained the data the squad needed. There was no need to kill him. Flipping the blade, she tapped his temple with the back end, putting him under.

Did you get what we need?

Looking up at the sound of Vasic's telepathic voice, having ignored him during the fight, she gave him an affirmative. "Get him to a hospital and contact the authorities," she said aloud for the benefit of their audience. "The threat has been neutralized." *I have Persephone's last known location. We'll go as soon as you 'port back.*

While Vasic took care of the body, she slipped the knife back into place and picked up the scanner she'd dropped. Then she walked deliberately toward the crowd. The onlookers parted in front of her, mingled fear and awe in their expressions. "Where's the gun?" she asked the human couple.

The man held it out to her, hand trembling. "I picked it up when you made him drop it."

Zaira knew that, had seen him do it and never forgotten the gun that could be turned against her. "Thank you. You minimized the risk to others."

A shaky smile. "You're an extraordinary young woman. Isn't she, dear?"

"Oh, yes," his mate replied with a beaming smile. "Why, that horrible man might have hurt us if she hadn't been there."

Not sure how to respond to that unexpected statement, Zaira turned to Vasic as the teleporter returned. *The valley first. We need more weapons and people.*

Chapter 77

THE LOCATION THE shooter had given her for Persephone turned out to be a shipping yard owned by a human magnate. Locked and gated, barbed-wire fence above the chain-link, the premises also had electronic surveillance, guards, and dogs. None of those were enough to stop a team of Arrows determined to get in, especially under cover of the night that had fallen in this part of the world.

While Mica took care of the electronics and Vasic silently stunned the guards into unconsciousness, another member of Zaira's team made sure the dogs were asleep. The sedative-laced meat they'd brought in after an initial reconnaissance had worked exactly as planned—the animals would be fine when they woke. No need to penalize them for the crimes of their master.

Going in ahead of the others while they cleaned up all suspicious signs, including hiding the unconscious guards, Zaira found a good position on the hulk of a ship being built and, putting the laser binoculars to her eyes, looked into the central building that functioned as the headquarters of the company.

It had six levels, was mostly glass and lit up like the Christmas tree she'd seen once in Times Square. That made it ridiculously simple to work out how many people were still inside. "Five," she murmured to Vasic and Mica when they appeared by her side. "Three on level two, one on level five, the last on level six." She increased the magnification on the binoculars. "I think level six is the CEO."

Mica took the binoculars. "Confirmed. I double-checked his image before we left." He glanced at Zaira. "We need him alive, yes?"

"Yes." She broke down and put away the binoculars into a pocket of her combat pants. "Persephone was taken to a basement level." And left there to die, according to the shooter. "Mica, you take the others and clear the building above. Vasic and I will head below."

It was stupidly simple to get in, the CEO apparently smug in his belief that his guards and dogs and fences would keep people out. The actual locks on the main doors were pathetic. But the ones on the doors going down to the basement? Those were significant.

They were also electronic, so she and Vasic couldn't simply break them.

"I can pull the door off its hinges," Vasic said to her. "It may be noisy."

"Wait." Touching base with Mica, she checked his progress. "Don't worry about noise. Mica has the CEO, and the other workers are corralled."

A shuddering groan as the metal door bent and bent before being torn away from the hinges. Placing it carefully against the wall, Vasic didn't attempt to take the lead position down the stairs. He knew as well as Zaira that this was her mission. If she'd failed Persephone, then she wouldn't hide from it.

Heart tight and head still an echoing aloneness, she spoke to Aden anyway. *We're heading into the basement. There's some lighting, but it's very dim. And the smell—bad.* Bad enough that it might come from a body that had just begun to decompose. *It's cold, too, but that's okay. That's actually good. Miane told me Persephone came from colder waters, that it's heat that's her enemy.*

No response, but it made her feel better regardless. Because as long as she talked to him, he wasn't dead, couldn't be gone.

We've reached the bottom. The space is sprawling.

Pockets of shadow pooled in the corners, but it was obvious the large open space filled with weapons and other supplies was empty of living beings. She and Vasic swept it anyway. *There are rooms at the end. Cells.*

Her anger burning ice in her blood, she stepped toward the first cage, looked inside. *It's too dark,* she telepathed to Vasic. *I'm going to shine in my flashlight. Shield your eyes.* Careful to angle her own eyes in a way that meant it wouldn't blind her, she shone the light within.

A startled hand went up, the thin man on the cot beyond looking at her with drug-hazed eyes, his skin yellow. Zaira switched off the light, her heart thudding. *That's one of the missing BlackSea people,* she told Vasic. *His facial features are distinctive even under the new scarring.*

We can't release him yet, the teleporter said. *We need more people if we're going to be freeing drugged hostages.*

Zaira nodded. Much as it infuriated her to see anyone in a cage, Vasic was right. The hostage could hurt himself or others in his current state. Walking on, she shone the light into the next cage.

This one proved empty, the cot neatly made.

Two more were occupied, one by a woman, the second by another man. The woman was another BlackSea changeling and she had the Halcyon pallor, but the older black man asleep in the other cot wasn't a sea changeling.

I recognize him, Vasic said unexpectedly just as her fully charged flashlight began to flicker. *He was a Council scientist. Specialist in explosives, I think.*

There was only one more cell left.

Gut churning and nausea shoving at her throat, she took a deep breath and shone the malfunctioning light through the narrow window. A tiny body lay under a thin blanket. Anger and sadness tore through Zaira . . . then just before the flashlight blinked off, the blanket moved. Shallow, so shallow, but it was a breath. "Vasic!"

"Move back. I didn't see enough to get a teleport lock." He wrenched the door off its hinges in a heartbeat and Zaira ran in to find the tiny little girl startled awake.

Terror filled her small, thin face.

Zaira didn't know what to do, so she did what she'd

always wanted someone to do for her as a child. She gathered that thin, scared body into her arms and said, "You're safe. No one will hurt you anymore." Her eyes met Vasic's.

There was no need for any further words.

He teleported them directly to the floating city where they'd been guests less than three days prior. Guns clicked around them as slanting rain plastered their hair and clothing to their bodies, but then there was a cry to get Miane and Olivia, running feet on the city that swayed slightly with the motion of the crashing, storm-lashed sea.

Zaira was startled when thin arms locked tight around her neck, Persephone's heart racing fast. "Shh," she whispered. "You're home. Mommy's coming."

"Mommy?" the child whispered, and then she said, "Mommy!" in a thin but joyous shout, having glimpsed Olivia racing toward her.

Passing over her precious burden to the crying woman, who covered her child's face in kisses, she was about to tell Miane about the other hostages when Olivia ran to the edge of the platform on which they stood and jumped straight into the cold, crashing water. Zaira moved instinctively to go after her but Miane got in her way.

"The child needs to shift," the alpha reminded her. "She needs the sea more than food, more than rest, more than anything aside from her mother."

Eyes wide, Zaira went to the edge of the platform and looked down. *Aden, I can't describe it,* she said in wonder, barely able to glimpse the truth below the crashing foam of the waves. *There's a glow, streamers of the softest, most beautiful light. I don't know what they shifted into, but they're extraordinarily beautiful.* Like glimpses of a dream.

Stepping away reluctantly when the lights faded, as if going into the deep, she turned to Miane. "We've found two more of your people. They'll need you."

ADEN was still in surgery when she and Vasic returned to the now clean infirmary corridor, both of them having taken two minutes to change into dry clothes because Ivy had pointed out that their getting sick right now wouldn't help

Aden. The empath had been at the valley when they returned to give Cristabel and the others a quick update.

By then, Vasic had already teleported Miane's people to the floating city, trusting her word that she'd share any useful data the captives remembered, while Mica was debriefing the scientist. He was in much better condition than the others they'd rescued—probably because his captors intended to use him long-term—and made it clear he'd be happy to talk once he'd had a chance to shower.

The CEO was in a black cell deep in Central Command.

"Do you need to go and further question the CEO?" she asked Vasic. As a human, the CEO had weak shields, though a Psy had clearly bolstered them somewhat. Still, they'd been easy enough to dismantle without causing damage. As a result, Zaira was cataloguing his memories and secrets even as she sat waiting for Aden to wake up.

"No," Vasic said. "He has no time-sensitive data and the two of us can give orders from here as we come across useful information from our deep scan of his mind." The teleporter stood with her in silence for over twenty minutes before saying, "Aden was here two months ago with Ivy."

"Your arm?"

"He stayed with Ivy throughout. She says that without him, she might have gone mad."

Zaira stared down the corridor. She wasn't like Ivy, wasn't comfortable with many people, rarely made connections. But Vasic was Aden's best friend and even when she'd seen him as a competitor for Aden's attention, she'd also always seen the loyal friend who'd stood by Aden through everything, and whom Aden would trust with all that mattered most to him.

Including Zaira.

"I can't lose him." Her every breath hurt, her chest was so tight. "He's a better person than anyone I've ever met, ever heard about. We need him. I need him." He made her feel as if she was all right exactly as she was, as if there was nothing wrong with her.

"Aden has a single deep flaw."

The only reason Zaira didn't turn on Vasic in violence for daring to say that was that she knew he'd never disparage Aden. "A flaw?"

"He has no capacity to care for himself," Vasic said. "He believes everyone else is more important and that's what makes him a great leader. But he needs someone to watch over him, to make sure he doesn't lose himself in his responsibilities."

"I know." Aden was her priority, her everything.

"Zaira."

She met Vasic's gaze ten minutes after they'd last spoken. "What?" It was a single angry word. If Aden died, she would find the door to the afterlife and drag him back out. How dare he think to leave her?

"Drink this." Vasic handed her an energy drink. "Aden will forgive neither one of us if he wakes to find you weak and exhausted."

She gulped down the drink, got up, began pacing, the rage creature angry and sad and scared. So scared. "How did he learn what he could do?" she asked just to fill her mind with something else. "What the mirror could do?"

She'd meant to ask him a hundred times, but somehow they'd never spoken of it. "He told me about Walker, how Walker taught him to shield." She paused. "Does Walker know?" That Aden was wounded, fighting for his life. "Aden would want him to know."

Vasic's winter-frost eyes darkened. "I'll go find him."

"Wait. Don't bring Marjorie and Naoshi," Zaira ordered, knowing Aden wouldn't want his parents to see him when he wasn't at full strength.

Walker was different.

Zaira didn't understand parental or maternal connections, but she'd felt Aden's emotions for Walker, knew the other man held a deeply trusted place in his life.

"No," Vasic agreed before leaving.

It took him precisely seven minutes to return with Walker Lauren. Zaira knew because she kept looking at her time-piece and calculating how long Aden had been in surgery. Too long.

Chapter 78

WALKER'S FACE WAS grim, his pale green eyes hard as he processed what Vasic had just told him. And yet, despite his obvious anger and worry, his presence was oddly stabilizing. Just like Aden's in similar situations. Father and son, Zaira thought.

Genetics didn't matter here. Walker and Aden had chosen their relationship.

Shoving up the sleeves of his blue shirt, Walker began to walk with Zaira, and when she asked him about Aden's abilities, he said, "I met him as a boy of six. So calm and strong and determined, and with the beginnings of what we named the mirror."

"You helped him shield it."

"At first, I simply grasped the subtlety of his telepathy," Walker said. "You know what he can do with it?"

"Yes, the Amplification Effect." Because Aden had two abilities close to the midrange, he could amplify one to a higher Gradient. Not everyone with two midlevel abilities could do it, but in his case, the effect pushed his telepathy into the 8.3 range.

"No one even considered him capable of it because his M abilities register at 3.2. That's extremely low for amplification."

Zaira knew all this, but she didn't care. Having Walker talk about Aden while Vasic listened and she asked further questions made Zaira feel as if they were surrounding Aden in their words, words that would remind him who he was to so many people, words that would hold him here. "He didn't think he could do it himself, not until you taught him."

"I recognized him, in a sense." Walker frowned. "His telepathy is like mine in that it's . . . quiet. That's taken as weak by some when the opposite is true—trained correctly, we can work with such stealth that no one notices our intrusion." He ran a hand through the dark blond strands of his hair, faint glints of silver catching the light.

"But it was the mirror that was the critical thing—I realized that at once as soon as I saw it, though it took me months to win his trust enough that he lowered his shields so we could work on the psychic level." Walker would never forget the boy Aden had been, so wary and careful. "Then, the mirror was embryonic, hardly visible. It was why he hadn't already been discovered."

"He once told me he began to trust you the second week of class," Vasic said quietly. "A child broke down in tears during a reading session and instead of berating or punishing her, you wiped away her tears and read her part of the text for her."

Walker didn't remember that particular incident, but he'd dealt with many like it. "They were all so tired and hurt and tiny." He shook his head. "Aden was the same age, but he was already looking out for the others."

"When he wakes," Zaira said, her voice fierce, "I'll allow him no arguments. I'm doing the looking after even if I have to tie him up."

"I'll help you with the rope," Vasic said.

Walker looked across to the teleporter. "Aden didn't know what the mirror was as a child and neither did I." All he'd known was that it was unique and that it sang of *power*. Instinct had told him he needed to teach Aden to hide it so the boy wouldn't be forced to use it for those who had less integrity in their entire adult bodies than Aden had in his littlest finger. "When did he figure it out?"

"We were twelve," Vasic said. "Aden was in anti-interrogation training."

Translation: he was being tortured.

Zaira's teeth ground down, hands fisted. Sensing Walker's

tension, she realized he, too, had understood the truth behind Vasic's words.

"The trainer made a mistake," the teleporter continued. "Aden realized the man was about to accidentally snap his neck. He couldn't stop him telepathically, not with his abilities leashed, so he says he instinctively reached for power." Vasic's tone was so even, Zaira knew he had vicious control on himself. "I felt him and didn't resist the power draw. I knew Aden would never do something like that unless he was in danger."

And that, Zaira thought, was why she had always trusted Vasic. Even when she'd been jealous of him, she'd known he wouldn't hesitate to stand with Aden against any threat.

"The trainer didn't realize Aden had gained strength?"

Vasic shook his head at Walker's question. "My telekinesis gave him the power to twist out of the trainer's hold. That sudden strength was attributed to a surge of adrenaline at being in danger."

Zaira heard Walker and Vasic continue to talk, but her mind, it kept searching for Aden. Her chest got tighter and tighter with every failure to connect. *Don't you leave me alone,* she commanded him again. *Don't you go.*

A warm weight on her hair, Walker's hand on the back of her head. "He's strong," the older telepath said. "Stubborn, too."

She didn't know why, but his calm tone, paired with the open emotion in his voice, smashed through her defenses. Maybe it was because of Aden's memories of him, but she didn't resist when he drew her into his arms, standing scared and angry and waiting against the warmth of him.

You finally won our argument, she said along the dead psychic pathway. *I chose to be better than my past today. Wake up so you can savor your victory.*

No response. Nothing but a blankness that made ice form in her blood, and the rage build again. Pulling away from Walker, she began to pace the corridor for what seemed an eternity.

And then she reached out to Aden . . . and his mind caught her own.

Twisting around as her blood thundered, she ran into the operating theater. A drained-appearing Judd was slumped against a wall, the doctor and nurses looking as tired, but

Zaira's focus was on Aden. To her shock, he pulled himself into a seated position as she watched. He was paler than he should've been, the skin at his neck appearing delicate and new, but he was conscious and unhurt and she could feel the wonderfulness of him inside her mind.

Opening his arms, he hauled her close. She held on tight, her heart squeezing so hard inside her chest that it hurt, her breath stuck in her lungs. She didn't care about that, or about the others in the room, leaving that to Aden.

He would watch her back. He always had.

ARMS steel around her, Aden breathed Zaira in. When he looked up, it was to see Walker and Vasic getting everyone else out of the room. Vasic had his arm around Judd's waist, the exhausted Tk only minutes away from a total flameout, while the doctor's face held lines of exhaustion. Her nurses weren't in any better condition, their feet dragging.

Walker met his gaze, the raw depth of his relief open. *Hold on tight to her. She loves you.*

I know. Pressing his cheek against Zaira's temple and sliding one hand in her hair, his other arm still locked around her, he basked in her fire, letting it banish the coldness of near death.

When she pulled away and shoved at his shoulders, he noticed she'd tempered her strength. "You aren't meant to get hurt." The words were gritted out. "You aren't meant to leave me alone."

Getting to his feet, his strength enough for that thanks to a blood transfusion, he closed the distance she'd created. She stood her ground but she was careful with how she pushed him, his lethal Arrow mate. He'd accepted that the bond might never form, her scars too deep to allow such trust, but she was his mate in every way that she could be; she had given him every trust she could.

Cupping her angry face, he said, "I'm sorry."

She pressed her fists against his abdomen and shook her head. "I'm never allowing you out alone again."

He loved her wildness, her spirit. "That'll make being the leader of the squad difficult."

"Shut up." A growl of sound before she hugged him again, a tiny Fury who'd claimed him as her own. "We found Persephone. Alive."

Hard, almost painful joy in his blood. "How?" He could feel exhaustion starting to drag him down, the work the medics and Judd had done not enough to erase the effects of the catastrophic hit he'd taken.

"I made the shooter talk." Pressed up against him, Zaira suddenly stiffened her body and slipped an arm around his waist. "You're about to keel over. Get back in bed."

"I will, but not here." Touching Vasic's mind, he asked his friend for an assist, shooting him an image of the location he wanted.

The remote teleport was flawless, and Aden and Zaira were standing by the bed in their cabin the next second. Pushing him gently into it, Zaira went to the end and unsnapped his boot clips before tugging one boot off.

"I never expected you to be so domestic," he said softly, feeling his heart expand to an impossible size.

"I told you to be quiet." She glared at him even as she removed his other boot, then stripped off his socks. "You're bloody. You need to be clean before you can sleep."

"I'm not sure my legs will hold me upright at the moment," he admitted, waves of exhaustion crashing into him. "Did the shooter tell you anything else?"

"It's what you thought," she said, coming around to help remove the shreds of his shirt. "This group wanted to assassinate you in order to subvert the stability not only of the PsyNet but of the world. *All* their actions are fueled by that single aim: to foster discord, fear, and panic."

Zaira disappeared into the bathroom and returned with a wet cloth. Climbing into bed behind him after nudging him to a seated position, she tugged him back against her and gently cleaned the blood on his shoulders and chest that the medical staff hadn't bothered with in the rush to save his life. "The group calls itself the Consortium."

"You missed a spot," he said, his mind heavy.

She kissed him for the teasing. "Do you want to hear the rest?"

"As much as I can before I fall asleep."

"We have one of the Consortium leaders in custody," she told him. "His memories confirm that the people at the top of the organization come from all three races—their plan is to take advantage of the post-Silence fractures to destabilize the world while putting their own empires in position to benefit from the ensuing chaos."

Sinking against her, Aden permitted his eyes to close. The Consortium's plan was predictable in a way—but only if you thought solely of individual gain rather than the good of the world. "Like an arms dealer who starts a war."

Zaira ran the clean side of the damp cloth over his chest. "Yes. And here's the other thing—they've made certain they can't identify one another. All meetings were done via audio and even the voices were disguised."

Compartmentalization at its highest. "Clever," he murmured. "One person has to know everyone, however."

"The instigator behind the entire idea." Putting aside the cloth, Zaira wrapped her arms lightly around his neck. "That's definitely not the man we captured, though once we put together all the clues from his memories, it's likely to point us in the direction of some other players."

"Does the Consortium want political power?"

"Not according to the shooter, but I'm getting faint hints of something else from the memories of the CEO we've captured—I haven't had time to mine all the data in his mind yet." She telepathed him the pieces she'd picked up so far.

Aden immediately saw what she hadn't, her brain not wired for politics. "The leaders of this group want to be the shadow powers behind the throne." It fit the cunning and slyness of their actions to date. "They want to manipulate puppets of their choosing while staying safe in their anonymous skins." Ironic, given how they'd fostered rumors saying he was nothing but a stalking horse for the real leader of the squad.

He went to vocalize that, but his lips barely parted before a curtain of drowsiness had him fighting to raise his lashes.

Zaira pressed her lips to his temple. "Sleep. We have things under control." Another kiss. "Vasic has promised to provide me with rope to tie you down, so don't tempt me."

That fire.

Aden curled his soul against it and fell asleep.

PSYNET BEACON: BREAKING NEWS

Nikita Duncan has released a statement on behalf of the Ruling Coalition quashing rumors of Aden Kai's death. Text as follows:

> An attempt was made on his life, but he is an Arrow. A simple bullet has never stopped an Arrow. Those who persist in believing otherwise will have to admit to believing in ghosts when Aden reappears.
>
> Anyone else who wishes to try to assassinate Aden Kai should take note of the fact that the assassin is alive only because the Arrows did not find him worth executing. He is also recovering from multiple broken bones and other injuries delivered by a woman half his size.
>
> Underestimate the squad at your own risk.

As always, the Arrow Squad itself has not responded to calls for comment.

PSYNET BEACON: LETTER TO THE EDITOR

I do not agree with the new direction taken by the strongest among us, do not agree with the fall of Silence, but I agree very much with the strength shown by the Arrows. Today's display by the female Arrow should silence any rumors of the squad going "soft" because of their choice to align themselves with the empaths.

Protecting the empaths doesn't make the Arrows weaker. It makes them even more ruthless. As Kaleb Krychek's bond with Sahara Kyriakus makes him the same. This is something I've come to understand in the past weeks, and it conflicts with my belief that emotions—and in particular, the empaths—are the enemy of our peace. That makes it no less true.

As long as the Arrows exist, no one can doubt our strength.

Ida Mill, on behalf of Silent Voices

Chapter 79

THE ARCHITECT OF the Consortium, the brain that had seen the direction of the world and laid a plan B in place just in case, looked at the images flowing across the comm screen and knew the group had failed in its first major action.

Abducting and controlling the water-based changelings had been easy because of the creatures' habit of roaming far distances alone or in pairs. The Consortium had also made certain not to target the strong—they had needed malleable puppets, not those who might break free of the drugs and other methods of control.

They still had a number in reserve, so *that* had been a success at least.

However, the water changelings had been but a single small stone on the Consortium's path to unrivaled power. They had created myriad small networks, situated pawns they could move about as they wished, held their hand until the fall of Silence sent a shock wave across the world.

A year of hard work while the architect of it all played both sides of the line, building the Consortium on one side while maintaining an "ordinary" life on the other. Unlike the others in the Consortium, the architect hadn't decided which side to support until the final instant. As it was, plan B was now plan A.

From the first recruit, the architect had researched and

targeted pragmatic and cold-blooded businesspeople across the racial spectrum. Everyone in the group had learned from watching the rise and fall of Pure Psy. There was no room for fanaticism in business or in power. Only the strongest and the smartest survived. Ego had to be left at the door, all of them meeting on a level playing field.

The architect didn't actually believe the founding partners were all equal, but that ideology served the purpose of the Consortium at this time.

Each had supported the business interests of the other partners. Of course, the architect acted as the intermediary who made certain nothing revealed the identity of any one party to another, all the while ensuring money flowed in the right direction. Where possible, the Consortium had created problems for those who were financial or business threats, or had nudged bad feelings to grow between normally friendly competitors.

But money, while enough to satisfy those on the lower rungs of the Consortium, wasn't enough for the upper. Their aim was to build a new world order, one in which the most ruthless and intelligent of all three races would wield power behind the scenes, working as one, while below them, the triumvirate remained splintered.

Stability might be good for the world, but it wasn't good for their interests.

Kaleb Krychek and the Arrows were two of the most solid beams holding that shaky stability in place and giving it time to become stronger. Krychek was a difficult target and one the Consortium had set aside in favor of focusing on the squad. To have excised the Arrows from the equation, whether through an assassination or by making the squad appear weak, had been their first major goal.

The result was a resounding failure that had turned Aden Kai into a demigod and elevated the near-mythic status of the squad. The news channels were currently obsessively playing the images filmed by eyewitnesses who'd seen the female Arrow take down the Consortium shooter.

What made the news media voracious in their interest, an interest shared by the public at large, Psy and non-Psy alike, was that the Arrow was petite by the standards of any of the three races. That petite woman had decisively beaten a man twice her size without sustaining a single injury. She'd also been pitiless in her treatment of the male, who had unfortunately known enough to have revealed the Consortium's existence and pointed the squad to one of the founders.

The image of Zaira Neve, her face cool, holding the tip of the blade to the shooter's eyeball, was being shown over and over. No one was horrified by her actions. Or if they were, the horror was mingled with equal amounts of awe. The Arrows hadn't only retained their position as the bogeymen you never wanted on your trail, they had become heroes who protected innocent bystanders.

"We have to pull the plug," the architect said to the Consortium's top tier. "We overreached by attempting to take out the Arrow leader." They should've focused on Nikita Duncan. Now even she was forewarned. "You'll notice one less member at this meeting. He was captured by the squad last night."

A murmur of consternation. "He won't be able to identify us?" one of the others asked.

"No. It's why we've always taken precautions veiling our identities from one another."

"Except you," another member pointed out. "If you get captured, we're all dead."

"I won't be taken. I haven't survived as long as I have by being unintelligent. We're all safe."

Regardless of the assurance, every individual at the meeting knew that in going after the squad, they had painted targets on their backs.

It was a risk the twelve people in attendance—and the missing member—had recognized right at the start, but back then, the Consortium had believed they had the pieces in place to initiate a total shadow coup. Aden Kai was meant to have died on that mountain after he was interrogated, his body to be dumped in a public location that made it clear the Arrows couldn't even protect their own, much less anyone else.

No one had expected the "field medic" to be a power, or for his female partner to survive her wounds. Now . . . "We need to go under for a small period as far as the wider world is concerned," the architect reiterated, careful not to couch it as an order. The perception of equality was what held the Consortium together.

Agreement from all sides.

"The Consortium will rise again," the architect said. "While the three races live in their separate worlds, we have created a group that takes advantage of all our different strengths and weaknesses. We will own the world."

"We will own the world!" repeated the others, the sound thundering around the room.

Chapter 80

ADEN APPEARED IN public a bare six hours after his surgery, after promising Zaira the entire operation would take less than fifteen minutes. It was easy enough to organize—with him taking a touch of power from Vasic to keep himself upright, he and the other man walked through a busy neighborhood as if on their way elsewhere. Giving the appearance that, to Aden, having major arteries and veins critically damaged was just a temporary nuisance.

People whispered and took camera-phone images from a safe distance.

Job done.

Two minutes later, they ducked into a disused building site and Vasic brought him home to a Zaira who scowled. "Get back in bed."

"Come with me."

As it was, he fell asleep almost as soon as his head hit the pillow and slept for fourteen long hours, leaving the squad in the hands of those he trusted. He woke, ate, fell back asleep. The next time he opened his eyes, he no longer felt as if he'd been hit with a sledgehammer. Touching his neck, he noted the sensitivity of the skin, but it was nothing major.

Not that Zaira would allow him to return to full duties.

It wasn't until a week later that the medics gave him a clean bill of health. He'd spent the interim time with his

Arrow family in the valley. The world was calm, no major issues on the horizon, though Aden didn't trust that calm. He didn't think their enemy had given up, and he was worried by how easily they'd manipulated countless parties.

However, he wasn't about to squander this chance to care for his squad. Not only the older Arrows and the children—all of them. Because as a result of the calm in the Net, most of his Arrows had been able to come home.

Some couldn't, of course. There were always serial killers operating somewhere in the Net, and they had to be hunted, but Aden made sure everyone was rotated back in on a regular basis. He didn't want anyone to feel like Edward, as if they didn't have a place in this new world, in this sun-drenched valley.

As he walked out after the final medical checkup, Zaira's hand in his, he saw children laughing as they played, two of the oldest active Arrows watching over them, and felt his heart expand. "We're doing it," he said to Zaira. "We're creating a better world for Arrows today and Arrows to come."

Weaving her fingers through his, Zaira nodded. "I've heard a rumor."

"Since when do you listen to rumors?" He felt a smile kick at his lips.

Narrowed eyes. "Since I'm trying to help you. Be grateful."

Breaking their handclasp, he wrapped his arm around her shoulders. "I am." And then, because he could, he kissed her in front of anyone who might be watching.

Cheeks flushed when she drew back, Zaira crooked her finger so he'd bend closer. "I heard that Cristabel and Amin have been seen walking together alone at night."

"They're senior Arrows," he pointed out. "They're probably discussing ops."

"Do you think they discuss them all night?" Zaira asked with a glint in her eye. "Because that's how long Amin was with her yesterday. In her cabin."

Aden blinked, felt his smile begin to deepen. "Confirmed?"

"By three different sources."

Aden wouldn't have predicted the pairing. Both were long-serving Arrows, and though Cris was older by eight years, Amin was equally Silent. "It's happening." His

Arrows were starting to see a better future for themselves, a future that didn't have to be devoid of pleasure.

"Yes." Rising on tiptoe, Zaira said, "We promised each other a night to ourselves. How about tomorrow?"

"Yes. What would you like to do?"

Zaira ran her hands down his chest. "I'll organize it. Dress in civilian clothes."

ONE night later, Zaira sat with Aden at a table in a tiny rooftop restaurant in Rajasthan, India. It was atop the second floor of what looked like a large family dwelling, the tables wood with embroidered cotton tablecloths. There was no roof, the desert sky drowning in stars above.

There was only one server, who bustled every which way, somehow managing to bring in meals without anyone having to wait too long—though if you had to wait, this location was . . . beautiful. Zaira wouldn't have understood that before her time with Aden in RainFire, but tonight, she saw the stunning clarity of the starlight, appreciated the warmth of the air against her skin.

She'd worn a dress, not because she had any particular desire to wear an item of clothing so much less efficient than her uniform, but because anything else would've made her stand out in this place. After settling on this location, she'd done her research, picked this white dress with its full skirt, modest neckline embroidered with colorful flowers, and cap sleeves as being appropriate to the local environment and customs.

Aden had followed her instructions and was wearing a simple white shirt untucked over old blue jeans, with the sleeves folded up to the elbows. His hair was long enough now that it fell across his forehead at times, and touched the collar of his white shirt. He was beautiful, too.

"Will you trust me to order for you?" Aden asked from where he sat beside her and used his free hand to pick up the yellow piece of paper on which were printed a number of dishes. His other arm was around her shoulders, fingers desultorily caressing her skin.

Each brush made her stomach tighten, the possessive

need in her conditioned to know that his touch meant searing pleasure.

"I chose this place for you," she said, knowing he was trying to push himself far beyond Silence and happy to walk beside him while he explored. "I'm not certain I can eat anything here. The spices will be too difficult to digest." She'd started to eat foods other than nutritional supplements, too, but there was a limit.

"Trust me," he said, fingers brushing her shoulder, and when the server came over, he made the order in the local language, the syllables flowing off his tongue as if he'd spoken it since birth.

"When did you learn?" she asked after the server had moved away.

"My mother taught me," he told her. "She learned it as a child from another Arrow, and the particular dialect is obscure enough that it acted as a 'secret' language at times." *Never totally, only in situations where we could be certain we weren't being recorded.*

Hearing his voice, and then his telepathic voice all in one smooth transition, it was so familiar now, so necessary. "Does Vasic speak it?"

Aden nodded. "I taught it to him, for the same reason. We made some adaptations so that it truly became a secret language—we don't use it any longer, but it's still there in the memory banks." *Would you like to learn?*

Yes. "Teach me."

"I will. At night." A long look, his thigh pressing against hers. *When we're alone.*

Electricity sparked through her, but she didn't want to rush, not tonight. This was their night and it was an important one . . . and perhaps she was scared, too. Putting her hand on Aden's thigh in an effort to calm her thudding heart, she looked out to the desert vista. This area wasn't heavily populated, so there wasn't a sprawl of glittering brightness.

Instead, the lights were yellow hued and scattered here and there, pouring through the windows of homes lower down on the slight hillside and coming from the campfires of the roaming desert dwellers who preferred a nomadic lifestyle. "Do you think there are changelings in this area?"

"There are rumors of desert eagles, but no confirmation."

They went silent as the food appeared. Aden had ordered something with lentils, as well as a flatbread and several vegetable dishes. He tore off a piece of the flatbread, held it out. "Try it."

She took a small bite, chewed, allowing the flavors to settle on her tongue. "I can eat this." Following his lead, she tried the other dishes, decided some weren't for her, while the lentil soup tasted good.

They ate slowly, with no rush, nowhere to go. Every so often, the server would come by to top up their water or ask if they needed anything else, but other than that, they were left alone. The conversation flowed as it always did between them; she'd never had to worry about not knowing what to say when it came to Aden.

At one point, they ended up speaking about the mirror, that part of the conversation almost fully telepathic. *I was surprised when Walker told me how young you were when you discovered the mirror. I would've expected Marjorie and Naoshi to know.*

They were Arrows on active duty and around only for short periods. Walker and I first glimpsed the mirror while they were away.

And you just didn't share the discovery when they returned, Zaira said, guessing he'd used the techniques he'd learned from Walker to hide the mirror's psychic evidence.

"No, I didn't." Aden's voice held no regret, nothing but a quiet confidence. *They'd been telling me I was a weak disappointment as long as I could remember—for all I knew, the mirror was a mutation that would just make things worse.* His lips softened unexpectedly, his mental tone different as he added, *Walker kept telling me it was a unique gift. That's what carried me through the years until I realized the mirror's purpose.*

Zaira's respect and liking for Walker Lauren kept growing. *Can you do it without permission?* she asked. *Draw power? Not like with Vasic when you were children, but with someone who doesn't have any reason to allow the draw.*

He bent close to her, lips brushing her ear. "Yes." *There were circumstances in which I had no choice—I took it from trainers who were hurting children, or from Arrows so far in Silence that they no longer had any idea of conscience.* Breath warm against her, he continued to pet her shoulder with those slow, caressing strokes that made her own breath hitch.

I didn't know at the time that I was making them stronger when I returned the power because I only ever drew a very basic amount—that small draw is why I was never caught. Vasic and I figured out the power differential when I was about fifteen, and that's when I knew exactly how careful I had to be to avoid detection.

Shifting back from her a little so she could see his face, he said, *As for the people from whom I siphoned power without permission, I don't excuse myself by saying I did it for a good reason. I made a choice to survive, and some of those choices were borderline.*

They didn't sound that way to Zaira, but Aden had always had a far stronger moral compass than she'd ever possess. *You worry too much.*

His smile lit up his eyes. *Will you teach me to play?*

It appears I have to. Picking up a piece of fruit from the dessert tray that had been left on the table when the meal was cleared, she held it to his lips. *Try this. They've put something on it.* A faint spice that didn't overwhelm.

He ate it, and it was intimate, the moment. She didn't understand why, except that it was Aden. Allowing herself to lean into him, she surrendered to the here and the now, to this instant under the starlight.

ADEN sensed Zaira relax totally against him, and something tight in him twisted tighter. He'd never felt her this way, never seen her shields fall this low. He could almost see her mind, the veil that hid it from him paper-thin.

It was tempting to tear through it, see all of her, but in so doing, he'd destroy the trust that bound them together and savage her. Never would he do that, no matter how much he craved the piercing intimacy of a true psychic bond, one that would hold even over the greatest distance without any conscious effort.

Fingertips grazing the silk of her upper arm, he sat with her under the stars until the restaurant began to go quiet. Rising to his feet, having already taken care of the bill, he held out a hand, giving her the choice.

Always, he would give Zaira the choice.

When she slid her hand into his without hesitation, he felt a warmth deep within, warmth that curled outward in fine tendrils that infiltrated every cell in his body. Getting up, she walked with him past the other tables and down the steps that hugged the side of the house. Hitting the ground, they began to walk along the narrow roads that formed the village in which this restaurant was located.

The houses were lit up inside, but there were few people on the streets.

"Can you guess where we're going?" Zaira asked, no urgency in her tone and her hand trustingly in his.

"Yes." The squad owned a home in this village, part of their network of bolt-holes for those who needed to go under. Oddly enough for such a small town, it was a great place to hide. "My father told me this village was founded by rebels hundreds of years ago," he said. "While they are welcoming, the people ask no questions."

"An interesting cultural tradition."

"A useful one." Walking with her down a narrow alley-way lit only by the lamps hung up on a balcony above, he said, "I assume the home is empty right now?"

"Yes, and no one will disturb us tonight." Zaira leaned her body against his.

His own body tense with an anticipation that was all the deeper because he knew the taste of her now, he led her to the door of the Arrow home and coded them in. The house was in the same simple style as those around it, made from the red sandstone prevalent in this region, but its hidden security features were of the highest grade. Entering, he turned on a wall sconce, then locked the door behind them.

When he led Zaira upstairs to the bedroom, she walked to the balcony doors and opened them to reveal the two lanterns that hung on stands outside, sending just enough light into the room that none other was necessary.

"You did this?" he asked, and when she nodded, he felt as

if he'd been given the world. He hadn't expected romance from his tough and lethal commander.

Picking up a lantern, she brought it inside and hung it on a curl of metal that stuck out from the wall and had clearly been designed for the lantern. "Close the doors."

He did so, drew the curtains. They weren't blackout curtains, would allow in sunlight in the morning, but at night, they shut out the world, cloaking the room in privacy. Turning after that was done, he found Zaira had moved toward him.

A soft kiss before she placed her hands on his chest and stroked down, the lamplight setting her ring afire. That he'd never seen her without the ring since the day he gave it to her was another unexpected and wonderful gift.

"Take this off."

Skin tight, he undid the top three buttons of his shirt, then reached back and tugged it over his head to drop it on the handwoven rug that covered the wooden floor. Zaira touched him again, the contact making him suck in a breath. It was always a delicious shock, the contact, like lightning through his veins. "Zaira."

Lashes lowered, she ran her fingers over his pectorals. "I like touching you skin to skin," she murmured, her breath kissing his chest. "I can feel your life, your strength, your need." Her lashes rose. "The tension in your muscles, it's for me."

"Yes." He cupped the side of her neck, his fingers curving partly around her nape and his thumb brushing her jaw. "You are my addiction."

ZAIRA felt her pulse kick.

Leaning in, she pressed her lips to his skin, just because she wanted to do it. His hand curved farther around her nape, the hold nothing she would've permitted any other individual. It left her too vulnerable, but she knew that right then, he was vulnerable, too—his body was taut, his muscles bunched, and when she tasted him with her tongue, a tremor shook his frame.

That felt good, too. To know that her touch gave him pleasure.

Bending his head, he pulled her hair away from the side of

her face to kiss her temple, her cheek. The heat and strength of him surrounded her, the slick strands of his hair brushing her skin. Sinking into the sensation, she turned and lifted her face toward him. And their lips were touching; the contact somehow reached into her stomach, made it flutter, stealing the fear that had the rage curled up into a tight ball of worry.

Her hands stroked up to his shoulders of their own accord, her body rising on tiptoe to better fit herself against him. Continuing to hold her with his hand around her nape, his other hand spread on her lower back, he angled his head, and their kiss grew deeper. But he broke it too soon. "What's wrong?" Eyes of deepest brown looking into hers. "I can feel your muscles about to snap."

Nails digging into his shoulders, she swallowed. "I'm afraid."

"Of this?" He brushed his thumb over her cheekbone, and she knew if she answered in the affirmative, he wouldn't berate her, wouldn't blame her, wouldn't reject her.

And in that reminder, she found her courage. "I got you a gift." Bending her neck slightly, she undid the clasp of the fine gold necklace she wore. It was long, had dipped between her breasts. Removing it, she pulled off the ring she'd slipped onto the chain. "This is for you," she said, not quite daring to look up. Possessive and feral she might be where he was concerned, but he also meant too much to her for this not to matter.

Taking the simple platinum band, Aden curled his arm around her shoulders. "Are you asking me to marry you?" he said and she heard the delight in his tone.

It made her look up, and his smile had every part of her ready to dance. "Yes," she whispered and kissed him. *Will you marry all of me?*

Aden went to answer when Zaira dropped her shields. It felt as if his mind and hers had been stretched to their limit and suddenly, the tension broke. Everything collided in a wild ricochet, his mind smashing into hers, hers into his, both of them totally out of control.

He saw the broken, jagged shards of her, saw the incandescent and stubborn fire that had never stopped burning, saw her endless, fierce love for him. He was her hope and her dream and her passion, and the knowledge brought him to his knees. She fell with him, her eyes silver mirrors when he looked at her.

"You love me *that* much?" she whispered, tears rolling down her face.

No answer was needed, his heart and soul bare to her, as bare as hers was to him. They just held on to one another as the storm crashed. When it finally began to subside, their minds separating but for a single link he knew no force on this earth could sever, they were both breathing hard.

As he watched, Zaira's eyes became her own and she met him on the PsyNet, the two of them looking in astonished wonder at the jet-black rope that tied them to one another, the twin strands both Arrow black. But hidden in the black was a brilliant fire that only became apparent if you stepped close.

"Thank you," he whispered back in the room in the desert, his voice raw. "Thank you for giving me you."

More tears before she threw her arms around his neck and held on tight. "You love me," she whispered again. "*All* of me." Drawing back, she kissed him again, and the intimacy was a punch of intoxication, the bond feeding him her pleasure as well as his. He had the feeling he could shut that off, but he didn't want to, wanted to drown in her.

He'd intended to give her romance tonight, too, but the bond pulsed with a visceral need he had to assuage. Realizing he was still gripping the ring, he pushed it into her hand. "Put it on me." He was hers in every way that mattered—the ceremony would be for others, for their friends and those in their care. This was for them.

Kissing his jaw, his throat, she looked down and, picking up his hand, slid on the ring. "All mine."

"Always have been."

Zaira rubbed her nose against his, and the spontaneous act of affection tipped him over. Shoving up the skirt of her dress as desire burned, he kissed her hard. She wrapped her legs around his waist, her tongue licking against his. Groaning, he reached between them and somehow managed to undo his jeans, shove down the denim and his briefs. It took a little more effort to kick them off, but he was highly motivated.

Naked at last, he nudged aside the gusset of her panties.

A single stroke of his finger through her wetness and her back arched, the sensations that came shooting back at him through the bond threatening to make his eyes roll back in his head. Then she bit him on the jaw and it was all over.

He thrust into her wet heat in a single, demanding push.

Clenching around him as their mouths tangled, Zaira moved with him, the rug bunching up under her body. Some small part of him realized she'd be bruised from being on the bottom, so he flipped them over, but they stayed locked together, his right hand holding the back of her neck and his left gripping her hip as they rocked together.

Her own hands were all over him, petting and clawing and owning.

When her body stiffened on his, her pleasure went straight to his blood, a drug punched into his system. He could no more stop the orgasm than he could let her go.

Chapter 81

KALING SINGH

ZAIRA WOKE NAKED in bed under the diffuse sunlight that filtered in through the curtains. Her ears and other senses told her it wasn't long after dawn, the village yet waking. The man who slept with his leg thrown across her thighs and his arm curved below her breasts, however, wasn't awake. Turning only her head so as not to disturb him, she watched him sleep.

His hair had fallen across his face, his features relaxed, and she suddenly realized how young he truly was. Twenty-nine a bare three weeks ago. Less than a quarter of the normal life span of a hundred and thirty. And yet he'd been a leader since as long as she could remember. He'd been that when he was a mere boy unlocking her manacles.

All his life, he had been forced to be older than his years, to make decisions that should've been made by those who'd lived far longer. All Arrows were forced to grow up fast, but Aden, he'd been born into a pressure cooker that had never let up. She'd seen how his parents treated him—not as a son, but as a soldier in their war.

That war might have been for the good of the squad, but it had stolen something from Aden. Even she, feral, bloodthirsty creature that she'd been, had understood what it was to be a child. She didn't think Aden ever had.

Will you teach me to play?

At the memory of his question, she thought of how she'd seen Ivy Jane laughing as she teased Vasic, of how the teleporter would quietly say something back that made the empath laugh even harder, her eyes bright. That was play and it was what Aden needed.

How extraordinary that she should be the one to think that, to believe that she could lead him into play. What did she know about such things?

"I know," she whispered almost soundlessly, "that he is more important to me than anything, even the squad." It was exactly as it should be—he needed to be someone's number one priority. And if he needed play, Zaira would learn how.

Last night.

The telepathic words were in his voice, and yet he was asleep, the words muffled. As if he'd heard her thoughts in his sleep through their bond—their *bond*—and given her an answer.

Last night had been play.

She hadn't consciously considered it that way, but he was right. It *had* been play. Just the two of them, doing what they wanted to do. No rules, no expectations. They'd ended up tangled on the floor after that first time, had lain there wrecked for long, long minutes before Aden finally groaned and got up, throwing her limp form onto the bed.

She'd lain back lazily and let him strip her, and by the time he finished, she'd revived enough to pounce on him. He hadn't complained, not in the least. Especially when she used her mouth on him—at one point, he'd muttered that she didn't need any manual. All she had to do was put her mouth near his erection and he was done.

The memory had her dropping a kiss to his throat, the rage inside her stretched out and lazy. Its insane possessiveness was as deep as always, but it wouldn't slip the leash, not now, because Aden *belonged to her*. Before anyone else, he belonged to her. It made her feel smug and content.

Zaira didn't think she'd ever been content.

"You look like a happy cat," Aden murmured when his lashes lifted. "I can feel you purring at the back of my mind."

Shifting to lie flat on her stomach, Zaira kicked up her legs. "Want me to stop?"

"No." He ran his fingers down her spine. "I like it."

They lay in silence so long that the village noises changed, became those of people going off to work or to school. Fine lines formed between Aden's eyebrows toward the end. Reaching out, she rubbed them away. "Tell me what you've been obsessing over since you woke from the surgery." She'd sensed that he needed time to think about it, had given it to him.

Placing one of his legs, hot and muscled, once more over her thighs, he absently massaged her nape. "The Consortium made us all dance to their tune." The hairs on his leg caused a delicious ripple of sensation down her body as he moved slightly. "We survived not because we were prepared, but because we were lucky."

Zaira scowled. "It wasn't luck—people talked to one another."

"But piecemeal." Rolling onto his back, Aden put an arm over his forehead. "What if Lucas had never said anything to me? What if Bo hadn't trusted me with the incidents that had affected the Alliance?"

She saw his point. "So, what are you going to do about it?" Aden always did something; that was who he was.

Glancing at her, he began to speak, laying out what he'd come up with over the past week of silent thinking. By the time he was done, Zaira knew that Aden's name would one day be written in history books, connected to a pivotal event that had forever changed the world.

"Let's do it," she said, her hand linked to his. "I'll watch your back."

His eyes met hers, his mind entwined with her own. "I know."

Chapter 82

BEFORE INITIATING THE plan that had grown inside him strand by strand, Aden spoke to his senior people, even his parents. The latter remained leery of contact with "outsiders," as they termed anyone beyond the squad, but they agreed with his viewpoint. As a result, he now stood in the communications hub of Central Command.

On the viewscreens in front of him were the faces of the Ruling Coalition, but one also showed that of Lucas Hunter. The DarkRiver alpha had been nominated by multiple changeling groups, including SnowDancer, to represent changelings at this first meeting.

Aden had been surprised the alphas had agreed to have anyone represent them as a group—they tended to be laws unto themselves. He'd heard Judd say that alphas "did not play well together." However, it appeared the changelings had set up an informal data network some time past, for much the same reasons as the ones that had led Aden here today, though the changeling network was limited to the packs.

On the screen next to Lucas was Devraj Santos, representative of the Forgotten; beside him, Bowen Knight for the Alliance. Another human—a silver-haired woman named Lizbeth Schäfer—was on the second-to-last screen. She was the head of a large humanitarian group that had provided major assistance in dealing with the aftermath of the Pure

Psy bombings; the group had also helped when the Net infection had driven so many Psy mad, leaving people of all three races traumatized.

While human, Schäfer did not ally herself or the organization she represented, Hope Light, to any one race, despite the fact that the membership was largely human with a scattering of changelings. Hope Light's motto was to assist where assistance was necessary and, post-Silence, they worked in close contact with the empaths. It was Ivy who'd suggested the organization be included in this meeting.

"She represents people who don't trust anyone else," Ivy had said. "Her group on its own is also a quiet but powerful force."

On the final screen was Miane Levèque. Technically, since Lucas was in attendance, she didn't need to be here, but Lucas himself had asked she attend. "BlackSea is unique," he'd said to Aden. "The fact that they cover the globe means they have a viewpoint other changelings don't."

Meeting the eyes of each of the attendees in turn, Aden began to speak. "It appears a group called the Consortium has come together to fill what they view as a void created by the fall of the Council and of Silence. The membership is composed of Psy, humans, and changelings."

Several people frowned but no one interrupted him as he shared the data the squad had been able to extract from the shooter Zaira had taken down, as well as the CEO still in their custody. "BlackSea has given me leave to share the fact that six of their people—five adults and a child—were abducted by this Consortium."

What Miane had been insistent he *not* share with everyone was that at least twenty-one more of her people remained among the missing. With no current knowledge of their situation, she didn't want to risk spooking their captors.

"Better to let the Consortium believe we haven't noticed the vanishings," the BlackSea alpha had said, her voice dark as the depths of the ocean that was her home. "Let the bastards think we're satisfied with the rescue of Persephone, Olivia, and the two other captives. It'll keep them from looking over their shoulders, make them complacent."

It was a sound approach. Even if it hadn't been, Aden

wouldn't have overridden her decision—such arrogance would create a fatal fracture in what he was trying to build. "I believe the water changelings were abducted and abused into compliance because BlackSea's people have the ability to covertly infiltrate territories across the world."

Miane's lips were a thin line, her eyes chips of obsidian rather than the translucent hazel he'd seen during less emotionally fraught moments, but she held her silence.

"Others, including owners of small businesses, have been coerced into the conspiracy without knowing who it was they served." Hashri Smith was a broken man, his business crumbling around him now that his powerful "allies" had discarded him. "The Consortium believes the world is fertile for chaos and sly destruction."

"In their minds," Ivy added, her voice clear and passionate, "the Psy are *already* in a state of chaos because of the fall of Silence and the ensuing hiccups as we try to forge a new path into the future. They want to push changelings and humans into the same state." A curl of her hair escaped her ponytail to kiss her cheek as she met his gaze again. "Is that a good summation, Aden?"

"Yes. All indications are that the Consortium is behind the incidents we've all logged that attempt to set one group against another."

Lucas's green eyes glinted panther-bright. "Identify them and we'd be happy to help you take out the trash."

"I agree with Hunter," Krychek said from his Moscow home. "We need to tear this organization to pieces before it ever takes root."

"That's the issue." Aden already had a team following every tendril of data they'd recovered from the shooter and the captured CEO, but so far, nothing. "Our captives confirm that the Consortium leadership learned from watching the disintegration of the Council and of Pure Psy—even the members don't know one another's identities."

He met the eyes of each attendee in turn. "Signs point to the Consortium having gone under until the heat dies down. I don't intend to allow the pressure to ease. The squad will continue to be vigilant and we'll alert each of you at any sign that they've reemerged."

"You want us all to keep watch, too," Lizbeth Schäfer guessed, fine lines spreading out from her dark gray eyes as she frowned in concentration.

Aden nodded. "The Consortium works by creating divisions along existing fault lines. By working together, we deprive them of their major weapon."

"I'll make sure to pass on the message through the terrestrial and aerial packs," Lucas said, folding his arms. "Miane, I assume you've already warned your people?"

"Yes. The news should reach even our most remote packmates within the next month." Miane's hair blew back in the wind where she stood, her comm panel apparently placed on an outdoor wall, since Aden could see waves behind her and her image moved in time with the motion of the sea. "The Consortium's tactics are dishonorable and cowardly and BlackSea has no argument with working with everyone to cut off their heads."

"The Alliance will also alert its network," Bo said, his flint-hard gaze turning to connect with Miane's. "We've lost a small number of people recently—they were hired away on plum contracts before disappearing from sight."

Miane's expression grew even more grim. "We should pool our data."

"Let's talk after this."

Lizbeth Schäfer had a troubled look on her face. "We've been working with a human settlement in Kenya that lost ten of its older teenagers six months ago," she said, her English flawless and accented with the rhythms of her native tongue—German. "The teens left saying they were heading out to join a group that would make the world 'a better place.' No trace has ever been found of them."

It fit the Consortium's MO, but it could as easily be a small guerrilla or mercenary organization that had seduced the teens. "We have to be careful not to see a conspiracy at every turn," he said. "That could hamstring us."

"Yes, I understand."

"If you wish," Aden added, "I'll send in a team to track the teenagers."

Clear relief on her face. "I would very much appreciate that. Many of their families are distraught."

The entire group spoke for over an hour, putting together more troubling facts that meant nothing on their own, but together painted a disturbing picture.

"I have a proposal," Aden said toward the end.

Once he set out that proposal, the discussion was vigorous, rough details hammered out so the various attendees could go back to those they represented to ask for feedback.

Switching off the system after the last person signed out, he turned to the woman who'd watched from the shadows. "It could take years."

"You'll do it." Absolute, unflinching faith from his mate.

"If we can hold the connections, forge them ever deeper," Aden said, "the world could become a fully functioning triumvirate again."

Zaira wove her fingers into his. "It'll happen. This is your destiny, Aden." Her kiss was fire and love and primal possessiveness. "Your parents dreamed too small when they wanted you to become the leader of the squad. You're about to lead the entire world out into a new dawn."

"My dream," he said, "is right here in my arms."

Firelight traveling through their bond, a psychic kiss from his dangerous, beautiful, perfect commander.

PSYNET BEACON: BREAKING NEWS

An unexpected new cooperation agreement, the Trinity Accord, has been negotiated and agreed upon between major elements of all three races. The aims of this agreement are to foster and maintain stability, both in world markets and for the personal safety of individuals. It has also been termed the first step toward creating a permanent United Earth Federation.

The Trinity Accord allows for the rapid sharing of data across signatory groups, and for the formation of mixed teams to deal with issues that affect more than one race. It is, however, more than an emergency network such as that managed by Silver Mercant. According to the papers released to the *Beacon,* Silver Mercant's network falls under the much wider umbrella of this "proto-Federation" agreement.

When asked for comment, Nikita Duncan, member of the Ruling Coalition, had this to say: "The Trinity Accord isn't only a political agreement, but one that opens up economic opportunities for all the signatories by breaking down the walls that previously hindered smooth and fast communication. Businesses no longer need be limited—an innovative Psy company can tap into the changeling or the human market and vice versa."

Nikita Duncan's interpretation of the Trinity Accord is one that is popular among the larger Psy families polled for this article. All came out in strong support of the Ruling Coalition for opening up new avenues of business as well as stabilizing the economic climate. "This is what our rulers are meant to do," stated Jen Liu, head of the Liu Group. "Not to isolate us, but to open up opportunities."

To check the efficacy of the cooperation agreement, the *Beacon* reached out through the listed liaisons for comment from a number of other parties. Responses were received from all, including one of the notoriously terse predatory changeling alphas.

"This agreement isn't a magic bullet," stated Hawke Snow, alpha of the influential and deadly SnowDancer wolves. "It's not going to fix the divisions in the world, but if everyone pulls their weight and no one attempts to subvert Trinity to their own ends, then it has the potential to eventually link the entire world together in a strong, functioning unit."

Bowen Knight, leader of the Human Alliance, was even more pragmatic. "The Trinity Accord is currently on probation—the formation of the Federation itself will take years of work because while the Alliance has had little friction with changelings, it has had significant issues with Psy. It remains an open question whether we can work together."

Kaleb Krychek, inarguably the most powerful Psy in the world, stated that he is a businessman and that the Trinity Accord is good for business. "Only idiots or those with blinkered vision will oppose it."

At time of press, the signatories to the Trinity Accord were as follows:

The Ruling Coalition.

The Arrow Squad.

The Empathic Collective.

Over one hundred predatory and nonpredatory changeling packs, including the SnowDancer wolves, the DarkRiver leopards, the BlackSea changelings, the StoneWater bears, the BlackEdge wolves, the SunGrass grazers, the IceRidge foxes, the DawnSky deer, the WindHaven falcons, the AzureSun leopards, the DesertRain lions, and the WaterSky eagles. Further signatories are expected.

The Human Alliance.

The Shine Foundation, as representatives of those who self-identify as part of the Forgotten population.

Hope Light, a nonpartisan humanitarian organization.

For the first time in *Beacon* history, the squad has responded to a request for comment, though in a way that fits its operating protocol. The following statement was remotely added to this article three minutes before we pushed Publish, confirmation of its authenticity provided by a psychic seal sent through the executive editor's highly complex shields.

Aden Kai had this to say:

"The Trinity Accord is a test. For the United Earth Federation to come into being as more than an idea, we must first pass this test. That responsibility lies with every man, woman, and child in the world.

"We can decide to remain in our isolated bunkers, becoming more and more obsessed with looking inward instead of outward, or we can decide to be great together. We can decide to stagnate, or we can decide to grow. We can decide to settle for the status quo, or we can decide to reach for the stars.

"Choose."

AUTHOR'S NOTE

I hope you enjoyed *Shards of Hope*, and that you're excited about all the ongoing developments in the Psy-Changeling world. I'm incredibly excited to continue forward and discover the lives and loves of characters new and old. There is *so much* I want to explore.

However, before we dive into the next arc of the series, I want to go back and check on all the couples from the previous books and novellas. Part of the joy of writing this series is being able to see how the characters' lives develop from book to book, year to year, but as I can only feature characters who have roles to play in any particular story, we haven't seen as much of some of them, and I'm painfully curious about what they're up to.

As a result, the next book in the series will be very (wonderfully!) different. First of all, it'll feature an ensemble cast. We'll also be taking a step back from the politics and the changing world to focus on the characters' personal lives, friendships, and of course, their relationships.

For those who are waiting for the pupcubs, I have a feeling they'll be making their long-awaited appearance.

This will be a book about family, whether those families are bonded by blood, by pack or squad, or through other bonds of loyalty. It'll also explore the intricate web of connections created between various disparate characters over the previous books and novellas.

I hope you're as excited about the next book as I am!

In further Psy-Changeling news, coming in August is a brand-new anthology of novellas set in this world. None of these novellas has ever been published, and all feature characters and parts of the world that have intrigued me over multiple books. One novella is set partly in the deep-sea station, Alaris, while another features a most unexpected DarkRiver-SnowDancer romance. The third novella involves two lieutenants and a mystery. There's also a special novelette focusing on Dorian (I always wanted to know how everyone reacted to his shifting!).

If you'd like to receive all the latest updates on these releases, as well as advance excerpts, direct to your inbox, swing by my website, nalinisingh.com, and join my newsletter. The Welcome newsletter features multiple free short stories set in the Psy-Changeling world, and as I write this letter to you, I'm hard at work on another newsletter story, this time featuring our favorite Arrows. I can't wait to share it with you, as I can't wait to share the next Psy-Changeling book and the upcoming anthology!

Take care and happy reading,
Nalini

M1516T0915